DEATH TAKES A FALL

DEATH TAKES A FALL

A COTSWOLD CRIMES MYSTERY

SHARON LYNN

First published by Level Best Books 2023

Copyright © 2023 by Sharon Lynn

This novel is entirely a work of fiction. The names, characters and incidents portrayed in it are the work of the author's imagination. Any resemblance to actual persons, living or dead, events or localities is entirely coincidental.

Sharon Lynn asserts the moral right to be identified as the author of this work.

First edition

ISBN: 978-1-68512-526-4

This book was professionally typeset on Reedsy.
Find out more at reedsy.com

For Dave and your unending support.

Praise for Death Takes a Fall

"Well-paced and brimming with heart, intelligence, and intricately crafted misdirection, *Death Takes a Fall* is packed with pulse-pounding twists and heart-stopping turns. Be prepared to stay up late with this fully immersive mystery because it pulls you in and doesn't let go."—Laurie Buchanan, author of the Sean McPherson crime thriller novels

"This fabulous second installment in A Cotswold Crimes Mystery series firmly establishes these books as must-read mysteries. American student Maddie McGuire is a quirky amateur sleuth who you can't help but love as she stumbles (literally) into a horrible criminal ring and puts herself (unwittingly) in mortal danger. The author skillfully builds the sinister plot against the backdrop of the seemingly idyllic setting of Bath, England accompanied by a brilliant cast of characters. Villains are hidden in plain sight, sending the reader on a marvelous twisting, turning jaunt as the culprits and their motives are unveiled. A charming, witty, and terrifyingly delightful mystery!"—Valerie Biel, author of the The Circle of Nine series

Chapter One: The First Discovery

Dew glistened on the round English wild blackberry dangling tantalizingly over the cliff. I reached for it.

Planting my feet, I calculated the distance, and if I stood on my toes, the reward would be mine, sweet and delicious.

As my fingers cradled the fruit, the gravel shifted. The toe of my hiking shoe caught as I overcorrected and tipped over the precipice. Flailing, I crushed the blackberry, juice squirting onto my face. My other hand gripped the closest vine, sharp thorns tearing my skin.

"Maddie!" Edward's voice barked my name as I slammed into a ledge. His head popped over the side of the cliff above, brown eyes searching for me. "Madeline!" He looked horrified, and then he schooled his features to neutral.

"Is that blood?" To his credit, he said it calmly.

Dabbing my finger into the goo oozing across my face, I probed. No pain, so I tasted it. "Blackberries," I announced. "I had no idea England was so steep," I added. Hailing from the Arizona desert, I pictured a hike in the Cotswolds as gently rolling hills cultivated over hundreds of years. Not 1000-foot rises into ancient, untamed forests.

Edward closed his eyes for a moment, probably relieved that I hadn't plummeted to my death. His lopsided grin appeared. "Y'alright?"

After patting myself all over, removing a thorn from my palm, and flexing my muscles, I stood on the limestone outcropping. My legs shook, and I didn't want to slide further down the escarpment, so I plopped on a sturdy rock. "I'm not hurt," I hollered at him.

My ledge extended about five yards from the trail. Even if Edward dangled half his body over the edge, and I stretched to my full five feet and nine inches, I wouldn't be able to grab hold of him.

"But I am stuck." I pulled my phone out and checked for a connection. Nothing. But maybe it was because I was on an international plan. "Do you have service?"

His head disappeared out of view for a moment, then returned, shaking. "No bars. We passed a farmhouse." He waved a hand over his shoulder. "I'll pop back there and make a call." Doubt tinged his voice.

I thought of ranchers in Arizona who answered their doors armed with shotguns. Worried, I asked, "The owners won't try to scare you off their property?"

Edward tilted his head. "Course not. I've got my warrant card." He searched my expression. "Would you rather I stay? I'm sure someone will be by shortly."

Concern for me, not for rifle-wielding farmers.

No one had passed us along the Cotswold Way since we began our hike from Birdlip to Painswick that morning. A train from Bath, my temporary home during my internship, to Stroud, followed by a taxi to the trailhead. Our driver was the last person we encountered.

Surrounded by thick bramble, beech trees and an enormous pig snuffling through the dirt hundreds of feet below me, I was in a lovely location, relatively speaking. "I'll be okay. I've been trapped in worse places."

Edward's face clouded over at the mention of my entombment, but I figured the more I talked about it, the less scarring it would be.

"Besides," I waved toward the faraway enclosure. "I have a pig for company."

Rather than celebrating my news, Edward's expression turned even more distressed. Anxiety in Edward presented itself as a tiny crease between his brows.

"What?" I demanded.

He stabbed a finger at the animal. "Be careful. Please. If you fell in there…" Shaking his head, he didn't finish his thought.

The pig lifted a snout toward us with a snort.

"He's cute," I insisted. Larger than any I'd seen at the county fairs of my childhood and colored with gray patches on pink skin, he looked like a cartoon. "I'm naming him Patchy."

"Patchy," Edward sighed faintly. "You're a mad one, lass." He puffed out his cheeks. "You're sure—"

"I'm sure. I don't want to be here all day. Any rope will do the trick."

"Do you need a flapjack?"

The incongruity of the question threw me. "How do you have flapjacks?"

He dug something out of his pocket and showed it to me. A square plastic packet. Extending his arm over the ledge, he dropped it on me.

Crinkly wrapping covered what looked like a granola bar. After opening it, I confirmed it. "This is a granola bar."

"Right. Flapjack."

Recognizing his stalling technique, I did not explain that flapjacks were pancakes. "A rope." I gave him a thumbs up. "Patchy will keep me company."

Another puff. "I'll be back as soon as I can."

His head disappeared, followed by running footsteps thundering away. When he said *soon*, he meant it.

Despite being stuck, I had a stunning view. The River Severn coiled far beyond green hills edged with hedges that cut the scenery into a patchwork. The cliff face's butter-colored limestone sprouted beechwood and more beguiling blackberry bushes.

My stomach rumbled, the granola acting as an appetizer. "Honestly?" I asked it. "You're the one who got me into this mess in the first place," I complained to my tummy. Another growl.

Somehow, I was under the impression that there would be a lot more pubs along the Cotswold Way. There are not, and I regretted my lack of preparation.

Giving in, I carefully lifted the nearest vine, searching for food. I discovered wild hops, not berries. Not quite as helpful at the moment, but once I got off this ledge, a locally made ale in a warm pub was my next stop. Being in a country where the drinking age was eighteen had its advantages, especially when dating a rule-crazy constable.

The prospect of a cozy dinner made me more hungry. "Fine. I'll forage. Like a bear." I couldn't remember whether England had bears. Worryingly, one of the supporters of Bath's crest was a bear, which didn't bode well for a girl trapped in the woods.

"But," I reasoned out loud. "The other supporter is a lion, and I know England doesn't have those."

Scooting as far from the edge as possible, I pressed my shoulders against the cliff face and wiggled toward the blackberry bush that had lured me here.

The fruits were smallish, each tiny pearl plump and inviting. Secure in my seating, I tugged on branches and plucked berries, popping them into my mouth. The subtle sweetness exploded with every bite, trickling down my throat.

I needed more.

One particularly thick bramble held fruity promise, but I couldn't tell if the ledge extended underneath it. I pulled back a curtain of leaves and was hit with an odd smell. As I dropped the branches, something blue on an ivory background caught my eye. Holding my breath, I moved the bush aside. Sunshine poked through a cloud, flooding the area and allowing the image to resolve: a unicorn head with a knife in its teeth.

I shuddered, struggling to see what surface the sinister image was painted on. Leaning forward to see it better, my hand settled onto something cold and pliable.

I froze, unable to blink. The dappled sunlight camouflaged something much larger than a creepy drawing.

Scrambling backward, a branch caught hold of my shirt, and I pitched sideways. Loose gravel gave way, and I slipped further down the escarpment. My hands flew out to find purchase, landing on dead flesh. The body shifted, revealing a girl a little older than me.

Horrified, I grasped a vine and pulled myself back onto the relative safety of my rock.

The young woman was naked, except for the tattoo penned into the side of her torso. Under it, a fresh gash, made with surgical precision, crudely stitched, curving from her back down and around to the front.

A deep sadness welled up in me, mingling with the horror. "I'll get help," I promised her, knowing, with a sick lurch, that I was too late.

Dizzy, with tears threatening, I pushed my way back to the sunshine. I needed to get out and let Edward know.

The rock face hadn't changed much since the last time I'd scanned it. I pictured the climbing wall in my old high school's gym. Straight up, thirty feet. Back in the day, I could scale it in less than half a minute. My current predicament had higher stakes but more holds and wasn't as high. The area also lacked a safety harness which I always used.

Certain that Edward would be back with a rope soon, I planned my path.

The route up and to my right rose steeper than the one to the left but provided a better landing if I slipped. Eyes raking the cliff face, I visualized each move, grateful for the distraction. Having a problem to solve allowed me to forget what I had seen.

"Edward?" I hollered.

No response.

Patchy, my pig friend on the farm below, snorted. I took it as encouragement, placing my fingertips on two rocks and my right toe on a third. With a hoist, the toe hold gave way, forcing my face into stone.

Carefully releasing my grasp, I rechecked my footing. Maybe it was better to stay put and wait.

"Hello?" I raised my voice.

Still nothing.

What if someone were looking for the girl? Before my rapidly thumping heart turned into panic, I scolded myself. "Focus, McGuire."

Testing another rock, it held fast. After a brief steadying breath, I moved up. Hand over hand, but always leading with my right foot, I concentrated on the ridge.

When I learned to climb, no one could ever convince me to move my left foot above my right. Every time I tried, I fell, so I gave up trying, focusing on getting fast using my technique. It worked. Slow and steady, my right foot led me up this wall.

Finally, my hands reached the loose stones of the trail. Turning my head to the left and then right, I calculated the distance to the nearest tree trunk. Neither direction in arms reach unless I leaned over and let go of the handholds. But the tree to the left was closer.

Leaning to the side, I extended my fingers. Closing on a leaf, I cautiously pulled the branch toward me, but the leaf snapped, and the tree moved away.

The effort caused my legs to shake, and I wasn't sure how much longer I could hold on.

The only way to get close enough to the trunk was to haul my left foot higher than my right and hook it over a low branch.

Slowly, the foot came up, but vertigo spun my head like a tilt-a-whirl. Too unfamiliar. I turned my hips to move my right foot. Pebbles rained down on me, eroding my footing.

"You can do it, Maddie." The voice of my mom, pragmatic and confident, came to me. She believed I could do anything. Thanking her, I tried.

Lifting my left foot, I willed the dizziness away. My stomach lurched, but I didn't dare slow. As my leg snaked over the branch, I launched off from my right foot and threw both hands, colliding with the trunk but clinging safely to the tree branch. After a beat, I lowered my feet to the ground and stepped gingerly onto the trail.

The momentary pride I felt from escaping the ledge quickly faded to horror. Legs trembling, they gave way, and I collapsed. On hands and knees, I scrabbled toward the edge, determined to confirm what I had witnessed. Tightness in my chest threatened to cut off my breathing as I peeked over.

The odd scent of flesh wafted through the clean smell of the forest.

A foot, clear as day, lay exposed from under the bramble.

Chapter Two: Old Nigel

Black dots danced before my eyes, again threatening to overwhelm me. I backtracked away from the ridge, turned, and sat flat, head lowered. Jaw tightening, I failed to keep tears from falling.

I balled my fists and counted first to five, then ten. The childhood ritual had the desired effect of calming me.

The promise I made to that girl. Help. I needed help, not for me, but for her.

Edward mentioned heading to the farmhouse we'd passed, so I retraced our steps.

The woods, which had shimmered with magic at the beginning of our hike, now creaked ominously. Tree roots appeared as long-toed feet, ready to ensnare unwary travelers.

Hoof beats clomped in the distance. I picked up my pace, speed walking toward the sound.

"Well, if you could climb up by yourself, why did I bring this great beast along?" Edward chuckled, indicating the massive, black-and-white draft horse he was leading by the reins.

Then he saw my face. "What's happened, lass?" His voice took on his best policeman's calm, but I knew from the Scottish burr he normally kept hidden that he was alarmed.

I wanted nothing more than to run to his arms and break down. But I promised the girl. "There is a young woman down there. A dead, naked," my voice caught. "Help her."

Nodding once, he handed me the reins and bolted to where I'd fallen.

One reason our relationship worked was that Edward didn't question my conclusions.

Pounding feet returned to me. "I see it," he reported, all trace of his Scottish brogue gone.

"Her," I corrected.

"What?"

"Her. Don't call her 'it,'" I insisted.

Face softening, he put both arms around me and squeezed. I was right. It felt nice, and I clung to him.

A moment later, he pulled away and spoke softly. "I'm going back to the farm to call this in. Stay here—"

"No," I interrupted.

"What?"

"I'm not going to stay here. I told her I would help."

Reaching for me, he pulled me into another hug. "You did, lass. I'll never know how you got up that cliff." After a kiss on the forehead, he added, "But I can run faster than you."

"Why would you run and not ride?" I patted the horse's neck, pulling in its great, solid strength.

"Ride what?"

All the chaos in my brain stilled as I stared at Edward. "Don't you know how to ride?"

"And where would I have learned that?" he demanded.

I shook my head, not wanting to get sidetracked. "I'll go. You stay here and guard the crime scene."

He squeezed my hand. "When you say it like that, it makes perfectly good sense."

The horse had a blanket but no saddle. "Give me a hand," I ordered, raising my foot next to the animal.

"Old Nigel, I believe," Edward offered as he made a cup with his hands. With a leg up, I swung my other leg over the back of the horse. Old Nigel was so wide that I felt like I was doing the splits to straddle him.

Edward handed me the reins.

"Are you sure you know how to control it?" There was a nervousness to the question that hadn't appeared when I'd tumbled off a cliff. If other matters weren't far more pressing, I would have pointed it out.

With a demonstration, I backed up Old Nigel several paces and turned him around. "Which farmhouse?" But I didn't need to ask. My mount was already straining to return home.

Edward explained the long wood and stone fence surrounding the building, and I loosened the reins, allowing the horse to gain speed, carrying me to an open gate. The weathered iron portal opened onto a stone pathway to the front door of a limestone farmhouse. Old Nigel tried to steer us toward his stable and food trough, but I aimed for the front door.

An elderly man barged out, demanding, "Where the devil did that young constable go? Who are you? And what do you think you're doin' to Old Nigel?"

I leaned onto Old Nigel's neck, looped my arms, brought my leg across his back, and lowered myself to the ground. He turned his great head toward me, blinking beautiful brown eyes.

"You're a good horse, Old Nigel. I wish I had an apple for you."

The man turned on his heel, leaving me to wonder if I should follow him or wait, but waiting wasn't an option.

"Sir?" I called, following him into the rustic entry of a sprawling farmhouse, searching for a landline.

"Ain't no *sir*," he answered as his sturdy, square body stumped into the kitchen. "Name's Nigel."

My hand paused mid-air, pointing at the telephone. "I'm sorry," I stammered. "I thought the horse was Nigel."

"'Orse is Old Nigel. Named 'im after me da."

Several responses went through my head, none of which were relevant. "Can I use your phone?"

"Ah," Nigel responded.

Since he nodded when he said it, I took it to mean "yes."

Drawing on my previous interactions with the police, I used my cell to find Detective Inspector Parikh's number and called it on Nigel's phone.

The DI was very polite until I identified myself.

"What," he asked with a long-suffering sigh, "have you gotten yourself into this time?"

Defensive, I barked my answer. "I do not go looking for dead bodies. England was supposed to be easy for me. I speak the language. I found my dream internship. I am behaving. But every time I relax, I trip over one!"

"Madeline?" DI Parikh's voice was authoritative but kind.

"Yeah?" I squeaked.

"Did you say you found a body?"

"Mmhm," I mumbled.

Nigel found what he was looking for in the kitchen but paused. He now stared with his ear cocked in my direction.

"Is Constable Bailey with you?" Parikh asked.

Shaking my head, I let him know, "Edward stayed with her. I rode here on Old Nigel to call you. We don't have any bars."

The words didn't make sense even to me, but the detective didn't press for clarification. "Do you know where you are?"

"The Cotswolds, near Painswick," I answered. "Nigel's house. Farm."

Even though I wasn't giving him anything useful, I couldn't think of the words to explain. Parikh, understanding as ever, asked, "May I speak with him?"

I thrust the phone in Nigel's direction. "Here," I said, with very little grace.

Nigel took the phone with one hand and, with the other, reached into the pocket of his well-worn woolen jacket for something. As I stood dumbly, he turned my palm up and filled it with sugar cubes. "'E's too spoiled for apples. Give my lovely these. There's a good girl."

Nigel nudged me toward the door, where the great black and white horse stood patiently.

Going to him, I patted Old Nigel, running my fingers through his white mane. A white blaze went over one eye and down to his nose, and he had enormous, furry white feet. Being near him brought me comfort I didn't think possible.

The scent of sugar must have been strong because he started nuzzling my arm. Lifting the cubes to his mouth, he snuffled them up with a gentleness that belied his size. Stroking Old Nigel's muzzle, I listened to his owner explain where we were to DI Parikh. The call seemed to end, although Nigel murmured a few more sentences before returning to me.

"You'll be wanting tea, then." Nigel made the statement in such a way that I didn't dare ask for coffee. Or a beer.

Darkness clung to the interior of the house, creating a claustrophobic atmosphere. The man sat me at his rustic kitchen table with its mismatched chairs. Bustling around the stove, he pulled a heavy kettle off an open flame and filled a thick ceramic mug. Plopping in a sugar cube without asking, he handed the steaming tea to me.

"Go on, then," he commanded. "Drink it down."

Wondering if the sweet cube came from the same grubby pocket he stashed the ones for his horse, I took a sip. Then another, and finished it, despite the heat. The tea revived me after hours of hiking. Unfortunately, my brain started spinning around my gruesome discovery.

The farmer refilled my cup, plopping in another sugar cube.

I longed to return outdoors and brush down Old Nigel.

From day one of horseback riding lessons back home, my ferocious instructor insisted I learn everything about the horse. She refused to teach girls afraid of the horse or the work that went into caring for it. In retrospect, she was terrifying, proclaiming that she "wouldn't teach no sissy girls." After a couple of years, my mom moved me into break-away roping lessons at a fancy stable in Scottsdale. Although no one there taught me how to pick rocks out of hooves. Not a task that comes up a lot in day-to-day life.

Still, rubbing down a horse sounded better than the questions that came my way.

Nigel, the man, not the horse, or his father for that matter, couldn't contain his curiosity.

"A constable took Old Nigel away, but an American girl brought 'im back. What's that you found, girly?"

Knowing I shouldn't share details, I stared at the steam twisting from the mug. The kettle ticked as it cooled.

"Which direction were ya comin'?"

Only two questions in, and I had had enough.

Scooting my chair back, I stood, then skirted around the table toward the entryway.

"Where be to, girly?"

Unable to decipher the question, I asked one of my own. "Do you have a horse brush? I got Old Nigel up to a canter. He could use a rub."

Nigel flopped his hand toward the stable I saw on the way in. "Ah. Help yourself."

Salvation, in the form of fresh air and a large horse, welcomed me outside. Squinting in the dappled sunlight, I looked for movement hoping for Edward's return. Or at least the arrival of the local police.

Seeing nothing but trees that reminded me of Snow White's escape to the forest, I turned to the stable. It struck me as cleaner than the house, and my estimation of Nigel went up a notch. The pile of fresh hay almost gleamed, the familiar scent taking me back to Boots' barn. Boots, a beautiful bay, had been my favorite childhood horse. I just knew that if I took good enough care of him, the stable would give him to me.

They didn't. Eventually, I discovered that boys were more interesting than horses.

But for now, having those memories to cling to kept me from shaking.

A comb, brush, and pick lay on a railing, and I snatched them as I went to the draft horse. Starting at his neck with a curry comb, I used a circular motion to loosen the dirt and hair. Switching to a body brush, I went over his full body and down his legs. It had been years since I last did the activity, and it tuckered me out.

Grateful for the distraction, I set the brush aside, swiped a lock of strawberry blonde hair out of my eyes, and grabbed the pick.

Lifting Old Nigel's front leg and bending it at the knee, I contemplated the state of his gigantic hoof. The worn shoes were clean, and tidying them didn't take long. "I'm glad your master spoils you. You deserve it."

By the time Edward returned, I finished the last one.

"Maddie, what are you doing?"

Intent on my task, it took me a moment to turn my head. Old Nigel mirrored my movement. Settling his big hoof on the ground, I gave the horse a pat on the rump. "Good boy."

Edward rushed to me, grabbed my shoulders, and maneuvered us away from the animal. "You can't do that! It could trample you."

For all the comfort I wanted at that moment, protection from a horse was not on the list.

Stamping my foot, I turned and looked at him, hands on hips. "Dude," I stated flatly.

The Americanism caused his crooked smile to form, and he had the grace to look at his shoes. "Sorry. I forget that you're from cowboy country."

About to point out that Arizona had thriving metropolises, an incredible arts scene, and vibrant indigenous cultures, a wild burro-crossing sign came to mind. To his point, the state was also home to quite a few cattle ranches. Cowboys, indeed.

"Right," I agreed. "Don't you forget it."

Both our smiles faded as the situation reasserted itself.

"The local force," Edward paused. "All two of them arrived and are securing the site. It will take the Gloucester DI and DS a few minutes to arrive.

"Won't DCI Bray and DI Parikh be here?" I asked.

"We're in a different area. Painswick is in Gloucestershire, not Avon and Somerset."

Annoyed, I shook my head. "What about the Gloucestershire, Avon and Somerset, and Wiltshire thing?"

When I found a disturbing clue during my first week in England, Edward described that the Tri-Force counties ran the most extensive lab.

Edward understood a distraction when he heard one and was willing and able to go off on a tangent to keep me occupied. "There are forty-three police departments in England and Wales, but they all follow the same laws," he lectured. "Scotland has one, but the laws are slightly different. This case will get handled by Tri-Force's MCIT."

I sighed. "Which stands for?"

"Major Crimes Investigation Team. Which means everyone you know will not be involved."

"But isn't Avon and Somerset part of the Tri-Force?" I wanted to know.

"They are their own team."

A thought occurred to me as I replaced the shoe pick on a shelf. We hiked for three hours before passing this farm. "Will they have to hike?" I asked.

Edward indicated the farm. "The houses along the Cotswold Way are down the slope enough to be on a street or lane." Again, to his credit, he pointed out what should have been obvious in a gentlemanly manner.

Of course, there was a road. How else would a farm get its bounty to market? "I've had a rough day," I said in my defense.

With a shake of his head, he agreed. "Indeed you have, lassie." After a quick kiss on my cheek, he asked, "Are you done with your wee pony, then?"

Possibly the worst description of Old Nigel one could imagine, but it had the desired effect. I laughed.

"Yeah."

He took my hand and guided me around the side of Nigel's homestead to terraced steps cut into the escarpment. As we scrambled down, Edward said, "DI Parikh cleared us to find our bed and breakfast."

A lane opened up when we got to the bottom, not visible from the trail. A funny snuffling snort caught my attention. Patchy the Pig, out of his sty and snuffling the field, poked his nose through the split-rail fencing.

As much as I wanted to say hi, exhaustion crept into my bones. "How much further?"

Steering us along the lane to a different house on the opposite side, Edward pointed to another set of steps. "A few more, then we'll be home free."

The stairs stretched to infinity as far as I was concerned, but down we went. Within a few minutes of what seemed like forever, we were in the village center.

Legs shaking from the steep descent, I looked up. "How long would it take if we stayed on the Cotswold Way?"

"About four hours," he responded. "Maybe more."

Whoever left that girl under the blackberry bushes worked extremely hard to get her there.

Chapter Three: Speculation

One horrifying discovery combined with a few hours of hiking, and I was done. Glancing around at the quaint village, the back of my brain registered the beauty of the architecture. But what I wanted was sleep.

"Where is the bed and breakfast?"

Edward swept a hand out. "Four or five houses along the Old Road."

"All the roads here are old," I pointed out.

Edward smiled, lifted my hand to his lips, and kissed it.

Melting, I relaxed enough to take in my surroundings. We stood on the corner of Old Road and New Road. Examining the materials in the street and building, I finally understood.

"This area," I indicated the New Road, "is clearly Tudor, 16th century." Moving closer to the Old Road, I squatted, touching a stone. "This is Roman." Roman architecture fascinated me, partly because cars drove over streets made 2000 years ago, and not one pothole marred the surface.

I stood and looked at Edward. "You knew?"

With a lift of his shoulder, he said, "Not exactly. But I love watching your brain work and figured you would tell me."

Blush rising to my cheeks, I turned to the Old Road and our B and B.

Edward, however, strode in the opposite direction.

"Hey," I complained. "A fluffy pillow is calling me."

"As are our dinner reservations." He pointed to a brightly painted wooden sign emblazoned with The Royal Oak just down the hill.

"It's a pub. Why on earth do we need reservations?"

Chuckling, Edward swept his arm to encompass the village. "If you haven't noticed, lassie, we're in a village. There are only two restaurants, and apparently, Michael is out of town visiting his grandkids in Stroud, so this is it. If we miss it, no food."

"I'm not hungry. We can grab cheese at the market later."

This time, he picked me up, difficult as we were the same height, and physically turned me.

Rebellious at being manhandled, I spun the second my feet hit the ground and stalked away.

"I know you're not hungry after what you saw," he said, following me. "But I also know you need food, or you will shake uncontrollably later."

He was right. He witnessed it happen the last time I came face to face with something equally disturbing.

Not wanting to give in right away, I took two more steps before acquiescing. Plus, as I flung my ponytail over my shoulder, I saw the Closed sign in the market window. Marching back to him like it was my idea to go to dinner, I took his arm.

Tactfully, he refrained from comment as we entered the crowded pub.

Packed to the brim with a cheery crowd, the aroma of fine dining greeted us. Near our table, in a faraway corner, perched a green and white quilted deer head complete with antlers to keep us company. The wooden tables looked as old as the building but were refinished so many times that they gleamed like obsidian.

Edward settled me in and went to the bar to order food. When he returned, he handed me a pot of hot tea and a brandy. What I really required was coffee to clear my head.

Pressing the brandy into my hand, he said, "Just a sip to keep the shock at bay."

I sipped, the sweet liquid warming my chest and calming my nerves.

Concern creased Edward's face.

With a smile, I held my hand across the table to him. "Thank you. It's helping."

His features relaxed. "Of course it is," he said, echoing one of my favorite retorts.

The brandy also sparked my appetite, not that I wanted to admit it. "What did the menu say?"

Written on a chalkboard by the door, I hadn't read it yet.

"I ordered," he said, looking toward the bar. "I didn't want you to wait."

As my head cocked in annoyance, he rushed on. "Courgette and lemon risotto and a burger. You can pick, or we can share both."

Suddenly famished, a burger sounded great, but I desired clarification. "What is courgette?"

Edward gaped. "You must have them in America," he said. "Squash. Long, skinny, green. They look like cucumbers."

"You mean zucchini? Italian squash? Summer squash? We have quite a few names for them. I don't think they need another."

"Italian squash, yes. Do you like them?"

"Love them!" Changing my expectation to a veggie rice dish, not juicy beef, I said, "I'll have that."

Beautifully plated food arrived, and I pounced on it. The creaminess of the risotto complimented chunks of zucchini and onion. A delicate hint of lemon accented every bite.

After shoveling half the bowl into my face, I checked on my date as he enjoyed what looked like a ham, cheese, and tomato sandwich.

"I thought you were getting a burger?"

Holding it toward me, he said, "I did."

"That looks like ham."

With a bite, he confirmed it.

"Burgers are ground beef," I clarified. "As in hamburger. That's where the burger part comes from."

Eyes narrowed, he considered me a moment before saying, "Anything on a bun is a burger."

That familiar sensation that I didn't belong in this country returned. Food had strange names, and I never knew where I was.

And I found another dead body. Dinner suddenly turned into a rock in my stomach as I wondered, "Why was she there?"

Shaking his head, Edward attempted comfort. "I'm sorry, lass," he said, full Scottish burr in evidence. "You shouldn't have to see a thing like that."

Impatient, I scowled. "No," I clarified. "Why was her body left in that particular location? It doesn't make sense. There isn't anything nearby. The murderer couldn't take the stairs because they're too far of a climb and much too public. Coming along the Cotswold Way is worse."

My eyes bore into his, daring him to tell me the situation wasn't my business.

Looking to the heavens, as he often did when my persistent nature surfaced, Edward sighed. "You won't let it go, will you?"

Arms crossed over my chest, I reminded him, "Last time I tried to ignore danger, it almost killed me. This time, rules or no, you need to keep me in the loop."

He tried to stop me, but I overrode him.

"I won't tamper or withhold evidence or take photos of things I shouldn't. But I need someone to talk to, and if it's not you, it will be my friends or random people I meet. Your choice."

As he opened his mouth, I thought of another point.

"And," I plowed on. "You can't claim it's being handled in a different office. I know for a fact that even if the MCIT is handling this, the South West of England is tiny, so you have to know someone who knows. Six degrees of separation and all."

When I paused for a breath, he managed to say, "Okay."

"Plus, you were on the scene when the body was discovered, so you will at least be involved as a witness, and you can talk to fellow officers when you're interviewed, and what did you say?" My brain finally caught up to my mouth.

"Okay," he repeated. "I'll keep you informed. DI Parikh actually said the same thing about wanting to be kept informed." He smiled, curling his fingers in mine. "Although without quite so much ranting."

"Emphasis," I corrected.

"Haranguing," he countered.

"Charmingly highlighting important details."

His lopsided grin appeared. "Run out of synonyms, did you?"

Rather than admitting defeat, I sobered, returning to the main point. "Do you agree? About how she could have been left there, I mean."

One shoulder lifted and dropped. "No vehicles or horses are allowed on the trail, but you saw how easy it was to ignore that rule," referring to my ride on Old Nigel.

"So you're saying that even though you're not supposed to, someone could bring a horse or ATV on the trail and dump a body."

"More often, it would involve poaching or moving farm equipment." He pointed to an access trail going up away from Nigel's farm. "There are manor houses and farms all along the way. They would have golf carts and tractors."

Turning in another direction, he pointed and said, "Remember the country home with the stone frog on the gate? They would use a motorized cart to transport potatoes to one of the villages."

I slumped. "If so many people come this way, why am I the only one who finds bodies?" In a small voice, I mumbled, "I don't like it."

Gathering my hands into his again, Edward said, "Of course, you don't, lass. But you did right by the girl today. You got her help."

Hoping the police would identify her and let her family know, I wondered if any other missing girls were lost in the ancient forest.

Chapter Four: Sherlock Holmes

Questions began with farmer Nigel the day before, continued with the local police, and ended with a female Detective Inspector who was very kind. I missed DI Parikh, though, with his trim beard and wire-framed glasses. All of it blurred together in my mind, and I couldn't remember what I said or to whom. With Parikh, I didn't have to explain why I was in the country. He was well aware of my college internship at the Roman Baths.

"Who was she?" I asked the detective inspector.

The DI shook her head. "We don't know. There are no local reports of missing girls."

"Find who did this." The thought of her alone twisted my heart. "Please."

The DI, whose name I couldn't remember, patted her dark hair before responding, reminding me of my dorm mate, Naomi. "I understand," she said in a way that made me trust she did.

In a daze, I wandered out of the B and B living room that our host Iris offered to the police for interviews.

"Send Bailey in, won't you?" the DI called as I slid the door closed and entered the cozy communal dining room where Edward waited.

After a surreptitious glance to make sure no one could see us, he enveloped me in a bear hug.

When he released me, I stepped back and looked into his face with a weary smile. "You're up."

The dining room's solid wood table held a selection of breakfast fare, including toast, oatcakes, muesli, yogurt, coffee, and a teapot covered in a knitted cozy. Two loaves of hearty bread, chock full of nuts and seeds, respectively, were meant to sustain hikers as they traveled to the next village.

My knotted stomach twisted further.

Grabbing a thick ceramic mug, I chose coffee, hoping to jumpstart my foggy brain. Between the shock of yesterday's discovery and the hours of hiking, I thought I would sleep better. But an unfamiliar bed set within arm's reach of Edward's had me tossing and turning.

Edward floated the idea of separate rooms for our Cotswold Way hiking tour, but I had to be all mature and cosmopolitan and tell him we could share. Frankly, I had envisioned pushing the twin beds together and taking our relationship to the next level. He had no clue what a big step that would have been for me.

Clearing the situation from my thoughts, I refilled the coffee and went to the door to the hallway stairs. The threshold, which I hadn't noticed the night before, created a triangle, not a square. To the right, creaky stairs lead to the bedrooms, and at an angle to the left sat the kitchen.

I stepped back, scanning the plastered walls, piecing the architecture together in my mind. The building, circa the 1600s, was made of butter-colored limestone. Guests entered through a beautiful portico, then passed through a boot room that opened into the dining and living rooms.

The stairs led to three rooms. One of those rooms seemed out of place, curling away from the house's footprint. With nothing better to occupy me, I trudged back down the steps and knocked on the kitchen door.

"Iris?" I called our hostess.

Quick, efficient, and caring, her long limbs bustled over to me. "You poor love. What do you need?"

With a shake of my head, I answered, "Nothing. I wanted to know about the bedroom we're staying in. Is it—"

"An addition? Yes, it is. My, you have a good eye. Sometime in the 1800s, long before the houses were put on historic preservation lists, an enterprising owner bought part of the first storey from next door. They share a common wall, don't you know? Well, yes, you must, or you wouldn't have asked. Added a full bedroom. When the en suite plumbing was installed,

I had to purchase extra insurance because the shower is over my neighbor's dining area."

My eyes bugged, fascinated by the creativity of the two-century-old design change.

Misinterpreting my expression for distress, Iris turned, snatched a scone from a cooling rack, and forced it into my hands.

"Eat. You need to keep up your strength."

Showing me upstairs, she called, "There are some mysteries on the bookshelf in the hallway. Have a lie-down and read."

I scanned the titles: *The Hound of the Baskervilles, The Study in Scarlet,* and *The Sign of the Four.* It shouldn't surprise me that every house I visited in England had Arthur Conan Doyle on display, but it did.

Even though I'd read it before, I snatched *The Hound of the Baskervilles* with a sigh. At least there were no naked dead bodies in Holmes stories.

As I skimmed the pages, I devoured the scone. Using my finger as a bookmark, I carried the book to the dining room, cut a slice of the nut bread, and covered it with butter. Sitting at the table, I read about the curse of the hound. Struggling, I couldn't remember the plot.

Soon the foggy, misty moors of Devonshire entranced me as the manor unfolded its secrets. Without realizing it, I ate half a loaf of nut bread and, sometime along the way, switched to a delicate teacup filled with Earl Grey and milk. Trying to stay a step ahead of Dr. Watson and Sherlock Holmes was a heck of a lot more fun than dwelling on our real-life mystery.

Except...I couldn't help but dwell.

The curse on the Baskerville line dealt with a lecherous old man trapping a young woman in a secluded home. The thought of the strange farmer Nigel holding a girl hostage brought on a full-body shudder so violent that when Edward said, "Hey there," I screamed. Loudly.

Edward wrapped his arms around my shoulders, Iris bolted into the room from the kitchen, and the female DI adjusted her necklace. I'm guessing because she intuited that I was okay and not because she wasn't concerned.

"Goodness gracious, me! What's wrong, pet?"

Hot blush flooded every inch of my skin. "Nothing! Overactive imagination. I'm fine, really," I said, waving away the fuss.

Picking up the volume from the table, Edward noted the title. "Why are you reading this, Maddie?" With the DI in the room, Edward's Scottish burr disappeared, replaced by a neutral accent. At least, I considered it normal. My coworker Simon described it as posh, like his. Edward had explained to me that a Northern upbringing would hinder him professionally.

All of which I pondered, not responding right away. Not wanting to admit I made a poor literary choice, I turned my attention to the detective inspector.

"You don't think Nigel held her captive, do you?"

Her intense look let me know she took the suggestion seriously. I appreciated it but didn't want to get the farmer in trouble for no reason.

"No creepy vibes came off him," I rushed to add. "He seemed odd but not off." I didn't admit I could be cutting him a break because of the horse.

Edward's hand rested on my shoulder. "You're sure?" he clarified. "Sometimes, you dismiss your instincts because you're not from here."

As much as I wanted to argue his point, I couldn't. It was the understatement of the century.

"I don't know." I shrugged. "My nerves are on edge right now, so I don't know what I'm feeling." Scrubbing a hand over my face, I concluded, "Ignore me."

With a sneaky flick of his wrist, Edward moved *The Hound of the Baskervilles* behind him, then popped it onto a shelf above the buffet.

Considering it, I pointed out, "I can reach everything you can, you know."

"Rubbish," he responded with a lopsided grin. "I'm at least eight inches taller than you."

For the first time, the Gloucestershire Detective Inspector laughed.

Ignoring them, I proved my point by stretching past him and retrieving the book. "I can't remember what happened." However, I didn't continue reading. Adding marmite to yet another piece of bread, I played over my encounter with Nigel. If I hadn't been shattered, would I have felt threatened? Closing my eyes, I tried to place myself into the farmhouse, but the image of the young woman I found surfaced, refusing to leave.

Slapping my hand on the table to clear the vision, I turned to Edward. "I'm going to the room." I held the book up. "To read."

Settling onto my narrow twin bed, I resolutely ignored the world and focused on the moors of Devonshire and Baskerville Hall, which got me precisely nowhere. The hound and love triangles weren't getting me closer to closure for my current situation.

Abandoning the novel, I switched to my phone to search Holmes short stories about dead bodies in the woods. *The Crooked Man* popped up, but as I skimmed the synopsis, all I discovered was that the man in question had the name of Wood.

"What am I doing?" I groaned, plopping onto the pillow.

The door opened, and Edward said, "Good question. Do you have an answer?" Sitting across from me on his bed, he waited while I thought.

One of the many things I liked about him was that he never pressed me, giving me space.

So why did I gravitate to Sherlock Holmes? How could an old plot help my current mess? It couldn't, but something in the story rang true.

Pushing onto an elbow, I turned to look at Edward. "I'm grasping at straws." That was close, but not all of it.

Edward heard my unfinished thought. "But?"

I stood and walked the room's length in two paces, pivoted, and returned. After a few circuits, an answer formed.

"A young girl kidnapped by an old man - it fits, doesn't it?"

Skeptical, Edward pointed out that Nigel was more weather-beaten than old.

Shaking my head in frustration, I said, "Nigel wouldn't leave a body on his property like that."

But someone in one of those secluded mansions might.

Chapter Five: Gwendolyn

All I wanted to do was return to work, my internship at the Roman Baths. The natural hot springs at the end of the Cotswold Way fueled habitation for over 2000 years. Bath, a stunning city of Georgian architecture, covered the ruins of a bustling Roman city. And I was lucky enough to be interning there.

That morning I got my wish.

The crackle of bacon lured me downstairs, where Iris laid out a full-English breakfast. While stuffing fried eggs into my mouth, Edward appeared with the good news. We were cleared to leave.

The drive through the Cotswolds, an "Area of Outstanding Natural Beauty" according to the signs, didn't hold the same level of enchantment when we took a train from Stroud. The fluffy white clouds cleared, allowing sunshine to ignite fall leaves in brilliant reds, golds, and yellows. The contrast with the deep green forest usually made me swoon, but not today.

This morning I longed for the warm, dry air of the desert and 100-mile views.

Edward must have caught my mood because he took my hand and squeezed.

Looking at our intertwined fingers brought a smile to my lips. "You promised me I wouldn't find any bodies on this trip."

A finger lifted, but he held on to me as he responded, "I specifically included the term 'in a bath,' so my promise is as good as my word."

The smile grew, spreading to my eyes and heart. It was true. If Edward said something, it could be counted on. He never wavered in his staunch belief in rules. A little annoying sometimes, but if I needed him, he would be here.

"Do you want to call the Priestlys and warn them of your unplanned arrival?" he asked as he passed a semi on the wrong side of the road.

Lorry, I corrected myself after opening my eyes. I would never get used to cars on the left, so I had no intention of driving.

I pondered his question. If I went to Ash Tree Cottage, where I rented a room from a lovely couple, I would have to explain why I was home. They had already cut a vacation short for me, so I knew Meryl Priestly would fuss over the situation. I'm pretty sure she missed her own kids and enjoyed having me to mother.

Then, she would insist I call home and talk to my mom in Arizona. The prospect held an appeal. Being cocooned in motherly love would do a lot toward erasing the memory of my discovery.

I allowed the idea to take hold for a few minutes before shaking my head. "No. Take me straight to work."

If I let my parents think I couldn't take care of myself, my mom would implant her well-meaning, loving hooks in and reel me home. Offers of redecorating her spare room for me would sprinkle every conversation. Her spare room. Not *my* room because she sold our house, the second I moved to Chicago for school.

Which posed another problem. Chicago and my dad in his corporate fortress. A possibility I didn't want to consider, but if I called him with this mess, he would set up a sales position for me in the blink of an eye.

No, thank you very much. I would not be a guest, and I would not be railroaded into a business job. I could take care of myself.

Something I proved with my work at the Roman Baths. Even though I had a rough start, I felt like a part of the Baths now. My aristocratic coworker Simon had developed a begrudging respect for me, and we were on the road to becoming friends. His aunt, Lady Vivian, who headed development as a volunteer, trusted me. A real live lady!

My boss Samantha Niven, Sam to her friends, welcomed me as a companion and confidant. The situation was practically perfect in every way, as Mary Poppins would say.

"You're sure?" Edward asked.

I squeezed his hand. "One hundred percent."

Sam and Simon would be curious about my early return but wouldn't pry for details. And when I was ready to share, Simon would play the older brother with useless advice and a dose of teasing to lighten the mood.

Edward pulled into the bus drop-off by the side of the Bath Abbey, a stunning gothic structure rife with history. After kissing Edward, I scrabbled out of the car. Walking across the square to the entrance of the Roman Baths, my confidence returned.

Not dressed in my uniform of tan khakis and a blue polo, it didn't matter. Maybe Dr. Daniels and Sam would let me sift dirt at the newest discovery site since I wasn't presentable as a tour guide.

My main goals at the Baths were to get Dr. Daniels to recognize me, remember my name, and invite me on as a member of his team. As of yet, he appreciated my work at the tesserae dig in the Baths' Undercroft but didn't associate my diligence with my face. Yet. He would, though. After all, how many bright-eyed, enthusiastic nineteen-year-olds were vying for his professional attention?

The Georgian-era entrance to the Baths always impressed me. The high, windowed dome allowed light to flood onto the excited tourists waiting for the ticket sellers.

Waltzing by like I owned the place, I headed to the unassuming door of the Oversight Office, where Sam kept her desk, scheduled tours, and ran things smoothly.

At the sound of Dr. Daniels' voice behind the door, I tapped before entering.

"Come in, come in. Nice to see your smilin' eyes!" Sam greeted me.

Dr. Daniels turned at my entrance, and recognition dawned. I straightened to my full height and stuck out my hand.

"You work at the Pump Room, yes? Fetch me a ploughman's with Stilton, would you?"

My arm fell as he turned away.

He thought I was Lily, who did work at the Pump Room next door, and she often delivered food to the Baths. We had the same long, wavy strawberry blonde hair that we tended to wear in a ponytail. The biggest differences were my height and her bright blue eyes compared to my green.

The archeologist recognized the server but not the Baths intern.

The whole exchange depressed me. Not only was I forgettable, but my friend Lily was in the hospital in Manchester.

Sadness must have shown on my face as Sam rose and put an arm around my shoulders. Convinced my boss was descended from leprechauns, a myth she did little to dispel with her bright ginger hair, tiny stature, and thick Irish accent, I couldn't help but feel a little magic in the gesture.

"No, Dr. Daniels. This here is Maddie, come all the way from America she has," Sam interjected.

"Is that right?" he said, making eye contact briefly. "You should take a tour of the Baths, then. Wonderful place," he suggested before looking away, unaware I regularly gave tours. "Quite wonderful," he added absently.

It wasn't until this point that I saw the object of his attention. On a chair, hidden by the open door, I still clung to, perched a young woman about my age. *Vying for his attention,* I growled to myself.

"And this here is Gwendolyn," Sam continued.

"You're Maddie," she exclaimed, excited. "How lovely to meet you, absolutely lovely. Simon told me so much about you. Adores you, he does, absolutely."

Her speech seemed artificially high-pitched, jaw clenched, much like Simon's when he spoke to his aunt. Aristocratic, I deduced.

"Do call me Dolly," she continued, oblivious to my confusion. "Please do. Absolutely everyone does."

"Maddie," I stammered, unable to think of a single interesting or polite thing to say.

Dolly tossed a long, straight, graceful sheaf of golden hair behind her ear, revealing perfect skin. Not a freckle in sight. Sky blue eyes with long natural lashes acted as beacons, making it impossible to look away from her.

A line from the musical *Wicked* came to mind. Something about loathing.

Unadulterated loathing.

"Well, of course, you are! Wonderful to meet you. Absolutely brilliant." Her graceful response covered my awkwardness. "Dr. Daniels here," she placed a delicate hand on his arm for a moment, then retracted it before it became personal, "was just telling us about that delightful discovery in the Undercroft. Have you seen it, Maddie? Of course, you have, Simon told me."

"Absolutely," I answered somewhat childishly.

Which, of course, was the wrong thing to say because Dr. Daniels then offered to take Dolly on a tour of the site, calling her by name. Technically, Simon showed me one evening for a few minutes, but I never had a proper visit.

As they walked by, the scent of expensive perfume wafted from her hair. Something my mother only wore on very special occasions. She stumbled over my shoe as she crossed under my nose.

Even that came across as elegant.

"Look how tall you are!" she exclaimed. "Simon's height, or yours, Dr. Daniels."

Unable to detect any malice or spite in her words only caused my dislike to blossom. No girl likes to be compared to a man, no matter how benign the comment.

"What was that all about?" I asked Sam, hoping for a bit of gossip and maybe some comfort.

Instead, I saw her crossing my name off the tour schedule, her face screwed up in concentration. Unpinning the work plan from the board, she muttered, "Wait, no. Is this right? I'd better check with Dolly."

Almost bowling me over as she turned and hurried to the door, she said, "Ah, Maddie, there you are."

Like I'd disappeared. "Still here." It may have come out a little more aggressive than I hoped.

Sam didn't notice.

"Could you be an angel and organize those papers?"

Without waiting for an answer, which would be yes in any case, she skipped out of sight and called, "Dolly!"

With a glare, I turned to the paperwork Sam mentioned. Donations and donor records, two months' worth. Opening the top drawer of the oak filing cabinet Simon purchased for the office, I found the proper folder and unceremoniously stuffed the first few sheets in it.

Filing. I was back to filing.

This activity kicked off a lot of my previous troubles. Plus, who wants an international internship that involves the most boring job on earth? No one.

I sighed. In truth, I did. I mean, I didn't want to file, but I would do anything to keep the internship so they could pretty much throw any demeaning task at me, and I would do it.

Rankled that Dolly waltzed in and took over my tours, I considered jamming all the papers into a single file and being done with it. But knowing my luck, I would be the one who had to sort and scan them into the computer.

"Sigh." I said the word aloud for emphasis.

"Back to your roots, as they say?" Simon entered the room quiet as a cat, as per usual. Blonde and handsome, when he wasn't sneering down his nose, he observed me with watery blue eyes.

Knowing how much I hated the task, Simon immediately settled into teasing me.

It took me a long time and a couple of dangerous situations to accept Simon's droll sense of humor for what it was. Wit, dry to the point of mummification, his calm, patrician bearing never cracked, even when joking. Now that I knew him better, I liked him for it.

And I couldn't wait to hear his thoughts about the absolutely perfect little Dolly. Some may be taken in by that tittering laugh and easy charm, but not Simon. He possessed the ability to see right through to people.

"Planting myself, it appears."

As much as I wanted to hear every detail about how Dolly appeared on the scene and then leap into my own tales of horror, I remained quiet. Decorum was key when dealing with Lord Simon Pacock.

With a twitch of a smile, he said, "I'll get Daniels to put you on sifting duty." While Simon coordinated the volunteers, Daniels had the final say on everything. "We're getting deeper into the room, so more fragments should be arriving soon."

"It will be a short sentence," I quipped. Then added, "Thank you. I can't believe I'm working an actual dig."

"Once Daniels has a better sense of the place, we will—"

"Absolutely!" The word, voiced by the ubiquitous Dolly as my mother would say, floated into the room, cutting Simon off mid-sentence.

"What?" I wanted to know. "What will we do?" Give me a pick and brush, and let me work inside the site? "Simon?"

His attention laser-focused on Dolly, who exclaimed, "Simon, darling, you're here!"

Big surprise. Half the office belonged to him.

"Maddie, Sam asked me to give you this and let her know if everything is acceptable," she said, handing me the revised tour schedule.

Her name replaced mine for the next two weeks. However, at the bottom of the grid, a scrawled note added that I would be sifting for two shifts a day. I'd be alone with a lot of dirt in a fluorescent-lit stairwell. Heaven!

"Of course," I said, pinning the schedule up and refraining from saying 'Absolutely.'

Dolly smiled. Sweetly.

It annoyed me.

But not nearly as much as when she took Simon by the hand and kissed him on the cheek.

"Uncle wants us to meet at The Gainsborough if you don't mind."

To my utter astonishment, Simon beamed. Beamed! I didn't have confirmation, but I suspected my newfound friend preferred his females that way—as friends. Were he and Dolly a thing?

I couldn't take anymore. "I'll see you all in the morning," I said to Dolly and Simon, passing Sam on my way out.

My head cleared as I slowly wandered by the train station, under the River Avon, and up the switchback path to Bear Flats. Ash Tree Cottage, Roger and Meryl's cozy home, would greet me with open arms.

The worn, wooden gate opened onto a lush garden with flower-lined stepping- stones guiding me cheerily to the front door. The ash tree's leaves hovered on the brink of turning yellow with the cooler weather.

Using a heavy iron key, I unlocked the mudroom door, or boot room, as they call it. I took off my shoes and padded into the living room sock-footed.

The scent of chicken soup wrapped me in a warm embrace. I arrived at the perfect moment.

"Hello?" I called as I moved through the main room to the kitchen.

"Maddie, dear," Meryl's muffled voice replied. "Is that you? Lend a hand, can you?"

Far from Meryl dishing out bowls of soup, I found her sprawled on the floor, head inside a cupboard under the kitchen sink. The extra-deep porcelain sink was half-full of standing water.

"Roger's not quite well, I'm afraid," Meryl informed me from her awkward position. "I made him soup, but too many noodles got in the drain."

Ducking to her level, I adjusted a flashlight, throwing light on her hands.

"Thank you, dear. I almost have it."

The 'it' in question was the j-joint, which she loosened in hopes of unclogging the drain.

Panic flared. The clog held at least a gallon of water at bay. "Meryl, no, wait!"

Dropping the flash, I popped up, thrust my hand into the sink, and felt for the plug - nothing but open holes in the drain. My eyes raked the counter, but the stopper remained hidden.

"Mind the torch," she complained, followed by a triumphant, "Aha!"

Abandoning my search, I turned to the cupboard with the mixing bowls as Meryl screamed, noodles and water cascading over her head.

I thrust the largest bowl under the torrent. Catching on, Meryl scrambled to kneeling, and we formed a bucket brigade with bowls and pans. Once the sink emptied, we snatched every available rag and sopped up the floor.

Standing with two drippy tea towels in my hands, I surveyed the kitchen. "I think we did it," I said.

Meryl burst out laughing.

Surprised, I looked at the state of her. A single noodle clung to her hair, half her red tunic wet, and she still found the hilarity in the situation.

As I removed the stray pasta, the giggles bubbled up in me. "That was impressive," I got out with a chuckle. "Where did the stopper go?"

Pointing under the sink, she admitted, "I took it with me to investigate. Thank the Lord you came home when you did, Maddie McGuire."

Grinning, I suggested, "Let's put the drain together before one of us turns the faucet on by mistake."

She shook her head. "No. I've done it before. Teflon tape and a wrench, and we will be ticketyboo." Picking up the plumber's tape, she added, "You go have a bath, you dear girl, and I'll have soup waiting in your room."

"That sounds amazing," I confessed, acknowledging my weariness. "Thank you."

"No, no," she said. "The thanking is all on my side."

As I plodded up the two flights of stairs to my studio, I realized no one asked why I came back early.

Chapter Six: Rhymes and Reasons

I couldn't blame Meryl for not fussing over my return with everything she had going on. I picked the Baths because no one would comment. Still, it felt lonely. With a sigh, I finished my soup, and went to bed.

Much as I would never admit it to my mom, a good night's sleep does wonders for putting things in perspective. The scent of freshly baked bread wafting up two stories didn't hurt either.

Just as I opened the door to what I referred to as my own private princess tower, my computer alerted me.

Accessing it, I found the beautiful and mischievous face of my best friend, Tori Gonzalez.

"Did you? How was he? Any regrets?"

The bonus of living next door to your best friend for eighteen years is that no preamble was necessary. "No, irrelevant, and plenty."

Her face fell. "I'm sorry. What happened?"

"You won't believe me if I tell you."

Squinting at the camera, she jabbed a petite finger accusingly. "If you tell me about a dead body, I will…."

My expression must have frozen because she didn't finish her threat.

"You didn't. Did you? Wasn't the reason for Bath is that it's so safe?"

The city of Bath has almost no crime. "Technically, I wasn't in Bath."

Tori covered her face and groaned. Peeking through her fingers, she sighed. "Seriously? How is that even possible?"

Scott, Tori's high school boyfriend, shouted in the background.

"He wants to know how we can help."

"Wow," I couldn't stop myself from saying. Scott had come a long way from the controlling jerk he had been.

Or I'd come a long way in sharing my friend. "That is so nice! You guys are the best," I added quickly.

"Good save," she commented but graciously moved on. "How am I supposed to ask you for favors when you keep embroiling yourself in death and destruction?"

"I'm not sure embroiling myself is entirely accurate. Becoming embroiled may reflect the situation better." I made a rolling motion with my hand, "Ask away."

"Does one become embroiled? Or is embroiling something that happens to you?"

"Not the question I was expecting. We've said embroil too many times. It doesn't sound like a word anymore."

"Have you ever heard Sing a Song of Sixpence?" she asked randomly.

"A pocket full of rye?" The tune surfaced, but I couldn't remember anything more. Recalling the last time Tori asked about a childhood song, I cringed. "Are you planning on ruining another nursery rhyme for me?"

"Not nearly as traumatic as the last one. Anyway, that one and Little Jack Horner." Expression turning evasive, she struggled with her question.

Wary, I demanded, "What?"

With eyes wide open and pleading, she looked like one of her Lupita dolls she started collecting when we were eight.

"Would you ask someone at the Abbey if either of the poems has to do with the Dissolution of the Monasteries?" Thick eyelashes fluttered. "Pretty please?" For her classes, Tori preferred to use primary sources for her research instead of depending on the internet.

Using my poker face, I pretended to think about it.

"You're the best! Thank you!"

I stared at the screen. "How did you know?" Giggling, she pointed through the camera. "Oh, please. You might as well have subtitles flash below your face."

"Never let me go to Vegas," I suggested before returning to the subject.

"So, yes, obviously, I'll go. Deacon Michael came on one of my tours and seemed to like it. He's all about education. Speaking of which, is this for your terrifying Abuela or for the class you're taking to appease her?"

Her highly devout grandmother agreed to pay for Tori's room and board if Tori majored in religious studies. It was a good deal, but Tori decided to double major so she could get a job when she graduated.

"The second. Last weekend Abuela gave my apartment an official tour. We made sure any sign of Scott was scrubbed away." Palms up, she said, "Must have worked because the rent is still being paid.

"Okay, enough about me. Tell me everything."

I did. About the blackberries and the peaceful, beautiful trail, my fall. And the girl.

"I wish I knew her name. Maybe then, I don't know..." I trailed off.

As usual, Tori didn't require explanations. "Because as long as people say your name, you're remembered, and you mean something."

Tears stung my eyes as I nodded. "Yeah. That."

"I'm sure Edward will tell you as soon as he knows. And," she continued, a sweet expression beaming at me. "I'll build her a Dia De Los Muertos figure."

Gobsmacked, my hand flew to my mouth. "You'd do that?"

With a look of supreme smugness, Tori said, "If you quit your blubbering, yes."

The Day Of The Dead, after All Saints Day, was a tradition Catholics from Mexico observed. In Arizona, it was as natural as celebrating Halloween. Skeleton figurines of loved ones decorated homes and businesses all year round. One year, Tori's Abuela allowed me to participate in making sugar skulls.

"I need to make one for an assignment anyway," she added in an off-handed way that didn't fool me for a second. Knowing how to make me feel loved was Tori's superpower. "I'll even add her tattoo."

"How can you put a tattoo on a skeleton? They don't have skin."

"Don't stifle my creativity. Unicorn head, right?"

"With a knife in its teeth. Kinda disturbing."

"Unique, though. It'll help guide her soul, as my grandmother would say."

"The nice thing," I said, pulling myself together, "is that this time, the death is very far from my door. Once the police have all my info, I can put the horrible parts behind me and focus on justice through remembrance."

"As opposed to justice through tracking down murderers."

"Exactly. Much safer."

Sausage and bacon crackled and snapped, adding their aromas to that of the bread. Nose twitching, I told Tori, "I better go. Meryl is cooking up a storm downstairs."

"I hate that I have to say this so much but stay safe."

"Right?" I winced. "Love you oodles."

The room I rented included a tiny kitchenette, but ever since my less-than-ideal introduction to England, Meryl insisted I breakfast with them. Hurrying downstairs, I entered the dining room to find her and Roger tucking into a full English - toast, eggs, bacon, sausage, mushrooms, and roasted tomatoes.

"Are you expecting an army?" I laughed.

Meryl preened, looking terribly pleased with herself. "The chicken soup did the trick, and Roger is much better." Gazing at her husband of thirty-five years with evident love, she extended a long arm across the table and patted his hand. "The old dear needs to build up his strength."

Roger Priestly, to my amazement, blushed at the display of affection. But he returned it in kind by kissing his wife's hand.

My parents, both wonderful people who were completely wrong for each other, had been divorced for so long that I never got to see a happy couple until now. The Priestlys were well matched, both exceedingly kind and gracious. Tall and lean, Meryl's intriguing shock of grey in her dark brown hair fit naturally by her silver-headed husband's side.

"I'm glad you're feeling better, Reverend Priestly."

"Ah, Maddie. Good morning." He gestured toward a chair. "Join us, and please call me Roger. There is something not quite right having the words reverend and priest in the same phrase."

The offer had been extended before, but something about Roger's height and venerable demeanor demanded formality, despite his easy manner.

"Tuck in, dear," Meryl insisted.

As I sat, a message came through on my phone. Not sure of the Priestlys' dining room rules, my hand hovered over it.

"Answer," Roger encouraged. "And," he added with a wink, "if it's that nice constable, invite him over."

Relieved, I picked up the phone and smiled at the message from Edward. Looking up, I said, "He is nearby. Is it really okay?"

Meryl indicated the massive amount of food on the table. "Please. Tell him to bring all his friends." After a beat, she added, "And his coworkers. And anyone he runs into on the street."

I conveyed the message, and Edward arrived looking smart and proper in his blue police officer uniform. Something warm and gushy blossomed in my chest at the sight of him.

With the artful editing of key facts, Edward managed to convey my shocking find to the Priestlys without mentioning murder. The explanation came out as a little disturbing and sad, but nothing to worry about. An impressive performance considering the amount of bacon and sausage he consumed during the telling.

I made a mental note to try the same technique with my mom when the time came.

"I'll add the poor soul to our prayer list," Roger said. "Do you have her name?"

Shaking his head, Edward said, "It hasn't been released to the public yet." He looked at the minister for a moment, coming to a decision. "For prayers, you can use Sherrie."

That bit of news surprised me. It meant the police had identified her.

"I'll need to tell Tori," I said. "She's creating a Dia De Los Muertos figurine for the girl."

Roger raised an eyebrow. "Indeed? I'd love to see a photo when the skeleton is complete. Perhaps we can double our prayers here by displaying Tori's work from Arizona."

Roger and Meryl met Tori when she visited me after my last ordeal. They, like most, found her delightful.

Touched, I responded, "That is so kind." Before I got overwhelmed, I tried to lighten the subject. "Tori's even going to include the tattoo, although I pointed out that skeletons don't have skin."

Meryl laughed kindly. "I'm sure your resourceful friend will figure it out."

The discussion eased my fears and anxiety. A name, prayers, and remembrance; everything I wanted for the girl and more.

Relaxing for the first time, I joined in the laughter. "You won't believe the image. A unicorn with a knife."

Picking up a butter knife, Roger used it as a horn, turning his head from side to side for us to see.

While we giggled, Edward froze, color draining from his face.

Plastering his official police persona over his features, he turned to Meryl and Roger and thanked them for breakfast. He kissed me on the forehead, whispered, "Gotta run," and left.

Blindsided, I knew one thing for sure—Edward recognized something about that tattoo.

Chapter Seven: Monasteries and Unicorns

Sated by Meryl's delicious cooking but unsettled by Edward's abrupt departure, I sought peace and work. After helping with dishes, I threw my hair in a ponytail and headed down the hill.

The Bath Abbey, a stunning example of perpendicular Gothic architecture, perches elegantly next to the Roman Baths Museum. An easy stop that wouldn't make me late to work, and I could check Tori's task off my list.

Entering the Abbey's main doors, I dropped a pound coin into the donation box and passed into the nave. The fan-vaulted ceiling took my breath away no matter how often I saw it.

As I stood gawking heavenward, a deep voice asked, "How are you doing, Miss McGuire?"

I turned to find the stern face of Deacon Michael searching my own.

"I'm fine," I said, not remembering what I should call him. Father, I thought, but not using a form of address seemed safer. "Thank you for asking. I'm surprised at how lovely it is every time I come in."

His smile transformed his face. "I'm glad you think so. Can I help you with anything?"

Retrieving my phone to pull up notes, I said, "Yes, actually, if you don't mind."

Nodding encouragement, he took me by the elbow and guided me to one of the pews.

We sat. "My friend is getting a religious studies degree and likes to have her information from first-hand sources." I glanced at him. "That would be you, if it's okay."

"Whatever you need."

"She has two nursery rhymes and wants to know which has to do with the dissolution of the monasteries by Henry the Eighth. The first is—"

"Little Jack Horner, I assume," Deacon Michael cut in.

"Yeah," I said, impressed. However, I shouldn't have been. I was here for his expertise on the subject.

"Yes, that one comes up a lot. It's based on Thomas Horner, who swindled the abbot of Glastonbury out of land deeds. He was supposed to deliver them as a bribe to Henry so the abbot could keep the main building. However, Horner kept them. Rather pleased with himself if reports are true."

"Stuck in his thumb and pulled out a plum and said 'What a good boy am I?' Plum land deal. Wow. I was raised with these books and never knew they meant anything other than a good rhyme."

"One is never too old to learn," the deacon said sagely.

Considering I was still in school and asking to be taught something, I found the phrase a little sanctimonious. But hey, I was in a sanctuary.

"The second one is Sing a Song of Sixpence," I said, double-checking my notes. "We know the interpretation that it is a secret pirate code is false," I added, proving my ability to fact-check.

"What's that?"

"Somebody wanted to prove how easy it was to spread urban legends by posting on the internet. It's one of the reasons we came to you."

Pleased, he continued. "Sing a Song of Sixpence, as you and your friend have discovered, isn't nearly as clear in its meaning. Songbirds were occasionally baked into pies as a fun surprise."

At my horrified expression, Deacon Michael paused, nodded agreement, and continued. "When there is no clear-cut story, people tend to jump to griping about Henry the Eighth. Blackbirds as monks and all." He shrugged. "I wouldn't put my name to it. We just don't know."

Thumb-typing as fast as I could, I took down everything he said. "This is perfect. She'll love it. Thank you so much!" I bounced a little on Tori's behalf.

As Michael turned to go, I thought of another question.

"Father?" I chanced the title, pleased when he responded with an encouraging smile. "I saw something, and I wondered if you might know where it was from." The image of the dead girl and her disturbing tattoo burst into my mind with a force I didn't think possible. My eyes slammed shut and then went wide, trying to banish the vision.

"Are you all right, child?" Michael asked.

Rubbing my hands over my face, I regained my composure. "Yeah, sorry." I contemplated telling him about my ordeal but realized I should not give details about an active investigation. "Question, do you know what a unicorn head with a knife in its teeth symbolizes? Or where it comes from?"

His head shook in the negative. "I've never seen anything like that. We have unicorns in some of the stonework in various churches, but nothing like what you describe."

Knowing I'd be late if I didn't leave right that minute, I thanked him and bolted. But I wanted to hear more about unicorn carvings and made a mental note to look it up later.

The Abbey's exit lay beyond the gift shop and deposited me at the Roman Baths Museum door. As I bypassed the line, Sam intercepted me.

"Top of the mornin' to ya," she said, her lilt turning the phrase into a song. I'm pretty sure she used the phrase for effect, leaning into her Irish heritage, but it worked. The morning seemed far brighter with her greeting in it. "The sifting rig is in the stairwell, all nice and upgraded for you. Go right down," Sam instructed.

The Archway area lay underneath the rest of the museum, well below street level. Set up as an educational wing, it emphasized the archeological process as much as the Baths.

I hadn't been down there since before Edward, and I embarked on our outdoor adventure, and I approached it nervously. The public elevator took me down to the Archway's main entrance to the Undercroft. Skirting tourists, I strode to the restricted area, showed my badge to the volunteer on duty, and checked in with Dr. Daniels.

"What?" he said, crushing any hope that he would ever remember me. "Not lunch, already?"

Coming to my defense, Simon appeared at that moment. "Ms. McGuire is here to sift. She will be stationed in the utility stairwell."

"What?" Daniels played the absent-minded professor to perfection. "What about that American student? She had a good eye."

If he wanted American, he would get it. Lunging in front of Simon, I stuck out my hand and proclaimed, "Howdy! Maddie McGuire at your service." My accent may have shifted to Texan to emphasize my point. "I am plumb excited to be on your team, Dr. Daniels. Panning for gold got me into archeology in the first place." I refrained from adding *yeehaw*.

Taken aback, Daniels' expression bordered on terror. Again, Simon stepped in. "If you need her, she will be in the stairwell."

"Quite right. Thank you, Simon, and you, er,"

"Maddie," I shouted as Simon dragged me away.

As we rounded the corner, Simon's facade broke, and he grinned at me. "You never say 'howdy,'" he observed dryly.

"If I'm ever going to get him to remember me, I have to do something," I insisted.

"He's going to remember you as a complete nutter."

"Mission accomplished," I said with a firm nod. "Everything set up?" I jerked my head toward my station.

"The doorway is partially blocked by the new table, but you can squeeze past it. We got you a comfortable chair, too."

Touched, I said, "Aw, thanks, buddy," at which he rolled his eyes and stalked back to his duties.

When I entered, gloom greeted me. The lower bank of lights flickered, but the second and third stories glowered darkly above. The door clicked shut, sealing me in.

Touching the sifting table, I said, "Hello, sifter," trying to shake loose panic that started to suffocate me. "How are you doing today?" Sweat prickled in my hairline. "Are we going to find good things?"

With every word, my voice turned more hoarse. Heartbeat pounding in my ears caused my hands to shake. Sure, the top of the stairwell would collapse onto me at any moment, I keened, shrinking into myself, arms over my head. Breath coming in restricted screeching gasps, I couldn't force myself out to safety.

As I shuddered, the banks of lights two floors above me burst to life. The extra twenty-four feet of space that illumination brought forward lifted some of the weight bearing down on me. The top fire door opened, then the other, allowing fresh air to filter in.

The changes in atmosphere gave me breathing room, although every inhale created another squeal.

I became aware of a soothing voice, an arm helping me to stand.

"Do be quiet," Simon cooed. "You'll bring the whole museum 'round."

The mild admonishment had the desired effect, as Simon knew it would. His embrace, far from suffocating, calmed me.

"Thanks, buddy," I said again, not wanting him to turn insufferable for this rescue.

We released, and I regarded him. "How did you know?"

Without admitting that the same thing happened to him, he glanced up. "It takes a while to trust the dark."

I did a couple of jumping jacks and waved my arms around. "Yeah. I'm good. Thank you so much. That's never happened before. Almost like scaring yourself to death." Another jumping jack to shake off my nerves.

"Hey, I have a question," I stated, anything to change the subject. "Have you ever seen or heard of an image of a unicorn head with a knife in its teeth?"

In the most elegant way possible, Simon shrugged. "The unicorn is Scotland's symbol, like your eagle. It may have something to do with the Scottish independence movement."

"What do you mean? You're the same country," I said with all the confidence of a foreigner.

"Some prefer Scotland to be a sovereign nation."

"What?" I repeated. "It's been over 400 years."

For some reason, the idea appalled me. My vision of the UK was one of tea, scones, and politeness, not political outrage and separatists. I had enough of that at home.

"May I point out that your colonies declared independence, and that has worked out really rather quite well for you?"

I huffed, and Simon asked, "Doesn't Texas threaten to secede occasionally?"

"First off, *it's Texas*," I said in a way that would have made my Dallas cousins disown me. "And secondly, most of Europe could fit inside Texas."

"Acreage does not a country make," Simon said, dismissing my arguments. He added, "I will see what I can learn about your be-knifed unicorn."

The dulcet tones of Dolly fluttered in. "There you are, Simon!"

As if he intentionally hid from her.

"Didn't I tell you he would be near the dig, Uncle? I absolutely did."

Jamming herself over the sifting table, Dolly finger waved.

The doorway opened into the hallway, not onto the stairwell landing. A large stone acted as a doorstop, propping it open. Another kindness from Simon.

"Come out here and say hello to Uncle," she invited us.

I wondered if the man in question was her uncle or if I misheard his name.

Not allowing me to work, Simon propelled me into the corridor.

Next to Dolly, who, annoyingly, looked straight off the runway, in khaki's and a blue museum polo shirt, stood a man of medium height, whom I assumed was her uncle. On the far side of middle-aged, with close-cropped salt and pepper hair and goatee, and piercing blue eyes, he had a commanding presence. About two tiramisus from overweight, he carried himself like a man used to the good life.

With a start, I realized Dolly addressed me. "And this is Simon's dear friend, Miss Madeline McGuire of Tempe, Arizona. She is the clever American who earned the internship here."

Gracious to a fault, Dolly's introduction made me fight the urge to curtsey. Aristocracy had that effect on me.

The blue eyes regarded me like something from a sci-fi movie, but when he smiled, Dolly's uncle was kind of handsome for an old guy.

"Maddie, may I present my uncle Clarence De Valence, Viscount Lisle?

And," she gestured behind him, "our indispensable butler, Winters."

"How do you do?" I asked, sort of bowing my head and extending my hand.

Thankfully, De Valence shook my hand, responding with the same phrase. The butler faded into the background, looking embarrassed to be a part of the introduction.

"How do you do? We've heard so much about you. I do hope you'll come for a weekend retreat and enjoy our facilities."

"Thank you," I sputtered, having zero idea of what he meant. Pointing to my stairwell, I excused myself, saying, "I need to sift."

"Quite, quite. Duty calls," he said before taking off at a brisk pace.

Settling into my new chair, I took my first allotment of dig-site dirt, logged the map area it came from, and dumped it onto the sieve screen. Using the wooden arms, I shook the tabletop back and forth until nothing remained but a few larger stones.

The dirt sifted into a five-gallon bucket. To kill time, I wondered if the Brits called them nineteen-liter containers. Maybe they rounded up to twenty.

"Is she all right?" I heard Dolly's concerned voice from the hallway.

Regretting my initial reaction to her, I almost called out that I was okay until I heard her say, "That sound! Rather awful, wasn't it? Gave me chills, it did."

"Awful? Try experiencing it instead of hearing it," I muttered under my breath.

"Momentary claustrophobia is all," I heard Simon's reassurance as they walked away. "She's a brick. No need to worry."

"Ooh!" Dolly squeaked. "I better get a wiggle on. Tour starts in ten. Cheers!" she called to Simon.

Unsettled from experiencing a panic attack and maybe a little bit of unaccustomed jealousy, I shook soil, and brushed rocks until I felt more myself. And then my mind started to wander.

My eyes strayed to the buckets, and calculations danced in my head. Dr. Daniels instructed that each waste bucket should be filled halfway so anyone could carry them. Since the containers had to go up three flights of stairs, I appreciated the decree. After each sifting reached the halfway mark, I stood, bent my knees, and lugged the bucket to the left side of the stairwell, one per step.

One-third bucket of dirt weighed about ten pounds, so each time I lugged one, I hoisted over twenty pounds. Using Newton's law of velocity, I figured if a bucket conked me in the head, it would be with about thirty-seven pounds of force.

Flexing my biceps like a strongman, I hollered, "I am invincible!" Except for the shooting pain in my shoulders, which cut my display short.

Another dump, shake, and sift, and my next bucket begged to be carried up. "Fine." My bravado from earlier failed me. Slogging the detritus up five steps, I settled it into place and paused for a breath.

That's when the top door closed. "Hey!" I called. "Someone's in here."

No response. I took a couple of steps up.

The door closest to me shut, and my heart skipped and stuttered.

"Hello? Could you open that, please?" My voice lost its strength, sounding hoarse and weak again.

The landings were cluttered with empty buckets that needed to be disposed of. *The crew up there is just cleaning and straightening*, I reasoned.

Patting the wall for stability, I took one step toward my station when the stairwell went dark.

A scream tore from my throat, filling the black void. Breath shallow, I forced myself to think. Someone should have heard me through the door Simon propped open.

Except, if the door were still open, there would be light, and there wasn't. Not any. No amount of blinking brought shapes into focus.

Claustrophobia smashed into my chest, pinning me in place. My heart pounded so loudly I couldn't hear or think. Swaying, my knees gave way, and I crumpled, tumbling down steps.

Disoriented and unable to see, I flailed to find purchase. My arms wrapped around hard plastic above my head, but whatever it was shifted, and dirt poured over me. Suffocating sand filled my mouth, nose, and eyes.

I forced my hands over my face, cupping my fingers to create a pocket of air until the dusty deluge stopped. Gulping in panicked gasps, I sucked debris into my lungs. Racking coughs tore through my chest.

When I could take a shuddering breath without hacking, I deduced that I had grabbed a waste bucket, not one of the stair rails. About twenty-two pounds of dirt now covered me.

I groaned. Because who put that dirt there? Me. And who would have to clean it up? Me.

Someone would pay for this humiliation.

With a shake like a wet dog, I dislodged as much soil as possible. Careful not to dump over another container, I felt around and oriented myself so that I sat on one step with my feet on the one below it.

Shifting to the side away from the buckets, I felt for the wall, then found the rail. Standing, I pulled my phone from my front pocket and pressed Home. It flared to life, then the battery signal indicated one percent and shut down.

"Are you kidding me?" I shouted at it.

Cell signals didn't reach the Undercroft, and I formed a habit of putting my phone in airplane mode to preserve its life. Also, I usually let Edward know when I'd be out of touch. I forgot both today.

"Fine," I repeated. "Absolutely," I added for good measure.

Three or four stairs to the main floor, where the table blocked my way. Patting for its edge and the protruding handles, I brashly stepped around it and stumbled over a chair leg.

Glaring into the inky nothingness, I moved more slowly, getting to the far wall. The landing's dimensions were easy to navigate, and I made it to the door without further incident.

Pushing the crash handle and stepping forward, I collided with the door, bumping my forehead hard enough to see stars.

"What the?" I asked.

It didn't have a lock, and even if it did, I could open it from the inside. Something blocked the door on the other side.

Scooting my foot over the floor, I searched for the stone Simon placed to hold it open.

Nothing.

"Okay then," I said out loud. "If Simon could pick it up, I should be able to shove it. Right?" I gave myself a reassuring nod. "Right."

Pushing my back against the bar, I planted my feet and used my quads to apply steady pressure. The slightest movement encouraged me, so I squeezed my eyes shut and doubled my efforts.

My feet slid slowly out from under me as I pushed, my back flowing down the door, pulling up my shirt.

"Jeez," I complained, once seated firmly on the floor with my legs straight out in front of me. I looked ridiculous.

Seeing the vague outline of my legs meant light, and that meant progress. On the floor, I bent my legs and shoved again, this time hearing the stone scrape. Once I had momentum, I was able to free myself.

Standing tall, I preened, pleased with my success. Until a skip of my heart reminded me that someone had trapped me, tortured me, on purpose.

Chapter Eight: Another Discovery

Dripping dirt rained off me in cascades of ancient filth. I shook myself, whacked at my hair, and wiped a grimy shirttail over my caked face.

Dolly appeared, looking astoundingly fresh and clean.

Pebbles fell off my clothes, making tapping sounds on the stone floor—tap, tip, tap.

"Maddie, good, you're free."

Her gaze raked over me, but her expression stayed as pleasant as ever. "Uncle meant it about you coming for a visit, and he wanted to make sure I invited you for the weekend. Facials and massages at the manor house. It's a medispa, you know, and it'll be absolutely wonderful to have you."

Without waiting for my answer, she sauntered away.

Tap tip tip tap tap. Bits of debris continued to fall as my nose started to twitch. Dust tickled my left nostril, and when I swiped at it with my sleeve, a sneezing fit took hold, adding to the cacophony.

A disembodied voice echoed through the chamber. "I say," a male voice called. "Are you quite all right down there?"

"Achoo!" I answered before gaining control. "Fine. Thank you," I added, struggling to control the sneezing fits.

"Aaaaachoooo!"

"I say!"

Covering my face with my elbow, I marched to the lady's room, interrupted by spasms. As a child, my mother insisted I take acting lessons, and one of the things I learned was a stage sneeze. With concentration, the force of the sneeze dissipates instead of creating a sound that peeled paint from the walls.

A tourist in the Archway public restroom gave me a wide berth as I headed to the stall, spasming and leaving a trail of debris.

Removing my polo, I gave it a thorough beating before slipping it over my head again. When I emerged, the mirror confronted me accusingly. My strawberry-blonde ponytail appeared dull and mousy brown. Uneven streaks across my face looked like a failed attempt at camouflage, and my shirt displayed alarming evidence of my sneezing fit.

"Excellent," I commented before returning to the stall.

The ponytail holder came out in fits and starts, snapping stray hairs. Leaning over the toilet, I flipped my hair over my head, carefully avoiding letting it dangle too close to the water. Both hands scrubbed and scratched, sand flying everywhere until I could see natural color again.

Back at the mirror, I scraped my hair back up and secured it before going after my face. Because I wouldn't be in a public space, I hadn't swiped on any mascara or lipstick that morning. Scrubbing with cool tap water did the trick. Unfortunately, the bathroom installed hand dryers, so I dripped and splattered onto my shirt, causing muddy patches as I stuffed my face under the blower.

Still, presentable. Ish.

Pushing open the fire door to my workspace and propping it open, I surveyed the damage I'd created in my panic. One overturned debris bucket and a lot of dirt on the stairwell. Nothing landed anywhere near the To Be Sifted pile, so I didn't need to worry about cross-contamination of sample areas.

A broom and dustpan cleared the area within ten minutes. "Huh." I thought it would take hours to clean.

Total darkness made everything worse.

Someone out there knew it, too, and plunged me into inky blackness with malice aforethought.

Sifting, I wondered why. What had I stumbled onto this time? I mean, other than Sherrie, the dead girl. That couldn't have anything to do with this, though. No one at the Baths asked why I came back to work early.

At that moment, Dolly entered with tea and scones. "Simon said you liked Earl Grey. Here, from the Bath Bun." She set my lunch on a freshly swept step, adding, "I don't know how you deal with those school tours. Absolutely exhausting."

For the first time, I smiled at my new coworker. "Right? It's like they suck all the energy out of you and fling it at each other."

Dolly laughed. "A perfect description," she agreed, reaching across my food to retrieve a small clump of dirt from my shoulder. Placing it in the discard bin, she said, "I'll need a massage after this week."

Brushing non-existent smudges from her khakis, she declared, "Once more into the breach, dear friends."

"Once more," I finished.

"That's right," Dolly commented. "Simon said you were brainy. I will need to keep on my toes."

As she left, the rest of the line from Henry V came to me. *Or stop up the walls with English dead.* Considering how close I'd come to losing my mind and becoming part of a stairwell, the imagery struck too close to home.

Did Dolly know the rest of the line? I sighed. *Did it matter?*

The very British snack revived me, sending my brain into overdrive as I sifted. I wanted Dolly to be a villain and laid out an argument for it. She took my job as tour guide, inserted herself between me and my boss Sam, and somehow bamboozled Simon.

Of course, since she had tours, I could work in the Undercroft, which allowed me to connect with Dr. Daniels. And bamboozled did not describe Simon.

However, no one knew I developed claustrophobia except Simon, who revealed the secret to Dolly not very long before the attack.

Brush paused midair, I turned this fact over. The timing lined up. Dolly complained about the keening sound I made, and Simon told her about my fears.

I had no way of knowing if anyone else was in the hallway to hear. Dolly heard, I was sure of that.

Lowering the brush to a large piece of debris, I removed grime, thinking. Everything lined up, with Dolly being the one who sealed me in.

"But why?" I asked no one. No motivation presented itself for Dolly or anyone else. I couldn't see any reason for someone to target me.

Frustrated, I jabbed at the chunk left on my sieve.

Blue glinted in the light.

The piece, less than a quarter inch, mainly composed of clay, but a tiny corner of blue-glazed ceramic adhered to it. The tesserae, little squares that made up the mosaic discovery, were predominantly blue and green. The overall image of the design hadn't been determined yet, so every piece of the puzzle was vital. And I found one.

This time, when my heart thumped, I didn't care. Excitement flooded me, but I stayed put, stilled my shaking hands, and made the necessary notes. Locating my find on the dig site map, I made a mark and added the coordinating numbers identifying where the piece came from. Placing it aside for Dr. Daniels to review, I stood, walked around the workstation, and bounced on my toes, unable to contain myself any longer.

A genuine archeological artifact. With the paperwork and storing complete, the reality of it made me light-headed. Practically staggering, I secured the area, moving the doorstop stone in front of the door to be sure, and called Dr. Daniels.

Before today, I had only unearthed one other thing in the hundreds of pounds of sifted dirt, which turned out to be a rock. This was different, and the head archeologist would want to know where it came from immediately.

Considering someone had already tried to sabotage me, I didn't want to walk off and leave my treasure for someone else to claim.

Practically skipping, I covered the length of the corridor to the Archway junction. In one direction lay the public area. The other, roped off, housed the dig site.

I hesitated. An American girl hollering at the top of her lungs to get the attention of an archeologist sounded like a bad stereotype. However, I didn't want to leave the hallway to my workstation unguarded.

"Hello?" I ventured.

Two tourists turned my way. I waved and ducked behind the wall before they could engage with me.

Crossing the barrier, I turned my head to monitor my area. "Dr. Daniels?" I called.

No answer.

No one had briefed me on the proper protocol for a vital artifact. Should I stay put and guard or report my findings?

Pulling out my phone, I shook it. Still dead. No way to call Simon and ask.

Unable to contain the news, I abandoned my discovery and reported to the dig team. Quickly.

At full speed, I ran down the hall to the first volunteer on duty. "I found something sifting," I said with no preamble, hand on my chest to calm my panting.

"I say," the man said, his voice familiar. "Well done."

"Could you send Dr. Daniels to the stairwell? I don't want to leave it alone."

"Right away." Keying a walkie-talkie, he reported my news to Dr. Daniels.

Walkie-talkies, what a great idea. I wanted one.

Feeling nine feet tall, I raced back to my sifting area and found Dolly moving the stone that I used to block the door.

Shock flared on her face before her expression returned to its perfect pleasantness.

"There you are," she declared in the same way she had when she found Simon earlier.

Warning bells rang out in my head. The stone was clearly in place to keep people out, and she moved it. The question was, did she move it before?

Dolly wiped her hands across her slacks to knock off the dust, then reached into her pocket and produced an envelope.

Handing it to me, she said, "Simon will text you all the details, obviously, but I so rarely use the family stationery."

The envelope, made of thick linen, displayed a small crest, blue and white stripes with red birds. I wondered if Simon and Lady Vivian had this kind of stuff. It struck me that I didn't know nearly as much about the people around me as I should.

Dolly looked at me expectantly as my brain dithered. Random thoughts and accusations warred with polite responses. "Uh, thanks," I said. Erudite, that's me.

As she turned to leave, she added, "Oh, and there is a plus one. Simon mentioned an Edward?" She phrased it as a question. Without waiting for my nod, she said, "We will absolutely have a room for him, too."

Still confused about what I had gotten myself into for the weekend, I opened my mouth long enough to look like a gaping fish before Dr. Daniels cut me off.

"Ah, Dolly," he went straight to her, ignoring me. "How nice to see you again."

They exchanged pleasantries, and I contained myself for exactly ten seconds, fists clenched in a slow count. "I found something," I interrupted.

Both faces turned to me. "Maddie," Dolly breathed, looking genuinely excited. "That's wonderful."

"What is it?" Daniels asked, banging the door open and walking into my sifting table.

"Tight squeeze." I held up the blue-glazed fragment. "I think it's part of the mosaic."

Picking up the artifact with tweezers and locating it on the dig site map, he grunted.

His eyes bore into mine. Intense concentration broadcast intelligence I hadn't seen before. "It's Maddie McGuire, correct? Our intern from America."

Everything else that happened that day disappeared. Dr. Daniels remembered my name. "Yes." Tears welled in my eyes, but I refused to let them fall.

"This is… yes. Yes."

Before he finished the thought, his absent-minded professor persona reasserted itself as he left the room, brushing past Dolly without a glance.

"Another tour calls," Dolly said as she left.

A weirdness settled over me. So many breakthroughs in my career happened in the past hour, but I didn't know what to do. I could follow Dr. Daniels, but if there was one chunk, there might be another, and I should work.

"Celebrate later," I told myself, settling back into my chair.

Not a single other exciting thing happened, either with archeology or claustrophobia, and once again, my mind began to drift.

While I couldn't think of motivations for Dolly or anyone else to attack me, one thing was clear - I may be heading into a trap this weekend.

Chapter Nine: The Medispa

The drive to Painswick manor-house-turned-spa took on a surreal quality. Like many things in my life lately, I had wound up in a situation entirely outside my control. Stuffed into the back of Simon's Citroen sedan with Edward, we listened to Dolly's constant stream of chatter about the delights awaiting us.

On the surface, it seemed great. Everyone excited, on our way to a weekend in the country with charming people.

But I couldn't recall ever agreeing to said weekend. Or driving with Simon. I had pictured a romantic journey with my arms wrapped around Edward as we zoomed on his motorcycle. Somehow, Simon talked Edward into going with them. Some excuse like storms in the forecast. *Like always this time of year*, I thought as a drizzle coated the windows.

Rain hardly ever came to the Arizona desert in the Fall. It was warm during the day, with the nights taking on an invigorating chill. Everyone was out and about, going to the Phoenix Zoo, hiking in the Superstitions, and having their last burst of pool parties or standup paddleboard outings on Tempe Town Lake.

The drought-resistant Bermuda grass got scalped, and bright green rye sprouted up for winter lawns decorated with cyclamen, bromeliads, and hibiscus.

Back home, it didn't mold or drizzle, and my hair always looked smooth, never frizzy.

I glared at Dolly's flaxen locks.

Edward poked my leg.

"What?" I said, wondering if he caught my scowl.

"I was asking how you kept your hair looking so nice in this kind of weather."

Add mind-reading to the list of Dolly's talents.

"Honestly?" I blurted out the rest before thinking properly. "I was just glaring at your hair. How do you keep it from frizzing?" Edward's look of horror was a not-so-subtle reminder that my upper-class settings skills lacked refinement.

Dolly, however, laughed. "A chemist's shop full of product," she said. "Otherwise, it looks like straw."

She didn't strike me as nearly as uptight about the aristocracy as either Simon or Edward.

On his best behavior, Edward's accent lost any trace of his Scottish burr, blending in seamlessly with the others. Leaving me as the odd man out, my American voice sounding strident even to me.

Sighing inwardly, I vowed to behave in a more civilized manner.

As we pulled into Painswick, the ninety-nine yew trees planted in St. Mary's churchyard greeted us. Legend has it that the devil won't allow the hundredth tree to grow. The manicured evergreens created lines of dark, dense green like something out of Alice in Wonderland.

Passing the world-famous Rococo garden, we turned through impressive iron gates. A discreet brass plaque set into the dark stone walls announced De Valence Court Medispa.

A valet appeared as if by magic and opened Simon's door as soon as the car stopped. The rest of us spilled out as another employee popped out of nowhere to handle our luggage.

Not that I couldn't carry my suitcase as it only contained my softest jeans, a couple of cute tops, pajamas, and toiletries.

Eyeing Dolly's bag and the elegance of De Valence Court, I sighed, tugging my jean jacket tight. When I packed, I hadn't considered that I might need a dress for dinner. Even Edward's bag was larger than mine.

I followed Dolly into the manor house. And my world shifted.

The gentle scent of jasmine enveloped me in a warm embrace. Candles, not LEDs, flickered within glass cylinders casting a peaceful glow in every nook and cranny. The entry hall functioned as a lobby for the medispa but also transported all who entered into a peaceful state of tranquility.

My mouth may have hung open.

Dolly clapped daintily. "You like it," she said to me. "I absolutely knew you would." She turned to Simon. "I told you so, didn't I, dear?"

If I gaped before, my jaw must have unhinged when I heard her call Simon "dear."

Especially when he responded, "You did indeed. Right as always, Doll."

The only thing worse than calling a grown person "Dolly" is to shorten it further to Doll. The woman in question didn't seem to mind.

Edward poked me, and my teeth snapped together, followed by a smile.

"It's lovely," I said with a vague hand gesture that took in the room.

The imperial staircase started on the third floor and curled down two sides to meet at the entry. The walls were decorated with waist-high wainscoting on all three stories. Doors to the second floor were only visible by the slightest gap as they were painted and paneled the same as the wall.

The tiled floor, disguised as white-washed wood, was covered in a richly patterned Persian rug.

"How do you live here?" I asked, unable to picture myself ever coming home to this level of opulence.

Edward sighed, which I took as disapproval but at least a step up from poking.

Dolly answered lightly. "I hardly ever come in the front door. Uncle and I have our home on the ground and first floors of the east wing.

"Above us are administrative offices for the spa, and above that, in the old servant's quarters are our old servants. Mrs. Pride, our full-time cook, makes the most brilliant shortbread you will ever taste. Mr. Pride oversees the garden staff and maintains the kitchen garden. Been married for donkey's years. And Winters, of course, the butler who manages the household and the spa administration. Uncle had the whole floor converted to a flat for the Prides."

At this point, I stopped listening, my mind spinning on the idea of a butler.

Like in a TV show.

Taking Simon's arm, Dolly led us to the opposite entrance. "It's the west wing that you'll want to see."

To the left, a large archway welcomed us into a pale blue relaxation room with oversized chairs positioned to ensure a measure of privacy.

"Where is the check-in?"

A tall man in a refined black suit entered, took note of each of us, made eye contact with Dolly, then retreated before either of the boys acknowledged him.

"That's just it. Winters confirmed we are here, but other than that, there isn't a check-in process," Dolly declared. "A brilliant idea on Uncle's part. Everything is filled out in an online form before you arrive, including your car. The valet checks you in. You are free to relax and not worry about the details."

Nodding, I had to admit the genius of it. The worst part of any spa experience was standing in line to check in or out after a relaxing treatment.

Again, as if by magic, four people appeared out of nowhere, sent by Winters, no doubt.

"Miss McGuire?" a petite woman with her hair in a bun asked. At my nod, she smiled. "This way for your massage. You must be tired after your journey."

Not really a journey, as it took just over an hour to drive. But who was I to say no to a massage?

"All your treatments will take place on the first floor," she said as we moved toward an elevator, joined by Edward and his guide.

Confusion must have radiated across my face because Edward reminded me softly, "Ground floor is zero."

Recalling a household exploration we once had, I nodded. The first floor was one story up.

The doors swished open to low lighting, tan walls, and gentle music. Eucalyptus and mint enveloped me, melting away tension before the massage started.

* * *

After dodging a few awkward questions about the various bruises on my shoulders and legs from my different falls, I melted into the massage. Completed, I wandered in a semi-catatonic state to the relaxation room on the first, no *ground floor,* I reminded myself, and collapsed into an overstuffed comfy chair, snuggling into a robe.

Also clad in a white, fluffy bathrobe and looking as relaxed as I felt, Edward arrived and plopped on the nearest chair. We stretched our hands toward one another, but the distance was too far.

Our hands flopped in happy waves.

"That was…" I trailed off.

"Aye," he agreed, forgetting to hide his Scottish accent.

Where you're from makes a difference, so he developed a posh accent whenever he was in public. It's a shame because his north country burr is dreamy.

Winters appeared, checking our state of serenity no doubt, but melted away before Edward could be bothered to turn his head.

I must have drifted off because the next I knew, we were going in the elevator to our rooms on the third floor. The elevator button read "Two," which took a ridiculous amount of effort to memorize.

Edward's room was close to mine—across the hall and down two or three doors.

Drifting after my technician, I entered the lavender-scented dream of my room. The clothes I'd worn into the massage room lay on the four-poster bed, laundered and folded. The cream-colored bedspread matched the flowing sheer curtains, the slipper chair, and ottoman.

A cherry armoire held my clothes and bag.

Opening what I assumed to be a closet, I found an en suite bathroom. Pure luxury.

For dinner, a tea cart rolled to my door, pushed by a cheery-looking middle-aged woman. Filled with healthy meal options and delicate pastries, I selected too much and ate my fill. The dishes went into the hall and were whisked away almost immediately.

There's nothing like living the good life to change one's perspective on unsavory events. This place was great. Life-changing, even.

The perfect setting to take my relationship with Edward to the next level. After a steamy, hot shower, I went through the trouble of blow-drying my hair, so my natural strawberry-blonde waves smoothed in a graceful fall.

Donning nothing but the big fluffy bathrobe and soft mule slippers the spa provided, I opened the door. An elderly gentleman, also in a robe, waved with a friendly smile.

Heart flopping in panic, I retreated.

"Of course, there are other guests. Get it together, McGuire," I chided myself, but my heart still skipped and fluttered.

With a straight spine, I smoothed my sweaty palms on the robe and moved once more into the hall.

Empty, thank goodness. Looking left to right to make sure I was alone, a silly grin spread across my face.

One step out, and a cool draft floated up from the floor, calling attention to my state of dress. Or lack thereof.

I retreated again.

"Maybe not quite so obvious. I don't want to throw myself at him," I said, searching for appropriately sexy underwear and bra. "A little decorum is charming." Trying to convince myself, I quickly redressed, checked my look, and tightened the belt on my robe.

When I stepped out this time, I confidently strode two rooms down and across from mine.

My hand hovered, poised to knock. Everything froze except for an uncertain buzzing in my ears.

"Was he two or three rooms away?" I couldn't remember.

I retreated.

Again.

Covering my face with both hands, I slogged through the misty post-massage memory. Edward went into his room first. I pictured his lopsided grin as he stumbled in. A painting of a woman on a white horse hung on the wall.

"Got it," I whispered, nodding.

Still deep in thought to keep the image fresh, I slipped open the door and bashed into something solid.

"Oh, I'm sorry!" I cried, stepping back to see Edward, an unaccustomed blush on his cheeks. He, too, wore the spa bathrobe, which made my mind spin about what was underneath. The buzzing turned into a warm frisson of anticipation.

"I thought—"

"I was just coming to see you," I said and wished I hadn't. "I mean," I floundered, "is your room the one by the painting?" I asked to make it seem like I was just curious.

My innocent look didn't fool him. Running a hand through his damp brown hair, he maneuvered around me, allowing the door to close with a snap. The snick of the lock echoed in my head, and I wished I hadn't cinched my robe so tight.

Longing to kiss him, to pull him to me, I fixed his collar.

And jabbered. "Because I was somnambulistic when we came upstairs after that massage. You seemed relaxed, too. Yours must have been as good as mine. The massage, that is."

Edward dragged the back of a finger along my chin, sending chills to my toes.

"Aye, lassie," he purred.

My voice went up a notch. "I was pretty annoyed on the drive here. I don't remember ever agreeing to come to this shindig, and here we all are, stuffed into Simon's car and spending a weekend in the country like some stock characters in a movie from the 1950s, and no one ever said the words, 'Do you want to join us?' Or anything like that."

Hands on my collar, Edward opened it enough to kiss my neck.

"Not that I would have said no," I babbled faster. "It's just that an actual ask would have been nice instead of just this, you know, assumption that I would say yes, no matter what. Although, to be fair, Dolly did give me a printed invitation which was really pretty nice when you think about it, but

I didn't do a traditional RSVP or anything."

"Mmmhmm," Edward agreed, kissing my collarbone.

"And, and, and…" I was running out of panic and wishing he would kiss me. Edward waited. This moment was supposed to be part of our Cotswold Way hike. Tori and I discussed it in detail before I left. Edward had never been part of those conversations.

A proper gentleman, my Edward, by action if not by birth. He wouldn't do anything I wasn't ready for. But he made his intentions quite clear, and despite my crazed ramblings, I responded in kind.

"You were checking the hallway to test that fantastic memory of yours?"

It wasn't the words but the way he said them. Thick, low, and passionately Scottish.

I grabbed the front of his robe and pulled him to me. The pent-up desire I felt since we started our Cotswold Way hike found its way into my reaction. I kissed him hungrily, hands roaming over his muscular back and broad shoulders.

One of his hands moved through my hair while the other pressed my back, melding us together.

I shuffled back toward the bed, never breaking contact. When we bumped into the footboard, we fell onto the pillow-top mattress together.

His bathrobe fell open, revealing abs so sculpted he looked airbrushed.

And, I noted, boxers. The relief I felt warred with my passion.

Are you sure? A little voice, that sounded annoyingly like my mother's, chirped in my mind.

While every nerve in my body screamed yes, I allowed my brain a tiny amount of logic. I saved myself, not because of religious reasons or a sense of propriety, but because I never met a boy who was worth it. Or worthy. Was Edward?

I nibbled his shoulder, thinking. A scar on his bicep caught my attention. Another, long and wicked, crossed his chest.

There was so much I didn't know about him, but what I did know, I liked. A lot. A gentleman in manners, if not status, intelligent, witty, and caring, Edward held many of the qualities that I held as important. Plus, that accent made me tremble with desire. Worthy indeed.

As I pulled the robe off his arm, I lightly bit his neck. A tattoo on his shoulder blade caught my eye. He rolled on his back, pulling me on top of him, which made me want to see it all the more.

"Come on," I said after a gentle nibble on his earlobe. "Show me."

Groaning, he responded, "It's a unicorn, lass. I didn't think you'd want to see it."

Tearing myself away, I sat on my knees, intrigued. "Like a Scottish Independence thing?" I asked as I tugged him onto his stomach.

The image hit me like a bucket of ice. The disturbing unicorn head with a knife in its teeth stared at me with menacing eyes. A red drop of blood stained the blade.

"The hell?" I squeaked, scrambling off the bed and bolting to the bathroom. Through the slammed door, I yelled, "Why do you have that? Why didn't you tell me you knew the girl? How are you involved?"

Opening a crack, I peeked at him. The rapid-fire questions hit Edward and hardened his exterior.

"You're telling me this was the tattoo you saw on Sherrie?" His tone and expression angry.

Half hidden by the bathroom door, I nodded, fists clenched in fury.

"You said," he pointed an accusatory finger my way, "that the knife was the horn."

Glaring at him, I stalked into the room. "I did not because it wasn't. It was that!" I jabbed his chest, hoping to poke all the way through to his back.

A different side of Edward lurks deep beneath the surface. I'd only seen it once when he was trying to get help for me. Like a coiled snake, threatening, dangerous, and ready to strike.

Hooded eyes bore into mine, any hint of passion obliterated. "Look again and tell me you're certain," he demanded.

"I don't need to," I spat back. "The stupid thing is seared into my brain. The only difference is your knife is dripping blood like in that Scottish play."

A low growl emitted from his throat as he snatched his robe and stormed out of the room.

Both my arms raised in the air like a saguaro cactus, I looked around, hoping for an explanation.

"What just happened?"

Chapter Ten: Abandoned

Refusing to go after Edward, I stomped around my room. I may have muttered obscenities under my breath.

I should have been the one who stormed out. Edward had the same tattoo as the murdered girl. Everyone I'd spoken to about it had never heard of it. Which meant Edward and the girl were connected somehow.

Is he secretly a serial killer, luring impressionable young women to the woods?

"No," I said out loud to assure myself.

The image of a rattlesnake ready to strike popped into my mind. Edward could be menacing, violence hiding under a calm surface.

"Don't be dramatic. That snake is for bad guys."

Still, the tremor in my hands betrayed my confusion and fear. That tattoo meant something, and I needed to find out what.

Digging my phone out of my closet, I tried using data to access the internet. One bar of service. No wi-fi in the spa. "Please use this time to untether yourself from the world and relax," I groaned, quoting the brochure in a horrible English accent.

The phone plopped on the bed while I paced, cursing, not being able to connect with Tori or anyone for support.

I froze, an unusual thought dawning on me. "I could talk to Simon," I said, listening to the absurdity of the suggestion.

My hand waggled back and forth. "Not bad. I might try it."

Of course, not until the next day. I couldn't go through the spa searching for his room. Simon wasn't like a close friend, but we shared experiences that created a bond. He could help, but I had to wait until breakfast.

Which meant attempting to sleep with all this adrenaline pumping through my bloodstream. No TV and no books, and I still wore my stupid sexy underthings.

Those came off, and cotton pajamas came on.

With the adrenaline ebbing away, darkness pooled in my chest. Tears splashed my cheeks. Perching on the edge of the bed, I drew my knees up to my chest and rocked.

This murder wasn't tied to me, I thought. My only obligations were to remember Sherrie and offer prayers.

Until now.

I pressed my palms into my eyes in a failed attempt to push back sobs.

Edward recognized the tattoo and didn't tell me. This time, it wasn't because of police policy. This was personal.

Then he abandoned me, but I was unsure how I felt about that.

Falling backward on the mattress, I balled my fists and puffed air to gain control of my emotions.

When only a searing headache remained, I sat cross-legged and clutched the sides of my head to keep it from exploding.

How could I trust him? Not only about the murder but as a boyfriend? As the man I finally decided to share myself with?

A roiling in my stomach caused a fresh round of tears, but no answers.

When the crying stopped, emptiness crept over me. Bleary-eyed, I stared around the room.

The only electric appliance, besides a lamp, was an elegant box with no visible buttons. When touched, gentle ocean sounds filled the room. A second touch emitted a mist of lavender. Between the two, the relaxing massage and exhausting conflicted emotions, I descended into a troubled sleep.

* * *

Alone in a black sea, waves crashed around me, soaking my hair, choking me. The wooden raft that kept me afloat creaked and moaned. Tossed between the mountainous surges, I clung to the edges of the platform, my face pressed to the rough boards.

A moment of calm caused me to look around, only to catch the slit eyes of a sea serpent rising from a coil over me.

I awoke with a start, then glared accusatorially at the white noise machine pumping out ocean sounds.

Shaking my head, I padded to the bathroom and splashed cold water on my face in a mistaken attempt to chase away the dream. However, the sensation made the nightmare storm feel real. Turning the tap to full hot had the desired effect, helping me to start my day.

More than ever, I wanted advice. I considered my plan of talking to Simon about Edward's tattoo.

Like Edward, Simon felt the intense need to follow rules. At least the rules that applied to him. Would something like the tattoo connection cause him to call Edward's superiors and have him investigated?

Turning the conundrum over in my head as I dressed for breakfast in a fresh pair of jeans and a pale green sweater that made my eyes pop, I decided to trust Simon. Mostly because he had no connection to this murder, so I reasoned he wouldn't see the need to intercede.

Unless he also sported a unicorn head tattoo, I didn't know about, but I couldn't picture that.

Confident in my logic, I went to the dining hall beyond the relaxation room. Set up with round tables draped in white linen; the room felt elegant and approachable.

The mingled scents of eggs, sausage, and coffee reminded me of my last breakfast with the Priestlys. A pang of longing cut into my thoughts. Remembering Edward, dressed in his uniform and eating like he'd never seen food before, made my heart turn over.

We had told Roger and Meryl about Sherrie, the Dia de Los Muertos figure, and the tattoo. I didn't give much detail. It was Reverend Priestly who used the butter knife as a horn. I didn't correct him.

Okay, so Edward didn't outright lie to me. He thought it was a different tattoo based on my vague description. But he could have said something about *his* tattoo. The similarities were striking, even if he thought they were different designs.

"You all right, miss?" a cultured male voice asked.

With a tiny yelp, I realized I'd been mid-step on the threshold for too long. The elderly gentleman from the hallway the day before looked at me, concerned.

"Oh, hi there," I said, tamping down the urge to flee.

The tattoo connection between Edward and Sherrie haunted me, dragging my thoughts in a negative spiral, even when smiling at the balding man with bushy white eyebrows and a hook nose.

Tightening the belt on his robe, he stood. "Major Pickering, at your service," he introduced himself.

"Maddie McGuire," I said, trying to place his name, sure it sounded familiar.

"Like *Pygmalion*." The major answered my unasked question.

It took me a moment to move from the George Bernard Shaw play to my favorite musical, *My Fair Lady*. "That's it! Only Pickering is a colonel in the play."

"That so? I supposed I have some work to do then," he said, grey eyes twinkling. "Care to join me?"

The dining room stood empty except for him, so I accepted the invitation and sat despite wanting to retreat. Small talk seemed beyond my capabilities today.

"A bit overdressed. One rarely sees color let alone shoes," he commented on my ensemble.

At that point, Dolly breezed in, also wearing a bathrobe. She stuck her hand out to the major. "I don't believe we have met. Gwendolyn De Valence."

Major Pickering stood again, introduced himself, and asked Dolly to join us.

"Delighted!" she exclaimed, pulling out a white upholstered chair and resting lightly on the edge.

"How long have you been with us? I have been in Bath trying to fill

Maddie's shoes on tours," she patted me on the arm like we were old chums. "I absolutely do not know how she does it. Exhausting."

"Nine days," the major responded to her question, ignoring the rest. "One more, then back to London. The bank can only do without me so long."

As lovely as the spa was, ten days sounded a bit… boring. He must have been here for a more invasive treatment than a massage, although he didn't look the type for liposuction or a nip and tuck. Maybe if you run a bank, you need solitude every now and then.

Or tattoo removal, my mind suggested unhelpfully.

"Where's Simon?" I asked with little grace, my thoughts jumping about like popcorn.

Plates of food arrived in front of Dolly and me while the major continued to tuck into his.

The sausage snapped, releasing smoky juices with a hint of fennel into my mouth. But one bite was all my stomach accepted. The grilled tomatoes and remaining meat served as playthings that I pushed around my plate.

Dolly's expression mirrored the major's, bordering on ecstasy, only what she ate looked burned.

"Is your food supposed to look like that?" I asked, indicating a rubbery disk of something charred.

"Mmmmm, yes. Black pudding is my favorite."

"Made with blood, you know," the major added.

"Ah," I responded, unable to think of anything appropriate to add. The fact did nothing for my already dark musing.

After another enthusiastic bite of black pudding, Dolly answered my original question. "Simon's staying at Comer Manor. No need for him to stay here when his house is so close. He and Lady Vivian will join us for tea."

Abandoned again.

A sudden loneliness slammed into me. Even though beautiful, the setting wasn't familiar, and I counted on my friends being with me.

Schooling my features to neutral like Edward always did when an emotion struck him, I took a tasteless bite of food.

"Maddie, are you quite all right? You look absolutely shattered."

With an inner eye roll at my so-called poker face, I confessed, "I needed to talk to Simon this morning. Edward was called away on important business," I added.

Acting classes, when I took them as a child, were focused on projecting emotions across the face, a natural for me. At no point did I learn to hide feelings, a skill I desperately required.

"Edward is a police constable," Dolly explained to the major, who nodded, uninterested.

"What a bother," she said, looking apologetic, then brightened in a snap. "Do you ride? We have lovely mounts in the stable."

The first smile I had since seeing Edward's tattoo graced my features.

"Wonderful," she said, not waiting for an answer. "I'm sure you didn't bring riding boots. I'll see if Mother's are still here."

With that, she scampered off.

I chatted with Major Pickering, only half listening to his responses, until a woman entered the room and called, "Time for your checkup, Major. Come along,"

Using both hands on the table for support, he pushed himself to standing. "Thank you for the company, Miss Maddie."

"My pleasure, Colonel Pickering," I said with a wink, giving him a promotion.

He responded in kind.

As soon as he shuffled away, my smile faltered. Wanting nothing more than to call a taxi and go back to Bath, I sought out Dolly and the promise of horses.

Not sure where to meet her, I pictured the house's floor plan. A flattened U shape, spa to the left, family quarters to the right, and the central courtyard we walked through when we first arrived.

Recalling a shorter building to the right, I bet it was the stables.

When I opened the front door, a somber man in a black suit asked if I required anything.

The butler. An honest to god butler. Winters, I recalled. Wishing I had more bandwidth to appreciate the experience, I said the only phrase that came to mind. "I'm looking for the stables."

"This way," he said, overtaking me and leading the way I was already headed.

When we arrived, Dolly came from a different direction. "Try these on," she said without preamble, handing me an exquisite pair of leather knee-high riding boots.

Sitting on a hay bale, I slipped off my tennis shoes and pulled on the boots. My toes could wiggle, but my heel didn't slip. "Not bad," I confirmed. "Thanks."

The groom appeared, again out of nowhere, like all the employees at the spa. I swear the place had secret passages. In this case, one big enough for two horses. A striking chestnut bay and black thoroughbred stood at his side, saddled and waiting.

Drawn to the larger bay, the same kind of horse I learned to ride on, I stroked the horse's soft, black nose. He responded with a gentle huff.

"Lancelot likes you," Dolly commented. "I'll take Merlin," she informed the lad.

With a leg up from the groom and grace that bordered on floating, she swung onto Merlin's back.

Not until that very moment did I remember that English saddles were different from Western. There was no pommel; it was half as long and not nearly as sturdy. If I could ride bareback, though, I could use this, I assured myself.

Except the stirrup wasn't in the right place, much higher than I expected, with no horn to grip for leverage. I guided Lancelot to the hay bale, stood on it, placed my left foot in the stirrup, and mounted the horse.

"I would have helped you miss," the groom said, offended.

I, however, felt rather innovative.

With both reins gathered in my left hand, I turned the horse to follow Merlin, but Lancelot had a mind of his own and tried determinedly to veer toward a patch of clover.

Barrel racing taught me two things. First, I was bad at it, but the second was never let a stubborn mount get the better of you. Using my legs and a firm hand, I turned him in the correct direction.

At Dolly's side, I patted the bay's neck. "Good Lancelot."

Dolly looked confused. "How did you steer him when holding the reins that way?"

"What way?" I demanded, instantly defensive. I knew horses, and no one in any country could tell me otherwise. This activity was supposed to calm me, not make me more upset.

"Why don't you use both hands?" she pressed, ignoring my obvious annoyance.

Lifting my right hand, I waved it. "Roping hand."

"What on earth do you rope?"

I shrugged. "Calves."

Her eyebrows shot up.

"Breakaway calf roping. The honda breaks away with the slightest pressure so the calf doesn't fall. No one hog ties anymore." I added, despite Dolly's confusion.

"Calves?"

"Baby cows," I clarified. "They're fast, and if they run away from the herd, wranglers have to know how to rope and catch them, or they'll get eaten by something. Probably a coyote." The more I spoke, the more I sounded like Annie Oakley living at the O-K Corral. I'd participated in a grand total of two rodeos when I was twelve years old. I kept a lariat and played with it when no one looked, but it's not like I'd ever been out driving cattle or living on a dude ranch. *Jeez*, I chided myself.

Giving up, I asked, "How am I supposed to hold the reins?"

Her expression smoothed over. Could everyone hide their thoughts but me? Yes, yes, they could.

"A Western saddle would flummox me," she admitted before demonstrating the English technique. "Hold the reins in both hands, so you have more control over the horse. And when he trots, you'll need to post, which is standing a bit." She demonstrated.

Nodding, I tried both. Lancelot responded with the slightest touch. The lack of padding on the saddle made it impossible to forget to stand when he trotted.

"Got it." Smiling, I turned Lancelot in a tight circle and backed him up to make sure.

Dolly stared at me. "That's amazing," she said, sounding sincere.

I nodded my thanks and asked, "Where to?"

Finally acknowledging my still sour mood, she led the way to a riding track around the property without another word. We neared a hedge, then turned onto a lane which brought me out of my gloom.

Ivy lined the edges of the pavement while spreading trees created an archway of green tinged with red and gold. The effect created a tunnel worthy of Narnia, which, I realized, was written very near here.

Oxford, where CS Lewis and JRR Tolkien met, was only a couple of train stops from Bath. Although I hadn't ventured there yet, it was on my list.

A flatbed truck rumbled by the cross street, breaking my reverie.

"Is it safe to ride on the streets?" I wanted to know.

"Of course," Dolly responded. "Why wouldn't it be?"

Because England has the fastest, craziest drivers ever, that's why, I thought, but chose not to voice.

Making a couple of turns, she stopped in front of a wide track. "This goes to Comer Manor," she pointed. "Simon's family seat. It takes forty-five minutes to drive, but you can walk this in just over an hour. We've talked about it but haven't done it yet."

When I failed to respond again, she turned around, and Lancelot followed her with hardly a tug.

"I'm sorry I'm lousy company today," I said to her back. "I love horses, and this trip is making me feel a lot better."

"I can tell you're a natural rider. Lancelot is smitten with you," she called over her shoulder.

More quietly, she added, "I wish we could return to horses for everyone. Eliminate cars and all that exhaust."

It was the first time I heard her voice sound natural, not artificially cheery or high-pitched.

The ride worked its magic on my mood, and when we returned to the stables, my eyes were bright with curiosity. Not bothering with the groom, who assisted Dolly, I used my trusty hay bale to dismount.

"Want me to unsaddle him?" I asked the stable lad removing Merlin's. I ducked around the horse, found the girth, unlatched it, and slid the saddle off without waiting for an answer.

"Oy there! Whaddaya think you're doin'?" The groom lost all pretense of politeness.

Undeterred, I turned to the lady of the house and, for the first time ever, pulled rank. "Do you mind if I brush him down?" I asked Dolly. "It calms me."

With a nod and a smirk I wasn't expecting, Dolly turned to the groom. "Tim, could you make sure Ms. McGuire has everything she needs?"

"Yes'm," he responded with a slight bow of his head toward her and a stern glare at me. "This way, miss," Tim said, taking the saddle from me. A glint of gold showed through from a tooth when he spoke.

The barn smelled of sweet, fresh hay and leather polish for the saddles and horses. But not manure. They must clean up hourly rather than mucking out a stall once a day. The brushes, too, showed no signs of dirt, as if thoroughly cleaned after each use.

As the lad polished the saddles until they gleamed and Tim cared for Merlin, I guided Lancelot back to my handy hay bale, climbed up, and ensured I brushed the horse's back thoroughly before moving to his legs. Not a sore or burr on him, unlike Old Nigel, who had seen some hard days.

Sure that if I started picking rocks out of his hooves, Tim would have a fit, I finished with the mane and tail. Thanking the men, I returned to the main house with a bounce in my step.

"Barkin' that one is," one of them remarked.

Chapter Eleven: A Manor in Peril

"Barking?" I barked once back in my room. "As in, barking mad? Simply because I want to care responsibly for a horse?" A chore that had been drilled into me by that first terrifying instructor in the desert near the boulders of Carefree.

Grinning, I wondered how Tim would have gotten on with that instructor. He wouldn't have lasted a day.

I leaned down to remove my shoes and looked at the butter-leather riding boots—Dolly's. My shoes were back at the stable.

With an eye roll at myself, I pulled the door open to head back to the stables.

Major Pickering, bald head gleaming, followed a valet loaded with suitcases to the elevator. Dressed in a three-piece suit, I recalled his statement about working at a bank. He looked the part, impressive and in control.

Without a glance in my direction, he strode past, pulled out his phone, and looked official.

Waiting till the elevator doors closed, I chose the grand staircase and managed to exit the front door before the elevator made its slow descent.

Ducking under a camera perched over the front doors, adding it to a map in my mind, I stayed in the shadow of the building as I went toward the stables. No one appeared.

Not hidden tunnels or magic but spying eyes that allowed the staff to appear at a moment's notice. I turned and counted. There were cameras over every door, on the gate, and on the roofline, at which point my count derailed. A lot, I concluded. The grounds up to the house were entirely under surveillance.

If I hadn't experienced the staff's miraculous appearances, it would have struck me as odd to have that many.

Again, I hugged the building to avoid the cameras and arrived alone inside the stables. All the tack, including the saddles, were behind a locked cage. They gleamed in the low light. The brush I had used on Lancelot was clean, drying in the pale sunshine. My shoes, however, were nowhere to be seen.

Retracing my steps, I made it back to my room unobserved. A pair of clean tennis shoes sat by the door. With a smile, I picked them up and went inside. Sure that the boots would make it safely to Dolly if I left them in the hallway, I kept them, hoping for another ride.

The white noise box dinged softly, and the word "message" displayed across the side. Approaching it with some trepidation, I again examined it, looking for a button. Grasping it to turn it over, however, activated it.

A soothing female voice said, "A facial has been scheduled for you at one o'clock this afternoon. A technician will guide you to the space. Please be so kind as to tap and hold for two seconds to confirm."

"Touch and hold," I said as I followed the directions.

The box glowed a lovely shade of pink and displayed the words, "Thank you."

After a brief shower to remove the horse scent, I changed into my robe and waited. The same woman who guided me yesterday promptly greeted me as I opened the door at ten minutes to one.

The facial included a scalp massage while the first mask sunk in and hand reflexology during the second. Heaven, pure and simple.

Done in time for tea, I brushed my hair and changed. Robes might be okay for the spa dining room, but I wasn't about to appear in front of Simon or Lady Vivian without looking my best. Or the best I had with me, which was jeans with a pretty top.

Entering the grand hall, Winters soundlessly appeared to escort me to the home's private residence in the east wing. With a backward glance at the hallway, I searched for a camera but saw none.

"How did you know I needed help finding the stable earlier?" I asked.

Without pause, he responded, "Lady Gwendolyn mentioned you required riding boots. I assumed you would appear soon to look for the stables."

Good old-fashioned butlering, then.

Glad that I wasn't under constant observation. I still looked for evidence of cameras but didn't find any. At least not in the private side of the manor house.

Winters opened the arched, wooden door to a library. Towering oak bookshelves lined each of the twelve-foot-high walls. Low-slung chairs upholstered in burgundy leather were arranged next to the mantle. A cheery fire danced in the grate, adding ambiance without making the room hot. A Queen Anne-style tea tray sat in the center of the seating area, covered in triangle-cut sandwiches and delicate tea loaves. Cut crystal bowls held jellies, jams, and clotted cream.

The only thing missing was the guests. Being the first to arrive made me unsure of what to do. Should I sit? If I did sit, was I supposed to stand when Lady Vivian came in?

What about Lady Gwendolyn? What the heck was up with that?

Sighing, I explored the bookshelves deciding against sitting. Classics of literature, leather-bound and beautiful, covered one wall. The following shelves included titles of alternative medicines, including several volumes on herbs. One, in particular, looked well worn and out of place from the pristine quality of the rest. Curiosity getting the better of me, I pulled it down and checked the publication date.

1748.

With far more care than when I unshelved it, I replaced the tome and backed away. Books older than my country made me nervous. The solid structures of Ancient Rome were my comfort zone.

The door banged unceremoniously open, causing me to jump. Glad that I hadn't flung the antique book across the room, I regarded the newcomer.

Simon, far from his unruffled norm, glared about the room. "Not here yet, then," he said enigmatically.

Torn between asking, 'Who?' and 'What's wrong?', both were answered by the arrival of Lady Vivian.

"How could you, Aunt Viv?" Simon demanded, exhibiting none of his customary calm.

Having seen Simon in near-death situations act with more composure, I froze, unwilling to draw attention to myself.

Dressed in linen slacks and a cashmere pink cardigan, Lady Vivian looked ready for a relaxing weekend. The scowl emitting from her velvet blue eyes could cut glass. Silver hair trembling in rage, her voice shook when she declared, "I expected more from you, Simon."

Whoa. They did not know I was in the room. I wondered if I could make it to the door without being seen.

"Me?" Simon practically spat.

At that moment, the door opened again. Clarence De Valence, with Dolly on his arm, entered.

Both Simon and his aunt schooled their features in an instant, Simon extending his hand to Dolly.

She glided to his side while Clarence went to Vivian.

During the distraction, I crept toward the door and got behind Clarence, hoping to give the illusion of just entering.

Simon caught the movement and gave me the briefest of smiles.

Five of us here for a happy afternoon tea. On one side, Dolly and Simon. The other, Vivian and Clarence. And me, not having a clue what was going on.

"I'll have the papers drawn up when I'm in London on Friday," Clarence said to Vivian, ignoring the daggers Simon's eyes shot at them.

"No business talk at tea, Uncle," Dolly tittered, trying her best to diffuse tension. "Oh, look, the cakes are already here." Gesturing to the food with an open hand, she directed us to our seats with polite murmurs, but she did not sit.

"I will just have the tea sent in, shall I?"

For once, I appreciated her social graces, mimicking her smile to lighten the mood.

All in all, not the best time for me to ask Simon for advice, I realized, slumping in my leather chair. He needed a friend, and I was the logical choice. But I wasn't sure I could keep my confusion, anger, and betrayal feelings toward Edward from spilling out.

For all its civility, tea bubbled with hostility under the polite conversation. Barbed comments rife with subtext I didn't understand peppered every exchange.

Giving up on enjoying myself, I created a game out of it. Every time I figured something out, I got a point. Making a mental list, I ticked off each fact. Clarence and Vivian did something Simon didn't like. It was related to business, and the due date was Friday.

I should get two points for that last one, I thought, then amended it to the papers would be drawn up on Friday and might not be ready to sign until the week after. Dolly's allegiance was unclear. A fact, but not worth points, I decided. Just to be fair.

The only other thing I could glean was related to Comer Manor, Lady Vivian, and Simon's country house. No information on why they were fighting over it, though.

Between four and five points. Not bad.

The door opened once more, and I suddenly found I was the only one still sitting. I was so wrapped up in my scoring system that I blocked everyone else.

"Simon!" I shouted in a manner completely unsuitable for the environment. But it worked.

Dolly's voice came through the open door. "Oh, yes. Maddie needs you. Why don't you two go for a walk." A brief pause followed by, "This way, Uncle. I wanted to…" Her voice faded as she walked away.

"You didn't want to talk to me, did you?" Simon asked, despite having heard my call and been told by Dolly.

"No. I was testing the acoustics."

He quirked an eyebrow, turned, and left the room before I could stand up.

"Hey!" I complained, scrambling out of the chair and sprinting to the door. Again, in a way completely unbecoming to me or the space.

I shouldn't have bothered. Simon waited, leaning against a wall, looking handsome and bored.

With an expression of superiority that could only be produced by centuries of careful breeding, he said, "Do be quiet. We are not on the prairie."

When I started at the Baths, I would have bristled at this kind of statement. Now, I knew he was kidding.

Mostly. Admittedly, he'd had better days.

"C'mon," I said, indicating the entry doors with a toss of my head. When he resisted, I got behind him and pushed. Discreetly. In a way befitting of a lord.

"Stubborn cow," I muttered as he leaned into me.

Planting my feet, I prepared for a mighty shove when he deftly stepped out of the way and sent me stumbling across the tiled floor.

Striding past me with the grace of a dancer, he held the door open as I regained my balance.

"You're a punk, ya know," I informed him on the way outside.

"No. I think not."

An anarchist with a mohawk probably came to his mind. I pictured Tori's obnoxious older brother.

"Yeah, you are." I nodded with a fond smile.

Our path across the driveway area brought a variety of spa employees out of their hidey-holes. A valet offered to fetch the car, a lad asked if our desire was to ride, and someone else wanted to know if we required a map of the town.

Helpful but also a bit creepy. The feeling of being watched, amplified with each person who appeared.

"How do you deal with it?" I asked Simon.

"The servants? We only have two. The household budget is quite small. Annoyingly so."

With a series of blinks, I took in this information. Point number six, Aunt Vivian, required money. Suppositions would need to wait.

The other thing that had my brain on the fritz was that Simon volunteered personal information without prompting. Or threats from me. Things must be really bad.

As he didn't offer any additional facts, I stated as neutrally as possible, "I've never seen you mad at your aunt before."

"And you think I am stubborn."

The statement made me think I'd missed a few lines of explanation, but I plowed ahead with the six facts I discovered.

Trying the first explanation that came to mind, I asked, "Is Lady Vivian selling the manor house to De Valence?"

He squinted at me. "Not *the* manor house," he growled, emphasizing the word the. "My manor house."

He stalked toward the garden, leaving me gaping.

Chapter Twelve: Shifting Perspectives

The ins and outs of British aristocracy baffled me at the best of times. Too many questions formed, and my attempt to force them all out at once resulted in the lamest response imaginable. "How?"

Simon expected more from my powers of deduction and observation. Without a word, he passed beyond a hedge into an expansive garden cultivated to look wild. A statue of an eagle loomed over the overgrown grasses. Pillars poked out of the overgrowth, creating the appearance of an abandoned Greek temple.

"This would be easier if you didn't make me guess," I said to Simon's back. Being only an inch shorter than him, I matched his pace easily.

An opening in a trailing ivy revealed a carved stone bench, curved to echo the wall of climbing roses behind it.

Plopping in the center, Simon hung his head. The look was not a good one for him. Casually arrogant suited him better.

I carefully positioned myself next to him, hip to hip, unsure if he would take the comfort. After tensing, he rested his head on my shoulder. Slowly he released, rigidity coming off of him in waves.

"I still can't be in the dark," he whispered.

Our collective experience, entombed in inky blackness, left its mark on both of us.

With a quick one-armed hug of my shoulders, his bearing returned.

"If you tell anyone about this, I will have you thrown to the dogs."

Punching him in the shoulder, I scooted away to give him room.

"Okay. Things I don't understand."

"Innumerable, I imagine."

Ignoring him, I said. "I thought these manor houses belonged to the whole family, so explain that. How can your aunt sell it if it's yours? Why do you care so much? I know you both live in town. And why does she want to?" I nodded, pleased with the clarity of my questions. "That'll do for starters."

"The house passes to the eldest son, in our case. Other family live there based on the gracious invitation of the current lord. Since my parents passed it to me when I was underaged, Aunt Vivian became my guardian. She wants to sell because it is in desperate need of repair."

"But you're rich." I slapped a hand over my mouth in apology. But he bought all kinds of stuff for the Roman Bath Museum, so I figured he had cash to spare.

"It's complicated."

"No, duh," I agreed with a smidgen of annoyance.

"Didn't you need something?"

I saw through his pathetic attempt to change the subject, and straight to an opportunity for an exchange, I confessed. "Yes. I found another body."

Both his eyebrows rose slightly as though I admitted to having asked for ice in my afternoon tea. In other words, total shock.

"Now," I said smugly. "Explain the complications."

Long-suffering as ever, his head drooped for a moment before facing me. "The trust my parents set up for my care expressly forbids upkeep or repairs for Comer Manor." Without drawing attention, he moved closer. "Even after I take control in three years, I will need to find a way to fund the repairs without the benefit of the trust."

My look of incredulity caused him to laugh. "I know, right?" he mimicked my favorite phrase with a perfect Hollywood accent. With another one-armed hug, he told me, "They were not expecting me to inherit at the age of ten."

That bombshell opened up a whole other can of worms. Simon orphaned at ten? I thought my parents' divorce ruined my life. I couldn't imagine losing them entirely.

Before I could find out what happened to his parents or offer condolences, he continued. "Maddie. Where was the body?"

A hitch formed in my throat, and I leaned into the comfort of his arm. Swallowing hard, I squeaked, "In the woods." I turned my face to his. "Why does this keep happening to me?"

I sounded pathetic, but Simon continued to comfort me. My weekend of taking relationships to a new level continued, but in a way, I didn't plan or expect. Something shifted during the last few minutes. Another wall dropped between us, and our level of trust went up, taking us to friends.

"Do you need intervention of any kind? Shall I call DCI Bray for you?"

The detective chief inspector had ties to aristocratic families, but I wasn't a suspect, so I didn't need that kind of help. "No. DI Parikh knows everything and turned it over to the Gloucester police."

I sat up, the answer to one of my questions dawning on me. While I didn't understand the aristocracy, Simon cared deeply for it. His house made up an integral part of that social class.

"We have to save that manor," I declared.

His sad smile strengthened my resolve.

"No, I'm serious. Can't you do house tours or something?"

Shaking his head, he answered, "We are on the Historic House registry, but we are not near a major road, so very few come."

Fine. "The point was you're willing to let strangers in."

"Only to three rooms. The plan for the medispa would take over most of my house, and it is smaller than this one." He waved a hand toward the three-story main building of the De Valence's home. "The plan Clarence proposed leaves us with very little space or control."

His face twisted. "It's a generous offer, and I am grateful to Vivian for trying to solve our woes and for De Valence's help. But..." He let the rest of the thought trail off.

"But nothing! Don't you dare stiff-upper-lip this situation. There must be something." Jumping up, I paced in front of the bench. I didn't know that much about Simon, but I was determined to help him.

"Maddie, I—"

"Don't argue with me. I will figure something out."

With supreme effort, he nodded.

Flabbergasted at the assent, I continued to brainstorm. "Make it a tourist stop, so more people come to the house. Prettiest village designation? Prettiest garden? Giant vegetable contest?" Okay, that one came from one of my favorite Halloween animated movies, but it had merit.

I paced faster, scoffing at the pseudo-Doric pillars supporting peach and pink roses. With all the Roman history in this area, why would they pick a Greek theme? Maybe they didn't know.

With a shake, I got myself back on track. "Bringing people to the area," I mused, but no more ideas presented themselves because the back of my mind caught hold of an idea. Try as I might, I couldn't bring it forward.

Turning in a circle, I relaxed my focus, letting the surroundings inspire me. When my gaze landed on the anachronistic column, my thoughts derailed.

"Seriously," I pointed to the column. "Why Greek? There is an ancient Roman villa, not ten miles from here."

"I'm afraid the poet Byron popularized the Greek ideal, supporting—"

Ignoring the rest of his lecture, I let the idea take hold of me. I turned it over, thought of it from several angles, and declared it valid. "Do be quiet." My attempt at his accent failed miserably.

Shockingly, he did and waited for me to wow him.

"How about you turn a part of your house into a Center for Archeology? Isn't there some national agency you could apply to for a grant ?"

"Say that again," he said, rising.

I repeated myself as Simon nodded.

"Is it an idea?" I asked, although I could tell from the small smile that he liked it. "It is. Good. It sounded like De Valence is drawing up spa papers on Friday, so if we can arrange a preliminary plan and present it to Lady Vivian, maybe we can stop the medispa."

Then, to cement our new friendship status, he offered a high five, which I returned with gusto. Casual, cool, and very much me, the gesture showed that he paid attention and was willing to compromise.

Or maybe I'd never seen him do it before, and this was no big deal. I took it to mean something important.

"Do you want to go for a ride? We need to celebrate."

A noise drew our attention. Peering through the rose vines, I saw a gardener retrieving shears he dropped. With an absent wave, he left.

I wondered how long he had been there and what he overheard. Would he report our exchange to De Valence?

Simon didn't seem to care, so I let it go, remembering eyes and ears spied everywhere on this property.

"You go ahead," he directed, striding purposefully out of the garden and to the front entrance.

Grinning at him, I turned right, heading toward the stable.

When I approached, I realized I didn't have the riding boots. Again. However, since the groom already thought I was crazy, I decided my tennis shoes would do.

No one appeared. Ironic, as it was the first time, I wanted someone to. As I stepped into the airy stables, the area went dark, and I fought down a bloom of panic.

My eyes adjusted, and the darkness coalesced into a large, chestnut bay. "Lancelot," I said, patting his neck.

He danced nervously until I stroked his nose and cooed softly.

Tim, the groom, suddenly appeared from nowhere and swiftly handed me the reins before turning to go. Preferring to be alone, his sudden departure suited me fine, even if it was a little odd. "Thank you, Tim!"

Lancelot and I walked to the edge of the yard. No hay bales stood nearby, so I decided to lead him by the low wall to boost myself up but decided better of it. Not wanting to use props, I hoisted my foot into the stirrup and managed to yank myself into the saddle.

Lancelot bolted before I could right myself, aiming for the stone wall. I managed to clutch the reins but wasn't ready when he jumped.

Flung forward, my face collided with his massive head, convincing the horse to launch me off. Slowing from a run, he bucked, back arched, turning wildly with each landing.

Jarring impacts rattled my teeth, making it impossible to take control of Lancelot or myself. Squeezing my knees to his withers kept me from flying off but did nothing to calm my mount. Bone-shattering hooves pounded the grass, churning chunks of plants and mud, making it impossible to see where to go.

Screamed commands fell on deaf ears as the enormous bay did everything to dismount me. Changing tactics, he reared, front legs extending over his head. With no saddle horn to stop me, I slipped. Burying my fingers into his mane, I kept from sliding off toward his deadly kicks. My shifting weight enraged him, and he returned to bucking and spinning, anything to dislodge me.

Ignoring my instinct to cling on for dear life, I pushed my hands together at the base of the horse's neck, kicked my feet backward out of the stirrups, threw my right leg across his back, and pushed against him with all my strength, before plummeting to the ground.

Chapter Thirteen: The Wound

When I learned how to dismount a bucking horse, the practice pony was neither big nor actually bucking. The skill didn't take long to master and, at a slow trot, looked like a movie stunt, at least in my mind.

When I pushed away from Lancelot, I misjudged how far down I would fall and overbalanced on impact. Stumbling on a rock as my feet hit the ground, I fell, ankle buckling without the protection of riding boots.

The muscle memory that got me to dismount safely, unfortunately, also made me keep hold of the reins, landing Lancelot's final buck a few inches from my arm.

Untangling my hand from the reins, I tossed them away. Lancelot calmed but continued to kick, front hooves pawing on the ground.

I rolled away from him, pushed to all fours, and breathed.

"Send help!" I heard Tim's voice cry. "That horse has killed her!"

Lancelot's eyes began to roll again while his great head jerked from side to side. With the groom's panic seeping into him, Lancelot could charge right over me and not even notice.

With an effort, I got to my feet and limped to the horse, cooing. Yelling at the groom would only make Lancelot antsier, so I ignored the man's cries. "We had quite a ride, didn't we, buddy." I pitched my voice low, using a lilt. "You're a good boy," I said, concentrating on calming emotions so he could pick up on them. "Good horse. Let's relax now."

Still jittery, he could take off at any moment, but I got close enough to snatch the reins. Holding tight but careful not to jerk him, I stepped near enough to pet his nose. When he nuzzled my hair, I let out a sigh of relief.

Until Tim, still screaming like a banshee, hopped on the fence and riled poor Lancelot up again.

"Shhhhh, shhhhh, shush. You're okay," I said, turning a ferocious glower onto the groom. "Shush," I sent his direction as well.

He did so.

Directing the horse and Tim simultaneously, I kept my voice low but added a commanding note. "We're going back to the stable and get that old saddle off you. You're okay," I assured everyone.

Recovering from the shock of almost killing a guest and personal friend of the De Valence family, Tim quickly and quietly ran to the approaching crowd, herding them to the house while I got Lancelot to his stall.

As I unbuckled the saddle, I noted how worn and patchy it was. Not at all like the gleaming tack kept locked in the front of the stable. When I turned it over, Tim returned and lifted it from me.

"Y'alright, miss?" he asked, concern in his voice, gold tooth glinting.

"Yeah, fine. Thanks," I responded, although my hands and voice shook with shock. A symptom I experienced far too often lately.

"That was some impressive riding, if I do say so myself," he offered.

That compliment cut through some of the buzzing in my ears.

When I first begged my mom for horseback riding lessons, she balked, saying horses were too big and dangerous. Wearing her down, she picked the no-nonsense trainer in the desert, hoping to discourage me. However, I learned to dismount from a trotting animal. When I showed her, she nearly fainted.

Today was the first time I understood her fear.

Searching Lancelot's big brown eyes, I swear I saw shame in them. "It's okay."

I climbed to the second rung of the gate to his stall so I could hug his neck. The muscles around his jaw relaxed, and I pulled back to smile at him.

As I balanced, he turned, presenting his back to me. I thought he might want to be brushed, but then I saw it. A small open wound positioned under the saddle area. Any weight must have been painful. No wonder he bolted when I swung into the saddle.

Rubbing his back for a few strokes, I gave him encouraging words, then hopped off the gate to find Tim.

And collapsed to the ground, still weak from the experience.

Tim and the other lad came running, threw a clean horse blanket over my shoulders, and helped me to my feet. A large technician, one of the masseurs, I thought, came to escort me to the house.

As we left the stable, I searched for the old saddle, but it wasn't anywhere in sight.

When I brushed Lancelot the day before, his coat gleamed with perfection. Before I could contemplate what his sore meant, the family greeted me in the welcome serenity of the main lobby. De Valence took over for the technician, supporting my wobbly legs.

"Dear girl, I simply cannot apologize enough for Lancelot's behavior. We've never had problems with him before. You're lucky to be alive."

"Be careful with her, Uncle," Dolly exclaimed, although quietly, befitting of the space.

He looked at his niece. "What do you think, my dear? Chakra balancing bath treatment followed by a healing mud wrap?"

"Absolutely," Dolly responded. "I'll contact Mary to set everything." Taking my hand, she squeezed. "I'm so sorry."

"As am I," De Valence repeated, guiding me to the elevator.

When the doors opened, Lady Vivian rushed out while maintaining her stately manner. An impressive feat that brought a weak smile to my lips.

"Treat her with the utmost care," she demanded with no preamble. Her pink jacquard suit jacket emitted the lovely scent of roses as she joined De Valence with an arm around me.

"How are you?"

The words were so full of concern that tears sprung from my eyes. "I'm fine."

The quaver in my voice belied the statement, but she patted my back. "Of course, you are, resourceful girl."

The pep talk had its desired effect, and I straightened a bit, relying more on my good leg. Something about being called resourceful by a refined English lady made me want to prove myself. "I'm okay," I reiterated, limping away from De Valence, who nodded his approval.

Crystal blue eyes flashing, he vowed, "I will speak to Tim and find out what is going on with Lancelot. Unacceptable," he growled, making me a bit worried for the groom. And the horse.

"It wasn't anyone's fault," I said, but something made me hold back the information about Lancelot's open wound. "There were a couple of wasps nearby. One must have stung him." Not true, but safer, somehow.

De Valence's handsome face relaxed. "Well then, we will call the veterinarian to come and give him the old once over." Lifting my hand and patting it, he said, "I am always at your disposal. Anything you need, let me know."

The support weakened my resolve to stand on my own, so I glanced at Vivian, who pulled her arms back ever so slightly. Rolling my shoulders created the same effect, adding strength to my stance.

I wondered why Simon hadn't appeared. After everything we went through earlier, I expected him to be there. The absence rankled me.

All the more because Edward not only wasn't there, but I didn't know where he was. Or why he stormed out when I had all the reasons to be angry, not him.

"Where's Simon?" I asked with more force than necessary, making it sound like a demand.

"Comer Manor," Dolly said. "He said he had important research to conduct, although he did not tell me what. He should be back by the evening meal. Do you want me to send a specific message or only to tell him about your accident?"

Shaking my head, I said, "Don't worry him. I'll talk to him when he shows up."

"Absolutely," she agreed, and I managed not to roll my eyes.

If I were honest, she struck me as a lovely person. Kind, friendly, charming. But something was not quite right, like she was hiding a piece of herself, which put my hackles up.

Of course, I had to admit my thinly disguised hostility didn't encourage opening up. Vowing to be nicer, I gave her a shaky smile. "Thank you, Dolly. Appreciate it."

The expression on her face proved my hostility hypothesis. Her return grin showed so much relief that my mother's voice echoed in my ears. *It's never a bad thing to be the most gracious person in a room.*

I took the advice to heart. Better late than never.

Dolly guided me through the spa treatments, warning everyone to be gentle with my freshly traumatized body. The bruises from my stairwell event and fall down a cliff were distant memories compared to the black and blue marks blooming across my legs and arms. My swelling ankle took on unnatural proportions.

* * *

The spa's healing treatments worked into my muscles as expected and promised. Exhaustion threatened to overwhelm me, but I wanted to go home rather than spend another night in the manor house.

Home. The word still carried a tang of bitterness since I didn't really have one. Picturing the house I grew up in, sprawling with vaulted ceilings, set in a giant yard complete with a pool, fire pit, and grapefruit trees, a lump formed in my throat. That place would always be home, even though my mom sold it the second I left for college in Chicago. I'd only spent two semesters at the university, so despite my dad living there, that city didn't feel like home any more than the condo my mom bought in downtown Tempe.

Except, no matter what, the desert called me when I thought of home. Warm, dry, with hundred-mile views. If I went there now, even in a guest room in my mom's condo, she would bundle me up and cook my favorite meals. Exactly like when I was learning to barrel race and would come home bumped and bruised.

"Sigh," I said aloud.

Today, I supposed Ash Tree Cottage counted as home. The Priestlys filled the house with family love, even when they were busy or away.

Decision made, I packed my bag, limping gingerly from dresser to bed to bath. Scanning the room, I didn't see anything resembling a phone to call the front desk, so I headed to the elevator and main lobby.

As expected, Winters appeared to take care of my every need. A cane for me, my meager bag loaded onto a trolley, and a gentle escort from the house to a waiting car. A little creepy, though. I wondered how anyone knew I wanted to leave.

As if on cue, Dolly, ever the perfect hostess, approached.

"Thank you, Winters," she said before giving me a brief and gentle hug.

"He kind of appears out of nowhere, doesn't he?" I commented.

"The Ubiquitous Winters, I call him," Dolly said, an appreciative smile aimed at his retreating back. "We would be absolutely lost without him."

She clarified, although I hadn't asked. "While taking care of Uncle and me, he oversees the staff for the house and the spa, keeps an eye on scheduling, and does the accounts. An absolute treasure he is."

I made the appropriate listening sounds, but my mind wandered to home as soon as Dolly said "ubiquitous." When I started kindergarten, my mom gifted me a full-sized, red leather-bound dictionary with gold edge gilding. I couldn't even lift the silly thing. "Every time you hear a word you don't know, look it up and put a mark by it," she told me.

Following her instructions until I left for college, and she ruthlessly packed the tome into storage when she sold my childhood home, I noted some words required multiple marks before I remembered them. Ubiquitous topped the charts with six tally tics.

My smile matched my host's, but mine was for my mom with her exquisite vocabulary. "That word doesn't fit the context," I heard her voice chiding me. "Choose a different one."

"Thank you and Winters for anticipating my departure," I said with a fair amount of formality.

Thoughtful, but considering I didn't have the chance to tell anyone my intentions, paranoia followed me into the warm interior.

The steward held the door open, saying, "The Viscount wishes to convey—

"

The lord in question ran out of the manor. "Miss McGuire," De Valence gasped, his handsome face pinched with concern. "So glad I caught you. I couldn't be sure you wanted to leave," he said in a fair impression of a mind reader. "But I wanted every eventuality covered."

The simple statement dispelled a lot of my anxiety about being spied on. Like with Dolly, I should accept that De Valence was kind.

"See that she gets to her door safely, Wiggins," he told the driver before shutting the door.

As we pulled away, a shudder wracked my body, bringing with it the thought that I missed something vital.

Chapter Fourteen: Rabbits and Hay

As Wiggins, De Valence's driver, whisked us down the A46 toward Bath, the pleasant rocking of the car coaxed me into a deep state of relaxation. Ivy nestled among sycamore and maple trees were starting to tinge red in anticipation of fall.

Oval-shaped gaps in the leaves formed watching eyes following the car's movement. One blinked, then erupted in flames at our passing.

Startling awake, my hand flailed, smacking the window. The view resolved into the welcoming Georgian architecture of Bath.

"Are you quite all right, miss?" Wiggins asked.

Trying to recall the number of times someone asked me that lately proved too much.

"Sorry," I responded. "I fell asleep."

"It'll take a moment to get through town," he informed me. "If you wish to continue to nap."

Rather than replying, I sat up straighter, working out the kinks in my shoulders and failing to scrub the dream eyes from my mind.

Ascending the roads to Greenway Lane, with its familiar landmarks, worked its magic, and I finally relaxed. As I unlatched the gate to Ash Tree Cottage, the chaos flooding my thoughts fled as I observed the Priestlys gardening in the late afternoon sun.

A smile spread across my face. Using my borrowed cane to hop down the steps and immediately over the short fence that created Roderick the Rabbit's enclosure. I sat on the cool grass.

"Hello!" I called as Wiggins followed through, fussing at me under his breath for not allowing him to support my injured ankle.

"Maddie, dear! How nice to see you!" Meryl called. "Hello," she directed at Wiggins.

"This is Wiggins." I gestured toward the man with my luggage. "Clarence De Valence's driver. He was kind enough to bring me all the way to our door."

Roger stood from his task, greeted Wiggins, and took my bags into the house.

Before Wiggins turned to leave, he must have conveyed my injuries to Roger because as the gate closed, he turned a concerned expression my way. Without a word, he went to Roddy's hutch, coaxed the large black and white rabbit out, and placed the bunny in my lap. Folding his long legs under him in a surpassingly spry movement, he sat next to me.

"Sprained ankle?" he asked.

I focused on the soft fur of Roddy's ears as I nodded.

"What's that?" Meryl called. Not waiting for an answer, she was by us in a few steps. "What happened? What do you need?"

I always prided myself on not being a crier. Never a damsel in distress. Not this girl. Lately, my emotions bubbled to the surface at the kindest word. Yes, I had experienced some crazy stuff over the weekend, but it wasn't the first time since my arrival in England. Vowing not to give in to another bout of tears, I raised my head and took in the joy in the situation. Loving friends, a sunny afternoon, a beautiful garden, and a sweet rabbit who seemed intent on nuzzling my hair.

"Bucking bronco." I explained what happened with Lancelot and my daring dismount. "You should have seen me," I said, cocky. "Straight out of a rodeo." Rolling my jeans away from my swollen ankle, I added, "Complete with the bumps and bruises."

Eyes wide, Meryl declared, "That needs ice."

"And elevation," Roger added.

Both sprang into action, leaving me with Roddy. Lifting himself, he stretched to his full height, resting his front paws on my shoulder.

"What are you doing, you wascally wabbit?" I asked, pulling him back to my lap.

Not content with cuddles, he reached for my hair.

Giving in, I released my strawberry blonde locks from the ballerina bun I had tied earlier for the spa treatments. Dust, grass, and a bit of hay rained out of it.

While my clothes had been laundered and shoes cleaned, I hadn't wanted to shower after my spa treatments. My hair still bore the marks of being dumped off a horse.

Roddy's nose twitched with delight as he examined the goodies now scattered about us.

A particularly large piece of hay still dangled from my waves. Untangling it, I offered the prize to the bunny.

"He looks delighted," Roger said, returning with a white cast iron chair from the boot room and a small table. After helping me to reposition, he produced a plump pillow and placed it under my foot.

"You don't have to do all this," I protested mildly, appreciating their efforts.

Meryl followed close after with a bag of ice wrapped in a tea towel. "Twenty minutes," she instructed. "Not a minute more."

"Thank you. It feels better already," I said, meaning it. Not wanting to dwell on my injury, I swept an arm to indicate the extensive garden and terrace of Ash Tree Cottage. "What are you working on today?"

Roddy's front paws found the seat of my chair, and he launched into my lap while munching another piece of hay.

"Removing pot saucers, raising pots, collecting masterwork seeds, mulching," Meryl listed, returning to star-shaped pink flowers and shaking them.

"Readying for the first frost," Roger continued, moving off to dig out sun-weathered peonies from a planter, leaving me to contemplate the rabbit.

"It's odd," I confided to Roddy softly. "That rabbits and horses both eat hay."

He offered no opinion on the matter, so I turned to appreciate the view. Greenway Lane lay at the top of Beecham Cliffs, and Ash Tree Cottage nestled into the hillside, creating a multiple-level home. The slope also formed a terraced garden. The path from the street past the enormous ash tree nestled in the front garden to the door fashioned one layer. Steps down to a patio decorated with potted plants led to a stone wall, the other side of which descended into the wilds below.

It was breathtakingly lovely, but was it enough to keep me here? The internship at the Roman Baths constituted a professional coup, but I never counted on finding a dead body.

"And where the heck is Edward?"

At my question, Roddy's ear twitched as if trying to locate him.

"It's no use," I informed the bunny. "The man and his tell-tale tattoo are nowhere to be found."

Every time I got close to contemplating the significance of Edward's unicorn head matching Sherrie's, my mind shut down. The only conclusion I managed to form was that any connection was bad. And in that case, did I want to know? But if I didn't know, how could I trust him?

The sprightly breeze picked up, bringing gray clouds with it. Goosebumps prickled my skin in the cooling air.

"Do I even want to trust him at this point?"

Roddy put his nose in the crook of my elbow. "Right," I agreed. "No good answers."

"What's that, dear?" Meryl asked, smacking dirt from her gloves.

"Uh." Which is worse? Talking to myself or talking to the rabbit? Choosing neither, I said, "It's getting chilly," and transferred Roddy to the grass.

As I moved my leg off its perch, the realization that it hurt presented itself. A lot.

My attempt to hide my grimace failed as Meryl called to Roger, and they helped me into the house. Once inside, I only wanted to go to my room and sleep. Looking at the narrow stairs, I realized that once I got up, I'd never get down until the swelling went away.

Meryl must have concluded the same thing as she guided me to the charming living room and settled me on the cream couch, elevating my foot to the armrest. After supporting my back with pillows and wrapping a blue afghan over me, she said, "I'll just put the kettle on. Tea?"

"Coffee, if it's no trouble," I said, needing something strong to clear my head.

Setting a side table within easy reach, she said, "No trouble," before heading to the kitchen.

Roger appeared with an armload of things, including my computer, phone, bathrobe, and hairbrush. With an embarrassed smile, he informed me, "All things I saw without digging through drawers or cupboards. Meryl will fetch your more personal things later."

As I opened my mouth to protest, Meryl appeared, coffee and milk in hand. "We simply don't see how you'll make it up the stairs with the ankle." She stirred milk into the thick ceramic mug and handed it to me. "So we'll move you into here until that ankle turns a less appalling color."

"I couldn't possibly," I began, but she had already closed the second door to the room.

The bright, acidic coffee danced on my taste buds, reminding me of home. Without considering time zones, I picked up my cell and called my mom.

"Salutations, beautiful, smart child!"

Heather McGuire's greeting summed her up perfectly. Despite her ridiculous vocabulary, her main goal always centered around supporting me.

"What would you think if I came home?" I asked without preamble, surprising us both.

It took a few beats for her to answer. I knew she wanted nothing more than to have me safe and sound on American soil, so it took a supreme effort for her not to jump on the offer.

"I fear there is more to this story than I am privy to," she replied in a neutral voice.

I sighed, not wanting to go into details. The one time I wanted her to give me all the reasons why I should be home, she decided to be logical.

"I found another body," I said, hoping the shock would motivate her into not only supporting me but insisting that I return.

"Oh, sweetheart." The pain and sympathy in her voice went straight to my heart. "Tell me everything."

I did, including Edward's tattoo. But not the circumstances under which I saw it. As a college professor, she could fill in the blanks. Although, I hoped she didn't.

"What did Tori say?" she wanted to know.

"I haven't told her yet," I confessed. "I wanted to hear your opinion first."

Taking a sip of coffee, I listened to her splutter and attempt to regain composure before responding. Certain that fifty sarcastic responses raced through her mind ranging from her being first to her being the best choice, I waited for her to find the right one.

With a Herculean effort, she contained herself and commented, "As you know, I have different criteria for you than your friends. Much as I want you to listen to me, I can't in good conscience offer my opinion."

"Mother." I wanted it to come out stern, but I sounded whiny. "What do you think?"

"What do I think?" Her dam of composure finally burst. "What do I think?" she repeated. "I think you should have never left for Chicago to go to school. I think you should be pursuing a degree in an employable field. I think your father should not have interfered and encouraged you to pursue an internship that was designed for an older student." She paused for a breath, continuing in a softer tone. "And I think you should return to being fourteen years old and needing me for everything."

A sniffle traveled the distance between Arizona and England, and I swallowed more coffee, failing to keep my tears at bay.

"But." Another sniff. "You can't. You have encountered horrors and handled them with uncanny resilience. When I visited, and you showed me the city and the Baths, you carried yourself with such confidence and grace that I recognized you were where you needed to be, doing what you were called to do."

Numbness spread through me, short-circuiting every synapse in my brain. My mother supported everything I did as long as she could keep an eye on me. Every time I mentioned archeology or going to England, her responses were kind, with an undercurrent of knowing I wouldn't succeed.

"My conclusion," she continued. "Is that you should stay."

"Really?" I squeaked, not knowing how I felt yet.

After a huge exhale, she contradicted herself. "No. Please come home. Go to school here, take my classes. Be my roommate."

At the offer, I recoiled. Supportive is one thing, but roomies? No way. Which, of course, she knew.

A chuckle replaced my quiet sobs. "That sounds amazing, Mom, but—"

"But suffocating. I know."

"You always know," I said in a quiet voice.

"Which is why you call me," she continued, regaining her superior tone. "Much as I want you home, you are doing archeology. Go back to work. Call me in a couple of days. You know, if you need anything, I'm here."

"I know, Mommy. Thank you."

After we said our goodbyes, I processed the conversation. Did I belong here? The Baths had Dolly to replace me, Dr. Daniels still didn't know who I was, Simon didn't need me, Edward was gone, and my ankle pulsated with white-hot pokers every time I shifted.

To top it all off, I needed to use the restroom.

A polite tapping from the door to the kitchen repeated itself.

"Hello?" I called, not sure if the knock was for me.

Meryl's head popped in. "Just had a thought."

Twisting to face her, I raised my eyebrows, encouraging her to tell me.

"There's no loo on this level of the house."

Chapter Fifteen: Giant Rodents

"I gathered some essentials from your studio and moved them to our daughter's room on the first story," Meryl informed me. "Roger will take these things upstairs," she indicated the nest that formed around me and my swollen ankle.

With that taken care of, she turned her attention to me. "I'm just not quite sure what to do about you." A worried expression creased her kind face. "Those stairs are steep."

Nodding in agreement, I told her my plan. "I've been thinking about that. Crawling will work going up. Coming down, I can bump on my bottom."

Meryl clapped. "I wouldn't suggest it to everyone, but you're young and agile. It's how our daughter navigated them most of her life."

With a supporting embrace, she helped me navigate upstairs, where Roger already had my temporary room set up.

"I'll just draw you a bath, shall I? Epsom salts will control the swelling."

Before going in, I called and then texted Edward. No response.

Putting him firmly from my mind looked like thinking about him every ten seconds, but it was better than constantly.

The bath helped a bit. When I collapsed on the plump feather bed, I fell into a fitful sleep.

* * *

The next morning, I considered calling in sick. No one would blame me. Of course, then I would be stuck with my brain spinning out of control over

Edward.

Flexing my ankle caused enough pain to put a check in the staying-home column.

As I picked up my cell, a text came through—'Rivers will be at your door in forty-five minutes. Good luck.'

Simon, texting on behalf of his aunt. Lady Vivian's driver, Rivers, took the rules of the road as vague suggestions, making any ride with him terrifying. Unless the lady herself rode, then Rivers maintained quiet composure.

I dressed, swallowed some painkillers, and recapped the bottle. Thinking better of it, I dumped a handful of the gel caps in my jean jacket pocket and then bumped my way downstairs, where a crutch waited.

Using it, I hobbled to the kitchen. Roger and Meryl left me a note stating in no uncertain terms that I should call them if I required anything. A fresh loaf of Meryl's homemade bread cooled on the cutting board. Toast and hot cocoa with a shot of coffee delivered the customary well-being I expected.

As I finished the dishes, Rivers rang the bell. We managed the car without mishaps, and I buckled in before Rivers could get behind the wheel. Gripping the armrest, I readied myself for the coming G-forces.

And, nothing.

Gentle, calm driving that obeyed every speed limit sign.

Confused, I asked, "Are you quite well, Rivers?"

"Oh, tip-top, miss. Never better. Lady Vivian told me about you and that horse. Be careful around them. You'd never get me on one of those beasts."

Before I got to England, my mother was the only person I knew who didn't ride. The idea depressed me, making me long for the wide-open spaces of the desert.

As we pulled in front of the Abbey, I said, "Thank you so much. I wouldn't have gotten too far walking."

"I'm not done yet, miss," he told me, turning off the ignition. "I'm to deliver you all the way to your sifting table, I am. And I'm not to take any arguments."

For once, I had no intention of complaining. Help sounded great.

Bypassing the Oversight Office, Rivers took me straight to my fluorescent-lit stairwell.

"Careful," I said when he slammed the door into the sifting apparatus. "The table is in the way. And, wait."

Something looked off. The light seeping around the door wasn't sharp enough.

Leaning my crutch against the wall, I placed a finger to my lips to caution Rivers and peeked at the landing.

My hand fluttered to my mouth as I gasped, not believing my eyes.

"Good. You're here," Lady Vivian stated. "Simon departed before I arrived but left specifications with Sam."

Transformed, the stairwell glowed with warm charm. The ubiquitous fluorescent still flickered on the floors above, but my area now had two floor lamps, creating a delightful atmosphere. A bright, full-spectrum LED cast clear light over the sifting table. In addition to the ergonomic seat Simon provided for my work, a new upholstered chair with a small tray sat in the corner, complete with water and snacks.

Overwhelmed by the level of kindness involved in the makeover of my workspace, I stammered my thanks.

Limping to my station, I found all my buckets within arms-reach.

"It's perfect. I can't thank you enough."

The door opened, and Sam stuck her head in. "Are you settled, you poor thing? I miss havin' you on tours, but Dolly is doin' her best."

She was pouring the Irish accent on extra thick today, and I wasn't sure if she was nervous for some reason or because it made me smile.

"I missed you, too."

She gave me an impulsive hug before leaving.

Contentment I didn't think possible flooded into me as I settled in to shake buckets of dirt. The thrill of discovering a corner of tesserae kept me focused and my mind off Edward and tattoos.

Three full hours went by with no obsessing - a record I felt proud of. Thinking, admittedly. Contemplating, yes. Considering, perhaps. But not obsessing. At least not for too long.

Pushing away from my workstation, I hopped to the easy chair, hooked my leg over the armrest to elevate it, and pawed through the snacks Simon and Lady Vivian left.

Several options not available in the US, so I chose one called Twiglets. An odd name, but when I opened the bag, I saw why. They looked like sticks. Small sticks. Twigs, to be exact.

"Entertain your senses," I read from the bag before popping one into my mouth. The earth-shattering crunch overshadowed the taste for a moment. Chewing, a salty, tangy, and pungent flavor, emerged. I tried another, munching so loudly that I didn't hear the approach of visitors.

"How are you doing, Ms. McGuire?" a male voice inquired.

"Huh?" I startled, spewing whole grain pieces on my shirt as I took in the form of Dr. Daniels.

Snatching my water from the table, I gulped too fast, coughing and spluttering.

He did not appear to notice. Daniels' head returned to the hallway where he said, "No, really, you must see," to someone. "The spitting image."

In popped Lily! My friend who served at the Pump Room next door. People mistook us for each other because of our matching strawberry blonde, not ginger, hair. The most striking differences were her startlingly blue eyes to my green, and I towered over her.

A terrible accident snatched her away for a month, and I missed her easy-going, genuine companionship.

"Lily! How are you? I wasn't sure you'd come back." Arranging myself to avoid more damage, I went to her. "Here. Take the chair."

With a delightful and slightly nasally chuckle, she waved me off. "No mither, I'm fine," she insisted. She pointed at my foot and asked, "What happened to you?"

I shrugged. "Jumped off a bucking horse."

"Good god!" Daniels exclaimed as Lily gasped.

"It wasn't the horse's fault," I rushed to assure them. "Someone put a burr under its saddle."

It was the first time I voiced my suspicion, and saying it out loud, it felt true.

Lancelot's gear wasn't the usual polished leather the spa used. The mount had been saddled when I arrived, and the groom unusually quiet. Plus, I'd brushed Lancelot the day before, and he gleamed with perfection.

"But why?" I asked myself as Lily and Dr. Daniels deposited me back in the easy chair.

"Because horses are dangerous," Dr. Daniels said, thinking the question was directed at him. "Now, do keep yourself safe. I'll send someone in to collect the sifted buckets." He turned to Lily. "Lunch?" He sounded like Winnie the Pooh.

"Ploughman's, yes. I have the rest of the order," she turned to me. "Except you."

Dr. Daniels wandered off, muttering what sounded like a To Do list to himself.

"Lily," I said, watching him go. "I checked the Pump Room menu. It does not have anything close to a ploughman's." The Pump Room, an elegant destination since Jane Austen graced the streets of Bath, served high tea and finger sandwiches. Not the chunks of hearty bread, ham, apple, and Stilton blue cheese designed to keep field hands productive all day.

She laughed. "No! I buy almost everyone's lunches from Mokoko or the Bath Bun. The maitre d' arranges for my time. He likes the prestige of providing food for the archeologists."

Turning at the door as she left, she invited me to catch up. "Let's get a brew later."

"Great!" I said. "Crystal Palace after work?"

She meant tea when she said brew, but the pub in front of the hanging tree had both beer and pots of builders with milk. We could both satisfy our brew cravings.

"See you there. Ta rah."

Unpacking the exchanges of the visit carried me through the rest of the day. First and foremost, Dr. Daniels came to see me to clarify that I was not the lunch girl. Great progress.

Lily returned. Fantastic news.

But the thing that kept popping out at me was the deliberate sabotage of

Lancelot. I did something to make someone angry enough to want to hurt or even kill me. *What?*

I knew nothing about Sherrie except that Edward's tattoo matched hers, which seemed more like a him thing than me.

Maybe discovering her body created the problem. Thinking back on our Cotswolds Way hike reminded me of The Hound of the Baskervilles. One of the women in the book was forced to pretend she was someone else. What if Sherrie was involved in a con of some sort and had been trying to escape? My stumbling on the body could have thrown off someone's plans. Whose?

Even if that were true, what did it have to do with the De Valence spa? Nothing, except that's where my accident happened.

Right before I went riding, Simon and I talked in the garden. At least one person overheard us. I had been helping Simon find a way to keep Comer Manor in his name.

Not knowing how much money the house and spa could make, I couldn't be sure that my interference qualified as a motive.

My musings accomplishing exactly nothing, I left the Baths. Remembering to turn my phone off airplane mode, I checked to see if Edward texted.

Nope.

With a pout, I hobbled through Abbey Green to the pub.

"Sigh," I said while pushing open the polished oak door of the Crystal Palace. Warm and filled with happy people, the pub smelled of roasting chicken and beef.

This time my sigh was a happy one.

At the bar, I ordered a half-pint of local ale. The bartender set it in front of me, and I stared at it, then at my crutch. A big swig took the ale to a reasonable level, but hopping across a room with a glass of beer struck me as a bad idea.

"Need help there, missy?" an elderly man's voice inquired.

Nodding, I turned to see Fred, a retired taxi driver who first told me about the hanging tree, the 200-year-old plane tree spreading its branches outside the pub.

"Hi, Fred." I smiled gratefully. "Yes, please. I'm waiting for my friend, so we'll need a table for two. Or three if you'd like to join us."

A shrewd look crossed his face, and I could tell he couldn't place me. Then he tapped his nose.

"The American intern, is it? Maggie?" he guessed.

"Close," I responded as he carried my drink to a low table near the coal fireplace. "It's Maddie."

Pulling up an extra padded captain's chair, he asked, "Now, how did you get in this state?"

"She jumped off a horse," Lily interjected, appearing out of nowhere. I was beginning to think I wasn't very observant.

"What's that then?" Fred's bushy eyebrows climbed to the height of his flat cap brim.

"Dead daft of her," Lily continued, setting her tea on the table and settling in.

Nodding in agreement, Fred held nothing back. "Never liked the things myself. Giant rodents, they are."

About to argue the point, I pictured both Lancelot and Roddy enjoying hay. I skewed the topic in a new direction. "If I may interject here. My dismount was spectacular. Movie stuntman quality."

"Mint," Lily said, grinning. She held her tea cup out, "Cheers!"

Fred and I clicked our glasses to hers. "Cheers!" we chimed.

As I contemplated another half pint, my phone rang. My heart skipped a beat anticipating a call from Edward before I could control myself.

Answering without looking at the caller ID, I practically squeaked, "Hi?"

"Maddie, is that you? This is Roger."

"Hi," I responded, disappointment sapping my energy.

"I should have thought of this earlier, but I'm here at the church. Are you still at work? I can give you a lift."

Getting home hadn't crossed my mind. Thank all that is good for kind landlords.

"That would be amazing! I'm at the Crystal Palace. Where should I meet you?"

"There's a road by the MS. Go out the door and walk away from the

Abbey."

Smiling, I hung up. Roger understood that not everyone had a sense of direction. He provided instructions based on landmarks, never saying things like "Go north," which means nothing to me.

"My ride's here," I told Lily as Fred had found a new group of folks to entertain.

"I'll take you there," she said, standing and gathering my crutch and jean jacket so I could reach them easily.

"Do you need a ride?" I offered on Roger's behalf.

She shook her head. "Got a temporary flat around the corner. No walking. No buses."

Roger's car idled on the street only a few steps from the pub.

As we drove through the winding streets, climbing our way up to Greenway Lane, that familiar sense of having missed something significant resurfaced.

Watching gardens flash by the window, one caught my eye. Tall grass, going to seed for the fall. It looked like hay.

Both rabbits and horses ate hay. Fred referred to horses as giant rodents.

"Roger?" Leaning forward, I asked, "How come both rabbits and horses eat hay?"

When I grew up, my PhD-mom was like a walking search engine. I could ask her anything. Turned out, Roger's grasp of useless knowledge rivaled hers.

"They have the same stomach, I believe. Or, more accurately, the digestive tract. Fascinating, really."

The same stomach.

The phrase doused me in a frigid chill.

Chapter Sixteen: AWOL

The same stomach.

Puzzle pieces danced around my head all night, and I formed an idea by morning.

Which, I thought bitterly, I would have discussed with Edward if he had called.

So, I turned on my laptop and contacted Tori.

"Ello, love," she answered, her English accent so much better than mine.

"Buenos dias," I answered.

"You know your Spanish accents aren't any better than your English ones."

"That's why I have you."

A grin blossomed on her features. "Granted. This must be bad, as you didn't pay any attention to the time zone. What's up?"

Quickly calculating, I realized it was almost one in the morning. "Oh no, Tori, I'm so sorry! Why don't you just ignore me?"

She giggled. "Mostly because I miss you, but partly because you've developed a shocking habit of finding danger."

"Nothing new on that front. Except for someone trying to trample me with a bucking bronco, me calling my mom and asking to come home, and Edward having the same tattoo as Sherrie, and then disappearing." I paused, tilting my head, ignoring her attempts to interrupt. "Yeah. We've got some catching up to do. But," I emphasized loudly, "I have an idea about Sherrie, and I want to run it by you."

With a dramatic sigh, she lifted both palms to the camera in a 'please continue' motion.

"You did a paper on the Kidney Foundation," I stated, remembering because the nonprofit I picked for the same assignment turned out to be a fraud. "Where is a scar for a kidney transplant?"

Tori bounded from her chair, turned her back to the camera, and lifted her tee, pointing along the side.

Frigid sweat enveloped me.

"What are you thinking? Did Sherrie have a scar?"

Mutely, I nodded.

"The police could use transplant information to identify her," she offered.

"Or," I said with a shudder. "If someone else needed the same kidney and didn't want to wait for it." Pausing, I gave her a moment to catch up to my way of thinking.

"Whoa, whoa, whoa." She cocked her head, distracted. "How on earth did you almost get trampled by a bucking bronco?"

With a brief eye roll, I clarified, "Actually, an English riding mount. He looks like Boots." Tori often watched me practice on my favorite horse at the stable, where I learned to barrel race. "There was an open sore under the saddle," I said, not wanting to go into my sabotage suspicions.

"Ah, K. So you're saying someone may have stolen Sherrie's kidney and dumped the body? Did you see a scar or stitches?"

One of the many things I loved about my best friend was her brain.

"Stitches," I confirmed. When I first looked, I thought it was a scar, but after spotting the healed slash across Edwards's chest, I realized that Sherrie's wound was different.

"Whoa," Tori repeated.

"Yeah," I agreed but wondered why a black-market organ harvester would clean up. "Why close the wound if they were going to kill her anyway?"

"If movies are any reflection of reality—"

"They're not," I inserted.

"But if they were," she continued. "They would put her into a coma and keep her until they needed the second kidney."

"That is disturbing, and I regret my choice to call you in the middle of the night."

"It's morning there," Tori pointed out." And no, you don't." A smug expression crossed her face. "Or," she held up a finger, "it's to keep things tidy. Stitches prevent blood - aka incriminating evidence—from oozing on the floor."

"Ew. Okay, if we're using movies as reality—"

"Which we're not," she inserted.

"It's always in the basement of some dilapidated apartment complex."

"Or," she interrupted my dark thoughts.

"You keep saying that."

Tori nodded. "To keep you from going to a dark place. Or, the girl had a transplant which is how the police identified her, and your hypothesis is unfounded."

"You're probably right." Hoping it was true, I offered a smile which she didn't buy for a minute. But she moved on.

While hopping around my temporary room to dress for work, I filled her in on Edward. "Call me later," I requested when Roger offered me a ride.

When we arrived at the drop-off point near the Roman Baths, I plopped my feet on the ground without thinking. A slight complaint from my sprained ankle, but not too bad.

"I think I'm healing already." I grinned. "But a ride home would be nice."

He waved a hand at me. "Of course, of course. Anytime. Every time for that matter." Putting the car in gear, he wished me a good day.

The intricate domed ceiling of the Roman Baths' entrance glowed with morning sunlight. As much as I wanted to work the dig site, going underground on a day like today created a pit in my stomach. Basking in the warmth, my steps toward the elevator were slow.

"Maddie, me darlin'," Sam's Irish lilt stopped my progress. "How is that ankle of yours?"

Flexing it, I said, "Much, much better. Sleep helped a ton." With a firm, only slightly painful step, I moved toward her. "Do you need me to do tours today?" I asked hopefully.

"Dolly requested some time off. Researching something, she said." Sam's eyebrows knitted together, concerned. "I can't fathom what's happening with Simon and Lady Vivian. I know you prefer to be at the dig, but—"

"I can totally be the tour guide today. I'll ditch the crutch and use a walking stick if I get tired. No problem." My smile felt manic, so I took a deep breath and relaxed my expression.

"It's my lucky day, to be sure. You look happy as I've seen you."

"It's the sun," I confessed. "I miss it sometimes."

The cane Lady Vivian allowed me to borrow still lay in the Oversight Office where I last left it, and it supported me nicely as I guided guests over uneven walkways. Easy.

The other advantage of tours included long breaks and phone service. First, a text to Edward. 'Not underground today. Text me. Now.'

After erasing the last three words, I sent the message.

Next, I steeled my nerves and called Detective Inspector Parikh.

"Yes, Ms. McGuire. How may I be of service?" Before I could answer, he added, "Please don't tell me you are in trouble."

"Surprisingly not, this time. However, I've been thinking."

An expulsion of a long breath from the detective. I ignored it. "The girl I found, Sherrie. Did she donate a kidney?"

"I understand why you are concerned and where you are going with this line of inquiry, but as I explained before, neither myself nor this office have any connection to the investigation."

"Okay, yes. Too detailed of a question," I said more to myself than to him. "How about this? In general, is black market organ harvesting an issue in England?"

There. I said it. Out loud. To an official person.

"I believe the correct term is organ recovery."

My head flopped back, and I rolled my eyes. "Okay. But is it?"

His sigh sounded more like a deep breath this time. Progress.

"You seem to forget that very little crime comes through this city. That sort of thing simply isn't done here."

"But you would hear of it, right? Even if it happened elsewhere?"

"Perhaps, but it would be none of our affair. Perhaps a newspaper would tell you more."

Not wanting to push my luck any further, I gave up. The newspaper comment gave me a new idea to pursue.

"Okay. Thank you for taking my call."

As I went to disconnect, Parikh said, "Ms. McGuire?"

"Sir?" I responded automatically, forgetting that sir meant something different in a country with royalty.

"Have you seen Constable Bailey?"

The hairs on the back of my neck stood, and my palms turned clammy. "Not since the weekend." I paused, unsure. Would he be mad at me for telling? "He hasn't been to work?"

"He did send a request for time off."

A brief silence when the world stopped moving before Parikh said, "I'm sure there is no need to worry, but if you hear from him, do let me know."

The connection severed, but I continued to stare at the phone, willing it to give me more information.

Edward had gone dark before but only in the line of duty. He loved being a constable, following rules, and working with the Avon and Somerset Constabulary. What could be so crucial that he left?

Unless the unicorn tattoo meant more than I wanted to believe.

The thought of another tour weighed on me like an anvil. How could I be informative and entertaining knowing that Edward was AWOL?

Chapter Seventeen: The Newspaper

Not my best day at work. Close to the worst. And I've had some pretty weird days at the Roman Baths. Thoughts of Edward spiraled from worry, fear, exasperation, and anger, but never ambivalence. I had to figure out what was going on to keep sane.

As I waited for Roger to finish his day, I sat in the cobblestone courtyard formed by the Abbey and the Baths. I sipped a luxurious cup of extra dark drinking chocolate from one of the corner tea shops, which, admittedly, made me feel better.

DI Parikh said something interesting before he sidetracked me with concerns about Edward. Going over what we said, I remembered to check the newspapers about black market organs. Not sure if British libraries carried back copies the way they do in the US, I resolved to go straight to the source. A reporter.

When I discovered an awful thing at the Baths, a reporter called Jeffery Dailey tried pretending to be a cop to scoop a story. I didn't let him past me, and Lady Vivian put him in his place. A smile crept across my face at the memory.

Not a top-notch journalist, more like a paparazzi snapping pictures and digging up dirt, Jeffery coveted my aristocratic connections, which would make him willing to talk to me.

Entering his name into a search bar, I came up with an email address. The query, 'Have you heard about black market organ harvesting in the Gloucestershire area?' should garner a response.

* * *

After dinner with the Priestlys, we moved my belongings back to my studio tower on the third floor. Or second if you're English. Who uses zero when counting floors? Brits, that's who.

Pondering the differences between the languages, I sent Edward the most direct, unambiguous text I could.

"Let me know you are alive so I can stop worrying. Parikh says you disappeared. No questions asked."

"There," I said, hitting send without much hope.

His departure had been so abrupt, and his lack of communication was too thorough for me to think my text would have an effect.

So when my cell rang with a FaceTime message from Edward, I almost hit the red button and accidentally declined the call.

"Wait, wait, wait. Did it work?" I said, sounding like my mother dealing with any technology ever.

"Ello, love," he said, a cheeky smile filling my phone screen.

I wanted to punch it.

"Where are you?" I insisted with more force than necessary. "How could you abandon me like that?" I mean, okay, yes, I was abandoned, but in a spa with horses. So not the worst thing ever. Before he could answer, I continued my barrage. "What the heck does that tattoo mean? Why didn't you tell me about it earlier? How do you know that girl? Why is the knife in your unicorn's teeth dripping blood? Where are you?" A repeat, admittedly, but quite relevant. "Why haven't you reported to work? What is going on? When are you coming back? Why haven't you texted me?"

"Is this your version of no questions asked?" he asked, looking annoyingly serene and unperturbed.

"Stop changing the subject and answer the question," I demanded.

The smile returned. "Which one?"

My hand slapped the desk so hard it rattled, knocking over my books on Roman architecture. "Any of them!" I practically screamed.

"Calton Hill. A kirkyard," he said, his Scottish accent thicker than ever.

"Neutral ground, here."

Hallowed ground, I thought he meant, but it wasn't important.

"See?" He slowly raked the phone around, showing a large circular monument, gravestones, crosses, and something unusual.

"Wait, go back."

The phone camera panned in the other direction until it landed on what caught my eye.

"Is that Lincoln?" I asked, thoroughly distracted. Yes, essential questions demanded answers, but I was easily distracted. And was it our sixteenth president?

"Is who what, now?"

I clarified, convinced I must be wrong. "The tall statue with the beard and curly hair. Go over there."

A bad horror movie shot of a camera being walked to a different location did nothing to calm my fried nerves, but when the movement stopped, there stood Abraham Lincoln in all his bronzed glory.

"Why?" I wondered.

The statue stood over a base which Edward read. "In Memory of Scottish-American Soldiers." The words ended with a carved relief of a slave being released from shackles.

"I never noticed it before," Edward said. "Good eye."

To me, Lincoln stood out like a beacon, impossible to mistake or miss.

"Why are you in a graveyard in Scotland with an American president when you are supposed to be here?"

My heart ached, which compounded the buzzing in my head.

I shook myself and asked, "When are you coming home?"

Edward's face whipped away from the camera as an angry voice shouted, "Just what the bloody 'ell do you think you're doing?"

Without another word, Edward severed the connection.

When I hit redial, it went straight to voicemail. After sending a couple of frantic texts, I tossed the phone on my bed. A new slew of questions swirled in my head as I squeezed my eyes shut, failing to block them out.

"Please be okay," I whispered in a small voice, sending it as a prayer for his safety.

Turning to my computer, I called Tori.

"My boyfriend is in a Scottish graveyard with an angry stranger, and I have no idea what's going on," I jumped in without preamble.

"Hey, progress! This morning he was missing. Did you ask about the tattoo?"

"How do you even remember our last conversation? I called in the middle of the night," I pointed out.

"You're better than watching tv."

Shaking my head, I commented, "Not my goal. Anyway, yes, I asked all the questions, to which he answered exactly one. That he's in a graveyard. In Edinburgh, I think. Before I could ask anything else, some angry Scottish man yelled at him, and he hung up."

"Weird."

"Yeah." I waited, but no additional advice came my way.

"You don't have any words of wisdom or reassurance for me?" I whined, sounding pathetic.

Her head bopped from side to side. "No?" She said it as a question. "I'm sorry, but I am totally out of my depth at this point. He is acting weird. That's it."

A puff of air escaped me. "At least I have confirmation that I'm not the crazy one."

But not that I wasn't a bad friend. Turning my attention to my bestie, I asked, "And you? What's new in your world?

Tori beamed. "Last night for dinner, I made tamales from scratch, set an amazing table, and invited my abuela to meet Scott."

This news topped any of my concerns. Tori's saint-like abuela expected convent behavior from her granddaughter. In exchange, Tori lived rent-free in her apartment. So did Scott, but up until last night, he had been kept a secret since they started dating in high school.

"How did it go? Did she look into his soul?" I wanted to know. A gift Tori and I were convinced the woman possessed.

"I'm sure. Fortunately, all her probing questions dealt with how he would take care of me."

"And since he's a cyber-security major, he will be guaranteed six figures right out of college," I concluded. My eyes widened as another thought struck. "He passed, didn't he? If she wants to know he's going to take care of you, she must assume you'll get married someday."

Her beaming face took on a glow. "And he passed." A happy sigh escaped her. "If I confessed we were living together, he might go down a few notches, but for now, he is expected at family gatherings."

"Something he has avoided for over two years," I pointed out.

"Not anymore," she said, triumphant.

Grinning, I said, "Congratulations, Tori! That is great news!"

We talked about nothing for a while, and despite not getting advice, I felt so much better. After instructing me to check my email, she hung up.

When I did, I opened pictures of her Day of the Dead figurine of Sherrie, complete with a tiny unicorn head on her hipbone. It was beautiful. I forwarded the pics to Roger. Content, I fell asleep.

* * *

No nightmares marred my sleep, and my bumps and bruises appeared more healed than not when I awoke. Things were good if I didn't think about any subject for too long.

After a morning of sifting at work, Lily arrived to take my lunch order. I leaped at the chance to run errands with her for some fresh air and to get to know her better.

"Why did you move to Bath from Manchester?" I asked as we rode the elevator to the main floor.

She grinned. "I'm the opposite of everything my brother is. He's at uni, living it up. Quite the lad, he is. Loves the bar scene, the big city rush."

The term "lad" threw me off. Her brother sounded like a frat boy to me.

We skirted the crowd in the lobby, and as I reached for the knob of the Oversight Office door, Dolly's voice rang through. Strident and sharp, her voice didn't sound at all like her usual accommodating tones.

Exchanging a conspiratorial glance, Lily and I kept the door closed and leaned in close to listen.

"I do not *care* what Maddie thinks. She can go back to America for all I care. Disappear forever."

Blood drained from my face as I crashed against the wall with a thud. I thought Dolly and me were becoming friends.

"Come!" Simon's imperious voice mistook my collapse as a knock.

Patting my shoulder, Lily searched my face, questioning.

I nodded, moving away from the door so no one saw me.

A squeak emitted from inside the office when she stuck her head in. I bet Dolly mistook Lily for me.

"Checking to see if Sam will be wanting any food with her tea," Lily announced to the room.

"How absolutely kind of you," Dolly responded, her soft, reserved, lying voice in place. "Why don't you bring her a strawberry scone?"

"Got it," Lily muttered as she closed the door.

With a tug of my arm, she unglued me from the wall and steered me outside. "Why are you surprised? You can never trust that lot."

"I thought we were friends," I admitted, referring to Dolly.

"Psh," she sputtered. "Those types stick to their own."

In a daze, I wandered from shop to shop with Lily as she collected goodies for the dig team. My initial mistrust of Dolly centered on the idea that she was after my job and stealing Simon away. And fine, her looks, too. Annoyingly pretty, that one.

But she fooled me with that fake gracious act of hers. I knew better than to trust her again.

Once I returned to my sifting table, my agitated brain tried to figure out Dolly's angle. Clearly, she wanted Simon. I wondered why. To paraphrase a line from Emma, she had no incentive to marry, as she was already titled and wealthy.

Although, maybe not very rich. After all, their family home doubled as a spa. I needed to keep an eye on her.

A knock on the stairwell door brought me out of my musings with a start.

"Come in," I squeaked, hoping Dr. Daniels hadn't caught me daydreaming.

The man who entered looked as different from Daniels as possible.

Paranoia crawled through my chest as I regarded the stranger standing between me and the exit.

The leather-jacket-clad man pushed a hand through messy, dark, wavy hair. The movement ran across his unshaven chin, creating a scratchy sound that caused the hair on my arms to stand. A black eye marred his features, heightening the bad-boy vibe.

I considered running up the stairs to the next floor, but his lean, muscular body looked ready to strike. I doubted I would get more than a couple of steps before he caught me.

Remembering the disorientation a load of dirt on the head caused me, I subtly reached for the Already Sifted bucket at my side and pulled it under the desk, ready to throw.

"Ello, lass. Not happy to see me?" the man said, a crooked grin forming.

Chapter Eighteen: The Tattoo

The thick Scottish burr filled my ears with conflicting emotions. First, undeniably, Edward looked hot, a confusing reaction that threw off my well-rehearsed responses to his reappearance.

The black eye required information, certainly. Bruises and cuts decorated his knuckles which also caught my attention.

What did I want to know first? The six million questions I threw at him when he called fled my memory.

"The hell?" I sputtered.

His grin widened, recalling my earlier impulse to punch him.

Slamming my eyes shut, I balled up my fists and counted to ten. When I released my fingers, a calm settled on me.

After assuming a pleasant expression, I stood, beetled around my work table, and approached him.

"I'm sorry," he started, but his voice turned into a yelp as I repeatedly slugged his arm.

"What." Whack. "Is." Whack. "Going on?" Whack, whack. The leather jacket deflected my blows, but I stayed the course.

Whack. One more for good measure.

"I like this one," another voice said, also in a thick Scottish burr. "Feisty."

The second guy who entered the room looked like a younger, thinner, taller Edward. That made two too many Edwards for my taste at the moment. My ire exploded in his direction.

"I have had it up to here," my hand indicated a place six inches above my head, "with surprises. No more. Not from you," I pointed at the stranger.

"Or you," indicating Edward. "Not one more unexpected appearance or disappearance. No more abandonment. No more pretending to be one thing when you're not. Not another person betraying my trust. I honestly don't even care what is going on anymore because I cannot handle it." I emphasized the last four syllables by punching Edward again. To his credit, he didn't stop me.

Instead, he hugged me and cooed in an irresistible lilt. "Dinna fash, lassie. I am so sorry, Madeline McGuire, and while ah dinnae ken if I can make it up to you, I will explain."

My struggles subsided, and I melted into his embrace. Not willing to cry in front of either boy, I steeled my heart.

"What's going on?" I repeated, my face buried in his dusty leather jacket.

He turned to the stranger who smiled like the cat who ate a canary, an expression out of place with, well, everything.

"Show her, James," Edward commanded.

Without a word, James shrugged his jacket to the floor and stripped off his tight-fitting black t-shirt. In addition to lean, sinewy muscles, six-pack abs, and a ragged red scar, he sported a unicorn head tattoo, complete with a knife in its teeth.

Tearing my eyes away from his distracting physique, I stared dumbfounded at Edward.

Whack. Wide-eyed and more confused than ever, I reverted to hitting. Whack, whack.

Lightning fast and feather-light, he clasped my hand, brought it to his lips, and kissed. With slow deliberation, he turned my hand over, opened the fingers, and kissed my palm. "Tha mi duilich," he said, eyes meeting mine, one of his swollen and bloodshot.

And my brain shut down, transformed into a fuzzy, limitless void. Emotions ricocheted like ping-pong balls, overwhelming me.

"Maddie," Simon's voice preceded his entrance. "Dr. Daniels—" Catching sight of Edward's bruised face, he paused. "I say, Edward is that you?" As he took another step into the room, the full force of shirtless James caught his attention.

I had my suspicions about Simon, but his apparent relationship with Dolly made me think I didn't know how to read English men very well. His reaction to James confirmed my initial analysis.

Simon's eyes traveled the length of James, who preened under the attention.

After a moment, Simon's facade slammed into place. "This is a national monument and place of business. Neither of you should be here. Please leave, or I shall be forced to call security."

Only Simon could use the word "shall" and not sound ridiculous.

Wordlessly, Edward jerked his head toward James, who donned his shirt and hooked his jacket over his shoulder. I could almost swear I saw him throw a wink at Simon.

"Who was that, and what is going on?" Simon demanded as James left.

Crumpling into the easy chair in the corner of my stairwell, I buried my face in my hands. "No idea," I admitted.

Edward lingered wordlessly in the doorway. I ignored him.

"Ah, well."

He said the phrase with such finality that I laughed. Looking at him through a gap in my fingers, I asked, "Did you say Dr. Daniels needed something?"

"Quite right. He wanted to know if you found anything from the debris in section C47. It looked promising."

Unfolding myself from the chair, I stood and checked my notes. "White rocks. Nothing exciting. To me, it looked like calcium deposits or hard water stains, not clay."

I handed him the inventory bag with the pebbles, then the clipboard with the chain of evidence. In his distinctive handwriting, he noted the bag number and date and added his signature, indicating he now had possession of the artifact.

"I will report your findings," he said with a pompous air I hadn't seen since we first met. Maybe Edward's skulking made him uncomfortable.

Pointedly getting Edward's attention with an intense stare, I motioned my head toward the door. He took the hint and left to find his friend.

"You okay, buddy?" I said, trying to shock Simon into relaxing.

A flush crept over his cheeks as he smiled. "Do be quiet," he kidded.

"Gotcha," I said with a grin, happy to know where I stood with someone. "Hey," I said, remembering his manor house conundrum. "What did you find out about your archeology center idea?"

Lifting his chin, Simon peered down his nose at me. A look of superiority I found both insulting and annoying. "I'm sorry, Maddie," he said, not sounding even remotely sorry. What is it with the aristocracy that they mastered condescending tones so thoroughly?

"We simply cannot discuss it. My fault, really." A statement that directed blame entirely toward me.

He turned on his heel and left me in stunned silence.

I jumped to my feet, whined at the pain-shooting daggers from my ankle, and plopped back down. "Dammit, dammit, dammit!" I hugged my knees to my chest. "No," I said to myself, resolute.

Rather than breaking down, I took a page from Simon's lot, as Lily called them, and summoned a stiff upper lip.

"No one," I voiced to myself, "is going to control my emotions. Not Simon, not James, whoever he was, not Edward, not Dolly. They can abandon me and talk behind my back, and I will do my job."

Self-righteous indignation lasted about thirty seconds before I noted that I wasn't doing my job. I was sitting in an easy chair shouting like Scarlett O'Hara at the end of *Gone with the Wind*.

"As God as my witness," I intoned in an admittedly ghastly Southern accent. "I will never be hungry again!"

With care, I gingerly made it to my table and continued my speech. "I will never stop sifting again!"

* * *

After a fit of feeling sorry for myself, I vowed to play offense. Mission One couldn't be Edward because too much happened. Dolly took that slot. Figuring out her deal required patience, acting, and stealth.

Tours ended before my shifts, giving Dolly time to sit in the office and complain about me.

One of the many great things about being fascinated by Roman architecture is that I could navigate the Baths Museum without being seen. Navigating through back hallways and ducking around archways allowed for good spying opportunities. With a confident stride, I approached the Oversight Office, glanced around, and pressed my ear to the door.

Dolly's voice, the real one that she used when telling the truth, filtered through the oak.

"Stupid, really," she whined. "I don't know why Uncle wants me to do archeology in the first place."

Interesting on two levels. One, she didn't want to be at the Baths any more than I wanted her there. Two, whom would she confide in? Surely not Sam, Simon, or Lady Vivian, all of whom treated the museum with the awe it deserved.

"Is it locked already, Maddie, me darlin?"

I jumped, knocking my forehead into the door jamb.

Deep in thought, I failed to hear Sam's approach.

"Ow," I responded. Dramatically, I jiggled the knob, turned it, and opened the door. "Silly me," I chimed.

"Sam, Maddie! Good evening. How were your days?" Dolly smiled, looking like an overly enthusiastic squirrel.

Sam responded pleasantly, and they prattled on.

No one else in the room must mean Dolly was talking to herself. Wondering if I could plant a bug or recording device, I quickly made my excuses and fled.

My phone didn't have service down in the Undercroft, so I wondered where I could leave it in the office. A voice-activated recording app must exist.

Plan in place, I exited the museum through the entrance to the stand where Roger hopefully waited.

An unshaven Edward and an unexplained, tattooed James stood lounging against a street lamp. If I didn't know them, I would turn in a different direction for fear of mugging.

Edward's cocky smile appeared when he saw me.

"You look like a thug," I quipped.

When James laughed, I turned on him. "And you! Did you do this to him?" I demanded, pointing at Edward's eye.

James held his hands up in a stop motion, then turned them around to show me his undamaged knuckles. "I'm not a brawler. I leave that to my brothers."

The thought of a third Bailey appearing conjured an epic eye roll on my part. One more thing I couldn't deal with. I skipped to the implications.

"Younger brother?" I asked, jerking a thumb in James' direction.

Edward nodded.

"Your older brother did this?" I asked, pointing at his black eye.

He dipped his head and bragged, "I did worse to him."

"That's not better!" I exploded, sick of not understanding anything and enduring too many surprises. I hated surprises.

A tall gentleman approached us, asking if I needed assistance. It took me a moment to recognize Roger.

Transforming like a magician, Edward stepped into his police constable persona. "Reverend Priestly," he said, every lilt of Scottish burr gone. "Forgive my rough appearance. I've been in Edinburgh to retrieve my brother from an unsavory home situation. James!" he barked as James giggled.

With a pathetic attempt to look serious, James stood straighter.

"May I present Reverend Priestly, Maddie's landlord? James, my younger brother, will stay with me for the foreseeable future."

In one exchange, Edward had revealed everything to Roger. Not to me.

My clenched fists were ready to start yet another barrage on Edward's arm; only Reverend Priestly's presence held me in check.

"Would the two of you care to join us for dinner?" he asked. "Meryl always has plenty of food."

Before I could stop it, my hand flew out.

Whack.

Edward's expression twitched into a brief smile at my reaction as Roger's eyebrows went up.

"No," Edward declined, with a quick, sidelong glance in my direction. "Thank you for the kind offer, but I need to settle James in at home." He turned to me. "Maddie, I will call you later."

As they left, James gave Edward a real slug in the arm and said, "Listen to that posh accent. Who do ya think you're fooling?"

Well, I thought. *Me*.

Chapter Nineteen: A Drop of Blood

What did I really, honestly know about Edward? Taking stock, I made a mental list.

He liked his grandmother, his brothers caused problems for his mom, who worked endlessly, and his father skipped out on them. Hometown: dodgy part of Edinburgh. Job: Constable. Going to university as part of his police training.

That's it. Ticking questions off my fingers, I enumerated my lack of knowledge. "Where did he live now? How did he wind up in Bath? Why did he never mention James before? If he's from a bad neighborhood, how did he become a police officer?" I paused for breath. "And what is up with that unicorn tattoo?"

"Maddie?" Meryl called from the dining room. "Dinner's on the table if you care to join us."

Hoping they hadn't heard my ranting, I shouted, "Yes, please! Be right there."

When I landed the internship, I tried to find the perfect place to live, and when this one came up, I thought I hit the jackpot. Empty-nester minister and his wife in a lovely neighborhood with a beautiful house called Ash Tree Cottage on Greenway Lane. We corresponded for months before my arrival, making my transition easier.

They made it clear that I provided my own meals. No exceptions. Which I expected, so no problem there.

When I got here, I realized "jackpot" didn't begin to explain my luck. Every aspect I thought might be nice turned out to be amazing, including the Priestlys.

They invited me to every meal and treated me like family. I hardly ever used the microwave or hot plate in my studio room.

"Thank you so much for having me," I said formally, the way my mom taught me. It didn't express my gratitude nearly enough.

"Don't be daft," Roger said, his hand flapping toward a place setting. "You're always welcome."

He picked up a fork and gestured at Meryl, then me. "Actually," he said with a grin. "I want to know why that nice constable had a black eye. It's big news in Bath if someone assaults an officer."

My eyes widened, and I struggled not to faceplant on the table.

"Leave the girl alone, Roger," Meryl suggested. "Can't you see she's distraught?"

"Distraught. Good word," I said, a thought forming. "I don't know why or how or where Edward's been. Maybe you can help me with something?"

"Of course," they both responded without hesitation.

"Remember the unicorn head tattoo I told you about?"

As the idea solidified, the red tartan napkins took on a brighter hue, calling attention to themselves. Unable to tear my eyes away, my appetite fled.

Already nodding, Roger confirmed, "Yes. It looked different than what I imagined. Sinister, with that knife in its teeth."

Out of the corner of my eye, I saw him turn to Meryl. "What was your impression, dear?"

My body shifted her direction before my head, away from the red napkin signaling danger.

Meryl's opinions were well thought out, informed, and insightful. Wise described her best, and Roger valued her.

Being the only child of divorced parents, I reveled in watching the give and take of a good marriage. Respect and trust mingled with love and friendship.

Would I ever be able to trust Edward again? Did it matter?

"Sinister. Good word, my love," Meryl told her husband. "The placement of the knife historically points to battle. The unicorn represents Scotland." She gestured to me, "At least in the UK."

Unicorns meant fantasy, magic, and purity to me. Or they used to.

Both Simon and Deacon Michael mentioned the Scottish independence movement when I described the tattoo. Meryl just confirmed a part of my fears. Edward, James, and Sherrie were involved in something violent, possibly subversive.

Bracing myself, I offered them more information, trying not to lead their conclusions. "I've discovered two other people with the same tattoo. Both alive," I added quickly, reacting to Priestly's looks of alarm. "What do you think that means?"

What it meant to me, if it were in the US, was a gang. The knife-dripping blood that Edward's tattoo depicted caused a shudder to rip through me. In the Southwest, adding a drop of blood meant only one thing. Murder.

"Rather sounds like a gang, don't you think, Roger?" Meryl asked.

Worst fears confirmed.

"Rather," Roger agreed. "Perhaps one fighting for Scottish Independence."

Meryl contemplated before saying, "Although, many a criminal hides behind a cause to wreak havoc. They may be using the ideal to lure young people in."

"Quite right, my dear," Roger agreed. "Do you remember that one time…"

I stopped listening as they relentlessly chattered on while my world crumbled. Who was I dating? The red tartan, another symbol of Scotland, lay discarded at my feet. Retrieving it, I made it through dinner by making proper grunts of agreement when necessary.

"May I clear your plates?" I asked, bolting up as soon as it was polite to do so.

After helping with the dishes, I braved the windy evening to look for Roddy in his hutch. "Hey, bunny," I cooed at him. A pink twitching nose on a white face appeared, followed closely by two long black ears. The rabbit hopped to me, and I hoisted him in my arms and carried him to the swinging bench under the spreading ash tree. Golden leaves tinged with orange rained around us.

"You know," I informed the rabbit. "It was you that sent me on the path of organ harvesting. Did you know you and horses share the same stomach?"

I looked up the fact and confirmed it was a similar digestive tract. "That's why you can both eat hay. Although I doubt anyone would try to fix you with a horse intestine."

Roddy bounded out of my lap at that, apparently offended by the idea. Then he hopped next to me.

His soft fur soothed my addled thoughts. I needed to clear my head before I called a friend. My go-to Tori might not know much about British gangs. Gathering the bunny for another hug, I mused, "Lily knows about stuff, and she's from a big city. Should we ask her?"

Roddy wiggled his ears in agreement.

"Okay. Thanks for your advice," I whispered into his fur as I carried him to his enclosure.

Once Roddy hopped back into his cozy home, I headed down the stone path, huddled against the chilly wind. In the boot room, I called Lily.

"I'm finishing at the Boater with some mates from work. I'll wait if you want to."

Watching the leaves swirl about the massive tree trunk, I tested my ankle and wondered if I could make the trek.

"That sounds awesome, b—"

"Dead good! See you," she interrupted and clicked off before I could explain the state of my sprain.

"Off to the church for a counseling session," Roger said, bursting into the boot room and pulling on a black overcoat.

Serendipity. "Could I ride with you? I'm meeting a friend at a pub on Pultney Bridge."

Roger dropped me at The Boater, admonished me to be careful on the stairs, and said he'd return to pick me up in an hour.

Lily picked a table on the main floor, only a few steps down from street level. On the far side of the bar, she chatted merrily with the bartender, who showed her a card trick. The other server seemed less than pleased at the attention Lilly received and barked an order for an ale. When the guy didn't respond, she pulled it herself with a glare at Lily.

"This is my friend from America," she said, catching sight of me. "Maddie, come all the way from Arizona. Wicked."

I waved at the bartender and ordered a half-pint of Bath Ales Gem, mostly because it had a rabbit logo on the tap. A deep amber, the sweet maltiness balanced pleasantly with barley. At home, where I wasn't of drinking age yet, I had a 'beer is beer' philosophy and drank as much as I could. Here, I ordered less and appreciated it more.

"Cheers," I said, lifting my barrel-shaped half-pint mug.

"Cheers," Lily responded, lifting her teacup.

Settling against the wall, I took in the watercolor mural extending the length of the opposite side of the bar. Pale blue with boaters along the River Avon made me long for a warm, sunny day.

"Do you have gangs in Manchester?" I asked without preamble.

Eyes wide, Lily nodded. "On the south side, yeah. Some," she lowered her voice, "even have guns."

Swallowing my initial response of "Well, duh," I remembered England and gun control. Most everyone I knew in Arizona had at least one gun in the house, mostly for hunting. "Do they have matching tattoos?" I asked, referring to the gangs.

"Oh, yeah," she agreed, her face with a serious cast.

Inhaling deeply to launch into my next question, I caught my ale's refreshing, almost oatmeal-like scent and took another sip.

Lily looked so distressed that I hesitated. "Last time I was here," I said, changing the subject, "I got hauled away to an interrogation room in Bridgewater."

Her expression turned sly. "Nah. You'd go to Keynsham if you were arrested, not all the way to Bridgewater. Bristol is closer, even."

"What's in Keynsham?" I asked, having only seen the name on the occasional train schedule.

"Holding cells. They always take you to the closest one," Lily said with an air of authority unusual for her.

Intrigued, I asked, "How do you know all this?"

She waffled with whether to tell me, but my pleading expression must have won her over.

"One of the lads my brother hangs out with came down here, got super pissed, and caused a huge ruckus. A constable came and explained where they took him."

I grinned. "Quite an adventure."

"Too much by half," Lily responded. Her gaze traveled to the other end of the bar. "Speaking of constables, isn't that yours?"

My heart flip-flopped at the mere thought, and one glance confirmed it. Edward lingered with a casual air, one arm hooked over the back of a chair.

Sensing our attention, he picked up his pint and sauntered to us.

"Ello, lass," he said with no attempt to hide his northern accent.

Grateful that Lily was there to keep me from flying off the handle or, conversely, leaping into his arms, both of which seemed like good options, I nodded my greeting. Cool and collected, that's me.

Then, Lily's phone rang. Of course, it did. And with that, she mouthed, "Sorry," grabbed her raincoat, and left me. Alone. With Edward.

Yes, technically, "alone" didn't describe the situation well, as a few patrons lingered, but I wanted backup.

"What?" he asked, although I hadn't said anything.

"Nothing."

"You were thinking of something," Edward replied, crooked grin in place.

"Don't you banter with me. I've asked enough questions for forty conversations, and you've answered a grand total of one. I'm done. I'm through. No more inquiries. Nada. Not me. This is on you."

"Questions, you call that? More like an interrogation." His response, accompanied by twinkling eyes.

"Queries," I countered, drawn into his spell, despite myself.

"Inquisition," he suggested.

"A poll."

"Third degree."

"That's your department." I smiled, knowing I scored.

Edward's face fell.

Mentally, I vowed not to ask another question. And no way would I beg for any more information.

But I looked at Edward's sagging expression and knew important things like a friend in need trumped any self-imposed rules.

"Edward," I said his name softly and nothing else until I had his full attention. "What's wrong?"

Shifting away, he busied himself adjusting his jacket.

I took his face in my hands, leaned in, and whisper-kissed his lips. "Tell me."

Red splotches appeared on his cheeks. "Three days," he said.

"I don't do enigmatic," I chided but continued to stroke his cheek. "What about three days?"

"That's all it took to screw up my life." Taking my hand in his, he continued. "I'm so sorry, lass. I thought we, ah, well. Too late, now."

"Still enigmatic." My racing mind tumbled at the possibilities of what "we" meant and how he destroyed his life.

"No synonym?" Edward's crooked smile clapped into place, and all his swagger returned. "Wouldn't your ma be disappointed?"

Distracted, I agreed. "She would. Still inscrutable," I conjured while catching hold of a different idea. DI Parikh's worried voice flashed in my memory, triggering the idea that Edward thought he lost his job. That scenario counted as life-ruining.

"Have you called the station?" I asked. "Detective Inspector Parikh was worried about you."

Before the words were out, he shook his head, repeating, "Too late."

"Look, Edward," I emphasized his name, trying to call him up from the depths. "I still don't know what's going on, but I know you are a good person, and good people always prevail."

"No good brother gave me the black eye," he muttered, his Scottish burr so thick I barely caught the words.

"Well, then, why did you bring him here?" I demanded.

Another head shake from Edward. "Not James. William, the eldest."

"Are all of you named after English kings?" A useless question. Jeez, sometimes I'm like a raccoon with shiny objects.

He shrugged, "Aye. William, me, then James. No sisters. All two years apart."

Three full sentences about his personal life. If the situation were less dire, I would cheer.

Rallying, Edward's public accent returned. The one he used as a constable, which Simon referred to as posh-no-money. "Tell me what you've figured out," he suggested. "It'll save time."

I took a moment to organize my thoughts, creating a Venn diagram in my mind, showing where the different facts overlapped. A puff of air escaped my lips, not knowing where to start.

Scrubbing the mass of circles from my mind, I created a mental flowchart, showing progress from one idea to the next.

"Okay, I'll start with Sherrie. Two things there, the tattoo and the scar. I'm just going to follow one track at a time."

Edward smiled, the first genuine one since his return.

"Sherrie's tattoo—I asked around about it, and no one recognized it. Then I discovered two other people with it." I paused to point at him. After a nod, I continued. "It suggests violence or battle, and the unicorn is the emblem of Scotland. And you're Scottish."

Eyebrows up, Edward almost laughed.

"Which," I conceded, "you know. So those, as they say, are the facts. Now for my suppositions. One, it's a gang tattoo. Yours is dripping blood which indicates..." I couldn't say murder. Not Edward. "Death," I substituted. "The gang talks about Scottish independence to lure in members but doesn't have a political agenda."

My palms came up with a shrug. "How did I do?"

"That's not what the blood symbolizes. You are the smartest thing I've ever met. You should be a detective."

Radiant with the praise, I explained, "Archeology has a lot in common with detective work. You find an unfinished puzzle with clues pointing in all directions and have to piece it together."

At that moment, Roger's head popped around the entrance. "Ready, Maddie?" he called across the mostly empty bar. "Oh, hello, Edward? Y'alright?"

"Aye, Reverend." Gentlemanly as ever, he stood, helped me with my jacket, and delivered me safely into Roger's car.

As we drove away, I realized he never told me what the blood on his knife tattoo symbolized.

Chapter Twenty: The First Accusation

Testing my ankle the next morning, I considered walking to The Baths until a gust of wind plastered wet fallen leaves to my window. When I pulled the lace sheer back and saw trees, bushes, and tall grasses bent to one side, I decided on the comfort of Roger's sedan.

A blast almost ripped the car door out of my hand when I arrived at the museum. Huddling in my blue raincoat, I fought my way to the entrance. Under normal circumstances, I missed having a view when I sifted in the Undercroft, but today my underground lair resembled a cozy den.

The comfort only increased when Sam appeared with two blue mugs of steaming tea. "Ahhhhh," she sighed, settling into my armchair. Pulling out a beautifully filigreed silver hip flask, she offered it my direction.

The flask was Simon's idea of a joke, ornate but a dig at one of the stereotypes related to Sam's heritage—that the Irish drink a lot. However, she filled it with honey from her sister's apiary.

Leaning across my table, I held my cup while she drizzled a stream of amber gold into my mug.

As my boss appeared happy and relaxed, I asked about the excavation she did when I discovered a body at the museum. Not that I would ever begrudge someone an opportunity to be at a dig site, but her disappearance had been ill-timed.

"Egypt." Another sigh escaped her. "While I love my Roman Baths, nothing beats the dry desert outside Cairo."

"Why didn't Simon take the opportunity himself?" I wondered.

Shaking her head, Sam said, "I don't know. Never goes to Egypt, that one."

Another mystery to be solved in addition to who put the burr under Lancelot's saddle and why. So much had happened since Edward's return that my ill-fated weekend in Painswick seemed like ages ago.

After chatting idly for a while, Sam furrowed her brows. "Do you think something is going on with Dolly?"

Squashing the impulse to respond 'Absolutely,' I considered why Sam asked. She wasn't the type to trick me into saying something I shouldn't, but that didn't mean she hadn't been sent by Simon, Lady Vivian, or even Dolly herself to trip me up. Also, I didn't need to make any enemies.

I sipped the strong builder's tea with a dollop of milk to buy time.

"Well," I said, swirling the liquid around the mug. "I'm not sure that archeology is Dolly's first love." There. As far as "something going on," this seemed informational without casting aspersions on her.

"Why do you ask?" I added, quick to shift the attention off me. My fingers found a loose bit of hair, and I wound it round and round, nervous.

Sam mimicked my stalling technique by examining her tea. "Forgetful, she is. And she sometimes has her uncle call when she can't make it." Sam's thick Irish brogue made the complaints sound charming.

"How odd." The most neutral phrase I could think of.

With a shrug, Sam changed the subject, launching into her fifteen-minute lecture about the Baths that she delivered daily as part of my internship training. When I spent more time guiding tours, she didn't feel the need. Now that I sat in a dusty, musty-smelling stairwell most days, she ensured I got the full intern experience. Her technique involved talking, asking questions to test my comprehension, and then leaving, which allowed me time to think.

"When do you think the Great Drain first clogged?"

I started winding my hair around a finger again. Should I know this? Did I miss it in my training?

"Go on, girl," Sam encouraged me. "Name a century."

"Well, I know the Anglo-Saxon Chronicles say the baths were destroyed in the sixth century," I began, glancing at her.

Nodding, she said, "And?"

With that confirmation, I declared, "Six-fifty, C.E. Or A.D." I added. The museum hadn't switched over to Common Era and Before Common Era, yet instead of the more religious notations of B.C. and A.D.

"Good guess!" She grinned. "Off by fifteen."

Without bothering to check my mental calculation, I asked, "Which is it? Six-thirty-five or six-sixty-five?"

A mischievous grin lightened her features. "Not years, centuries."

I gaped in disbelief.

"That's right," she continued. "In 2009, the Great Drain clogged because of bad city engineers from the 1960s."

"Honestly? That is so cool! Not the bad engineers, but that the Roman builders knew so much and executed it so beautifully."

"Brilliant, isn't it?" she agreed. "They had to fix it, or the Baths would have flooded."

An image of Meryl removing a pipe and releasing jammed pasta popped into my head. "Flooding can be disastrous. I have first-hand experience."

Sam insisted on hearing the story, and we spent far more than her allotted lecture time chatting.

When she left, I pictured the Great Drain, almost tall enough to stand in. The build-up of over forty minerals in the water created intricate water patterns out of rock. Stained red with iron, the opening, which still dumped water from the hot springs into the Avon River, steamed and gurgled.

Which I contemplated for exactly twenty seconds before mulling over what Sam had meant about Dolly.

One thing, she did miss a lot of days. Despite my mishaps and injuries, I missed work less often than her. She didn't strike me as unhealthy or negligent. But she didn't come across as someone who would badmouth me behind my back either, yet she did.

And forgetful. "About what?" I asked out loud.

Between tour routes, schedule timelines, and facts about ancient Romans, there was a lot to learn, but none of it difficult.

Finally, the odd thing about Dolly that Sam didn't mention: Simon. Did Dolly suspect what I did about Simon? If so, why did she still hang on his every word?

The door to the main hall opened, and Simon's head popped around the corner.

"Speak of the devil," I said, then regretted it. With a wince, I hoped he wouldn't ask me to explain.

"What's up?" I plowed ahead.

"The bag with the white pebbles from C47. I need it."

Squinting at him. "You have it."

Edward's appearance and James' tattoo clouded my memory of the exchange. Still, I remembered Simon signing the log when he took that bag.

"Don't you?" I asked, not sure if I should trust my memory.

With a curt nod, he said, "I did," before brandishing the clipboard at me. "It says here you signed it into your custody after me."

The signature taking possession of the artifact looked like mine, but I had zero memory of signing it.

"That's weird." Standing, I came around the table. "Maybe it's in the office. I need to stretch anyway. I'll go look."

As I passed him in the hall, I took the log clipboard and headed to the elevator. Approaching the Oversight Office, I slowed. Dolly's exasperated voice carried through the door.

"Drat," I muttered, clunking my palm to my forehead. With Edward's return, I totally forgot to plant my phone in the office to record conversations.

I paused, listening.

"Yes, Uncle," Dolly's half of the conversation came through.

On the phone, I thought.

"Of course I understand, but—" she continued but wasn't allowed to finish her thought. "I know that, however—" A pause, then, "But why can't I do that from De Valence manor?" Another break before, "Yes. Of course." Her voice raised in pitch, falsely cheery. "Absolutely."

For the first time, I considered that she knew how obnoxious the word sounded.

With a double rap of my knuckles on the wood, I entered.

"Oh, hey, Dolly," I said. Cool and casual, that's me.

"Maddie! How are you today? Is your ankle healing?"

Honestly, did she have to be so considerate? It made it difficult to remember that I caught her saying she wished I were back in America.

Lifting my foot, I swiveled it. "Yes, thank you. It's mostly better. Running a marathon is out of the question, but it always was."

A charming giggle crossed her lips at my quip, and I fought against being pulled in.

"Hey," I repeated. "Is that artifact bag Simon lost in the desk?"

A small crease marred her brow. "He asked me the same thing," she said, opening and closing drawers while I checked the file cabinet. "I remember something." She frowned in frustration.

Under her breath, not meant for my ears, she continued. "I'm going mad."

Even though I heard, I wanted her to elaborate. "What's that?"

Bright facade firmly in place, she apologized for not being more helpful. "It's not here, I'm afraid. Any luck?"

My eyes scraped over every inch of the office, looking for another hiding place. When I landed on the tour schedule, I stopped. Furrowing my brows, I double-checked the time on my phone.

"You're supposed to be on a tour right now."

"Am I?" Dolly's eyebrows shot up, and she looked the epitome of innocence. "I thought it was you today,"

Shaking my head, I said, "No, Sam took me off guide work." I scanned the schedule line by line anyway.

And yes, two random time slots had my name added to them. The current tour wasn't one of them, but no one told me about the others. Why those times, and who changed them?

"No. Today is you," I let her know, causing her to flee.

"Ta, Maddie! I absolutely don't know what I would do without you!"

Her situation reminded me of Sherlock Holmes and *The Red Headed League*. In the story, a man found a job based solely on the employer needing someone with red hair. He stood in a line of applicants before being interviewed and getting the job. He went to Holmes because the employer disappeared.

De Valence, Dolly's uncle, seemed intent on keeping her employed or at least occupied at the Baths, far from their spa and home. Employed because of who she was, not any real need on anyone's part.

Wracking my brain, I couldn't remember what happened in the Holmes tale. Any clue as to why Dolly suffered exile at the Baths, the most fascinating place on earth, would help me.

With a huff at her ingratitude at being able to be in the museum every day, I added looking up the end of the story to my mental checklist of things to do. The Priestlys had a copy of The Complete Works of Sherlock Holmes.

Trivial matters like how a short story ended fled my mind when I returned my attention to the tour guide table.

Heat prickled at the back of my neck as my fists balled up tight. Panicked, I reexamined the dates and names in each little box.

There, first thing this morning, my name.

I missed a tour.

A high-pitched buzz skittered around my head. No one told me about the revisions or that I landed on the schedule. Not Sam's handwriting, so who then?

Someone was trying to make me look bad. And succeeding.

Before I could calm myself, Simon strode into the office.

"Did you find it?" The lack of any preamble turned the question into an accusation.

"Look, Simon," I began. "I don't know what's going on here. Someone put me on the schedule and didn't tell me." I pointed to the clipboard. "I have no idea why my name is on the log. Why would I need those stones? I'm not on the research team yet."

Adding "yet" was a ploy to implant the idea of elevating my position. It was worth a shot, even in my panic.

"Ah, yes. Well, I'm sure it's nothing," he said in that infuriating way that made it sound like the single most important thing on earth.

With a yank on the door handle, he left before I could further plead my case.

Glaring fiercely through the wall, I hoped he felt my indignation.

As I bounded through the door and around the corner after Simon, I collided with someone.

"Hey! What's the Bob Murray?" a heavily accented voice complained.

"I'm so sorry," I apologized, backing away. "My fault. Are you okay?" I wanted to know. Until I saw who it was.

Jeffrey Dailey, the reporter who tried to sneak past me to enter a murder scene, stood before me in all his smarminess.

Hands on hips, I fixed him with a stare. "Who is Bob Murray?" I asked, which I realized was not the strongest thing to lead with.

"Wha? Oh, no one. What's your hurry? If I know you, you're off to somewhere interesting."

I wish. "No, not really." Curiosity took hold of me against my better judgment. "If you're from London, what are you always doing here?"

He held his hands up in a stop motion. "You called on me, remember? I don't need none of your accusations."

Did I? I scrunched my eyes closed in disbelief at my stupidity. In my quest for finding information, I had emailed the reporter asking for anything he could find on black market organs. Never in a million years did I imagine he'd show up at the Baths.

Lady Vivian loathed him and with good reason. Positioning himself as the voice of the common person, he vilified the aristocracy in his articles.

"Let's talk outside." *Before anyone sees us together*, I added in my head.

Without waiting for a reply, I scuttled toward the exit.

Unfortunately, he caught up with me before I reached the door. "Still rushin' about. What is it you don't want me to see in here?" He gestured with an arm, and Lady Vivian suddenly appeared through an archway.

I hadn't seen her in days, and now she shows up? And, to make matters worse, with Clarence De Valence at her side.

Heart sinking to my toes, I urged, "Come on," hoping she wouldn't spot us.

"Hold on, hold on," Jeffrey stalled. "What's all this then?"

Eying Lady Vivian and her companion, he pulled out his phone and made to take a picture.

Accidentally on purpose, I jostled his arm, spoiling the shot.

"Out," I commanded with less force than I'd hoped. "Please," I added, my stomach turning in knots.

Once we were clear of the building, a steady drizzle began. I motioned toward a fudge shop patio table with a yellow and pink umbrella. We stood awkwardly under the scant protection, not wanting to sit on wet benches.

"Me aunt left me a cottage in Freshford," Jeffery volunteered.

"What?"

He shrugged. "Why I'm not in London."

When I pushed at his unexpected forthcoming, he pounced. "So what's all this about Lady Vivian and Lord Lisle? Another expensive medispa that no regular folk can afford? Ruinin' the countryside, they are."

Oh. Em. Gee! I shouted in my head. How could I have contacted an actual reporter? Simon, his aunt, and De Valence were going to kill me.

Short of breath, I plopped onto the wet bench.

Rubbing his hands together like a cartoon villain, Jeffery grinned. "That's it, then?"

"Pull yourself together, McGuire," I muttered under my breath, willing my fists to unclench.

Determined and reasonable, I placed my hands on the wire mesh table and conjured a pleasant smile.

"No." Not really a lie, as I still hoped to help Simon find a way around the sale of Comer Manor. "Family friends, that's all." Gaining confidence, I pointed an accusatory finger. "And I better not see anything in the paper about this. Not," I jabbed the air for emphasis. "One. Word. Got me?"

Mock-offended, Jeffery put his hand to his heart. "'Ow could you accuse me of such a thing?" He shook his head, feigned disbelief dripping off him like gobbets of oil. "What with me drivin' all the way here just to check on my old friend."

Try as I may, I couldn't stop the eye roll. "Look, Jeffery. I admit that I contacted you looking for information to help a friend with a homework assignment," I improvised. "I did not invite you to show up at my doorstep. And it is unprofessional of you to take advantage of what you think you saw.

Isn't there some sort of code against printing libel in this country?"

A shrewd look crossed his features before he managed to look hurt. "Would I do that to you? No, no, I would not. The things I get accused of, I tell you—"

"Good," I interrupted. "Thank you." Another eye roll. "What do you mean, 'drove all the way here.' You just admitted you live in a village outside of town."

"Clever one, you are," he said with a grin. Coming to some sort of decision, he turned serious. "I'll tell you what I know about organs and the black market, but I want your guarantee of a story if another manor house sells out. Deal?"

His hand stuck out, and as I shook it, I saw Simon and Dolly.

Snatching my hand away, I prayed they hadn't seen me with the reporter, skulking in the rain, apparently making a deal.

I turned away, heading back to the museum.

"Let me know if you find any more brown bread," he called after me, causing heads to swivel in our direction.

Brown bread? More cockney rhyming slang. In my head, I substituted letters and didn't get very far. Starting and ending with "d."

Dead. Brown bread meant dead.

Chapter Twenty-One: The Forgery

Mind spinning like a Tilt-a-Whirl, I stumbled back to work. Dead. Did Jeffery know I discovered another body, or was he referring to the scene I stopped him from entering before? If he did know about Sherrie, how? Asking Jeffery about the black market was such a bad idea that I could kick myself.

Not just a reporter, a paparazzi wannabe for a tabloid. My silent prayer that Lady Vivian, De Valence, Dolly, or Simon hadn't seen me with Jeffery came to a halt when I calculated the odds. Not good. Of course, one of them saw us.

"Drat," I muttered as I walked into the Oversight Office, hoping to find Sam to clear up the tour changes.

Lady Vivian perched behind the desk, transforming the space into something regal. No Sam.

I froze, knowing better than to say anything aloud in front of Simon's aunt, as questions would follow.

"Hello." I smiled politely, waiting to be acknowledged.

After receiving a nod, I asked, "Do you know where Sam is? There were changes to the schedule I…" I trailed off, knowing she wouldn't wonder why I wanted Sam.

"Ms. Niven is giving a private tour to a major donor." Folding her hands before her, manicured light pink nails clicking softly, she eyed me. "It is expected that one be ready for any eventualities, even if they are first thing in the morning."

A dark hole opened inside my chest, filling with dread. The changes on the schedule were hers, and I missed a tour that morning.

And she knew.

The chill settling into my bones from my damp clothing turned colder. "Yes," I agreed, not knowing what else to say. Then added, "Ma'am. Uh." *Drat!* "I mean, Your Ladyship. Yes, Your Ladyship. I will make sure to check the tour schedule every morning before heading downstairs to the Undercroft."

Her velvet blue eyes narrowed momentarily before relaxing. Another nod.

An obvious dismissal, I turned to go before the clipboard caught my eye. The bag I sifted still hadn't resurfaced, and I wanted another look at the log. About to ask permission to take it, the phone interrupted me.

As Lady Vivian turned to answer, I snatched the log and headed to my sifting station.

The piled-up backlog of excavated material in my area wasn't too bad. I worked through it, extra careful not to miss anything. After a reprimand from Her Ladyship, I could do without being accused of shoddy fieldwork.

Once caught up, I limped to the easy chair in the corner to study the log. Between the long period of sitting and still damp khakis, my muscles stiffened, and bruises swelled. Elevating the sprained ankle lessened the throbbing, but I wished for more of the deep rich tea Sam brought me this morning.

Suppressing a shudder, I turned my attention to the clipboard, studying my signature. Not remembering signing it caused goose flesh to crawl over my skin.

"Get it together, McGuire," I chided.

Then, using a trick of my dad's, I pulled out my phone and snapped a picture of the log. Turning the phone to its brightest setting, it didn't take long for me to see that the signature was a forgery. A tiny heart instead of a dot floated over the "i" in Madeline.

Not in a million years, would I use a heart in my name. Around my name, yes, if it also included a boy's. But no female who wanted to be taken seriously in her career used hearts in her official signature.

Some women would if they didn't care who saw it or if they were above reproach. Aristocratic women, for example. Especially those who didn't even want to work at the Baths.

Wracking my memory for an example of Dolly's writing proved difficult. However, no one else had access to the log, there was no better candidate for someone who used tiny hearts in their handwriting, and Dolly said she wanted me gone.

Honestly, though, I didn't think she would stoop to framing me.

That pang of disappointment resurfaced, despite my self-admonishment to not be taken in by her charm. Why hate me? I wasn't the petite, aristocratic, rich beauty. Granted, I could've been friendlier, but I didn't do anything to make someone want me fired. Jeez.

"Who do I tell?" I asked the room.

Not Dr. Daniels. He might not even know about the missing bag, and I sure didn't want to be the one to tell him. I ruled out Lady Vivian as I didn't want my presence to remind her of my absence this morning. That left Simon, the man smitten with the woman I wanted to accuse.

Excellent.

As I moved into the hallway, the musty scent of damp rock and dirt enveloped me. "Smitten with her," I said aloud, contemplating what I suspected about Simon versus visual evidence. "Strange." The flat sound of my voice sank mournfully into the stone of the narrow passage, causing me to scurry.

Moving too fast for the small space, I rounded the corner at full speed and collided with someone again, but this time I bounced off and landed on the cold, stone floor with a shriek.

"Do be quiet," Simon admonished, holding a hand to help me up.

"Is it possible," I began, eying him, "that I'm getting clumsier?"

He laughed, despite the obvious effort he took not to. "There are more things in heaven and earth," he quoted Shakespeare.

"Than are dreamt of in my philosophy," I paraphrased the rest. "So, you're saying that yes, I can get more clumsy. Just what I need."

Simon made a twirling motion with his finger, and I slowly turned in a circle.

"Presentable?" I asked.

"I have seen you looking worse," he conceded. "A little smudged, but no one will notice."

"Okay, well, I'm glad I ran into you."

"Literally?" he asked.

"No, that part hurt," I said, rubbing my backside. "As in, I was looking for you."

Simon raised an eyebrow by way of asking why.

Handing him the log, I jabbed a finger at my name.

"Charming," he said, a faint smile gracing his lips. "Dolly dots my I with a heart."

Bingo! I knew she wanted me out.

"Cute," I responded vaguely. "Anyway, the point is, I don't."

"Don't what?"

"Dot my 'i' with a heart. Never have. Never will."

Narrowing his eyes, he asked for clarification. "This signature is a forgery?"

With a nod, I said, "Not my signature. Looks like it, but it's not mine."

"Who on earth would want those rocks?" he wanted to know.

I wished to explain my conspiracy theory that no one wanted the rocks but instead wanted me gone, but I thought it wiser to let Simon come to that conclusion on his own.

"Why did you want that bag? Is it important?" It would certainly help my position at the Baths if I had made another groundbreaking sifting discovery.

But, no.

Simon shook his head. "Not even remotely. They need to go to the cleaning lab, be put with the others of its kind, and then be photographed and drawn."

"Wait," I held up a hand to stop him from walking off. "We have a lab? When did we build a lab?" More importantly, why hadn't I seen the lab?

"Of course we do," he sniffed. "It's on the second floor of the National

Heritage Center. We've taken over one of the classrooms." He paused, considering me. "Didn't you know?"

Following along, I said, "Clearly not," and refrained from adding, "Duh." "When can I see it? Now?"

"It is really rather a tight space, and Dolly is up there now."

I couldn't stop my eyes from going wide in surprise. "Why does she get to see it before me? I have the archeology degree, I have seniority, and I—"

Managing to stop before blurting out that I actually wanted to be here, and she didn't, I concluded, "I would love to help clean artifacts."

I put on a pleading expression, fluttered my eyelashes, and said, "Pretty please?"

Unaffected, Simon answered. "Ask Sam to find a time for you. Dolly is there sketching. She is a gifted artist, and Dr. Daniels liked the idea of pen and ink representations to accompany the photographs."

"Like Carter in Egypt," I said, nodding. Howard Carter had King Tut and other discoveries photographed and drew the pictures himself. At the turn of the century, photography was expensive and sometimes unreliable, and his drawings were annotated with field notes.

The added sketches of the Baths created a different dimension to the find. "Cool," I said, meaning it.

"Indeed," he agreed. "Didn't you wonder why you were put back on tours?" Simon wanted to know.

Perturbed, I answered, "Yes. I asked you about it."

"Did you? Ah, well. That's why, then."

Before the urge to strangle him took over, I counted slowly to five and said, "No one told me about the change in tour schedules. I missed one this morning." *Six, seven, eight, nine, ten, breathe.* "Your aunt was disappointed in me."

At the mention of Lady Vivian, Simon slowed and wrapped a brotherly arm over my shoulder. "I am sure she will forget about it quite shortly," he said in a way that made my error seem indelible.

"Right." He released me. "Back to sifting. And look for that bag," he called over his shoulder.

With a fond scowl at his retreating form, I returned to my sifting table.

While the details were still clear, I went over our conversation. What seemed so unbelievably apparent to me had slipped under Simon's upturned nose.

Fact: The missing bag had little to no value. Just rocks. Fact: My signature was forged with a heart over the 'i.' Conclusion: Someone wanted me to look bad.

Fact: Dolly used a heart to dot the 'i' in Simon's name. Fact: Dolly was a gifted artist, meaning she could copy signatures. Fact: I heard Dolly say she wanted me gone. Conclusion: A strong argument could be made, based on admittedly circumstantial evidence, that Dolly was trying to undermine me, get me fired, and kicked out of the country.

The question that remained, though, was whether her dislike led to sabotaging Lancelot to incapacitate me. Or kill.

Chapter Twenty-Two: The Second Accusation

The next day arrived with a clear sky, a deep blue promising warmth. Lured in by its appearance, I sent Roger ahead without me, choosing to walk and build up strength in my ankle.

I realized my mistake as soon as I called goodbye to Meryl and stepped into the garden. Fall leaves swirled around my feet in a light but persistent cold breeze. Returning to the mudroom, I grabbed a green plaid scarf from a hook on the mudroom bench and wrapped it securely around my neck.

Chilly air stiffened my muscles and slowed my pace. Gingerly, I made my way down the steep sidewalk to Bear Flats. The only indicator as to why the neighborhood had such an odd name was an incongruous polar bear on the roof of a pub. Past that crouched a steeper hill winding to the tunnel under the main road to the train station. Wishing for handrails, I got to the subway and saw it had been repainted. Poseidon mural out, local parks mural in. As much as I missed the Baths Museum pediment painting, the deer and bunnies lightened my mood.

Until I emerged and the wind slapped me in the face.

Scrunching my nose into the plaid of the scarf reminded me of Scotland, which of course, turned my thoughts to Edward.

Unsure of everything I thought I knew about him, I found myself avoiding contact. Gone were the hourly checks to see if he texted, the afternoon phone calls, and the evening strolls by the Avon River. Did I miss them? And him?

A cold pit in my gut hinted at the answer. I ignored it.

Crossing over the dark green river, I paused, watching the narrow boats strain against their ropes as the wind picked up speed. One vessel, blue, unadorned, and old but well-maintained, caught my attention. A man poked his head out of the saloon, surveyed the area, saw me, and retreated.

The dark hair and the way he moved reminded me of Edward, but I couldn't be sure. If it was him, what was he doing on a boat?

A particularly nasty gust hurried me toward the safety of the Roman Baths, taking with it my unanswered questions.

Once inside, I sought out Sam and explained my forged signature and why I missed a tour the previous morning. If all else failed, I wanted my internship secure.

"See?" I held the picture of the signature on my phone to her. "I do not use hearts in my signature."

An impish smile graced her features. "Of course, you don't use wee hearts," Sam agreed. "You don't need to go explaining things to me, now, lass. No one thinks you lost the C47 bag. It'll turn up where we least expect it. It will."

When Simon accused me of losing the bag, he made it sound like the end of the world. By now, I should know better than to listen to him when he's focused. Way too serious.

"Really?" I practically squeaked, unable to contain the relief. Tension melted out of my shoulders as I sank into one of the office chairs.

Nodding, she said, "It was me own fault you didn't get notified of the schedule. I told Dr. Daniels to pencil in your name and forgot to tell you. I took yesterday's tour myself. Hadn't done one in years and had a blast." She paused, head cocked to one side. "We did run thirty minutes long." With a shrug, she concluded, "But we had fun."

My ankle held up to the walk well. Putting my weight on it, I rose and checked for any guide sessions today. Three, the first in twenty minutes.

"Thank you so much," I said, meaning it. "I'm looking forward to talking about the Baths today. Ancient dirt makes a lousy conversationalist."

Sam laughed before settling into her fifteen-minute archeology lesson.

Today's focused on how the common people of the Roman Baths communicated with the gods. The hot springs were direct links to the Underworld, so tossing a coin or gift into the water went straight to Sulis Minerva. Some people even wrote backward mirror notes on lead leaves so that only the goddess could read their secrets.

"I wonder how those folks would feel about having their notes displayed in a museum?" I mused.

Sam took the question seriously. "We have to be careful with the past. Preserve it, study it, but also have respect for those who came before."

"Exactly," I said, sensing this topic was important to her. Not sure of my opinion, I said my goodbyes and went to meet my tour group.

* * *

After three tours, my ankle throbbed, and my stomach growled. I peeked inside the elegant Pump Room for Lily, but they were hosting a private event, and she only had time to give me a wave.

After grabbing a croissant sandwich to go, I sat on one of the wooden benches in the square by the Abbey and watched tourists crane their necks to see to the top of the bell tower. The flying buttresses created a line of arches that held the graceful tower.

"Exquisite," I breathed aloud.

Wanting to share my good morning with someone, I called Tori, flatly ignoring the time zone difference.

"Why can't I see you?" she greeted me.

"I'm using an app on my phone. Which, weirdly, is less phone-like than the one on the computer." I smiled. "Why are you awake or available or whatever you should be doing right now?"

"I'm about to go into hibernation. I've been awake for thirty-one hours and fifteen minutes, and I'm starting to hallucinate."

"Whoa, whoa, whoa. What the heck? Why?"

"Mostly because I'm an idiot."

"No, you're not," I responded immediately.

"Thank you, but yes, I am. I did not have my cloud backup turned on, and my computer got fried during an electrical storm."

In the Arizona desert, hot air from the ground mixed with cold, moist fronts and created spectacular displays of sheet lighting. Stunning, but the absolute power of the storms was also dangerous and deadly. If lightning struck the street, the deafening sound and blinding light were a prelude to the power surge that could take out all electronics.

"Oh no," I sympathized.

"Oh yes. Fortunately, Scott is a genius and helped me find and recover a lot of it. Luckily, I email things to my mom to proofread sometimes."

"It's good to know Scott has some purpose," I joked, having come to appreciate her boyfriend.

"Watch it," she warned.

"Too soon?"

She laughed. "You know I am *diabla loca* when I'm tired. We're unplugging everything and going to sleep for the next day." After a jaw-cracking yawn, she said, "I'm glad I got to say howdy. I've missed you."

"Me too," I agreed. "Give Scott a hug for me. *Adios!*"

"What have I told you about using Spanish? I don't understand how your accent can be so bad."

"*Buenas noches*," I sang and hung up before she could complain further.

Sighing happily, I took stock of my situation. My bruises healed, and Sam trusted my work. The breeze had even died down, and the charming square radiated with autumn warmth.

On the other hand, Simon's mood bordered on mercurial, and I didn't know what to think about my relationship with Edward.

A fluffy grey cloud moved over the sun, bringing a chill. I snuggled my scarf around me, gathered my things, and headed back to work.

With a smile, I opened the Oversight Office door to discover a scowling and most displeased Lady Vivian. Sam was nowhere to be seen.

Without knowing why, my hands turned cold, and sweat broke out on my brow.

"Good afternoon," I said politely.

"No," Lady Vivian disagreed. "It is not."

Too afraid to ask why, I stood stupidly with my blue jean jacket halfway off, dangling from one arm. I took a step backward.

"Have you," she said, freezing me in my tracks, "any idea where this story came from?"

Although she primly placed the tabloid newspaper on the desk for me to read, her hands shook. I assumed with fury.

"Another Country Village To Be Ruined," the headline ran, with a byline of none other than Jeffery Dailey.

My eyes dried up in their sockets as I stared, unblinking, unable to look away.

He couldn't have, my brain protested. He promised he wouldn't run anything about Simon's manor house or the De Valence medispa purchase.

Cromer Manor will be the next victim in the ever-expanding greed grab by local aristocracy. Is no village safe from these capitalistic money-makers? The spa's services are so high no one local can pay, even though the locals are the ones who pay the price in the end.

"That doesn't even make sense," I sputtered, unable to focus. "You can't complain about the aristocracy and capitalism in the same paragraph. They're two different socio-economic systems."

"That is hardly the issue," Lady Vivian snapped. "Why were you speaking to this," she stabbed a manicured pink nail toward the newspaper, "reporter?"

"I wasn't," I protested, caught myself, then clarified. "I mean, I was. But not about that. About Sherrie, the girl I found in the woods. Remember? I just sent an email to him. It was all his idea to come here to the Baths. It wasn't my fault that he saw you and Clarence De Valence. He drew his own conclusions about that, and I told him not to print anything based on his conjecture, and he promised he wouldn't, and he gave me every impression that he was sincere and—"

"Stop," she commanded, her voice quiet and hard as diamonds. "I'll be speaking to Ms. Niven about the internship."

The internship, not *my* internship. Dark spots danced at the edges of my vision, mingling with unbidden tears. My nose filled, and I fought sniffles.

"And." Lady Vivian paused, making sure she had my full attention, then went on relentlessly, "the status of your student visa."

Chapter Twenty-Three: From the Abbey Roof

Lady Vivian just threatened to deport me.

Despite the skin on my face tightening, I would not allow myself to cry in front of her. No way. Not this girl.

"I would hope," I began but stopped when I heard how high and thin my voice sounded. After clearing my throat, I said, "That you will consider the good work I've done both on tours and sifting debris from the new dig site."

The glare she delivered cut through to my heart. Which, frankly, pissed me off. I mean, this was my life she dangled in the balance.

"And not," I emphasized, "allow personal inconveniences to color your once high opinion of me."

At my declaration, Lady Vivian stood.

My knees almost buckled.

Not allowing my weakness to show, I turned on my heel, marched out of the office and the Baths back to the square.

Once clear of the building, hot tears stained my cheeks, and no amount of sniffing stopped my running nose. Sobs wracked my body as I ran bleary-eyed to sanctuary. Heading into the gift shop of the Bath Abbey allowed me to bypass any line at the main entrance so I could aim straight for the bathroom.

Finally allowing myself to break down, I collapsed onto the radiator, my head resting on the cold white porcelain of the sink, and cried. Loudly.

A quiet knock on the door alerted me to the fact that I was making an appalling amount of noise.

"Yes?" I answered thickly. "It's taken," I added needlessly.

Rather than a woman's voice asking about using the facilities, a man responded. "Are you quite well, my child?"

Father Michael. It must be.

"Just a moment."

Splashing cool water on my face, blowing my nose, and finishing with more water, I got myself under control. The reflection in the mirror did nothing to improve my mood, my eyes red-rimmed and swollen, a small smatter of freckles standing in stark contrast to my now pale complexion.

"Sigh." Then, louder, "Coming."

The entryway was empty when I opened the door. Peeking around the corner, I found Father Michael sitting discreetly on a chair in the sanctuary.

As I approached, my personal trauma dropped away as I took in the space. Open and airy, breathtaking as always, but something was different.

The pews were missing. Without them, the open floor flowed seamlessly to the columns that drew my eye up to the fan-vaulted ceiling with its intricate flower pattern.

"Where did the pews go?" I asked, plopping into the chair next to the deacon.

His eyes traveled around the room, then settled on me. "It was a difficult decision, but this is better, don't you think?"

Nodding, I agreed. "The dark wood of the pews kept the focus on the floor instead of…" I indicated the heavens above with a wave of my hand. "They were beautiful, though, with the carvings at the ends."

By way of answering, he stood and invited me to walk with him. "We kept some on the far side of the choir. The ones with historical or artistic significance."

I hoped the one I used in the scavenger hunt of the Abbey that I created for Edward made the cut. The carving of a green man, which, frankly, looked more like a monkey or maybe even a fox, was the starting place for the expedition.

"This one is my favorite." He indicated a carving that looked like a house at the end of a pew. The detail drew me in, and I wanted to shrink down and explore inside.

"It's amazing," I agreed.

Sensing that I was ready, Father Michael asked, "Is everything quite all right?"

The phrasing coaxed a smile from me, because, obviously not. "I screwed up, and think I may be deported," I admitted.

Saying it sucked the heat from my body, and I slumped onto the dark wooden bench.

"I see."

The response calmed me, not demanding answers or explanations.

"I'll miss the Abbey."

His eyebrows raised, questioning. The church played a role in my discovery of a dead body at the Baths, but overall it provided me with an architecturally splendid safe haven.

"Yes. I love it here."

"Quite right," he agreed before standing. "Have you ever been to the roof?"

My eyes crinkled with delight. "The roof? Honestly? No." Excitement pushed my ennui to the side. "Can I?"

His smile matched my own. "We have tower tours scheduled almost every day." He chuckled, surprised that I didn't know.

"Well, Ella wasn't the best docent," I said, referring to the woman who caused many of my problems when I first arrived in Bath.

"To say the least," Father Michael agreed, a furrow appearing between his brows. "Come," he invited. "I will make sure you are on the next tour, free of charge."

"Oh no," I protested. "You don't need to do that. I can pay."

"Consider the tour part of your free counseling. A community service, if you will."

As he spoke to the guide, I looked for signage about the tour and found one. It read, 'Bell Tower and Roof Tour: £10.'

Spotting the price, I pulled an orange-colored ten-pound note from my front pocket and slipped it into the donation box.

Father Michael ushered me into the group as the guide explained about the number of narrow, steep, spiral stairs and the built-in breaks we would encounter.

A clunking and shuffling sound followed me as I ducked into the undersized door to the stairwell. Turning around, I saw a thin guy with shockingly blonde, spiked hair and way too much photography equipment to haul alone.

"Do you need help?" I asked, pausing on a turn.

"Eh?"

"Can I carry one of your cameras for you?" I clarified, holding out my hand.

The expression on his face went from harried to relieved.

"You're a lifesaver, you are." Extending a black bag with a thick strap, he said, "Here, this one isn't heavy."

So as not to hold up the group behind us, I slung the bag over my shoulder and continued to make my way to the bell tower, our first stop.

The square room housed the ropes that the bell-pullers used. The contraption, called a spider, descended from the ceiling so the pullers could stand in a circle to coordinate their movements.

Although fascinating, my mind refused to focus, twisting every thought to my imminent deportation. Where to go when I flew home? Tempe, to my mom's new condo, to stay in a guest room? Or Chicago, where I could pick up a few classes. Maybe work for my dad.

"Jordan," a voice said, causing me to squeak.

"Yip!"

I turned to see the guy I'd helped extending his hand in greeting. "Thank you. My name is Jordan."

"Hello. How nice to meet you," I responded, ignoring the fact I just jumped out of my skin. Cool, that's me.

"I'm Maddie. Are you a professional or an over-equipped amateur?"

Aiming his camera at the ceiling where the bell pulls perched, he said, "I work for a country living magazine. Country churches are the theme for this issue, and I'm using the Abbey as the crowning glory of the Cotswolds."

"It is at that," I agreed.

From that room, the tour split in two, half of us heading behind the clock face. I stuck with Jordan since I still carried his equipment. On our way along the single-file walkway, we passed the keystone for the vaulted ceiling. Henry VII's stone masons built the structure with no mortar, just fifteenth-century physics.

My mind flitted to the high rises of downtown Chicago. Those buildings also held many firsts, including the dawn of the skyscraper, but the idea of going back to school in Illinois made everything look grey.

Granted, we were in a limestone structure that had a lot of grey bricks, but that wasn't the problem.

I loved the City of Bath, the Roman Baths, the Abbey, and everything about my internship. Going back to America caused my mouth to go dry.

After the clock and a view of the bells, our group went along the outside edge of the roof with only a 400-year-old balustrade protecting us from falling off. Another skinny, pointed door opened onto our final staircase. These, in an even tighter spiral, were more worn and uneven. Without a rail, we clung to a bell rope threaded through iron eye holes screwed into the wall.

Jordan trudged behind me, keeping a running commentary of the sites he visited on this assignment. Wishing I could devote more attention to the personable photographer, I made polite sounds I hoped passed as friendly.

When we emerged on the roof, the wind, combined with the view, took my breath away. Standing on the tallest tower of the Abbey, the view revealed tree and ivy-covered hills surrounding Bath, which rolled to the clean lines of the limestone Georgian architecture most buildings boasted.

The rain stopped, but the wind accelerated, whipping my ponytail into my face.

Ignoring it, I drank in the view, starting opposite the Baths.

Jordan approached, so I offered him his bag. Shaking his head, he said, "I have everything I need. Thank you, again."

I smiled weakly and gestured to a field on the far side of the river. "What's that?"

"Rugby pitch," Jordan explained. "Come on, you Bath!"

He grinned like I should know what any of it meant, so I tried to smile again before moving to a different wall.

The view was so picturesque that tears threatened to spill again. How could I ever land another opportunity like this? Emotion squeezed my throat, making me wobble. With a hand on the cool stone of the tower, I took deep, calming breaths before moving to look at the Pump Room and entrance to the Roman Baths.

A familiar form moved suspiciously, checking behind and around her every few seconds.

Dolly.

Grateful for the distraction, I watched, wondering what she was up to.

Instead of gliding across the pavement, she flitted, stopping and starting with glances over her shoulder. It took forever for her to move around the corner to the same fudge shop where I met the treacherous reporter, Jeffery.

"OMG," I muttered like a middle-schooler.

Jeffery swaggered toward the same table where he betrayed me and greeted Dolly.

Chapter Twenty-Four: Shadowing Dolly

Dolly said she wanted me back in America, and Jeffery wrote an article that managed to achieve that goal. And now they were having a secret meeting.

Standing on my toes, I moved my head around the various gothic accents on the Abbey Tower to secure a better view.

"Hello," Jordan said, causing me to jump. Again.

"I'm sorry," I said, extending his bag. "Do you need this?"

He shook his head. "No." He held up a camera with a massive telephoto lens. "I wondered if you wanted a better view."

Not believing my luck, I nodded like a bobblehead and gathered the camera to my chest. Placing the strap over my head, I aimed the viewfinder at Dolly and Jeffery.

My goal was to get a front-row seat to observe what happened next.

Despite the high-tech Single Lens Reflex in my hand, I couldn't take a picture. I didn't think my new photographer friend would send it to me, considering he was on a job. My phone's camera would be too grainy from this distance to serve as proof that Dolly was up to something shifty. Evidence that I required to convince Lady Vivian to keep me on at the Baths.

"Anything interesting?" Jordan asked.

"Uh, very," I said, despite aiming the lens at a local shop and not the idyllic view. "This doesn't have wi-fi, does it?" I asked, already certain of the answer.

"No. I take the SIM card out and download the photos to my computer." Removing the strap from around my neck, I returned the camera to him.

"Thank you so much for this," I said. "You have no idea how much I appreciate it." I also extended the bag to him, a plan forming in my mind.

"I hate to burden you, but I need to run."

Jordan glanced wearily at the multiple equipment bags, so I quickly added, "I would be happy to carry it downstairs and leave it with a docent if you like."

Smiling, he took it one step further. "I have what I need. I'll follow you down."

Bag over my shoulder, I offered a brief grin and returned to the weathered wooden door and crossed the roof.

The winding stone stairs slowed me, despite needing to get to the square. Jordan stopped a couple of times at arrow-slit windows to take artistic shots, but I hurried onward, clinging to the bell rope handrail.

When I emerged into the sanctuary, I paused only long enough to give Jordan his things and accept his business card.

"Thanks," I responded before turning to the gift shop and bolting outside.

Phone at the ready, I rushed through the doors and managed to shoot before Dolly and Jeffery separated.

Not enough.

The photo showed the pair passing each other, not conspiring together.

"Fine," I hissed and took off after Dolly as she glided toward Manvers Street.

At first, I practiced stealthy ninja skills, dodging behind pillars and in alleyways to avoid being seen and walking on my toes to keep the heels of my boots from clicking on the stone sidewalk. Not a glance in my direction from Dolly.

As she waltzed inside the train station, I appreciated her lack of awareness. The Bath Spa station wasn't very big, and I had to wait outside in the dripping cold while she bought a ticket from the kiosk.

Once Dolly headed through the gates and up the stairs, I charged in, swiped my BritRail pass, and followed.

The pass allowed me to go anywhere, anytime, and it could only be purchased by non-British citizens. I pictured myself darting across England when I first got it, but I loved Bath so much that I hadn't traveled anywhere else yet.

The long platforms didn't afford any place to hide, but Dolly seemed lost in her own world. I pulled my collar up and slouched against a wall, wondering which train we were going to take.

The displays showed one to Swindon arriving next, the military time throwing me off for only a moment. Add twelve to everything. Easy.

Huddled against the fresh bout of rain, I waited.

Finally, I glimpsed the yellow band of a Great Western Railway as the deep green train pulled smoothly into the station. Straightening, I located Dolly as she hopped on board.

I followed suit, hitting a glowing button to open the doors of a car adjacent to hers. Finding a seat, I avoided spots with a red "Reserved" light above them.

I popped up to watch every station we stopped at to make sure she didn't get off. Which, honestly, got boring, and I suspected I looked a little crazy.

"What am I doing?" I whispered, doubt bouncing in my brain. I didn't plan out what to say to her, didn't know what I thought I would catch her in the act of, and didn't know how to react if she caught me.

My adrenaline spiked at Swindon when my vigilance paid off. Dolly stepped off, and I followed her down the stairs and to the platform across the tracks. This train proved a challenge, as it was much smaller with only two cars. But again, Dolly didn't bother to look up.

Apparently, here she didn't feel the need to look over her shoulder every few seconds like she did in front of the Baths.

This told me that neither Lady Vivian nor Simon took trains, but also that she probably wasn't going anywhere interesting.

The doors closed, taking me, who knew where, and the doubt returned as my excitement over successfully shadowing another human ebbed.

You're grasping at straws, McGuire, I thought.

Deciding to disembark at the next station and return home to the comfort of the Priestlys, a familiar cold settled into my chest. Still, a plan felt better than no plan.

When we pulled into Stroud, I quickly shuffled onto the platform and spotted Dolly, just a few people ahead of me.

Walking with purpose.

Okay, one should not ignore serendipity. It was like the universe was telling me, "Hey! Go that way."

Not one to pass up an opportunity, I followed her, not bothering to wait for the next train. My BritRail pass gave me access anytime, so I didn't need to worry about ticketing.

My quarry marched up the street, past a taxi, and into a pub.

The place practically vibrated with good cheer, so I went in and found a quiet table by a brick wall with an arched window in the corner. If she looked, Dolly would see me, but with the temperature dropping outside, I chanced it.

Besides, the pub had table service, and when a big guy with a goofy smile asked what I wanted, I couldn't resist a meal.

"What's good?" I asked.

"Woodchester sausages with mash is me favorite," he said with a West country accent.

"I'll have that then and a half pint."

"Right," he responded before I could tell him what kind of beer I wanted.

My dinner fate in my server's hands, I pulled myself together and thought things through. First off, a call to my dad.

Thankfully, his answering machine picked up, so I wouldn't have to go into too much detail. "Hey, Dad, it's me." Like, anyone else called him Dad. "I might need to come home from England a little early. Would you mind terribly helping me with a plane ticket to Chicago? And maybe we could talk about getting me an internship at your company?"

Your company, I thought. I didn't even know what they did. Dad headed up sales and marketing for one division, but I never wanted to be in the corporate world, so I didn't bother to pay much attention to what he sold.

With a sigh, I muttered, "At least I won't starve."

Asking for a way home and a job was one thing. Well, two things, but I drew the line at living with him and his new wife. Yasmine was great but not that much older than me.

I called my dorm mate, who lived one door down the hall from me during our freshman year. "Hey, Naomi."

"Madeline, girl, what is up? How is England treating you, mon?" Using the Jamaican accent, she fell into when near her grandmother, her voice welcomed me.

"You're not busy, are you? I didn't even think about the time difference."

"Na, no worries. Everyone is asleep. Tell me everything."

"Well," I started but couldn't finish. "A lot. But the important thing is I'm coming home, and I wondered if you still had an empty bed in your dorm room. My dad can spin his magic to get me in mid-semester."

"Da hell, Maddie?" she said, her native Chicago accent returning. "You okay?"

"I'm okay. Just making contingency plans."

"Plan with me anytime, girl. I gotcha."

"You're the best. Love ya, girl."

"Back atcha. Call when you have the detes."

The detes, or details, would come later. For now, having a vague idea of my future felt, well, depressing, but better than floating in limbo.

My sausages arrived with a delicious, malty red ale. I thanked the server and dug into a fluffy, golden pile of mashed potatoes drenched in a deep red onion gravy. Heaven.

Devouring a hearty meal helped my mood. Practicality reasserted itself, pushing out the pity, and with the return of my spine, confrontation sounded like a good idea.

I would march up to Dolly and demand to know what she was doing with Jeffery, the reporter, and why she tried to kick me out of the country. Tried, not succeeded. Not yet, anyway.

Peering around the pub, I saw her leaning against the bar, chatting up a good-looking guy. Quickly snapping a few pictures for evidence, I watched for a minute. Their body language said flirty, but I found that my ability to read people in England wasn't nearly as dependable as in Arizona.

Still, what was she planning with her handsome new companion? Plotting the downfall of another coworker?

"Wocher doin' all alone, gurly?" a gruff voice inquired.

Snapping out of my internal interrogation, I saw Nigel, the farmer who helped me call the police when I found Sherrie. I translated his question to, 'What are you doing all alone, young lady,' and responded accordingly.

"Hello, Nigel. How nice to see you. How's your horse?"

"Old Nigel be fine," he aimed for the bar. "Ta."

A text message came through from Lily. 'Up for a brew?'

"Not right now. I'm in Stroud on a wild goose chase. Do they have those in England?"

'Stroud? Why?'

Why, indeed? I didn't want to confess that to Lily, though. 'Following a De Valence.'

The texting with my friend was cut short by the dulcet tones of Gwendolyn De Valence. "Maddie? Is that you?"

Chapter Twenty-Five: The Ultimate Betrayal

Busted.

"Oh, hey, Dolly." Cool, that's me. "What are you doing here?" I asked, taking the offensive.

She perched on a chair at my table. Uninvited, I might add.

"How absolutely lovely to see you!"

Was this girl for real? Not a hint of guilt for destroying my internship, imperiling my career, and getting me deported.

Glancing back at my phone, I texted Lily. 'I've been fired, and I'm trying to find out why.'

'No!!!!' Lily's response was immediate and comforting.

Dolly waited politely.

After rejecting responses that ranged from, *Yeah, right,* to *Why did you betray me?!?* I repeated my question to her. "Why are you here?"

With a slight scowl of consternation, she admitted, "I've been here before. But…"

She trailed off, glancing in the darkened corners of the pub.

"But what?" I insisted, not caring to be gentle. "Why here? Why now? Who was that guy?" I indicated the young man who currently chatted up a busty brunette.

The vague expression returned to her eyes. "I am not—" She shook her head, interrupting herself, then searched my face. "Have you ever felt like you've been someplace before, but you haven't really?"

Unconcerned with her intensity, I shrugged. "Sure. Deja vu. Everyone has." I returned to my texting. To Lily, I sent the message, 'I'm going to get myself in more trouble, but I have to know what's going on.'

The tiny shake of Dolly's head batted away my explanation like a gnat. "No," she said flatly. "It's not that." Leaning close, she confided, "I don't remember being here. The man at the bar, Stuart, remembered me. And I knew where the bathroom was."

Closing my eyes, I pictured the pub's layout, compared it to every other bar I frequented, and pointed. "Is it behind that wall?" I asked, opening my eyes.

The crease between her brows returned. "Well, yes," she admitted. "But—"

My finger traveled, pointing to the flirt at the bar. "Let me guess. Did he say, 'Haven't I met you before?'" A classic and very outdated line.

Lips pursed, she looked like she wanted to cry. "Yes, but I…"

My eyebrows went up, impatiently waiting for an explanation.

Voice quiet, she said, "I really cannot explain it."

Unable to ignore her distress any longer, I relented. "Maybe you had too much to drink?" I suggested.

"I guess I could have. I get lightheaded pretty easily."

"Still," I began, putting myself in her shoes. She mentioned forgetting things before. It must be terrifying to have gaps in your memory. Despite everything warning me not to trust her, I sympathized. A little. "You should remember getting here, though, and having the first drink, if not the second."

Relaxing against the back of her chair, she agreed. "Exactly right. Only bits and bobs come back. How am I supposed to do anything with my life if my memory is already failing?"

Pleading and earnest, she looked heartbreakingly vulnerable.

I recalled what I overheard through the oversight office door. Dolly's uncle, making her take a job, and her wanting to hide at the manor house. I took it to mean she was bored, but perhaps fear of losing her mind ruled her arguments.

"Listen, Dolly, we've had our differences, but you strike me as being really smart, caring, and, well, frankly, together." I couldn't believe I said it.

Wanting nothing more than to scream at her for ruining my life, I offered comfort.

Was this ploy of hers another way to mess with me? If so, it worked.

"You're so kind, Maddie. I've appreciated having you as a friend."

Sincerity sang through in her voice and expression. I fell for it.

"You're not losing your mind," I maintained. "Maybe you reacted to something. I know someone whose brother is allergic to alcohol. He goes kind of crazy."

Hope blossomed on her beautiful face. "Do you think so?"

Nodding, I confirmed it. "You probably just can't handle agave or juniper or something."

To my complete and total surprise, a single tear trickled artfully down Dolly's cheek. With a practiced hand, she whipped it away, removing any evidence of the social foible.

"It is an absolutely smashing pub," she said, cheer covering any emotion she showed earlier. "Don't you think?"

Two cups of tea in thick mugs clunked on the table. "'Ere ya go. 'Ave some tea," Nigel offered.

Dolly blinked rapidly at the man, so I explained. "Dolly, this is Nigel, a farmer in the Cotswolds. Nigel," I said, turning to him and indicating he should sit. "This is Lady Gwendolyn De Valence."

Placing a knuckle to his forehead like a serf from a movie, he said, "Pleased to make your acquaintance, my lady." He turned to me, any pretense of good manners fleeing. "I added sugar," he informed me.

With a fake smile plastered on my face, I responded, "How kind."

Picturing the sugar cubes kept in his grubby pockets for Old Nigel, the farmer's draft horse, I took matters in hand. With a spoon, I pretended to stir and fished out the offending cube and dropped it on the rocks of the potted plant behind me. Stealthy.

Much as I loved horses, I could do without linty pocket treats intended for the beasts in my tea.

Mission accomplished, I rejoined the conversation which had turned to countryside living.

Dolly and Nigel established the proximity of their properties and exchanged niceties about local politics.

"Nigel owns a delightful black and white workhorse named Old Nigel," I informed Dolly. "Giant, but sweet as a kitten."

"Do you?" Dolly exclaimed with the proper amount of enthusiasm. "How absolutely lovely."

The same phrase she used to describe meeting me, but I let it go.

"My first pony was black with a white blaze on this nose," she told Nigel as she splashed milk into my tea. "Just the sweetest thing." Another dollop. "You like yours white, don't you?"

On occasion, Dolly served as drink and lunch server for the dig team. "I do," I said, although only sometimes. Mixing things up suited my style better, but I added, "Thanks for remembering."

Sipping his tea, Nigel nodded, a sweet grin on his face. The pub environment suited him. On the farm, he came across as watchful and concerned. Here, he relaxed, one of the regulars, having a pint. Or, in Nigel's case, a cuppa with cream and sugar.

I also started to unwind, feeling contentment I hadn't felt in weeks. Dolly wasn't so bad, really. I grinned at my companions, and Dolly's return smile matched mine: happy-go-lucky. She, in fact, looked enormously pleased with herself.

Nigel nodded approval, apparently happy to facilitate a pleasant evening among friends.

But, that seed of distrust about Dolly stubbornly grew, marring my enjoyment. Never properly explaining why she came to that pub added to my suspicions. Earlier, I let the fact slide that she lavished attention on a great-looking guy. However, when I revisited them, her explanations seemed weak.

"Her name was Biddy Boop. Isn't that just absolutely the cutest little name for a pony you could ever imagine?" Dolly droned on, happy as a clam.

My head was too foggy to figure out why Dolly was acting so jolly all of a sudden. I stood, the action tipping the table, sloshing our drinks.

"Do you need something, Maddie?" Dolly asked with wide-eyed innocence.

Plopping back onto my chair, I said, "Tea," surprised at how short my eloquent answer became. Another attempt came out, "Need tea."

"I'll get it," she volunteered. "Nigel? Anything more for you."

"Aye," he agreed, apparently content with our company.

At that moment, my server returned. "Y'alright?" he asked.

"Another round, garçon," Dolly ordered with a giggle, and I wondered if she downed a pint or two before I arrived. "Three Builders." She scanned the table. "With sugar." Clinging to the small metal pitcher in front of her cup, she told him, "We have milk. This will be plenty."

In a fit of silliness, I texted Lily, 'Having a brew tea,' with a smiley face, teapot, tea cup, milk bottle, and heart emojis.

'Y'alright?' came Lily's response.

When our round of drinks arrived, Dolly immediately dumped the pitcher into my cup. Again, without asking.

'Being drowned in milk. By That Lot.' Smiley face, milk bottle, teacup, teapot, castle emojis.

Dolly turned to Nigel. "Do you take milk?"

"Aye," he nodded.

"And more milk, please." The dazzling smile she bestowed on the server erased any hint of annoyance he showed at having to do a second errand.

Dolly and Nigel became more animated as I withdrew, feeling spacey.

When my chin dropped to my chest, I yanked my head up.

Fail.

It only came about halfway before slipping toward the table. I could, I reasoned, let my eyes close and use the table for support.

"No," I muttered.

Something was terribly, terribly wrong. This girl did not fall asleep in public. I took in Dolly's expression, her smile appearing demonic.

"Y'alright there, gurly?" Nigel asked.

Staring into his dark, obsidian eyes, I compared them to the warmth of Edward's soft brown.

Ignoring his question, I pulled out my phone to text Edward. Let him know where I was. Tell him I missed him and that we could work everything out. Except, my fingers were too fat for my skin.

Clumsy.

Tired.

"Miss?" A gentle shake nudged me back to the present, and with it, realization followed hot on the heels of panic.

Never let anyone put anything in your drink in a bar. Every girl in the US knew that, even those of us not technically old enough to go to bars.

Dolly and the milk. She put something in the pitcher, then made sure I downed it all.

I leaned over to whisper to Nigel, miscalculated my balance, and pitched forward into him.

"Dolly drugged my tea," I managed to get out.

Chapter Twenty-Six: The Van Ride

Although my words slurred, Nigel took my claim seriously, even though once I said them, it sounded stupid.

I mean, honestly, why would Dolly spike my tea? She couldn't sell me off to the highest bidder. People would notice.

Or would they? Edward was so concerned with James that I barely crossed his mind. The Priestlys would think it odd that I didn't say goodbye, but once they found out I was fired, their conclusion of "too embarrassed to face us, poor dear" seemed logical. Everyone at the Baths already thought I was gone.

"Did she, now?" he asked, eying our tablemate.

No matter how little I thought of Dolly, human trafficking took it a step too far. On the other hand, my drink had been tampered with, and she controlled the milk.

Nigel pushed away from the table. "Come with me, then."

Helping me to my feet, he supported my stumbling. Scents of hay and pipe smoke mingled with occasional hints of rotting vegetables.

"Patchy," I murmured, reasoning that the pig's slop stained Nigel's thick-soled boots.

Rather than responding, he opened the side doors of his small black farm van, poured me in, and strapped me to a bench.

The seat's dark, cracked vinyl reeked of spoiled leeks and spinach but welcomed me to safety. Unable to help myself, I collapsed sidewise, allowing my eyes to close. Even though I would have to wash my hair three or four times to remove the stench, I silently thanked the old farmer for saving me before I descended into oblivion.

* * *

A loud bang jarred me awake. Disoriented, I panicked at my surroundings before remembering that Dolly drugged my tea.

Then what?

Nausea swelled my belly and thickened my tongue.

Another rough bump caused my dinner and the offending tea to come up. Spewing like a college freshman at a frat party, my body rejected everything.

Bleary-eyed, I spied my surroundings. *Some sort of work truck*, I thought before catching the profile of the driver. The farmer. Good.

Getting rid of the food offered a bit of relief. *I will offer to clean it up for Nigel,* I thought before drifting off again.

* * *

Head pounding in possibly the worst hangover anyone anywhere ever experienced, I bounced along upside down, rushing blood throbbing in my ears.

Being carried over someone's shoulder fireman-style, I concluded. Roughly.

About to complain about my treatment, Nigel's voice cut into my brain like a knife. "Dump 'er in that room," he commanded.

Limp, at the mercy of the brute who carried me, I held in tears.

How could Nigel do this to me? Anyone who took such good care of horses couldn't be bad, could he?

Yes, yes, he could. A very bad man. Not my savior, my captor, Nigel working with Dolly. Mind spinning at the implications, I couldn't pull the pieces together.

Facts flitted to and fro, tantalizing me with helpful information and jumping away before I could grab hold.

No one knew my location, including me. If I got away, how would I find the train station? Without my BritRail pass on my phone, how could I board? No passport. No money and no one to save me.

Dammit.

Ire rose, cutting through the fog of self-pity and drugs.

If anyone was going to save me, it would be me. And right now, playing dead was my best strategy. Knowing I was awake would get me another dose of whatever went in my tea, so I flopped along, draped across a shoulder like a sack of potatoes.

When the lighting changed, I chanced cracking my eyes enough to see through my lashes.

The rough canvas of my hijacker's oil jacket didn't give me a lot of information. When he turned a corner, I let the momentum flop my head to the side. A pale blue door, barely visible against the wall, pulled open, and my handler dumped me unceremoniously on a narrow table. Unbalanced, I couldn't stay in place without holding on, so I crumpled painfully onto the floor.

Not a glance from my jailer as I thudded to the white marble tile. He pushed out the door and allowed it to close, whisper quiet.

Jerk.

Twit, idiot, clod, ignoramus, imbecile, moron, stupid head! I flung insults at the jerkwad who treated me so horribly, rallying my emotions.

Not moving, I listened.

Not a sound.

Again, looking through the camouflage of my lashes, I checked the room. Serene low lighting permitted enough to see without stabbing knives into my eyes. A small room, too dark to distinguish between gray or blue walls. A table-bed like ones used for massages, but no other furniture. A white tank on a tripod lurked next to the bed.

Sure I was alone, I opened my eyes fully.

Surreal confusion battled with logic, and I swooned.

Flat-out swooned.

What the hell, McGuire? I chastised myself. What was I? Some medieval maiden in distress? No. Not me.

Bracing myself, I flung my eyes open, taking in my prison. Soft, blue light glowed from the edges of the ceiling. A simple but elegant oil painting of a flower hung on one wall. The air smelled of eucalyptus and mint.

A De Valence Spa treatment room. How could that possibly be? Dolly wouldn't be so stupid as to kidnap me and bring me to her home. There must be a villain handbook somewhere explaining these things. Bringing drugged kidnap victims to a secret lair had to be in it.

Still, confronted by the evidence, I stuck with my conclusion and prepared myself for the next step.

Flexing my fingers and toes, I gave my brain strict instructions not to throb or blackout as I pushed upright.

Ignoring my admonishments, black dots swirled in my vision, dancing in time to heavy metal drumming in my head.

Long exhales. Three of them. The cacophony didn't stop, but controlled breathing erased the blackness in front of my eyes.

Before deciding to stand, I took stock of myself. A bruise on my ribs ached dully from lurching against my seatbelt in the getaway van. No new trauma to my ankles, but my knee already sloshed, swelling caused by the fall from the table.

I straightened my leg and bit back a scream, stabbing pain in my knee shooting up through my hip and down to my feet.

Choosing to remain on the floor, just for the time being, I assured myself, I checked my pockets. A spare scrunchie, the twin to the one holding my ponytail, and a piece of cinnamon gum. My purse, stocked to the seams with useful items, was gone. Still at the bar unless Dolly, that traitor, picked it up.

My jean jacket still hugged my shoulders, but those pockets held nothing but a few aspirin and lint. My boots' chunky heels might serve as a blunt instrument, but they didn't have helpful shoestrings.

I slid to a wall of cabinets by the sink. Towels in one, everything from pro-collagen marine cream to vitamin-C exfoliants in the next. A treasure trove but useless. Not even in glass bottles, the product line boasted non-bpa carbon-neutral plastic.

The final cabinet held gel-filled cooling eye masks designed to reduce puffiness. I grabbed three and, going up the cuff of my jeans, placed them on my wounded knee. Not ice, but the cooled chemical worked its magic almost immediately.

Bracing my sore leg, I put my weight on the other, my hands on the table, and pulled to standing.

My moment of triumph fell flat when I heard voices in the hall. Reversing the movements, I lowered to the floor and resumed the position I'd fallen in.

"Take the lady to her room," a low-voiced man directed. "Use the wheelchair."

Wheelchair?

Confused.

Again.

I didn't do well with confusion. Clear-headed, logical, and smart suited me.

Eyes closed, I strained to hear more.

"Across the landing, third door on the left," the directions continued.

A grunt, then Dolly rang out, "Hello. Who are you? I seem to have forgotten."

In the long list of things that weren't right at this moment, Dolly's question shot to the top.

"Bloody 'ell," a second, whiny man exclaimed. "You said she was out."

"Relax," Low Voice assured him. "She won't remember a thing."

Chunks of the jigsaw fell into place. Dolly confused with gaps in her memory. De Valence wanting her out of the manor house.

What were they doing here, and how many times had they drugged Dolly?

"If she won't remember," Whiny-man began, his voice with a cunning edge that turned my insides to water, "how come I can't have a go?"

Chapter Twenty-Seven: The Treatment Room

My eyes shot open, fear coursing through my veins like ice. No. No, no, no, no, no. They could not be contemplating that. Not to Dolly. No.

Unzipping my boot, I loosened the heel, ready to charge into the hall and protect my friend with my only weapon.

"No," Low Voice replied, with something that sounded like a smack.

Good.

"The Old Man has her checked. You don't want to wind up like Tim, do you?"

Every single line that came out of these guys was worse than the last. Okay, yes, good that Dolly wouldn't suffer a terrible fate at the hands of the disgusting henchmen, but only because De Valence had her checked. I wondered how he would feel about being called an old man. Served him right.

Also, what the what? What kind of psycho drugs his niece and then checks to make sure no one got to her?

Feeling like Alice in an even more disturbing version of the rabbit hole, I then realized I knew Tim. The groom who let me brush down Lancelot. Why wouldn't they want to wind up like him?

At least Dolly was relatively safe. Home, and under someone's protection, no matter how twisted.

"What about the ginger, then?" Whiny's voice came through the door, referring to me. His leer crawled over my body despite the wall between us.

Low Voice took way too long to respond, and it was not reassuring when he did.

"That one's unconscious," he explained before adding, "Boring."

High-pitched buzzing engulfed my head, and my stomach lurched. Willing the bile down, I fought panic. The bravado that created my confidence to defend Dolly vanished.

"So?" Whiny asked, ratcheting his depravity meter even higher. "She's still fit."

The panic broke, turning into incredulity.

Again, what the actual hell? Who did these two toadstools think they were? Nothing. Absolutely nothing.

Bringing up a self-defense course my mother made me attend, during which I mostly flirted with the instructor, I remembered SING. Solar plexuses, instep, neck, and groin. How to disable attacking males in four easy steps.

As I unzipped my second boot, Low Voice clarified, "Besides, they'll need to prep her for surgery. Get the lady out of here."

Surgery.

The word carried the weight of doom. A tiny squeak escaped me as more of the puzzle turned into a picture. Sherrie, whom I mistook as left nearby randomly. Sherrie, with a surgical scar where a kidney would be. De Valence, flush with money when other manor houses floundered. De Valence, getting Dolly out of the house and drugging her when she saw anything. The spa with special treatment rooms and medical staff for long-term guests.

De Valence was harvesting organs.

A question about the unicorn tattoo kept the complete picture from forming, but everything else was clear. Including that I had to escape this room and this house. With Dolly. I required corroboration against this lot, and she needed explanations she would never get if I left her behind.

"Right," I whispered. *Easy.* Heart pounding loud enough to be heard on every floor, I made a keening sound when I inhaled.

Too much noise. You're supposed to be unconscious.

The thought provided a distraction for me, and it helped. Thinking properly, I wondered why I wasn't out. I ingested enough milk for any drug to take hold.

Only the milk wasn't spiked. Dolly's drugged lady-of-the-manor brain obsessed with ensuring the pitcher provided everyone with the proper amount of creaminess. Not nefarious, but overly polite.

Since she controlled the pitcher, Nigel couldn't have used it. Besides, Dolly and I reacted differently to the drugs. I passed out, and she was awake but unable to remember.

It couldn't have been in the tea. I drank enough of that to knock out a horse.

My heart skipped a beat before accelerating.

A horse who ate sugar.

Nigel put cubes in both our mugs. Dolly's contained something like a roofie, I reasoned. Her vapid conversation, manic expressions, and memory gaps were all symptoms of the date rape drug.

The sugar that went into my cup had to have been laced with a knockout chemical. I fished it out before the full dose had a chance to release. Vomiting on the car ride purged the rest of it out of my system.

Cursing myself for being a lousy judge of character, I turned my attention to my captors.

No sound seeped into the treatment room. Did that mean no one guarded the door, or that one left and the other didn't have anyone to talk to?

Rolling over to push myself up, I bumped my inflamed knee on a table and groaned before I could stop. The cooling masks lessened the swelling, but pain radiated in every direction.

Before Low Voice or Whiny could catch me, I plopped to my original fallen position.

Through slit eyes, I watched the play of light under the door. Since it was brighter outside my door, I could see the movement of shadows.

Nothing.

Maybe I had gotten lucky.

Slowly, carefully, painfully, I sat up, keeping an eye on the strip of light.

Darkness, the size of a shoe, blocked the door.

Toppling back into place, I readied myself for attack. The light returned, indicating the person walked away.

Maybe.

My jaw throbbed from grinding my teeth together. Not knowing, not acting, wreaked havoc on my body. Stiff joints and aching muscles complained, and I closed my eyes against the pain.

* * *

With a jerk, I awoke, not knowing if ten seconds or ten minutes passed.

The shadow by the door ebbed and waned. Pacing. My jailer must be walking back and forth, hopefully to fight boredom.

I could work with that.

When I pulled myself to standing this time, I determined not to go down again without a fight.

Taking stock of the room, I contemplated the machine on a tripod. A vaporizer for facials. The controls only went to forty-three degrees Celsius. After a quick mental conversion to 110 degrees Fahrenheit, I discounted steam as a weapon. Not hot enough to cause discomfort.

A fluffy robe lay across the bed. Removing the belt, I held it between my hands and gave it a tug. Strong. I stuffed it into my jean jacket pocket.

With a hop, I pivoted to the cupboards and found two drawers. One had lip-plumping balms, useless. The second contained strips of cheesecloth to apply during facial masks. Tiny and lacking in structure, they were also useless.

Fifty lashes with a wet noodle, my dad used to joke when I acted up.

The thought of my dad made me smile. Goofy and friendly, he always lightened the mood, no matter how terrible things got.

I wished Dad were here now to help me make a plan. He never offered solutions but always kept me from taking myself too seriously.

Something about him sparked an idea, but I was too muddled to grasp it.

Holding still, I pictured him teaching me to drink coffee without my customary caramel and whipped cream, telling puns to the servers.

"Why was the worker fired from the orange juice factory?" he would ask.

"Because they couldn't concentrate!" His laugh so infectious that everyone joined in despite themselves.

I had to get out of here, hear his voice, and roll my eyes at his dad jokes.

"Think, McGuire," I whispered.

Jokes. The joke held the key.

Fifty lashes? No, nothing there.

I checked the doorknob. No lock. Great news for getting away, horrible for keeping Low Voice and Whiny out.

The bamboo massage table could be moved in front of the door, but it didn't have enough weight to stop anyone from entering.

Pausing, I recollected my treatments and being dumped in here. The door opened into the hall. A table on this side constituted a tripping hazard at most.

"How do I jam you closed?" I asked it in a whisper, the thought of encountering Low Voice or Whiny almost paralyzing me.

Eyes raking the room again, I selected and discarded options. Towels were too soft and slick, eye-gel masks too gushy, and facial supplies too big.

With a sigh, my head slumped back.

And the universe revealed the answer.

The hinge that closed the door had an elbow design bent closed. As it opened, the arm would straighten. If I prevented the hinge from straightening, I could effectively lock the door. All I needed was a strap.

Pulling the sturdy robe belt from my jean jacket, I made a simple slipknot, fed it through the hinge, and looped it into a square knot. Sending thanks to the summer camp teacher who taught me to macrame, I tested the door with a gentle push. It held tight.

If someone tugged on it from outside, the slipknot would tighten, jamming the door closed.

The accomplishment and newfound safety calmed me enough to think. Picturing the layout of the spa, we were in the west wing treatment area above the guest rooms. If someone were below me, I might be able to cause enough of a fuss to draw the household.

But the noise would attract my guards first.

I checked for vents to crawl through, but the house's heat came from radiators.

Opening the cupboard under the sink, I saw only a regular two-inch pipe.

"Not like the Romans," I whispered, wishing for the Great Drain at the Baths, tall enough for a person to walk through.

There it was again. An idea trying to force its way to clarity.

Recalling Sam's lecture about the drain not clogging until 2009 and clearing it before the museum flooded, the solution solidified.

"A wet noodle," I breathed, the connection finally snapping into place.

Meryl's sink, clogged with noodles, formed a tidal wave of water and chaos.

Counting on the fact that the spa doubled as a home and guest house and that De Valence enjoyed the finer things in life, I figured a leak would cause enough response or distraction that I could escape.

Invigorated by the plan, I returned to the drawer with cheesecloth strips, scooped them out, and deposited them on the bed.

"Right. What's next?" Barely audible, the sound of my voice kept me from thinking about Whiny and his evil desires.

With a shudder, I contemplated the drain. Clogging it and letting the water fill the sink, gush over the counter, and seep to the door would take forever. And it may do irreparable damage to the historic home.

"The owner is more important than the house," I reminded myself.

Raking over the room, my eyes landed on the facial steamer. Not hot enough to do damage, but it had a long, expandable hose.

"It might work," I whispered, the idea forming a blueprint in my mind.

Creeping to the machine, I stepped on the base and gave the hose a mighty tug.

Rattling. No progress in loosening it.

A primal scream formed deep in my soul. One thing! Couldn't one thing be easy? Stuffing the robe in my mouth, I released the frustration into a muffled sob.

The light under the door darkened, a foot paused, a person listening.

Chapter Twenty-Eight: A Trail of Breadcrumbs

Silence filled the room. *Go away*, I chanted in my head while praying the terrycloth belt would hold.

The light returned, and my captor resumed pacing, not bothering to check.

Returning to my plan, I took time to examine the contraption. Four screws held the hose in place.

Nothing in the room resembled a screwdriver. My pockets were empty except for a hair tie.

I balled my fists up, holding back panic, nails biting into my flesh.

Nails.

With a shake of my fingers, I stuck my thumbnail into the slot of the screw and turned.

It budged.

Encouraged, I worked my position around for a better angle and removed a screw.

The second came out more quickly than the first, followed easily by the third.

When I slipped my nail into the final screw, I nearly wrenched it off my thumb, cracking it to the quick.

A squeak of pain escaped. "Ow."

I limped in a circle, rechecking the room, my jacket flapping at my sides.

Quieting the offending clothing, my fingers brushed against the silver buttons. Their thin edges gave me an idea.

The rim of the button fit in the screw's head. With a few turns, the screw released, and I removed the hose triumphantly.

Using my hair scrunchies, I secured one end of the tubing to the faucet. Fully extending the hose across the narrow room, I put the opposite end at the base of the door. To keep it from snapping back, I set the massage table on it, careful to ensure it didn't squash the plastic flat.

Step one complete, I then swiped the cheesecloth strips off the table and stuffed them in the end of the hose.

Too excited for my own good, I twisted quickly toward the sink, and pain shot through me like a bullet. Nausea threatened again as I straightened my knee.

The gel masks had gotten warm, so I replaced them with fresh ones and reminded myself to be careful.

With slow, deliberate moves, I returned to the sink and turned it on. Water sluiced into the hose, stopping at the cheesecloth dam.

"The doc is almost ready," Low Voice called.

Frozen in place by the implications of his words, my head swam.

Doubt diluted my resolve. I couldn't fight these two. Impossible.

'Of course, you can, resourceful girl,' Lady Vivian's voice blossomed in my thoughts. Even though she fired me, the power of her compliment gave me strength. I would get out of this just to prove my worth.

The cheesecloth reached its absorption capacity, water pooling at the hose's mouth.

Taking one noodle of cheesecloth halfway out of the hose, I fed it under the door, the capillary action drawing the water into the hall.

I waited, watching the light by the door fade and brighten with Whiny's pacing.

Tread, tread, tread.

Tread, tread, squish.

Squish.

"Bloody 'ell," he whined.

Squish, squish.

Whiny tugged on the door.

Heart in my mouth, I waited.

The door held fast.

A string of expletives escaped from his mouth.

Do it, I willed him.

The light changed enough to indicate he bent to the floor, testing the carpet, discovering water.

"The old man is gonna kill me," he sniveled.

"Do it!" I braved a whisper.

"What's this?"

Finally, he took the bait, tugging the cheesecloth I fished under the door. With it, buckets of water gushed into the hall.

More cursing. My mother would tell him to choose more interesting words.

Continuing his complaints, he ran off with a panicked call for help.

Reaching up, I released the robe belt from the door hinge, stuffed it in my jacket, and gingerly ran to Dolly's room. 'Across the landing,' they said and three doors down.

I opened a door, the lights blazing, and discovered Dolly slumped on a plush bed.

My eyes rebelled against the sudden change, and I flopped my hand at the wall switch until the crystal chandelier switched off, leaving a subtle glow from a table lamp.

On the table sat Dolly's phone. I lunged for it, collapsing in a heap, pushing buttons.

It was locked.

Crawling to Dolly, I turned her over to use her face to unlock the phone.

She popped up like a jack-in-the-box.

"Oh, hello, Maddie. How are you?"

Squelching a squeak, I shushed her. "Quietly now," I said. "I need to use your phone."

While I aimed it at her face, she explained, "Absolutely no problem. But we don't have cell service here. Uncle insists on serenity." She giggled. "Even if he has to enforce it."

Grinding my teeth with a growl, I refrained from throwing it against the wall. The device was still useful. I opened the camera app and started recording.

REC: "Hi, this is Maddie McGuire at the De Valence Medispa with Dolly, and weird stuff is happing." As good of a preamble as I could muster.

I turned the camera on her. "Dolly," I began.

"Hello, Maddie. How are you?" Face gracing confused, she put a finger to her lips. "Or did I ask that already? Do forgive me. I really am rather muddled."

"It's okay. Do you remember where you were tonight?"

"A pub," her bright smile faded. "I think. It's the strangest thing. I think I was in Stroud." A line creased her brow. "How did I get home?"

A tremble in her voice conveyed the depth of her emotions.

"It's okay. What else?"

A decidedly unladylike giggle escaped her. Disturbing. I made sure the camera recording light glowed red.

"Why did you go there?"

The frown returned. "I think I was there before. But, I can't...." She shook herself and then looked at me and the phone. "Hello, Maddie. How are you?" Dolly repeated.

I couldn't accuse De Valence of organ harvesting with this video, but I could prove that Dolly was not right.

"Did you see anyone at the pub?" I asked, making my questions neutral. I didn't want to influence her answers.

With a pert nod, she said, "Well, you, of course, silly."

Patience, I vowed.

"Yes, I was there. Anyone else?"

"Well," she began, heartbreaking concentration marring her features. "That cute boy. Stuart, I think. He said I'd been there before, but I can't remember."

Distressing as this was for her, the information and proof would help us. The sounds of approaching footsteps meant the house knew about the flood.

Time was running out.

"Did you drink anything?"

"I don't really drink much. Except for tea!" Her face brightened. "You and I had tea with that farmer. Nigel, wasn't it? With the black and white horse. Too much sugar, but I drank it down. Can't be rude, don't you know?"

That was enough. The exchange lasted about two-and-a-half minutes. A lifetime in terms of us getting away safely.

"Okay, Dolly, we need to leave. Is there a back stairway?" Throwing logic to the wind, I added, "Or a hidden tunnel?"

Fingers to temples, she asked, "What is wrong with me?"

I wondered if enough time had elapsed for the drug to wear off. "Drugs is my guess. The good news is you aren't going crazy."

"Oh, quite good." For the first time, she took note of our surroundings. "Why isn't the fire lit?"

I'd been so preoccupied that I hadn't taken in the details of her bedroom. Decorated in period Georgian style, a fireplace graced the wall to the left of her bed, windows on either side.

"No time. We need to leave. Now."

"Right. No. No tunnels or hidden stairwells."

Rolling off the bed in a move worthy of a prima ballerina, Dolly came to rest by my side.

"It's dangerous, isn't it?"

Nodding, I said, "I think they were going to remove my kidney." Saying it aloud turned both arms icy, and I began to shake.

In an uncharacteristic show of emotion, she hugged me. "I don't know how much help I'll be. My legs are rubbery."

"That's okay. I was planning on dragging you out, so the fact that you're coming to is great."

"Do be quiet. Nothing about this particular situation is great."

I grinned. "That was. You sound like Simon."

Looking at the room with its pale cream walls, blue floral Persian rug, and canopied bed, I didn't find anything that resembled a weapon.

"Okie dokie," I said in a tone that brooked no arguments. "We're going out the window."

Immediately arguing, Dolly said, "No, Maddie, we can't. We're on the second floor."

"No problem. My friend Tori and I used to sneak out of her bedroom all the time. We just need a rope for you."

I looked hopeful.

Dolly shook her head.

"Fine. Bedsheets it is."

Without a word, Dolly crawled out of my way and allowed me to strip her bed.

Handing her a corner of the fitted sheet, I twisted and made a knot every two feet to add strength. I repeated the process with the flat and tied the two together.

American king sheets were eighty-four inches, roughly square. That gave a hypotenuse of about 118 inches or nine-and-a-half feet. Taking into account knots, I had around eighteen feet of rope. Two stories up would be twenty or twenty-four feet. We could drop the extra yard to the ground.

Securing the sheet rope around the foot of the heavy oak canopy bed, I pulled it to the window and threw open the sash.

And groaned.

The second story in England meant the third floor, which meant at least ten more feet of rope, to reach the ground.

"Oi! What's this?" Whiny in the hallway. Way too close for my liking.

Low Voice answered, "One of them eye thingies women use. What's it doing here?"

Raising my eyes to the heavens, I shook my head, then patted my knee. Sure enough, only two of my makeshift ice packs remained.

"Breadcrumbs, right to the door," I murmured.

However, unlike the treatment rooms, Dolly's door had a bolt. With as much stealth as I could muster, I raced to the door. Ever so slowly, I slid the lock closed. They wouldn't charge right in. Not to the lady of the manor's room.

Turning to Dolly, I whispered, "We're running out of time." Much to my surprise, she mimicked my handiwork with a mattress pad and cream jacquard bedspread.

"Resourceful girl," I complimented her, echoing Simon's aunt.

With the thicker bedspread rope, I wrapped Dolly in an impromptu sling. "You're too wobbly to climb."

"You are too wobbly to keep me from falling," she pointed out.

It was true. Dammit.

"Fine," I said. "We'll make a pulley system."

Gathering the sheet around a bedpost, I added the robe belt to counter-balance her weight. With the sheet across my back and my good leg braced on the wall, I sent her out the window.

"I can do this, I can do this," she repeated in a mantra, her voice getting higher with each bit of fabric I let loose.

The strain on my good leg caused it to shake.

Whiny or Low Voice tested the door, rattling the knob and pushing against the bolt.

Dolly's weight shifted, and I stumbled into the wall.

A shriek quickly muffled, and then the rope when slack.

"Oh my god, I've killed a lady."

Chapter Twenty-Nine: The Fall

I couldn't bring myself to look. How far down Dolly had been before I fumbled the rope meant anything from a broken leg to a shattered spine.

It didn't matter if she was drugged. At least she had been alive and unmarred. Darkness danced at the edges of my vision as I held my breath in panic.

Something hit the window.

How could I explain this? To the police. De Valence. Lady Vivian. To anyone.

Tick against the glass.

And Simon. We were friends now, despite his rather snotty attitude lately. He would never trust me again.

Tick. Louder this time.

Dolly might need help.

She definitely needed help.

Tick, tick, tick in rapid succession.

No matter what happened to me, I had to look and wake the household.

Remaining in the shadows, I raised my head and peeked over the windowsill, narrowly avoiding being pegged by a projectile. I stuck my head out the window until I saw a shape.

Dolly throwing pebbles to get my attention.

Barely visible in the gloom, she gave a thumbs up.

"Thank goodness," I muttered. A few deep breaths cleared my head, allowing my blood pressure to return to non-life-threatening levels.

"Focus."

Securing the sheet rope around my back and seat, I used the leverage to support myself in a clumsy version of rappelling. Foot on the wall, I part climbed, part leveraged the pulley to work my way toward the darkness below.

Dangling fifteen feet above the bushes, I slipped sideways, and my inflated knee bumped into the wall. Daggers shot through my body, causing my hands to spasm and release.

"Maddie!" Dolly's voice sliced through the dark night as I tumbled, one shoe flying off.

The need to tell her to hush trumped every other thought in my mind. My arms flailed to the sheets. Finally, one caught, and I used a spiral motion to wrap the material around my biceps. While I continued to slide, my momentum slowed.

"Shhhhh," I hissed.

Supporting herself on the wall, Dolly reached a hand toward my leg. "Two meters. Almost there."

Under normal circumstances, a six-foot drop wouldn't be a big deal, but not now. "Thanks," I whispered, using both hands to lower myself closer.

"One meter," she reported after a lifetime of inching.

"Half," she said, and I dropped.

"Are you all right?"

"I lost a boot," I said, remembering that I unzipped them to use as weapons.

"I am very impressed we made it outside," she began. "But neither of us is in any shape to escape on foot."

Negative, but true.

"Do the cars in the garage have keys in them?" I asked, but her head shook no before I finished the question.

"Locked away in the valet's station in the lobby. Besides," she added sheepishly. "I don't know how to drive."

"Honestly?" I asked, distracted by this news. I'd been driving for four years, since I was fifteen, and pestered my mom for my permit.

Dolly's expression told me to drop it, redirecting my attention to different things. Like not being sliced open and eviscerated.

I shivered at the word. Sometimes my mother's insistence on a strong vocabulary backfired.

"Think, McGuire," I chided while I watched Dolly's eyes slide closed, still under the drug's influence.

Leaning close, I gave her a shake. "Come on, Lady Gwendolyn. You are needed."

Her return to consciousness brought the strength of centuries to the call. "Thank you, Miss McGuire," she intoned formally.

Pointing across the field to a tree-canopied trail, she said, "That leads to Comer Manor and Simon."

Nodding, I said, "Good idea. I remember you showed me when—"

My hand hit the air multiple times in excitement. "When we were—"

"Riding!" Dolly finished. "Right. I'll fetch the horses."

With a rush of purpose, she stood too fast, wobbled, and crumpled to the ground.

"Do you know how to ride bareback?" I asked after checking her over.

She shook her head.

"The tack is locked away," I reminded her. "We will both ride Lancelot. Without a saddle, his broader back will hold our weight better than Merlin."

Patting the ground, I looked for my shoe.

"What on earth are you doing?" she whispered.

"Boot."

"You cannot possibly think you will make it to the stables. Your knee is so swollen I can make it out through your jeans."

"I know where the cameras are," I countered. "I can sneak to the stables without being seen."

A wicked smile graced Dolly's features. "And do you know how to get by them on a horse?"

I had to admit that I didn't. Tilting my head to the side, I raised an eyebrow, questioning.

"You think I don't know how to avoid every camera installed on my own property? Please."

"Awesome," I said, returning her smile before reality crashed our party. "Can you stand?"

"If I go slowly, yes." And she proved it. "Hide," she suggested before stumbling deeper into the shadows.

Good idea, I thought as I worked myself into a bush. Hidden from view, I pulled out Dolly's phone and cursed myself for not getting her password. Checking it anyway, I discovered it didn't matter as there still wasn't any service.

Unable to call for help, I resolved to find my missing shoe. I scooted around on my seat, exploring under bushes with my hands. When my fingers brushed against a new surface, I reached for it.

Spikes pierced my palm, and I yanked my hand away, hoping I didn't wind up in a cactus patch hidden in the moonless night.

"Did you find her?" Low Voice's words carried around from the front of the house.

"I just started lookin' now, didn't I?" Whiny grouched.

Exposed, I wiggled until my back hit the limestone wall.

Something soft dangled by my shoulder, causing the hair on the back of my neck to stand. Squinting, I braved a glance.

The bedsheet rope. A bright, white beacon pointing at my hiding place.

The only bright side, the building's bricks were creamy, butter yellow, so my hiding place remained safe unless a light shone on it directly.

The beam of a flashlight bobbed around the corner from the front of the house.

With a groan, I nose-dived to the ground. Unable to outrun anyone in my current state of sprains and twists, camouflage was my only defense.

Something moved by my head. Picturing any of the venomous creatures that inhabited my Arizona desert, I froze.

"Chuff, chuff, chuff, chuff," sounded near my ear.

With careful deliberation, I turned my head and came face to face with an irate hedgehog.

Under different circumstances, I would have been enchanted. But I didn't need anything drawing attention to me.

"Shh," I pleaded, not remembering if they were dangerous. Hedgehogs were illegal to have as pets in Arizona, but I didn't know why. I hoped it didn't bite or have rabies.

It puffed. "Chuff, chuff, chuff," continuing like a steam engine.

"What's that?" Whiny demanded, the flashlight bouncing closer.

"Psst, huff, huff, huff, psst," The poor little thing hissing in distress, trying to shoo me away.

Squeezing my eyes shut, I willed it to be quiet.

"Just a bloody hedgehog," Whiny declared and moved toward the front of the house.

"Sorry," I whispered to the creature when two thoughts struck me.

One, I was in a hedge, and the little animal sounded like a snuffling pig. Hedge. Hog. Wow.

Two, I grabbed his spines and not my boot, making my hand itch like mad. Still better than a cactus, but no wonder the little creature was so upset.

"Oi, Brett!" Low Voice called for his partner in crime.

Whiny responded under his breath with an unflattering term before muttering, "Don't use my name, you bloody arse."

A second beam of light joined Brett's, doubling the chance of finding me.

Pressing as flat against the wall as possible, I wormed away from the pair. Every bump and bruise plaguing my body screamed, slowing my progress as flashlights played across the garden.

A soft glow erupted beneath my arm. Dolly's cell, coming to life from my constant wiggling.

I slapped my hand over it and dragged it under my heart hammering. Sweat prickled my brow despite the cold night.

"Over here!" Brett, aka Whiny, called.

Chapter Thirty: The Boot

Stock still, I waited, shielding the phone from betraying my position. Their lights didn't suddenly illuminate me. They hadn't seen the shine of the cell.

However, my hedgehog friend chose this moment to press his advantage, waddling toward me. Puffing up like, well, a puffer fish, his chuffing began anew.

"Shoo," I mouthed.

"Chuff," it responded, louder than before.

At some point, my captors would investigate why the hedgehog was making so much noise. They would see the bedsheet, find me, and….

Not finishing the thought, I fought down the high-pitched scream that formed at the back of my throat.

Army crawling backward, I inched away from the angry creature.

When his spines smoothed, his chuffing stopped, and so did I.

Wanting nothing more than to put my head down in the dirt and sleep, I instead tried to find further proof of my predicament.

"Stupid password," I muttered at the phone.

My eyes flew open. I never unlocked my phone when I took a gazillion pictures in Bath.

Checking, Dolly's cell worked the same way.

I pressed the camera icon on the lock screen. Input switched to video, I pressed record on the odd chance my Brett or Low Voice said something damning. Video running, I closed the device into my jacket pocket, wishing it had a zipper.

"Find her?" Low Voice answered, the lights pointing at something in the middle of the lawn.

Hoping the cell's mic caught their words, I held my breath.

"No, Brad," Brett spat. Annoyance with each other telegraphed through every exchange. "I would have said, wouldn't I?"

"Don't use my name, you eejit," Brad demanded.

The lights picked out an object on the ground, the beams creating a monstrous effect on my captors' faces.

At the very least, I had first names. Not much, but something.

Curiosity finally forced my head up to examine what they found. When a twig snapped, it echoed through the night like a gunshot.

Slamming my eyes shut, I counted to ten, pins and needles crawling like ants across the length of my body.

Nothing. They hadn't heard.

Peering through the hedgerow, I recognized my boot. The spin must have flung it.

Away from me.

Brad slapped Brett hard enough to make his head snap.

"You let her get away, didn't ya?" Brad accused, shining light into Brett's eyes. "Do you know what the Old Man is going to do to you? Pig slop!"

"Ahem," a voice cleared. "This way," a third, cultured voice commanded. I couldn't swear it was De Valence, but the way the two thugs snapped to attention didn't leave much doubt.

"Tell the doc, uh, doctor, we'll be right there with the donor."

Donor.

The shivering returned, cold from the ground seeping into my sore joints, terror filling my soul.

The clip of fine shoes on pavement indicated that the third man walked back to the house.

Brett's face, grimacing in pain, reflected across the lawn. Brad had him by the hair. "Find the ginger and get her to surgery," he growled before dropping his partner and stalking away to his boss.

"Coming, sir," he called.

My teeth started to chatter, despite clamping my jaw shut. Immobilized, frozen, and hunted, I watched the flashlight move from the boot toward town.

Knowing Brett could return any moment, I wormed away again, adding distance from the noisy critter and makeshift rope.

"Dolly," I sent quiet encouragement. "Be careful." Then for me, "And hurry."

Reverse army crawling went faster than worming, but also made more noise. If Brett returned, he would hear me.

Huffing with exertion, I continued inching away from the rope. As soon as someone braved busting through Dolly's bedroom door to find me, they would scour the area in earnest.

As I crawled, rocks and branches attacked my hands and face.

A sudden breeze cut across my legs, and I found myself exposed, having exited the bushes at the back of the house.

Adjusting to my bloody hands and one knee, I stared at a pair of work boots.

The scream died in my throat as Dolly's voice rushed to explain, "I found an extra pair in the stable."

Sturdy, with ankle support, I tossed my remaining dress boot into the bushes and pulled on the old pair. Only then did I brave standing.

"They're looking for me. For surgery." I shuddered, reaching for Lancelot.

"What have we gotten ourselves into?" Dolly asked before dropping to all fours next to the horse.

"Uh?" Eloquent. That's me.

"Step on my back to mount the horse."

"Dolly, I—"

"You're a foot taller than me," Dolly exaggerated. "I cannot possibly pull you up."

"Point," I conceded before placing the foot of my good leg on her back and throwing the other over Lancelot. He pranced, unused to the sensation of a person with no saddle. Dolly had thrown a blanket over his back to protect his coat.

Flexing my strong ankle, I held my arm firm. "Grab hold, then use my foot as your stirrup."

Dolly's determination outweighed her drug-addled brain, and she managed to land behind me without too much fuss.

Lancelot's prancing turned into pawing, and I feared he would bolt.

With a gentle pull on his reins, I leaned forward and whispered, "It's okay, buddy. Settle."

He stopped pawing the ground, but muscles jumped under his skin.

"Shh, shh, shh," I tried to calm our mount to no avail. He could sense my fear, smell it on my skin.

"Dolly," I changed tactics. "I need you to mirror my movements. Wrap your arms around tight and snug your legs against mine. You'll be tempted to control him yourself. Don't."

Wordlessly, she did as she was told, but her grip was weak.

"Good," I said, encouraging her. She rested her cheek on my back. "Don't fall asleep. I need you."

I felt her head come up.

"Tch, tch." Urging Lancelot, I caressed his flanks with my heels. He stepped forward at a stately pace.

Sighing, I guided him to the back of the property and toward the path to Comer Manor.

The possibility of safety somehow made the horror of being caught again worse. Every sound amplified, posing a new threat. Trees reached out with long, wicked talons. Shapes emerged and faded. The feeling of being watched itched up my spine.

"I feel like flippin' Snow White," I whispered, hoping to garner a laugh from Dolly.

Nothing.

"You know?" I prompted. "When she escapes in the woods, and the forest looks evil?"

Pressure released from my waist, and Dolly canted to one side.

"Dolly!" I shouted, immediately regretting it. We were moving slowly to avoid noise, which meant we could still be in earshot of De Valence Manor.

My outburst had one desired effect: Dolly's grip tightened around me.

"So sorry," she murmured. "My fault."

"Are you okay?"

"Mmmhmm." A slightly positive sigh.

It would have to do.

"Tch." Lancelot picked up our pace.

On high alert, I kept watch, head swiveling from side to side, unblinking. Although, the panicked buzzing in my ears made me less effective as a guard.

The canopy of the ancient trees blackened an already dark night. Our horse could see better than me, but I worried an exposed root, sticking out like a demonic foot, would send us all toppling.

As my eyes scanned the impenetrable wall of ivy and birch to my right, a claw raked my left cheek, pulling at my jacket.

"Ahhhh!" I screamed, releasing the reins to bat at my assailant.

Before registering that my hand grasped a branch, Lancelot reacted, prancing sideways before rushing forward.

Plunging toward his neck, I scooped the reins back into my hands, but not before Dolly let go.

In a split second, I chose to control our mount over grabbing her. If she fell while Lance ran, he could deal a deadly kick.

Fighting the impulse to yank him, I eased him back, cooing, "Steady, boy. Steady."

A canter slowed to a trot.

"That's it. Steady."

The trot transitioned to a jittery walk, allowing me to transfer my attention to Dolly.

"Hey," I called. Loud, but after all the noise we made, another shout wouldn't matter.

Twisting to see her, I swung my arm around to steady her.

Eyes fluttering open, she said, "Yes?" then pitched to the side, head aiming for the hard ground below.

Chapter Thirty-One: A Perfectly Acceptable Moment of Hysteria

"No!" I screeched, dropping Lancelot's reins and grabbing Dolly by the edge of her sweater as she tilted toward the ground.

The fine, bunny-soft wool slipped from my grasp, and I dug my fingertips into her flesh, causing enough pain to wake her.

"Ouch! AHHHH!" Her cries added to my grunts as I attempted to stabilize her.

I might be bigger, but deadlifting one hundred lbs of squirming human is beyond me.

"Take my arm!" I shouted over her screams.

The noise disturbed an already antsy Lancelot, and he picked up his pace.

With my right hand, I clutched Dolly by the waist of her jeans and buried the left into the horse's mane. With that handhold providing a tiny bit of control, I slowed him.

And I started to giggle.

What a ridiculous situation. Snorting with laughter, my grip loosened.

Dolly cartwheeled an arm back and landed a steel-vice hand on my leg, right below my swollen knee.

With a screech of pain and roiling nausea, I came to my senses. Clamping my jaw shut to escaping whines, I pulled on Dolly's jeans, leaning to the opposite side to create leverage.

Her leg shifted from flopping to slipping toward the correct side of Lancelot. I snaked my foot around her calf, anchoring it.

Unless we both fell off.

A snort of laughter blurted out of my mouth, quickly becoming a squeal of pain.

"Don't you dare," Dolly commanded in a way that would have made a queen proud—particularly impressive delivery from her perpendicular angle.

Effective as a good shake, I pulled myself together.

"Umph," I grunted with the effort of a final tug and got her on the horse's back.

Dolly's hands shook as they found their way around my waist.

Petting Lancelot's neck, I praised him. "Good boy. Thank you for not running off."

"Well, then," Dolly said. "That was an adventure." Shaking hands were the only sign of her state of mind.

"Indeed," I agreed. "Tch, tch. Come on, boy."

Soon enough, artificial light bloomed at the end of the trees.

"Look, Dolly," I breathed in relief. "We're almost there!"

Urging Lance forward, I heard Dolly gasp.

"Mrph," she said, as excited as I felt. She slapped my back a few times before her hands fumbled toward the reins.

"I got this," I told her, rushing toward the light and safety.

"No," she gasped, and I finally recognized urgency. "Stop."

Stop. What an odd thing to say. I didn't want to stop. I wanted to go in a full gallop. But there was terror in her voice.

"Whoa," I said to Lance, who ignored the command. "Hey, whoa," I said, using more force. He acted like Old Nigel heading to his barn.

"Oh no," I said, realization dawning on me. Horses always picked up speed when they sensed home. Home. De Valence Medispa.

"That bench we just passed is on our property," Dolly explained.

"We're going the wrong way," I finished.

While we dangled, Lancelot must have walked in circles, and I didn't realize it when we started again.

Staring at the light, I ignored Lancelot's insistent strain toward home, but

I didn't move him away. Tears stung my eyes, burning down my cheeks.

Smack. Smack. A dull rapping on my shoulder.

Almost. We were so close, and now we were back where we started. The thought was unbearable.

Smack.

Thwack, thwack, thwack in rapid succession.

It didn't matter. Nothing mattered. Everything I did turned out wrong. Why bother trying to run?

"Get it together, McGuire." The admonishment from behind me sounded strange in Dolly's posh accent. But it worked.

With a swipe at my face, I nodded.

"Come on, boy," I whispered, turning Lancelot around.

He resisted, testing my waning strength.

Summoning every lesson my first riding teacher ever gave, I took charge. "Oh no, you don't," I said with more confidence than I felt.

Lancelot relented, plodding dejectedly away from his stall.

I sniffled. One more tear leaked out, either in relief or pity for myself.

"Grrrrr," I growled. No one had the right to turn me to putty, and it happened one too many times that day.

"I say, did you just growl?"

"Yep," I practically spat. With another inarticulate sound, I said, "I don't know about you, but I'm getting pretty sick of being hunted."

"Agreed."

"We've made so much noise already," I started to tell her my plan.

"They have heard us or not. Either way, we need to leave," she finished for me.

"Pronto," I agreed. "Can you hold on tight?" I avoided adding *this time*.

"Too right," she said.

Seated on our mount, I started us off at a trot that quickly moved into a canter. I didn't want to take him faster as our weight on his bareback could strain him.

"Hurry," Dolly urged in my ear.

Without much encouragement, Lancelot opened up, charging forward, our weight clearly not a concern.

Cold autumn air leaked through my jacket, chilling me and turning Dolly's hands icy. It wouldn't do to arrive at our destination with hypothermia, so I slowed Lance's thundering hooves.

Brrzzzzz.

In the relative quiet of our slower pace, the sound of a chainsaw filled the night.

Which didn't make sense. Who in their right mind would cut down trees at this hour?

The buzzing shifted, becoming louder and more constant.

"Oh no." Dolly sounded panicked, lifting her head. "The ATVs. Get off the path."

Not a chainsaw, an engine with no muffler. Brain fog still clogged my thoughts.

"Where?" I asked, the tangle of ivy and trees creating a wall on both sides of the track.

Dolly let go of me, saying, "Help me down." Flexing my foot, she stepped on it and swung her other leg over. Landing with a wobble, she steadied herself before holding her hand out for the reins.

I turned them over, and she led Lancelot and me toward impenetrable vegetation.

I bemoaned, "Sorry I insisted on the big horse. I don't know that we will be able to hide him."

Dolly ignored me, her eyes intent on finding an opening.

"If we let him go, he will head home, and maybe they won't find us."

"Tch," she said, hushing me before walking straight into a solid mass of ivy.

A light bounced high and cut across my back for a second, the engine's whine loud as the wheels left the ground. He must have jumped a tree root.

He was close.

Turning back to report the news, I found myself alone. Dolly gone.

"No," I whispered. No way. She wouldn't leave me, not after everything. She would not.

"Come on, you stubborn cow." Dolly's voice, talking to the horse as he shook his head.

Angling toward Lance's neck, I flattened myself.

I knew she wouldn't leave me.

Unable to see anything, I trusted my friend and gently nudged the horse forward.

Vines slapped my face as we plowed through. After a moment, we opened into a folly, a random garden structure designed to look nice and do little else.

Lancelot's horseshoes clanged on the stone floor of the miniature temple. Barely big enough for the three of us, the horse danced in nervous steps.

"Hey, shh, shh, shh." While I stroked his nose, Dolly removed his blanket and ran her hand along his back.

He settled with a snort just as an ATV roared by.

Then stopped.

Our pursuer must have only gone a few yards past our hiding place before something halted his search.

Lancelot chose this moment to verbally express his displeasure in a piercing whinny.

Dolly and I froze.

The ATV's engine cut off.

Silence.

Heat ticked off the cooling motor like a clock counting down our doom.

Go away, go away, I chanted in my head.

Work boots crunched on the gravel.

Pacing, turning, pausing, the relentless sounds of the rider searching for us. A flashlight beam pierced our hiding place and remained steadfastly on my face.

Chapter Thirty-Two: Exposed

I slammed my eyes shut against the light that penetrated our vine-covered enclave. Still as a statue, I willed the intruder to mistake my hair for fall foliage.

A hand reached through bushes, exposing us further.

No way was I going to allow us to get caught. Not after escaping the treatment room, climbing out a third-floor window, encountering angry hedgehogs, and stealing a horse.

A horse! Big and unpredictable, a lot of people were afraid of them.

"Move Lancelot," I ordered Dolly, maneuvering the horse's powerful hindquarters into kicking position.

"Maddie? That you?"

The voice sounded familiar, but I didn't trust my muddled brain to respond.

"You think you can keep your wee horse from trampling me?" he asked.

No one would call the giant bay "wee" except a Scot.

"Edward?" My voice wafer thin. Hope turned my resolve to goo, my body shook, tears returned in full force.

"I don't mean to interrupt this lovely reunion," Dolly interrupted as I blubbered uselessly. "Are you quite sure you were not followed? We do seem to be in a bit of a predicament."

Understatement of the century.

"Right," I said, rubbing my face. "We're in trouble."

"Quite a kerfuffle going on at the spa," he confirmed.

As much as I wanted to know how he found us and that he wasn't followed, escape was higher on the list.

Emerging from the secret garden, I saw Edward's motorcycle. Not an ATV.

"Does your phone have service? We need the police. DCI Bray, preferably." I paused, inventorying our state. "Can you take Dolly to Comer Manor at the end of the road? I'll take the wee pony," I said, giving Lancelot an affectionate pat.

Flexing muscles in his jaw indicated Edward wanted to argue, but he didn't. Nodding, he sent a text, then removed the spare helmet from the back of his bike and handed it to Dolly.

I returned Lance's blanket to his back and looked at him. We were both exhausted.

"I'm sorry." Speaking to him quietly, I stroked his neck. "Just a bit further. Do you think you can make it?"

I swear he managed to look offended at the suggestion that he was not perfectly up to the challenge.

Patting the horse, I instructed Edward, "Help me up."

Cupping his hands at knee height, he held them out. I stepped in and returned to my mount. If Lancelot could carry on, so could I.

"Don't stray too far ahead," I cautioned.

"You go first. You'll not find me taking my eyes off you again," he promised.

With that encouragement, I guided my mighty steed in the correct direction and set out at a gallop. The roar of Edward's motorcycle followed us.

Lancelot's cadence changed after a few minutes, and I realized I couldn't run him flat out for too long. Dolly said they could walk from the De Valence home to Comer Manor in a little over an hour. Walking at a brisk rate meant three miles, but more likely closer to two-and-a-half as a leisurely stroll.

Too far to make Lancelot gallop. I slowed him to a canter, hoping the motorcycle wouldn't plow into us. Edward matched our pace seamlessly.

Exhaustion crept over me, starting at my toes and traveling into my legs, making it challenging to stay on.

Slowing further, I slumped forward, my fingers numb from clinging to the reins so tightly.

Lancelot huffed, jerking me into awareness.

"Thanks, buddy."

I straightened.

That's when I saw the light. Unlike at the spa, a warm yellow spilled softly through the foliage.

Without waiting for direction, Lancelot sensed the finish line and surged forward. Pulling into the curved driveway, I recognized Simon's Citroen.

"Thank goodness," I breathed. "Sanctuary."

Edward cut the engine on the motorcycle and checked Dolly. Although dazed by the ride and everything else, she answered his questions well enough.

Swaying unsteadily, I wondered if my hands would ever relax enough to let go.

"Let's get you down offa there, lassie," Edward offered.

Covering my hands in his, he infused me with warmth. "Come on, lassie. I've got you."

Unwilling to give up control, my body refused to move.

Lucky for me, Edward recognized shock when he saw it and continued his gentle urging until I practically fell on him. Although the same height, he was much stronger than me, and he turned the action into a tender embrace.

Dolly led our savior horse to a stable yard and took charge when she returned.

"Right," she said regally. "Are you quite ready?"

Nodding, I stood tall and agreed. "Quite."

One step in, I began to topple, my knee unable to support my weight.

Edward jumped in to support me. "Let's try that again, shall we?"

A sorry sight, we arrived at the grand manor house door. I was all for plowing in, but Dolly politely rang the carved brass bell.

A very tall, thin, white-haired man opened the door and bowed his head to Dolly. "Lady Gwendolyn," he intoned formally, not batting an eye at her bedraggled appearance. "I shall inform the Lord of your arrival."

Like we were expected.

Looking me over without a hint of judgment, he asked, "Ms. McGuire?"

I nodded.

"Wonderful. This way."

"Hawthorn," Dolly addressed the butler. "I've put our mount in the stables. Could you call a groom from the village to care for him and send me the bill?"

"Of course, but no need. I will take care of it."

"No, no. I insist. Completely my fault the poor thing is so knackered."

Hawthorn assented with a nod. "I'm sure Rupert will be happy to care for his immediate needs."

I assumed Rupert was a groom, but Dolly asked, "And how is your nephew?"

It was amazing how they were making normal conversation when I could barely keep my eyes open.

"Precocious as ever." Hawthorn chuckled, a fond expression on his wrinkled face.

Wondering how old Rupert was, I hoped he was up to the task of taking care of Lancelot.

As Edward assisted me into the library, he kept checking the door as if he wanted to bolt.

"Sit with me," I insisted, choosing an intricately carved wooden bench and avoiding anything with fabric. Leaves and dirt rained off me in little showers with every step.

"Of course," he assented, but his muscles coiled so tightly he could spring up and hurtle away at any moment.

"What happened to not taking your eyes off me?" I teased. Catching sight of myself in the gilt-framed mirror, I regretted it.

A bruise I didn't remember getting ballooned under my eye, angry red and purple. My hair hung half in and half out of its ponytail, wispy and carefree but rather like a demented mushroom. A dense cover of mud and mulch clung everywhere else.

All in all, pig slop described me best.

Excellent.

Simon rushed into the room with a casual air. He needed to teach me that technique.

Taking in his guests with a glance, he nodded at Dolly, who looked smudged and a bit ruffled but otherwise elegant as ever.

He addressed me. "Find yourself in a bit of a mess, then?"

"Nothing some female ingenuity couldn't handle." If there was one thing I learned about dealing with the aristocracy, hysterics simply would not do. "But, a bit of assistance wouldn't be amiss."

"Shall I call DCI Bray?" Hawthorn inquired as he helped a woman his age with a tea cart.

It had been maybe half a second since we arrived. When did he call for tea, and how the heck did they make it so fast? Magic, this staff.

"I took the liberty of contacting DI Parikh and asking him to pass along the message," Edward told the room.

"Mrs. H.," Simon addressed the woman. "Would you be so kind as to create an ice bag for my friend? She seems to be swelling. Visibly." Removing a silk handkerchief from his pocket, he shook it once and handed it to me.

"Better make it two," Dolly added.

With a startle, Mrs. H. assessed my appearance.

"Right away," she said and scurried off.

I dabbed and wiped at everything that wasn't swelling. Chunks of mud and bark thunked to the antique rug at our feet.

Pig was right. I couldn't be trusted in a nice house.

Returning with a tray of towels and ice bags, Mrs. H. offered one to Dolly before coming to my aid. She took Simon's dirty handkerchief from me and stuffed it in her housecoat pocket. Next, she handed me a towel, warm and lemon-scented.

As I gingerly cleaned my face, she pulled an ornately embroidered ottoman in front of me, covered it with a plain, clean towel, and lifted my foot to it with the utmost care. She removed the riding boots Dolly had given me and tut-tutted at the condition of my torn and bleeding feet.

When the ice bag went on my knee, I expected more immediate relief.

"Eye masks," I moaned.

Both Mrs. H. and Edward looked at me, waiting for an explanation.

Pointing, I asked, "Could you go up my pant leg and remove the eye masks? I used them as makeshift ice packs."

Edward obliged, removing one. "How many?"

"Three originally, but at least one fell out by Dolly's room. The other might be in the bushes or on the path. Like a trail of breadcrumbs," I added with an eye roll.

Mrs. H. lifted my hand and turned it palm up. Covered in a rash, the sight of it exploded in a fit of scratching.

"What did you get yourself into, Miss?" she asked, separating my hands.

"Hedgehog," I said, then laughed. "Pigs and hogs, hogs and pigs." Nonsense bubbled out of me, but it felt necessary. I kept circling back to pigs.

"Patchy," I spat in what sounded like more babbling.

With a cocked eyebrow, Edward said, "Your cliffside companion?"

I shook my head and then nodded, causing a wave of dizziness to wash over me. Edward wrapped an arm around my shoulders and said, "You've thought of something."

"The farmer, Nigel. He did this to us. Drugged our tea somehow."

Disentangling himself from my grasp, he stood. "I'll report this, try and catch him tonight."

And he left.

Again.

Chapter Thirty-Three: Confrontations

Yes, the information I provided to Edward was a vital clue. Yes, it required following up. But he literally just promised to keep me within eyesight. And while, no, I don't feel the need for protection or supervision twenty-four/seven, I would like for my boyfriend to sit with me for a while after being drugged and almost forced into organ donation.

If he still qualified as my boyfriend, that is. I mean, I still had zero idea what's going on with the unicorn tattoo, or his brother, or his work, or how he found us. A boyfriend should share that kind of info.

Holding an ice bag with soft fabric and a screw top to my cheek like a film heroine from 1955, I sighed. My love life should take a backseat to everything else, but I couldn't keep the facts straight.

Dolly's eyes had taken on a haunted, vacant look. I didn't know if she would be much help when we explained our predicament, as she called it, to Simon.

"You seem to have developed a knack for driving people off," Simon commented.

I smiled despite everything. "Right? The farmer who helped me after I found the girl. He drugged us and dumped us at the spa."

A full-body spasm shook me, and Simon, in an overwhelming and uncharacteristic show of emotion, took my hand.

"Simon," I squeezed his fingers around mine. "They were prepping me for surgery. Organ harvesting."

"Recovery is the proper term," he corrected.

The same thing Parikh said. "Fine. Whatever. I think you missed the point."

The accusation caused a raised eyebrow from Simon. "Drugged, yes. Dolly hasn't been quite right of late."

"Exactly," I pounced at the slight hint of agreement. "And—"

"However," Simon overrode my following statement. "To my knowledge, all of her organs are intact."

"No. Well, yes, but they drugged her to keep her quiet. I got a different one." I batted the words away like gnats. "I know it sounds crazy," I confessed, but then I couldn't remember what I wanted to say next. If convincing Simon was this hard, the police would never listen to me. Let alone accusing De Valence of masterminding the whole thing.

To keep his involvement secret until I could privately talk to DCI Bray, I kept my mouth shut. Any hint that Dolly and I knew the truth, and he would scrub the place clean before anyone could find evidence.

"I should tell all this to the police first."

Simon patted my hand, then stepped away.

"Dolly," I called her to my side.

How much did she remember, and did she suspect her uncle?

"You're cleaning up quite nicely," she commented.

A bold but well-intentioned lie.

"You never looked dirty in the first place."

"Yes, well, mud wouldn't dare cling to me."

The comment sounded like something Simon would say, and I liked her for it.

"So far, all I've managed to do is sound crazy. What do you remember?"

The library door swung open, and Lady Vivian Pacock demanded, "What is that person doing in my home?" An imperious finger pointed my way.

Simon bristled. "My home, Aunt Viv."

"I thought I made myself clear that you were to leave the country immediately," she continued over Simon.

Not to be outdone, he stomped on her words. "And she has rescued Dolly, so if you could attempt civility...." He trailed off, looking from her to me.

"Aunt Viv, you can't fire Ms. Niven's team members. Or mine. I've told you that."

I wondered how many times she'd tried to have interns fired in the past. Jeez.

Ignoring both of them, Dolly rushed to the man standing behind Lady Vivian. Clarence De Valence.

Did I warn her not to tell him anything? I meant to. "Dolly, don't—"

"Oh, Uncle," she cried, the calm she exhibited crumbling at the sight of him. "It was awful. They've been drugging me and doing illegal surgery at our home!"

Sigh.

"Rubbish," he said, stroking her hair. His crystal blue eyes impaled me from across the room.

Wishing Edward hadn't abandoned me again, I bolstered myself and refused to look as intimidated as I felt. It's hard to pull off swagger from a seated position, foot propped on a fancy footrest.

Fine. *Let Dolly tell our story*, I decided. They would believe her.

"No, Uncle. Really. It's been awful. I have been forgetting things—"

"That explains it, then," De Valance interrupted. "You have been avoiding your wellness treatments. Once you start those again, you will be perfect."

"Of course, yes, but that's not it at all," Dolly corrected and tried again. "Tonight, I went to a pub in Stroud."

"Now," De Valance took over. "What were you doing at a place like that? You know Michael puts on a brilliant trivia night."

The gall of this man, talking of trivia night when he masterminded a deadly black-market surgery.

"Yes, of course," Dolly repeated, frustration showing in her balled-up fists. A girl after my own heart.

"But the point is, Uncle, that I went tonight because I felt I had been there before. And people remembered me."

"All the more reason for you to avoid it," De Valence said, missing the point by several miles.

The cunning he exhibited in controlling her made my skin crawl. Muddling her logic, distracting her line of thought, he could continue to drug her for years, and no one would know.

"Really, my dear. You must understand how your actions reflect on me and the spa."

The dialog sounded vaguely familiar, but I couldn't put my finger on it. A father figure berating a young woman, telling her she's not good enough.

When it clicked, I almost shouted it. "Oph." I cut myself off, sending what could be interpreted as an insult into the air.

"Ow, oh oaf!" I covered, not having to pretend pain in my knee. Subtle, that's me.

Ignoring me, Dolly kept trying to explain. I wanted to scream.

My mom's module about women's support systems in Shakespearean plays returned to me. Her brother told Ophelia she was not good enough and then left. Her dad told her she shouldn't think, her mind too close to that of a child. He would think for her. Then, he was murdered. She had no one left to think for her, and she wandered into a stream and was pulled under by the weight of her garments. Suicide or confusion, either way, her lack of support was to blame.

Dolly had steel in her, which meant subjugating her required higher stakes.

As I readied myself to enter the fray, Lady Vivian interjected that we should shower.

"No." I stated it in a way that brooked no argument.

"Rubbish." "But Maddie." "Do be quiet." De Valence, Dolly, and Lady Vivian all argued.

My assertiveness skills, could use some work.

Simon, bless him, held a hand up and nodded to me.

"None of you will believe us unless we have proof. We need to be tested." They stared.

"By the police," I added for good measure.

"Absolutely," Dolly agreed and marched across the room to stand beside me.

Struggling to control my emotions at the sudden show of support, I took another swipe at my face with the towel Mrs. H. provided.

With a glance between us, Simon called for Hawthorn. The stately butler entered the room as if by magic.

"When will your niece be picking up Rupert?" Simon asked.

"I believe her car is just pulling up," Hawthorn responded without a hint of questioning on his face. I bet Simon could ask for a diamondback rattlesnake, and the man would procure one from his jacket pocket.

"Bring her to us, would you?"

Hawthorn bowed his head in acknowledgment, left, and returned with a middle-aged woman in nurses' scrubs.

"Lady Vivian, how delightful to see you," she said, going to shake the dowager countess's hand.

"Lovely to see you again, Abigail. We do apologize for disrupting your evening, but Simon needs your expertise regarding these young women."

Her statement confirmed my notion that she and Simon communicated telepathically.

Abigail looked at me and jumped.

Peeking at my reflection, I discovered that removing the dirt did not improve my appearance. A jumble of red, blue, and purple decorated most of my face.

"I'm fine," I said unconvincingly as she rushed toward me.

Simon approached and corrected her course. "These women have been subjected to a crime and possibly drugged. Can you take samples as evidence?"

The nurses' professional demeanor snapped into place. "Yes. Blood?"

With a nod, Simon glanced at me. "And urine?"

"Yeah, probably."

"If you have any idea what you were given, it will speed the results," she said.

"I think Dolly was given some sort of roofie. Me, a knockout drug."

Fierce eyes bore into me, the blue of De Valence's stare cold and calculating.

"Be careful," I muttered sotto voce. "People may not want you to find anything."

Tracing my eye-line back to De Valence, she vowed, "I'll be careful."

Standing, she directed the situation. "Lady Gwendolyn, you first. Come along."

I wondered if I would see Dolly again that night.

Chapter Thirty-Four: Stirrings in the Night

Nurse Abigail returned for me. Taking me to an artfully appointed but oddly proportioned bathroom, she collected samples. Meticulously labeling and bagging them, she sealed them into her medical bag.

"Don't you worry, now," she told me. "I know what to do."

A pair of silk pajamas and a pink robe perched on the counter. She pointed to them. "Shower now. Lots of hot water. I've left a salve for your bruises, and you'll need to ask Mrs. H. for more ice when you're through. Off you go."

No encouragement required, I started to strip down before she closed the door on her way out.

The water clunked in the pipes and came out of the tankless water heater contraption in fits when it first started. Steam enveloped me almost immediately, melting away dirt and horrid memories.

Drying off, I took stock. My legs, once show-off quality in sundresses, now looked diseased with discoloration and swelling. Moisture made my wet hair appear dark, bringing the red to clash with the pink robe.

The salve Hawthorn's niece left had a greenish tinge, and while it felt amazing, it created the appearance of gangrene.

At least Edward wasn't here to see it.

Cinching the robe tightly around me, I went back to the library to discover the police had arrived and were gathered in a far corner.

Including Edward.

I puffed a breath of air and went to Dolly's side. The pink robe complemented her complexion, and her freshly scrubbed skin glowed.

No one spoke, and the tension crackling between Parikh and Edward could have charged a car battery.

"What's happening?" I whispered.

Dolly shrugged. "I don't know. They've been glaring at each other since your constable arrived."

Coming to a decision, I took Dolly by the shoulders and turned her toward me. "Whether you remember it or not, we've been through a lot together."

She made to interrupt, but I held up a hand. "Let me finish. I need to tell you this." A deep breath. "You are annoyingly lovely."

A brilliant smile erupted on her face. "And you are inspiringly kick-ass."

My eyes bulged in shock, and she giggled at my reaction.

"Not to mention the center of every man's attention. Talk about annoying," she said with a flip of her damp hair.

On impulse, we hugged.

"Maddie, my bonnie lass!"

Edward registered my entrance and, from his expression, had noted that a thorough cleaning had not helped my appearance.

"I'm fine. What is going on?"

With a stony face, he admitted, "I couldn't find the farmer."

I glanced sidelong at De Valence and confided, "There is someone else in charge they referred to as the Old Man."

DI Parikh inserted himself. "I'll need to interview you now, Miss McGuire."

"Yes, sir. Of course. Whatever you say." Edward's words conveyed a sarcasm he never used at work.

"Your assistance is no longer required, Mr. Bailey," Parikh said with a formality unsuited to the occasion.

Mister. Not constable.

"What is going on here?" I asked again.

"We need to take your information, please. This way."

I shook my head. "No. This is like being in a Daphne de Maurier novel. Everyone all polite, with a layer of seething hatred behind every word. "Edward, why are you so mad?"

Stoic silence.

"Detective Inspector Parikh," I tried a different approach. "What has Edward done?"

The compact man removed his glasses and pinched the bridge of his nose. "Mr. Bailey," he said, emphasizing the word "mister," "did not call in his location. As he moves every three days, he needs to report his location to us." With a glare directed at Edward, he added, "Even if time off was requested. And taken without approval."

So much to unpack. To start, why did Edward not wait for approval? Even more confounding, why does he move every three days?

I poked Edward in the ribs. A smirk appeared and vanished.

"Why didn't you call in?"

A granite statue had more emotive power.

"Fine. I'll talk for you," I decided. "Being a constable is the single most important thing in Edward Bailey's life. If he did anything to jeopardize that, it was for family. He went to Scotland to rescue his brother."

"Scotland," DCI Bray interjected.

Edward bowed his head.

"What's wrong with Scotland?" I wanted to know.

"The Avon and Somerset Constabulary does not allow just anyone off the streets to be an officer," DCI Bray informed us.

If that was supposed to mean something, it required clarification. "How did Edward pass the vetting process?" I asked, knowing he had a rough childhood in a dodgy part of Edinburgh.

"A recommendation and a promise. A restriction, if you will," Bray said.

Did they teach "infuriatingly vague" at the police academy?

Looking at Edward, I willed him to talk.

He did. "To not return to Edinburgh."

Oh no. Not helping, I disclosed the most damaging evidence possible to Edward's career.

"Which explains why he didn't call in his location," Parikh fumed.

Instead of explaining, Edward turned to stone.

"To get his brother," I said, indignant on his behalf. "He had to fight a gang leader and everything."

Parikh finally looked Edward in the eye. "Is this true, Bailey?"

"Aye," he responded, the Scottish accent he normally hid at work out in full force. "Fought William for James. And warned him not to send anyone else."

Bray muttered something like, "Good Lord," but otherwise remained impassive.

"Like a gothic duel?" I asked, incensed at the idea.

"Aye. A bit. He let me win," Edward offered.

"Win? With the damage he inflicted?"

"He could have killed me. He didn't."

A fact I could have lived without.

"Did he reveal who their contact is?" Parikh asked, which lost me for a moment.

Not to send anyone like Sherrie? Reading between the lines, I reasoned that William, Edward's elder brother, was in charge of the gang that Sherrie and James were in. And they must have sent Sherrie to England for some reason, and Edward didn't want James or anyone else to suffer the same fate.

I listened harder, searching for facts to confirm my theory.

"No, sir. The only thing William said was, 'Watch out for snow.' I dinnae ken what it means."

They stopped talking. No more facts or confirmation, but I had to do something to fix what I broke.

While the tension eased, I pounced at the opportunity to help Edward.

"So, yes, he violated a rule, but for family. And he got a clue." I turned my swollen, blackened eyes on Parikh. "That has to count for something, doesn't it?"

He replaced his glasses and said nothing. Sometimes the British gift of not showing emotions made me crazy.

Managing not to stamp my fuzzy slippered foot, I turned my appeal to Bray. "Doesn't it?" I demanded.

"Ah, well," Bray said, and everyone seemed to accept that the matter was closed.

Edward kissed my forehead and asked, "Would you like me to drive you home in the morning?"

I nodded, watching him go as a pit opened in my stomach.

Which picked that exact moment to growl. Loudly.

Hawthorn jumped to action before Simon could raise a finger. Small sandwiches and scones appeared after a few moments.

Dolly and I attacked them before being guided to different corners, Parikh with me and DCI Bray with her.

"What happened?" Parikh asked me with a concerned tone I appreciated.

"I'm going to start at the end and work backward because I'm less fuzzy about those events."

He nodded.

"Edward found us on the trail as we escaped on horseback."

"How did Constable Bailey know where you were?"

Constable, not mister. Perhaps my unwelcome intervention made a difference.

My brow furrowed. How did he know? I shook my head, leaving that mystery for another in a long line that Edward still needed to answer.

Suppositions aside, how many of my guesses were correct? Saving his younger brother James from what appeared to be a black-market operation sounded like the Edward I knew and loved.

Whoa. *Loved*? Or just an expression. I mean, what did I really know about him? The list I made before lacked way too many details. Like where he lived.

"Miss McGuire?" Parikh interrupted my train of thought.

"Huh?" Eloquence personified. "Sorry. My brain went down a rabbit hole. What was the question?"

Deftly, Parikh changed the dynamic of the interview. "Why don't you just tell me whatever comes into your head? No more interruptions."

Firmly pushing thoughts of Edward aside, I babbled bits and bobs, as Lily would say. "We used bed sheets to climb out of Dolly's bedroom. I lost my boot. There were two of them. Captors, not boots. Well, actually, there were originally two boots, but I only lost one. Brett found it."

My eyes got wide. "Brett! One was named Brett. And then I turned Dolly's phone to record." At this, I stood, excited. "I recorded our escape in case they said anything. The recording might be muffled from my pocket, but it's worth listening to."

"You might be right," Parikh agreed, also standing. "Where is it."

I patted my robe pocket, rolled my eyes at myself, and said, "My jean jacket."

With agility I didn't know he had, Parikh bolted up to the bathroom and returned with the dusty garment.

I turned out each pocket.

Nothing.

"It must have slipped out when Dolly fell off the horse," I moaned.

"I remember that," Dolly exclaimed, her interview halted by Parikh's behavior. "Fell asleep, and the next thing I knew, you tried to pull me up by my skin."

"It's not my fault your cashmere sweater had no purchase," I countered.

Both Bray and Parikh watched this exchange bemused.

"How did you come by the horse?" Bray asked Dolly.

Parikh, however, left the room, beckoning Simon to go with him. When the detective inspector returned, he explained, "Simon will guide one of the locals down the path in a search."

"Did you call it?"

Parikh nodded. "Straight to voicemail."

He added, "I think sleep will do more for your memory than my questions."

Exhaustion hit me like a brick at his words. With his butler magic, Hawthorn appeared and helped me to a small but sumptuous guest room.

Crawling under the cool covers, I waited for sleep to overtake me.

But it didn't.

"Come on," I said out loud. "Can't anything be easy?"

Something niggled at me, a chore perhaps.

"Lancelot." Deciding I would sleep better once I confirmed the horse who saved us was well cared for, I slipped on Dolly's boots, careful to tuck in the silk pajama legs, and ventured out to the stables.

As the only horse, he was easy to find.

"Hey, buddy," I greeted him. "Thanks for everything."

His huge hooves plodded toward me, and I saw that his coat gleamed and a clean blanket covered his back. Oats and fresh water sat in pails in his pen.

"Rupert did a good job, didn't he?"

"He always does," a male voice commented.

Too tired to scream, I twitched and said, "Hey, buddy," to Simon.

"The same greeting as the horse?"

"This horse saved my life. I'm quite fond of him," I defended. "How long have you been here."

"I followed you out," he admitted. "We found Dolly's phone, but the battery died. The police are charging it now."

"It was awful, Simon. Dolly kept saying the same polite thing over and over. I hope the recording proves something."

Simon picked up a handful of oats and held them out to Lancelot. "I'm sure it will. Thank you."

Not articulating the rest of his gratitude didn't matter to me. What mattered was that Simon believed us.

"I followed her into the pub in Stroud after your aunt fired me."

"You are not fired," he reiterated.

"Thank you." I shoulder-bumped him. "Nigel, the farmer where I found the girl's body, was there."

Lancelot snuffled the oats. "Nigel would have sugar for you," I commented, and electricity shot through me.

I grabbed Simon's arm. "Sugar. I'm sure he drugged us with sugar cubes. I fished mine out and dumped it in a plant behind a corner table. We need to go back and find it."

Chapter Thirty-Five: Bunny and Horse

As much as I wanted to charge to the pub, Simon convinced me of the wisdom of sending the police. "Chain of evidence and all," he explained in a rather pompous tone.

As he called DI Parikh and gave instructions, he guided me to the guest room. "I just want to go home," I whined.

"Safer here for now," he whispered. "Your constable will be here in the morning."

"Tomorrow," I ventured, nervous about his response. "You won't close ranks on me? Let De Valence sweep it under the rug?"

Simon graced me with his best down-the-nose sneer before softening. "It's a valid question," he admitted with a brief hug.

As I drifted into a dreamless sleep, I realized he didn't answer.

* * *

The following day I couldn't move. Every single solitary muscle in my body ached and throbbed.

"Ow."

At one point, someone lit the small fireplace in the corner, laundered my clothes, and left a tea tray on the nightstand.

I eyed it, willing it to be coffee.

A pot of tea with milk and a side of oat cakes and jam.

"Alas," I sighed, wishing I was home with my mom to take care of me.

Immediately regretting my ingratitude, I shimmied upright and poured myself a cup.

The steaming, creamy beverage warmed my insides, and I admitted that maybe the Brits were onto something with this tea thing.

Contrary to DI Parikh's hope, memories of the previous night continued to evade me. Random questions crowded my thoughts. Where was my purse? Is there coffee downstairs? Do you toast oat cakes or heat them in an oven?

When I forced my mind toward the events that took place at the medispa, memories skittered away like a nervous horse.

The horse, Lancelot, I remembered, but the ride came and went.

Rubbing my temples, I gingerly swung my feet to the thick carpet and padded around the room. Small, but with high ceilings and ornate crown moldings, I went to the only piece of furniture other than the bed and nightstand. A delicate secretary perched under the window. Pulling open the writing flap, I discovered stationery.

I sat on an embroidered stool and, employing DI Parikh's method, let my mind go and wrote every thought without editing or thinking. My mom sometimes had her students try stream-of-consciousness writing to discover themes that stood out in plays. Today, I used it to spur my subconscious into revealing its secrets.

Ten minutes of constant writing created two pages of world-class drivel. Not surprisingly, Edward appeared quite often, but a few things stood out.

Grabbing more sheets of paper, I created two lists, one titled Questions, the other Memories.

Colored markers would have been terrific at this point, but I underlined everything in my ramblings that held value.

Questions: How did Edward know where to find me? Why did De Valence allow the kidnap victims in his home? Were the captors part of Edward's old gang? And, because I missed it, where was my purse?

Memories: Farmer Nigel found us at the bar and gave us the drugged sugar. Nigel stuffed me into a van. Two men, one with a low voice and one a nasally whine, dumped me in a treatment room and kept watch. A room prepped for surgery. Which I flooded to cause a distraction.

I paused, something critical staring at me. Their names, maybe? Important, but not correct.

The names started with B, both of them, I noted to keep the thought from distracting me.

Not that many memories flooded the paper yet, so what was I missing? I reread the lists.

The van.

It smelled of rotting vegetables. Not essential, but the conjured scent caused my stomach to turn.

I vomited in the van. That was it. If my blood didn't show drugs, that would.

After organizing all my notes, I dressed, noting that Mrs. H. must have done laundry in the middle of the night. I owed this household so much.

Navigating the stairs proved challenging as I wasn't willing to bump on my bottom in Lady Vivian's home. Determined, I clung to the polished wood banister and sort of hop-stepped to the foyer. Not the most graceful descent on earth, but at least it qualified as upright.

Hawthorn greeted me. "Mr. Edward is waiting in the library." After a brief hesitation, he gestured to a chair by the door. "I'll fetch him for you, shall I?"

Much as I wanted to protest, my knee took the lead, and I plopped on the seat. "Thank you," I called as he retreated. "And thank Mrs. H. You've both been so kind."

He paused, turned, and said, "Think nothing of it." But he said it with a smile.

Comer Manor showed its age more than the medispa. Pipes rattled, radiators hissed, and floors creaked. Still, it exuded quiet elegance. White marble floors kept the atmosphere light against the richly stained wood wainscoting. Tall, mullioned windows boasted hidden gems like terracotta soldiers or a bronze stag outside.

Very befitting of Lady Vivian.

I should be furious with her, but I couldn't summon the energy. She did what she thought best for Simon and the manor.

And, annoyingly, I still craved her approval.

Edward appeared, sparing me from further contemplation on that front.

He extended a helping hand, but I gave him my notes and remained seated.

"Could you make sure DI Parikh gets these? I used his interview technique to dredge up memories."

"Right away," he said without a hint of Scottish brogue.

The Northern accent that caused my heart to flutter was less appreciated at the force. I hoped that the return of his posh cadence meant something positive for his career.

When he returned, he asked before helping me to my feet, "Ready?"

"I am," I answered.

At that, he scooped me up and carried me outside. "This way is faster," he said as I spluttered indignantly.

A tiny Smart Car sat poised at the end of the parking lot. I recognized it as belonging to a friend of his mother's, but I had yet to meet the friend.

Settling in, I eased my knee straight and arranged the seatbelt to avoid my absurd number of bruises.

"The first question on your list," he said once we were on the road.

"Yeah?"

"Your friend Lily saw me at the Boater and said you were acting strange. She didn't want to call the police, but she'd seen me at the Baths with you and figured I was the boy you always went on about."

At that, he raised his eyebrows with a glance in my direction.

Blushing, I said, "Okay, so maybe I talk about you to my friends. It's no big deal."

"She showed me your texts. Strange didn't cover it."

I squinted, trying to recall. "I don't remember texting Lily," I admitted. "What did it say?"

"The line that concerned me said, 'tea brew brew tea' or something like that and ended with a string of emojis."

"I never use a string of emojis," I insisted.

"Exactly."

When I concentrated, a hint of the text with Lily came back. This level of confusion must have been terrifying for Dolly, who had consistently been given drugs designed to erase her memory.

"So, what, you went to Stroud?" I asked. A smidge overprotective, but also very sweet.

He nodded. "To the pub closest to the train station. You weren't there, but since you were following a De Valence, I went to the medispa. Lights on with people shouting. Rough voices that shouldn't have been there," he added. "People were searching, and so I took the trail."

"Thank you," I said, meaning it. We would have made it to Comer Manor, but sparing Lancelot a second rider helped.

"The horse was easy to spot. Lucky they didn't think of it."

With a cold spasm, I said, "They're used to their victims being drugged and incapacitated."

Acknowledging my discomfort, Edward changed the subject, and we chatted about nothing for the rest of the drive.

* * *

Edward left me safely deposited on the couch with Meryl happily fussing over me. "Roger is going to head back the way you just came," she told me as she iced my knee. "He's got a bit of a surprise."

Not having the heart to tell her my distrust of surprises, I commented, "How exciting."

"Here he is," she exclaimed, and I expected to see her husband.

However, Roddy hopped around the corner, jumped on the sofa, and nuzzled my arm.

"How did you get inside?" I asked the rabbit, stroking his silky fur.

Smiling, Meryl confessed, "It turns out he's quite a brilliant companion. A good ear for listening."

I laughed, running my hands over his long, black ears. "He's a d-ear."

"Hear, hear," she agreed as we exhausted our hearing-related puns.

"You are a good bunny, aren't you?" I murmured. "You match Old Nigel, don't you? Digestive tract and coloring."

Old Nigel, the draft horse. Who was looking after the horse if Nigel, the farmer, was on the run?

Kissing Roddy on the head, I moved him aside and addressed Meryl. "Did you say Roger was headed near Stroud?"

"Yes." Her raised eyebrows invited further conversation.

"Do you think he could drop me off for a few minutes? I want to check on some farm animals. The farmer is," I paused and grinned, "on the lam."

"Brilliant," she told me, then grew somber. "Is he really, though?"

I told her about the farmer's role in my difficulties and that Edward searched for him.

"Is it quite safe for you to go?" Her concern wrapped me in a warm hug.

"He knows the police are after him, so he wouldn't go home. I'm sure they'll send someone to look after the animals, but I want to make sure the horse and pig have water and food. Hopefully, they have someone watching the place, and I won't have to get out of the car."

On reflection, a constable standing guard seemed like the most likely scenario. Still, I couldn't leave Old Nigel with someone who didn't know horses. If a guard was there, I could give him instructions. Easy.

I went to grab my phone to tell Edward my plan, remembered I didn't have it, and shrugged. We would be back soon enough.

On the drive, I filled Roger in on the bare minimum of my misadventures, keeping the tone light. Every so often, talking jarred loose a memory, and I made a note of it on a scrap of paper I stuffed in my pocket.

Memories List II. De Valence might try to cover up evidence in the treatment room. Same floor as Dolly's room.

Scribbling over De Valence's name, I added 'Someone,' not wanting to derail the investigation because of my accusation. The pen jabbed a hole in the note, and I sighed.

Roger asked, "Is everything quite all right?"

"I miss my phone," I answered, side-stepping the million other reasons for my current state of unease.

For his part, Roger looked appalled. "Where is it?"

If he reacted like this about a phone, I couldn't imagine his response to drugs and kidnapping.

I flapped a hand in the direction we traveled. "Stroud, somewhere. It got left behind."

And was now, hopefully, with the police. Not having it made getting updates difficult.

"What if you need me?"

I smiled at his concern.

"I'm sure everything will be fine," I said, hoping they weren't my famous last words.

Chapter Thirty-Six: About Pigs

Employing a sixth sense I neither possessed nor understood, Roger drove directly to the country lane at the base of Nigel's farm. A weathered split-rail wooden fence lined the property, including a taller, more solid sty enclosure.

"I'll just check for fresh water for Patchy." Eyeing the stone steps that climbed to the farmhouse, I decided, "If he's taken care of, the horse will be too." No way could I navigate that climb.

"Patchy?"

I grinned, "My name for the pig. Cute, isn't it?"

With a shake of his head, Roger declined comment. He asked, "Why don't I just stay, since it won't be long? Keep an eye out, as it were."

The idea held appeal, but I already imposed on his errand. Dressed for business, he couldn't help. I'd be wasting his time.

Plus, the setting oozed peaceful tranquility.

"You go ahead, and I'll be done by the time you get back," I assured him.

Swinging my legs out of the car, I planted my feet gingerly before standing. The ride had lulled me into thinking the pain subsided, but no. A few steps eased my stiffness, and the smile and wave, I bestowed on Roger were genuine.

A breeze from the river valley floated up, crisp and clean, carrying the musky, sweet smell of autumn leaves.

As I approached the sty, the wind shifted, handing me a nose full of the aroma of pig slop.

"Bleck." I grimaced, trying to shake the scent away.

Scanning the area didn't reveal a gate, so I stood on the lowest fence rail and swung my leg over the top. Before slipping down, I used the vantage to search for signs of people. The field appeared fallow, but I didn't know anything about farming. It could be normal for fall.

No light or fire smoke escaped from the farmhouse. The area appeared free of humans, but my skin itched with the thought of eyes following me.

Swiveling my head, eyes raking every inch of the property, I finally saw movement from the shadowed wall of the sty.

"Who's there?" I demanded like I owned the place. "Come out now. The police are on their way," I ad-libbed.

Footsteps rustled twigs, dragging through mud. Menacing groans emitted, conjuring images of zombies crawling out of the ground.

Retreating off the fence, I scrabbled toward the road, pursued by a blood-curdling scream.

After hobbling a few steps, I realized that "scream" probably wasn't the correct word. A squeal described it better. Maybe even an oink.

"Patchy," I breathed, retracing my steps to climb the fence to the pig's enclosure. "I should have thought of that, seeing as I came here to check on you. Sorry for thinking you were the undead."

"Snuffle, snuffle, snort," Patchy responded.

"Now, let's see how you're doing." All business-like to avoid feeling so silly.

My knowledge of pig care rivaled that of farming, as in nothing, but I was on a mission.

Unlike the rest of the farm, the pigsty had a four-foot solid fence with crossbars on the outside. Standing on the lowest crossbar, I could see the entire enclosure, including a tiny Quonset hut at the far side.

The food trough had evidence of vegetables and bread, but as pig slop came pre-spoiled, it was difficult to tell how long the feast had been there.

Searching the ground, I found a stick. Climbing to the second bar, I could extend far enough to poke through the slop.

After discovering an entire zucchini, I concluded that the constabulary fed him. "At least you have food," I commented before losing my footing and pitching forward.

Splat, I landed in the fetid mud.

"Ew," I said, pushing myself up to all fours. My hand landed squarely in pig poo.

"Ew, ew, ew, ew, ew!"

Patchy snorted.

"No offense," I muttered, picking up something that glittered gold in the muck and stuffing it into my already filthy pocket.

Looking at the fence, I wondered how I could have gotten so off-balance.

Nigel's lined face appeared, twisted and unrepentant. "Soo-ie! Pig, pig," he shouted.

Stupidly, my brain thought it odd that farmers in the US called pigs to dinner the same way.

Dinner.

Before I had time to think that through, four hundred pounds of English swine barreled toward me.

Rolling to one side, Patchy missed me. Snorting, he turned, scooping a stray carrot into his teeth and decimating it in less than a second.

A carrot is not much thicker than any of my fingers.

"Crap," I squeaked, crawling to the food trough, rejecting the hut as too far. Every movement sucked me into the mud, hampering progress. I managed to clutch the cement trough and pull myself into it.

Patchy couldn't control his momentum and slammed into the edge hard enough to tip the trough on its back legs.

Using the motion, I grabbed the top of the fence, swaying unsteadily as the concrete below me rocked.

When it righted, I stood tiptoe on the rim and reached for the top crossbar on the far side of the fence. Flinging one leg over, I expected the force to carry me over and tumble to the ground. Stuck on top, the uneven wood slats dug into me.

With an evil cackle, Nigel whacked my shoe, trying to tip me back into the sty.

The injustice of it all pissed me off. I came here to check on his animals, after all.

Blindly, I kicked with the foot he hit and was rewarded with "Oof" and a distinct lack of laughter.

Swinging my other leg up, I started to slide off the top but was yanked back.

Patchy grabbed hold of the leg of my jeans.

Still clinging to the top rail, I thrashed both legs and howled like a banshee. A ripping, snorting cacophony, and finally, my jeans ripped at the knee, freeing my foot.

Toppling to the farm side of the fence, Nigel came after me with a pitchfork.

"Honestly?" I complained as I lunged away from the tines. They stuck fast in the wooden fence.

Nigel tugged, and I scuttled around the corner.

My screams attracted the attention of the constable patrolling the area, and with an "Oi, you!" a chase commenced. Nigel's bandy-legged gait was surprisingly fast, followed by an older constable with a steep, uneven staircase to navigate.

Laying on the ground, covered in pig poo, adrenaline seeped out of me, replaced by cold fury.

"I've had it up to here," I raised my hand to my forehead, a piece of pig poo falling on my shirt. Disgust replaced my ire.

As Nigel crabbed further from his pursuer, a police car pulled into the lane, blocking the path. The DI from Gloucestershire Constabulary leaped out, apprehending the old man quickly.

"Old man," I muttered. Maybe my captors had referred to Nigel and not De Valence. But then, why use the medispa? I supposed they had to have a surgical suite somewhere.

"Help is on the way," shouted the DI, who looked like my dorm mate Naomi.

Alone in the chilly afternoon, covered in who knew what, I contemplated pigs. I never thought they were dangerous, but Patchy's intentions were clear. I was food. The unreality of the situation kept me from freaking out.

Unblinking, I stared at the road and waited for help.

The buzzsaw of a small engine preceded the entrance of an ATV pulling a trailer. Edward hopped off and waved.

Not caring how gross I looked and smelled, I waved back and pushed to standing. Unsteady but determined, I picked my way to the fence as he bounded toward me.

"I think Patchy tried to eat me," I squeaked.

"Lassie, why didn't you tell me you were coming here?"

"The police have my phone. I think. I'm not one hundred percent sure about that. It got left in the pub."

"My number is by the landline in the Priestlys' dining room."

True. I put it there myself. That would have been smart.

"It's okay," he said, holding his arms out for a hug.

"I'm covered in pig poo and rotting veggies. I'm not hugging you," I insisted.

With a squint, he turned and ran back to the ATV's trailer, grabbed a blanket, and returned.

Enveloping me in the scratchy wool, he squeezed tight. "Have you never seen *The Wizard of Oz*?" he asked randomly.

"Yeah?"

"Everyone goes crazy when she falls in the pig pen," he explained.

Pulling the blanket tighter around my shoulders, I indicated the ATV. With Edward for support, we got to it, and I plopped onto the trailer.

"Because she hit her head."

"And they needed to get her away from the pigs before they decided she was an afternoon snack."

"Ew." I shuddered.

Sitting next to me, he hugged my shoulders and refrained from inhaling.

"Which station are we going to?" I asked, knowing I had to give a statement.

"The spa," he said. "You can—"

"No!" Surprised at my reaction, I continued more quietly. "No. Too soon. Too awful."

"I know, lass, but DI Parikh wants you to look at something. You can get cleaned up there. I messaged Roger to meet us."

Resigned, I huddled on the trailer, bumping noisily along country lanes until we pulled up to the rear entrance of De Valence Medispa.

"You should have sent him home. I've ruined his trip," I said once the engine cut off.

"I suggested it," Edward said, picking up on our subject before the drive started. "He wanted to see you for himself."

Edward held out a hand, and I shook my head.

"Come on, lass," he murmured.

Raising my eyes, I looked at the building, shuddered, and shook my head again.

"It's okay," he decided, sitting next to me.

After a few moments of silence, I asked, "Do you still have your job?"

He shrugged. "They don't seem angry and haven't said anything." He smiled. "They might just want me around to control the likes of you."

"Well done on that front," I said, stench radiating off me.

We waited until DI Parikh exited the building and approached. Stopping a few feet away, he told us, "DI Tillman has entrusted me with collecting sty-related evidence."

Was that irony I detected?

A police photographer and a white-clad technician bustled after him. Both drew up short when they got close, my offensive odor greeting them. Resuming their professional demeanors, they approached, clicking and scraping, respectively.

As their collection process slowed, DI Parikh turned to leave.

"Wait," I said, reaching into my pocket and retrieving the golden nugget. Extending it to them on my palm, I braced myself before saying, "I think it's a gold tooth. Like the groom's."

Chapter Thirty-Seven: The Old Man

"It might not be," I explained to the police about the piece of gold in my hand.

The chunk went into an evidence bag.

"But it looks like an eye tooth, and one of the grooms fired from the spa had one. Tim." The horror of the accusation punched me in the gut, and I hunched over, chanting, "No, no, no, no, no."

Edward pounced, returning the blanket to my shoulders and pulling me into his warmth. "That's enough for now," he said in his posh voice. "Let's her get cleaned up."

To my surprise, Parikh added a protective arm around my back, and they led me to a boot room with a small shower enclosure. The techs put mesh over the drain to collect anything else that might fall off me.

The hot water scorched my skin as I scrubbed every surface. Finally, I emerged to find a spa robe, slippers, and yoga clothes.

"At least they're not pink," I commented, tired of wearing clothes I didn't own.

Both top and bottom were too short, the leggings landing mid-calf and the top exposing my belly button. It felt better to wear real clothing, but the outfit required the robe's decorum.

Fluffy and clean, I searched the back of the manor house for the police.

"Miss McGuire," Winters, the De Valence butler, intoned. "This way, please."

The guy must be triplets to be everywhere at once. He guided me to a small sitting room that opened onto a side patio. Hot tea and scones awaited me.

Winters poured tea with an absurd amount of formality for a girl dressed in too-small yoga clothes and a fuzzy bathrobe. The fine bone china teacup, almost paper thin, was exquisite. However, the gold rim triggered a spasm as I thought of the tooth I found.

Hot tea sloshed, staining my slippers as I bobbled the cup. Fumbling it to a side table, I managed to avoid cracking it.

"Maddie!" Edward's voice, calling from outside.

Without batting an eye, Winters said, "I will refresh the pot."

"Thanks," I answered, wanting coffee but not bothering to ask for it.

Opening the window, I called, "Yeah? Why are you yelling?"

"Parikh wants to speak with you."

"Okay. Meet you in the lobby." I headed toward the main entrance of the house.

Converging, we discovered Roger perched in a wing-backed chair with a skeleton in his lap.

"Reverend Priestly," Edward greeted him.

"Roger," I began. "I am so sorry to cause all this trouble."

"Glad to be here. This way, I can get you home safely." He held out the macabre figurine.

As I looked, it turned from a skeleton to a delicate remembrance—the Dias de los Muertos figure of Sherrie in a three-dimensional representation of Tori's art.

"She's perfect," I breathed.

Roger beamed. "Rather than a picture, I felt this would bring the prayers the girl deserves."

"You're so sweet," I said, rushing to him for a hug. "Thank you."

Laughing, he patted my back in a fatherly way. "You are most welcome."

When I pulled away, he asked, "Now, when can we be on our way?"

"Unfortunately, Reverend, we will need Miss McGuire's presence for a few more moments," Edward told him. "I do have a car with me and can deliver her to you if you wish to leave now."

Roger searched my face, and when I nodded agreement, he gave me another pat and said, "Good show." As he strode away, he called, "Give her phone to her."

"Ah," DI Parikh said, patting his coat pockets until he found a cell. "Yours, I believe." A purse followed.

Nothing beats getting your phone back to make you feel whole again. "Thank you."

"This way," Parikh continued and started up the stairs.

Wide-eyed, I turned to Edward for intervention.

"Perhaps the elevator," he suggested. I could have said it myself, but my brain's capacity to deal with problems was at an all-time low.

"Of course," Parikh said.

Once alone in the elevator, the detective inspector removed his glasses and polished them. "Miss McGuire."

I readied for an onslaught of disappointment.

"I wish to express my regrets that your experience in the Cotswolds has been," he paused, selecting his words carefully. "Less than peaceful."

Laughing, I countered, "Horrifying, you mean?"

Glasses perched on his nose, his laughter joined mine. "More accurate."

When we stepped into the hall, another spasm of terror wracked me.

Rather than treating me like a wilting flower, Parikh turned all business, removing a tablet to take notes. "What do you remember?"

The severity with which he asked the question didn't allow me to wallow. I reported the facts dispassionately. "I was carried. The man had an oiled jacket. He dumped me on a massage table, and I fell."

Once we reached the landing, I went three doors down. "Dolly's room?" I checked. Parikh nodded.

Turning around, I returned to the treatment room closest to the landing. "This is the one I was in."

"You're positive?"

Sure, I double-checked anyway. "Yeah."

He tapped through his notes. "You said you created a flood."

"I did."

"There is no evidence."

De Valence. I knew he would clean everything up if we gave him the chance.

"There must be something," I said, opening the door.

The facial steamer was intact in the corner, a fresh robe lay across the bed, and no sign of water damage marred the carpet outside the door.

"I locked the door. Dismantled the steamer and used the hose to sluice water to the hall."

"How did you lock the door?" he asked, noting the lack of mechanism.

Pointing to the elbow bracket, I said, "I wrapped a robe belt around that so that if you tugged, the elbow wouldn't straighten."

He beamed at me.

I didn't know what to think of it. Parikh wasn't one to be impressed.

Together, we moved the massage bed under the door. Parikh crawled on top, stood, and shone a light on the hinge. Using tweezers, he removed several strands of thread after taking a picture.

"Clever. Tell me about the water."

I explained my logic and implementation.

With a curt nod, he dropped to his knees and picked at the carpet on the threshold until a corner came loose. Again, he poked with a flashlight and tweezers until a square section lifted.

"Under here."

Indicating that I should look under the carpet, he scooted to make room.

I squinted, then relaxed, allowing the area to come into focus. A line, razor-thin, traced an outline of a T.

"The padding's been replaced," I said, looking at Parikh for confirmation.

"Feel there," he directed after giving me a smile.

Lightly tracing an arc across the line, warm, springy, tightly woven on one side. Cool, flat, and moist on the other.

"They missed some," I concluded. "This proves my escape story."

"I am beginning to see why our young constable depends on you," he said.

His response was fantastic on multiple levels. Edward appreciated my insights, it sounded like he was not fired, and Parikh didn't mind my interference.

After walking him through the sheet rope process and Dolly's room, we joined Edward, Dolly, and De Valence in the library.

Striding in with the confidence of someone whose story had been validated, I missed my chance to join Edward when I crossed the room. Tucked into an alcove by the door, Parikh took the spot, whispering instructions. It definitely seemed like Edward was back on the force.

Dolly stood near the viscount, who stalked indignantly in front of the oak bookshelves. "The situation is unacceptable," he preached. "Quite."

Several scenarios of me accusing Lord De Valence, Viscount Lisle, played through my mind. They all ended with disbelief on everyone's part, annoyance or anger with me, and no action taken against him. Hoping the police would take point on The Old Man inquiry, I remained silent. Nigel didn't tick enough mastermind boxes.

Turning to Parikh, De Valence demanded, "What have you found? Where is the proof?" Marching to his niece, he patted her gently on the shoulder. "And what has been happening to you? Unacceptable," he repeated.

"I'm fine, Uncle. Absolutely no reason to worry." The haunted look in her eyes belied her words.

Slipping away from his protective arm, she glided to my side, repeating, "What did you find upstairs, Maddie?"

Winters opened the doors wide, gestured to the tea cart, and stepped back, remaining in the hall. Deferential to the situation, but the butler couldn't help but listen in.

Surprising me, De Valence stepped in to play host, pulling the tea into the room and pouring. Despite his large hand, he handled the delicate china deftly. The doors closed, but I didn't hear the latch catch. Winters, listening for gossip.

"Proof," I said, casting a meaningful glare at De Valence.

"Proof?" His voice sharp, colored by something else. Anger?

At what? That his minions didn't clean up their mess very well?

"Thank you, Winters." DCI Bray's voice preceded his entrance as the butler opened the room. The doors again hung open until Bray snapped them closed.

"Right. Everyone here?" he asked, surveying the room with keen eyes behind black-framed glasses. He ran a hand over his gray crew cut. "Good."

Before he could speak, I barraged him with questions. "Did you get our blood tested? Was the sugar cube in the plant at the pub? Where was the van?"

Edward's gaze floated to the sky, asking for patience, no doubt.

When I was alone with Parikh, I hadn't thought to ask him anything. Working together for clues, I was part of the team.

However, the detective chief inspector was called in because of his ties to the aristocracy. The other should be here, too, to make sure all the loose ends got tied up.

"And where is the DI from Gloucester?" I added.

"Otherwise occupied," Bray said, ignoring my previous questions. "Please, everyone," he pointed to the jacquard couches positioned in a U-shape in the center of the library.

"If I may?" He glanced at me.

I shrank down, pulling my robe around me, and I swear I saw Dolly smirk.

"We will start with the immediate threat to Miss McGuire. The farmer is at His Majesty's pleasure just now. DI Tillman and her team are getting details, but we know that gang members in Scotland were sent as mules for drugs and sometimes did not return."

"Because of Patchy?" I interrupted.

"The pig," Edward clarified.

"Ah, yes. Well," Bray stammered, glancing at Dolly. "The pen revealed some disturbing evidence."

Bray went on to explain that Nigel used marginalized individuals for organ transfers, then disposed of the bodies. Drug traces were found in the sugar, Nigel's van, and samples from Dolly and me.

At least no one thought I was crazy.

Dolly and I hugged. "You're going to be a lot happier knowing you're not losing your mind."

She squeezed. "You have absolutely no idea," she said. "Come along. Your clothes should be ready."

After changing, Edward took my hand, and we got in his friend's SmartCar to drive to Bath.

Just as I was about to ask if I could meet this friend, I realized that no one at any point asked why they used the spa or questioned if Nigel was The Old Man my captors feared.

Someone was covering up for De Valence.

Chapter Thirty-Eight: Watch Out for Snow

Not wanting to burden Edward with my fears concerning De Valence, I said, "I realized after the fact that I could have called you on the Priestlys' landline."

One eyebrow raised, he flashed a crooked grin at me. "Madeline McGuire, is that an apology?"

I punched him softly on the arm. "This time, I wasn't obstructing anything. I forgot landlines existed. Plus, I was with Roger, so I thought it would be okay. I wanted to make sure the farm animals had food and water."

"You have a good heart."

The compliment flattered me, but it didn't ring true. "Do I? I've been awful to Dolly. I accused her of forging my signature on a dig bag and meeting with reporters to get me fired."

"Who did those things?" he wondered.

I shrugged. "Don't know. The reporter thing was probably my fault. Lady Vivian hates me."

"I'm sure that's not true."

"She referred to me as 'that creature.' Simon says she doesn't have the authority to fire me, but the atmosphere at the Baths is decidedly hostile."

Now that I didn't have Dolly to blame, I had to fix the problems myself. Simon's manor house was still in peril, too. After the police validated my evidence, I thought everything would return to normal.

But no.

If anything, I had more to do.

Grateful to Edward, I exited his car with plans for lunch the next day. Inside, the scents of home greeted me. Meryl made hamburgers and mac-n-cheese for dinner. American comfort food for their international student.

* * *

Roger returned the photos Tori sent of her Dias de los Muertos doll and took his statuette to the church. Deciding the more remembrances, the better, I stopped at the Abbey after Roger dropped me off at work.

As always, a sense of well-being enveloped me on entering the Abbey. Despite everything that happened, the sanctuary made me happy to be in Bath.

"Maddie?" Father Michael's voice, quiet but welcoming.

"Hello," I said. Suddenly shy, I didn't know what to ask him about the pictures.

As always, he waited patiently.

"I ask you for a favor every time I come in."

Agreeing, he said, "Which is, after all, my job." With a smile, he asked, "Is this about your friend's homework?"

It took me a moment to remember Tori's research on nursery rhymes. "No, but she, Tori, was really grateful. She went with the Little Jack Horner poem as it had the most clear-cut story, but she focused on the greed of the landowners rather than Henry. Thank you so much."

"You will find that quite a lot of people will do anything for land."

His statement struck a chord, but I didn't have time to process it as he asked, "What do you have for me today?"

A quick shake to clear my head, and I showed him the pictures of Sherrie's figurine. "This is a Dias—"

"De los Muertos doll, is it not?" He took the pages from me and peered. "Exceptional detail. The tattoo," he tapped the unicorn head. "Is this the one you mentioned?"

Searching my memory, I couldn't remember if I mentioned Sherrie before.

As much as I didn't want to go into it again, Father Michael deserved to hear the whole story. Telling him everything, from finding her to discovering the tattoo on Edward, the gang in Scotland, being drugged, I finished with my fear that someone would get away with masterminding a black market in human organs.

He didn't offer platitudes or solutions, just a sympathetic ear. When I didn't offer more, he picked up the thread for me. "Would you like me to hang the pictures with an offer for prayer?"

"Would you mind?" I asked. "I know it's not the same belief system, but—"

A raised hand stopped me. "Prayers for those who have passed on are universal."

Checking my watch, I squeaked. "Eek! I'm late for work. Thank you for everything."

"So you still have a job?" he asked, reminding me that I sought the Abbey for solace after Lady Vivian fired me.

"I do. But I also have a lot to fix. Thanks again," I called as I scampered out of the church and to the Baths as fast as my injuries allowed.

Angry bees swirled in my stomach at the thought of seeing Lady Vivian, so I took a couple of deep breaths before opening the Oversight Office.

Neither Sam Niven nor Lady Vivian was inside.

Without looking up from the document he was reading, Simon commented, "I hear you were nearly devoured by livestock."

"It gives a whole new meaning to eating like a pig," I responded, rushing gingerly around the desk and giving him a very American, inappropriate-for-the-workplace, hug.

Before anyone could see, I resumed the proper decorum.

"I am glad you're not dead," he admitted.

"Where do you need me today?" I changed the subject, not pressing my luck with more displays of emotion.

"Everywhere?" His question bordered on distress. The fact that he was dressed for tours and not for the dig site indicated how short-handed we were.

"As long as I have a walking stick, I can navigate tours," I assured him.

Examining my still bruised and scratched face, his expression telegraphed disapproval.

"Perhaps you could be a runner for Dr. Daniels." Doubt tinged his voice.

More walking but less public, a runner carried messages and finds to the departments scattered across the museum.

Nodding, I affirmed, "I can do that."

"Do be serious, Maddie," Dolly declared as she entered the office. "You should be in bed."

"As should you, my dear," Simon said, standing and offering his chair to her.

"Nonsense," she responded. "I am really rather quite tired of a haze blurring my thoughts. I am ready for work. The tours are mine."

Simon beamed at her, admiration clear on his face. "Right," his voice all business. "First one starts in ten minutes."

"First things first. You are all invited to Painswick Manor for dinner this evening." Eying me, she added, "Including Edward." Her gaze traveled to Simon. "And Lady Vivian."

Before either of us protested, Dolly continued, "And yes, Maddie, I know you are traumatized, but quite frankly, so am I, and I need to host a dinner party to help me feel like myself again."

Simon attempted a way out for us. "Really, Dolly. My aunt is in no mood to see Maddie. Or me, for that matter."

Add to that my aversion to De Valence, and the party seemed destined for failure. Except that maybe I could find a way to trip up the viscount or trick him into admitting something. *Strike while he's not expecting it,* I thought. Not that we had a choice with Dolly on a mission.

"Nonsense." She stood. "Off I go, then," Dolly said while slipping her cell out of her pocket. "Simon will drive us. Meet at six by the Abbey Green."

I received a text moments later from Dolly. 'Don't let him fool you. Lady V was absolutely frantic about your condition.' Followed by a smiley face.

Grinning, I hearted the message.

To Simon, I said, "No tours for you, which means you can run. I should sift?"

Before heading downstairs, I texted Edward about dinner and that I wouldn't have service while in the Undercroft. I added a note to Roger letting him know that the Abbey now displayed the picture of Tori's Day of the Dead doll and that I would be having dinner out.

'You're sure?' Roger wanted confirmation, and the comfort of his protection enveloped me.

'Yes. Thank you so much!' I texted back, hoping his protection would extend to the De Valence Medispa.

* * *

The ride to dinner rang with good cheer. The same car and the same people as the first time I visited Painswick, but this time I was happier. Dolly, far from being the threat I pictured, turned out to be an ally.

We chatted about inconsequential matters, and much to my surprise, I relaxed.

"You were right about a get-together, Dolly. I already feel better."

She turned around in the front seat, and I had a moment of panic as she took her eyes off the road.

"I do, too. My goodness, what is wrong?"

Laughing, I patted the headrest. "I still forget that the driver's seat is on the other side of the car. You're the passenger."

A short while later, we arrived. Clarence De Valence himself opened the door for us. "Welcome, welcome," he greeted us, shaking hands with the men and extending a slight bow to the ladies.

"Vivian is in the drawing room. Let's collect her and go into dinner."

The evening passed pleasantly with no talk of murders, kidnapping, drugs, or revealing newspaper articles.

The conversation hadn't presented an opportunity for me to lure De Valence into a verbal trap. The idea started to feel ridiculous as the evening drew on.

The eerie recollection of relaxing my guard at the pub surfaced, reminding me of being drugged. Checking all my senses confirmed my normal state.

To put a nail in the paranoia coffin, Lady Vivian even asked after my various injuries and complimented my bravery in rescuing Dolly.

The fact that she and I both required rescuing was glossed over by all, including me. Honestly, I wanted it to be over. Nigel was in custody, and he confessed. I had my internship. All was right in my world.

Except, why this medispa?

"Let's adjourn to the drawing room, shall we?" De Valence suggested.

Dolly walked by me, explaining polite society manners. "It used to be that the men went to the drawing room for cigars while the ladies were shunted off to the sitting room. My mother put an end to cigars or cigarettes anywhere on the property ages ago."

As much as I wanted to ask what happened to her parents, I didn't think it was the right time.

"Thank goodness," I remarked.

"Indeed."

While not large, the drawing room was designed around small group conversations. De Valence and Lady Vivian headed to wing-back chairs in the corner.

Seeing Simon's scowl, Dolly placed a hand on his shoulder. "I made Uncle promise not to discuss business of any kind."

Relief, followed by casual friendliness, reflected on his face.

Impressive, I thought. Dolly subverted trouble in advance and knew exactly when to bring it up to Simon.

Each time the conversation veered toward the situation, Dolly maneuvered us to safe ground expertly. It was an epic display of how to host a party.

Until Lady Vivian commented, "At least this terrible business is all behind us."

"But why this spa?" I said before I could stop myself.

A stunned silence, followed by everyone looking at me.

Turning to Edward, I asked, "How did Nigel get access to the surgical suite in this spa?"

"Woe, alas. In our house?" Dolly quoted Lady Macbeth.

While a heartbreaking sentiment, Lady M was lying when she said it. It kind of gave me the creeps.

"I am not privy to case notes and am back on the force on a probationary status," Edward explained.

"But you must have heard something," I prompted. "Shop talk?"

Blowing air in a long, steady stream—rather dramatically, I thought - he told us, "The Gloucester force is convinced the connection will be explained when your captors are in custody. In the meantime, Nigel confessed to drugs, kidnapping, and disposal."

Disposal of *what* he left to us to fill in.

"But," I started, leaning forward.

"You start far too many sentences that way."

"If someone answered my questions, I wouldn't," I countered.

He sighed in a way that made me think he had given up trying to thwart my curiosity.

At that point, Lady Vivian and De Valence joined us, listening.

Why now, I wondered? Returning to my original plan, I studied De Valence. His salt and pepper hair looked like freshly fallen snow over black ice. The image reminded me of something Edward told us.

"But what about what your brother said?" I asked.

"What brother? James?" Simon asked while Dolly repeated, "What did he say?"

A polite knock on the door interrupted us, much to Edward's noticeable relief. From where we sat, the door blocked everything, but a decadent selection of desserts was wheeled in on a cart.

"Perfect," Dolly chimed. "Dessert will go down a treat, don't you agree?"

Hopping up, she practically skipped across the room, murmured, "Thank you, Winters. I'll take over," and pulled the dessert trays toward us.

I've always said if it's not chocolate or caramel, it's not worth the calories. So when Dolly pointed to a chocolate-caramel mousse, I almost knocked over the coffee table to get to it. Preferring to stand after the long meal, I lingered by the door, drenched in sugary joy.

"Edward," Dolly, ever the hostess, restarted the conversation. "What did your brother say?"

"William," he responded, clarifying the brother in question. "He's entrenched in a gang. The girl Maddie found, Sherrie, was in the same one." Looking directly at Lady Vivian and De Valence, he admitted, "As was I."

The air in the room sparked with tension. Dolly looked pleadingly at the desserts, hoping to bring the party back to life.

Simon stared daggers at his aunt until she finally said, "A shame."

Ouch. The phrase was the English equivalent to "Bless your heart" in the US South. Nice enough sounding, but a cutting remark.

However, surprising us all, Lady Vivian continued. "The situation sounds most intolerable. You have done yourself proud, young man."

The tension broke, and Edward blushed under the attention. Actually blushed. Unbelievable.

"As most of you know, I went to Edinburgh to retrieve my younger brother and to warn William not to send any more members to England."

It took me hours of contemplating clues to figure all this out, and he relates it to everyone else in a couple of sentences. Jeez.

"The one warning William gave was, 'Watch out for snow.'"

Eying De Valence, I scrutinized his response. He looked bewildered.

"That doesn't make any sense," Simon insisted.

"What does it mean?" De Valence asked.

Giving up, I quipped, "As in 'Winter is coming'?" referring to a popular fantasy series.

No chuckles, just blank stares. "You know?" I prompted. "Game of Thrones. 'Winter is coming' was the catchphrase. Remember?" The one time I attempted lighthearted, and not mystery conspiracy, and no one got it.

De Valence stood, and all eyes turned to him.

Switching gears again, I watched his movements. Had I found the thing to catch the conscience of the king?

Why my mother's use of Shakespearean quotes invaded my brain at the worst moments, I'll never know.

On the contrary to showing guilt, De Valence offered a clue. "Our butler is called Winters."

"What butler?" Edward asked, also coming to his feet.

"You've seen him," I insisted. "He's everywhere."

"The ubiquitous Winters," Dolly and I said in unison.

Edward shook his head. "No, never."

At that moment, the butler in question pushed open the door where I stood with a dessert cup in my hand.

When I turned and opened my mouth to invite him in, he lunged at me, arm around my throat.

Chapter Thirty-Nine: The Vagus Nerve

The bone china clattered to the marble floor, shattering. The sound jarred me to action.

In my self-defense class, the one I spent flirting and not learning, the instructor taught us how to escape from a chokehold in three easy steps. I remembered one of them. Tuck your chin into the crook of the attacker's elbow to protect your windpipe.

Once I achieved that, the black dots swirling in my vision lessened enough for me to realize that his other hand rested on my temple.

"Let her go, White," Edward barked.

No longer using the refined accent of the butler, Winters' Scottish burr emanated violence. "I'll snap her neck," he shouted. "You know I can."

Blanching, Edward backed away, out of view.

Any thoughts I had of kicking or biting fled. I stood stock still, not breathing, not blinking. Getting out of a hold was one thing, but our intro class never covered someone wanting to flat-out murder us.

Finally getting the answer about why all this happened at the De Valence Medispa paled at the idea of having my head twisted off.

Winters shouted directions. Nothing penetrated, words became meaningless. My body tilted back, dragged down the hall to the front doors. Tripping and stumbling, every misstep put more pressure on my throat. As I struggled to keep up, I strained to hear what the others were doing. No use. Panicked buzzing overrode every sound.

Vision graying, I swayed unsteadily, releasing a stream of vitriol from Winters.

A memory triggered from my childhood. Tori's older brother, picking on us. Too big for us to defeat, we turned into jelly deadweights, throwing off his balance.

I went limp, praying it wouldn't trigger a final snap of my neck.

He stumbled, then pressure released.

Playing dead, I flopped on the cold tile.

Something large dropped next to me. Chancing a look, the tuxedoed form of Winters lay on the floor.

A boot kicked a vicious blow to Winters' rib cage before the shoes' owner squatted, a gentle hand moving hair from my face.

"Y'alright, lassie?" Edward said. "You're safe now."

Pushing to seated, I stared at Edward, willing him to explain.

He didn't.

"Did someone shoot him?" I asked, my mind still muddy from lack of oxygen.

Edward scoffed. "We don't carry guns, lassie. You know that."

I did know that. What I didn't know was what happened. A low warning growl emitted from my throat.

"Right," he said, helping me to my feet. The rest of the company parted, making way for me to sit on the couch. "Vagus nerve in the side of the neck. Push it just right, and your victim…" he coughed. "Ahem. Push it, and your aggressor," he corrected, "faints."

"Is he secure?"

Dolly scampered out of the room and returned moments later, with heavy-duty gardening jute. "Maddie. I know you said something about roping. Do you know how to hogtie someone?" Displeasure at her fake butler clear, she wanted him punished.

Edward took the rope and tied Winters to a banister just as the man awoke and unleashed a nasty assault of Gaelic.

"Wheesht," Edward commanded. Surprisingly, Winters complied.

"How did you get behind him?"

Edward pointed to the open French window. "Out the window, through the door."

Head dropping into my hands, I scrubbed my face. "I don't understand," I confessed. Turning to Dolly, I asked, "I thought you said he had been with your family for years?"

Dolly shook her head, handling the betrayal better than her uncle.

Ashen-faced, De Valence stared at the fallen butler in horrified disbelief. Simon went to his aunt, touched her arm, and nodded to the viscount.

A delay of only a moment, then she strode to the decanter and poured amber liquid into a cut-crystal tumbler. Handing it to De Valence, she spoke to him in firm but quiet commands.

With a glare toward Winters, Dolly explained, "No. We've had our cook and gardener for years. They have the flat above ours." She jabbed a finger toward the prone man. "That," she spat the word, "came to us two years ago. The ubiquitous Winters." Raising her voice, she shouted with a fair amount of decorum. "Spying on us! How dare you?"

Looking like a caged predator, dangerous and ready to strike, he smiled.

Still confused, I said, "I thought you liked him when you introduced us at the Baths."

Dolly stamped her foot and turned away. "Well, look at this place. We went from barely making it to looking at expansion plans once he took over schedule and bookkeeping."

Color drained from her face. "Oh, my. What have we done?"

Echoing his aunt's movements, Simon poured a brandy and handed it to Dolly as he guided her to a loveseat.

I turned to either side in my chair, wondering where my comfort disappeared, until I saw Edward in the hallway. Back and forth in front of his prisoner, he marched, speaking with his neutral accent on the phone.

Softly, I padded toward them, listening.

As Edward reported the crime to the police, Winters sneered, mocking him. Using both Gaelic and English, he poured poison into Edward's ear. A second Hamlet metaphor that would have made my mom proud.

When Edward ended the call, I piped up, "How are your ribs?" Gleeful at the pain shooting across Winters' face when he moved.

"Police brutality, that is," he complained. "I'll have your badge."

"I did it," I said, covering for Edward's brutal kick. "Self-defense."

Edward gave me a warning look.

Eyebrows raised, I tilted my head.

He winked.

"Well," Dolly said, coming into the hallway. "This rather puts a damper on my after-dinner surprise for you."

"She hates surprises," Edward and Simon said in unison.

Touching, really. Edward and I discussed my aversion to surprises, using the quote from Jane Austen's *Emma*, but Simon must have figured it out on his own. That man continued to amaze me. He gave every impression of ignoring everyone, yet he observed everything.

Nodding, I said, "It's true."

"Very well. Not a surprise. Lancelot wishes to see you."

I grinned. "Very well."

We walked out the front door to the stable. Lancelot raised his noble head when we approached.

Stroking his nose, I let him know what a good horse he was. After a moment, he stepped away from me, turning his head toward the next stall.

At first, I didn't see anything, so I moved closer. A huge, black and white draft horse stood at the back of the stall, munching oats.

"Old Nigel!"

The farm horse plodded to me at the sound of his name. Dolly slipped me a handful of sugar cubes which he snuffled out of my hand.

Turning to Dolly, I could barely contain my happiness.

"We couldn't let the sins of his master affect his fate, could we?"

She returned the hug I enveloped her in.

As we approached the house, Gloucestershire Constabulary vehicles arrived on the scene.

I told everyone about Dolly rescuing Old Nigel to cheering and applause. But when we settled into silence, the atmosphere closed in.

Shock washed over each of us in waves. However, Dolly always maintained a stiff upper lip to talk the others through. By the time we were called in for statements, we were relatively coherent.

DI Tillman took us to the library one at a time. Not trusting the activity to a constable, she wanted to gather every nuance and impression.

As I waited my turn, I organized my thoughts, making lists and points. And most importantly, questions to be answered. Something eluded me, but I couldn't pinpoint it.

When summoned, I said, "You look like my dorm mate back in Chicago."

DI Tillman raised her eyebrows.

"Are you Jamaican?" I asked.

"My family came to England from the Caribbean." Smiling, she asked, "Do you miss her?"

I nodded but said, "I have a hard time admitting my various disasters to her because she was so excited when I got my internship. I spend most of my time talking to my BFF from childhood. Best friend forever," I added at her questioning look.

"Are you ready?" she prompted.

I started with Sherrie's body and went through my escape with Dolly. Shaking my head, I said, "I'm missing something, though."

"It will come," she said.

"Did the recording I made with Dolly's phone help? Can you identify Winters from it now that you know it's him?"

She made a noncommittal sound as she took notes.

"Is incapacitating a suspect by pushing the vagus nerve standard police training?"

A shake of her head. "You'll need to ask your boyfriend about that."

The word boyfriend sent a spontaneous fission of joy through me.

"So," I began, although I knew I was pushing my luck. "Was Sherrie supposed to have been pushed down the escarpment to the sty?"

A sigh, then DI Tillman told me, " That does seem to be the case."

"Why didn't they double-check?" I asked. I mean, jeez, how sloppy can you get?

"Brett was not the most reliable of henchmen," she smirked.

"Are Brett and Brad in custody?"

A curt nod.

Her patience wearing thin, I soldiered on. "Was the gold I found in the sty a tooth from Tim, the groom? Did they feed him to Patchy because he failed to kill me using Lancelot?"

With a sigh, she set her pen down and gave me a stern stare. "I don't know how they do this at the Avon and Somerset Constabulary, but this is an interview, not an exchange of information. I ask the questions."

"Yep. Got it," I assured her. "Same with DI Parikh. He never tells me anything. Neither does Edward, which is extremely annoying sometimes."

Mistaking my statements for acquiescence, she looked at her notes with a nod. Before she could move on, I asked, "Why did Winters stay around after I escaped?"

No response.

"My guess?" I offered despite the lack of engagement. "Profitability and greed."

Nothing. Then she asked, "Tell me again why the drugs didn't affect you."

I did, and while she was distracted, asked, "Winters's real name was White?" In the scuffle, I thought I heard Edward say it, but I wanted confirmation.

"Yes," she said without elaborating.

"Snow White Winters," I said.

DI Tillman did not appreciate the comment. "If you know you're not supposed to ask questions, why do you continue to do so?"

"American persistence," I said with a bright smile.

She sighed again.

"I'm sorry. But, when I ask something someone doesn't know the answer to, they go find it out. So occasionally, not often, but sometimes, I'm useful. But today, I'm trying to trigger what I've forgotten. It has something to do with Winters."

And danger, I didn't add out loud.

Chapter Forty: An Unexpected Visit

As much as I tried, I couldn't dredge up the final piece of the Winters/White puzzle, so DI Tillman sent me home in a taxi. The police were busy "processing the scene," which someone actually said. I thought the phrase only came up in TV shows.

The Priestlys were out, so I called Tori.

"Hola," she greeted me.

"Finished hibernating?" I joked.

"Si. Me, Scott, and my computer. Thanks for asking, although I recognize it as a delaying tactic. What new horrors have befallen you?"

"Befallen? Have you been chatting with my mom?"

No one could speak to Heather McGuire for long without picking up Elizabethan words.

Tori laughed. "How did you guess? She called to check on me as a thinly veiled ruse to check on you. I'd been asleep, so I didn't have any updates. As such," she paused, waiting for me to answer her question.

"Did you know pigs can eat people?"

"Everyone knows that. Didn't you ever wonder why the farmhands freaked out in *The Wizard of Oz* when—"

"When she falls. Yeah, I know. That's because she hit her head," I insisted.

"And because…" stopping, she eyed the camera. "You?"

I nodded.

"I swear I'm going to put a pet microchip in you."

"Deal," I agreed. "I kinda want one at this point."

After explaining about Patchy, Nigel, and Snow White Winters, I changed the subject to something happier. "I have a surprise for you, though."

"Really?" Unlike me, Tori loved surprises.

"Roger took your Day of the Dead pictures and had a friend make a sculpture."

Wide-eyed, she breathed, "Wow, I'm touched."

"That is in his church, and your pictures are in," I held for a dramatic pause. "Wait for it."

"The Bath Abbey? Seriously?"

"You didn't wait for it," I complained, then smiled. "But yeah. Cool, huh?" Thinking of Sherrie reminded me of Sherlock Holmes. "I was totally off the mark with *The Hound of the Baskervilles*, though. Not really kidnapping and nothing related to love triangles."

"That's not what the story is about. He wants the Baskerville manor house. It's about real estate."

"Maybe I should have finished reading it," I said. "De Valence is trying to buy Comer Manor through Lady Vivian, but Simon doesn't want to sell. So, right story, wrong interpretation."

"Exactly."

* * *

The next morning at the Baths, I wasn't sure how to approach Lady Vivian. The artifact bag still hadn't surfaced, and no matter what, she was still mad about the medispa article.

Pausing outside the Oversight Office, I listened for indications of its occupants.

A distinctly American male voice said, "I'm taking a bath on this whole visit, if you know what I mean."

Given the city and museum's name, the pun was so bad that it reminded me of... "Dad," I whispered.

Rushing into the room, I caught Lady Vivian and Sam laughing. At a Dad Joke. My dad's joke. Nothing in my world made sense.

"Dad!" I squealed, running to his arms.

"Pumpkin!" he exclaimed.

I hated my childhood nickname with the white-hot intensity of a thousand burning suns. He gave it to me before my hair color softened and became closer to blonde. And right now, it was the best word in the entire world.

"No one is going to send my little girl home. Not when she belongs here."

"Of course not," Lady Vivian affirmed. "Maddie is a vital part of the dig team."

Sam added, "And a popular tour guide."

Color me bewildered.

Bracing for a verbal thrashing from at least Simon's aunt, my emotions ping-ponged with the sudden changes, blocking rational thought.

"Thank you, Milady," my dad said, and I groaned.

"Oh, Ed. Call me Viv," she tittered.

Actually tittered.

Too much had been unbelievable lately, and my world slipped into surreal.

The thing was, everyone considered my dad attractive. Also charismatic, and he could sell a parka on a desert island. Apparently, he worked his charm on Simon's aunt.

"Maddie!" Sam exclaimed. "Where have ya been hidin' your da all this time? A treasure he is."

Far from being embarrassed by the attention, Dad preened under it.

"That's my dad," I said, trying not to sound mortified. "Can I show him the sifting site?"

Dragging him from the office among calls of "Give him the full tour, Whatever you need," and "Take the day if you like," I marveled at his ability to turn every situation his way. And my way, too, in this case.

"Come on. Turn your cell to airplane mode. The Undercroft is way underground."

"I've gotta hand it to you, Pumpkin. This place is amazing. I always knew you were a genius, but you've outdone yourself."

Even though he spoke like I discovered and excavated the museum myself, I beamed at his compliments. "Thanks, Dad. And not to sound unwelcoming, but why are you here?" The trip wasn't planned, and I hadn't received any notice.

"You called," he said simply.

That I did. And he came. Sometimes I forget how lucky I am.

"I was going to come to you," I said, although now that I had my job back, I'm glad I didn't jump on the first flight out.

He shook his head. "No, you belong here."

I squeezed him. "Thank you," I whispered again.

As we arrived at my sifting station, he looked dismayed. "In a stairwell?"

"There's not a lot of space down here," I explained with a loving pat to my sifting table.

Pointing to the easy chair that Simon and Sam provided after I found a body, he amended his opinion. "Surprisingly homey."

After I explained the process of receiving, filtering, examining, and disposing of ancient soil, he picked up a handful of sifted dirt. "And I heard you found something."

I grinned. "Two things, so far. Dad, you have no idea what a thrill it is."

Dirt fell off his fingers, tap, tip, tip, tap. The tapping drowned out his response, taking me back to my claustrophobia attack when someone shut down the lights and locked me in.

"Just a sec," I said to him, pulling out my cell, needing to tell DI Tillman what I remembered.

"No service," he reminded me.

"I need to call someone," I explained, but not enough to tell him about my suspicion. "Let's get you back upstairs, and maybe we could go to the Pump Room for lunch."

Even with Lily's employee discount, I could never afford to have tea there on my own.

Once the elevator doors opened, I ducked into a side hallway and called the Gloucester DI. With a sigh, I noted there were way too many police officers in my cell's contact list.

"Hi. It's Maddie."

"I could tell by the accent," she said, laughing.

"Right. The thing I remembered. When I first met De Valence, Winters was there right after I had a panic attack from claustrophobia. When I returned to work, someone used that information against me, closing all the doors and turning off every light. Sealing me in."

Even now, the recollection sent a shudder through me.

"Find out from Winters or White if he did that." It didn't matter a whole lot now that his other evils were exposed, but I wanted to know. I'd blamed Dolly before I knew she was far too kind for sabotage.

Before DI Tillman let me go, she asked more questions, clarifying timing. When I finally hung up, it took me a minute to find my dad.

There he stood, talking with Edward and James.

"Oh no," I muttered, an entirely different kind of panic gripping me.

Dad and Edward had met before when my dad came to visit, but only enough to say "Hello." Not an entire exchange. And not with James, the gang-member along.

And if my dad dared reveal my nickname, I would explode.

As I approached them, Edward took me aside, leaving Dad and James.

"That's not a good plan," I complained, pointing at the pair.

"He'll behave," Edward assured me about James.

"Not what I was worried about," I muttered, distracted by the object in Edward's hand. "Is that the C47 artifact bag?"

With a nod, he told me, "James. Old habits die hard."

Snatching it, I hurried to the Oversight Office, not caring if anyone followed.

Fortunately, Sam sat at her desk. I extended the bag in her direction, and words failed me. What was I supposed to say? That my boyfriend's brother tried to frame me? Or was I careless enough to show a stranger our process so he could forge my signature?

"Missing bag," I said. Eloquent, that's me.

"Is this the one with the forged signature on the log?"

My eyes bugged a little, but I remained calm.

"Don't be lookin' so panicked," Sam chided. "I know you don't use hearts to dot your i. Do you know who took it?"

Again, speechless. The door opened, rescuing me.

Uninvited, James, Edward, and my dad joined us.

"That would be me, darlin'," James confessed without a hint of contrition. "Me brother's trying to set me on the straight and narrow. I'm afraid it'll be a long journey." He turned to me. "I am sorry. Truly."

Huh. I believed him. Probably wishful thinking, but maybe he would go straight.

"I should ban you from the building," Sam commented without rancor. James managed some charm of his own.

"He's a good artist," Edward added in his neutral accent, creating a marked contrast to his brother. "But he uses his talent for evil."

Without knowing anything about anyone, my Dad offered, "Maybe Dolly could give you some lessons. Her work is top-notch."

Raising both eyebrows, I asked, "When have you seen her work?"

A finger upward, he explained, "In the lab."

The lab.

Where artifacts were cleaned, photographed, and cataloged, and some were sketched by Dolly.

The lab I hadn't seen yet.

Puffing air through my lips, sounding like a horse, I marched toward the hallway vacillating between being annoyed and impressed at my dad. And James. And Sam, for that matter.

Bursting through the door, I squeaked in shock.

Chapter Forty-One: New Information

Lady Vivian's pink form filled the doorway. Redirecting my energy to avoid knocking down a lady, I collided with the door jamb.

"Hi," I said uselessly.

"Quite," she answered, sounding like De Valence.

Dolly and Simon avoided bumping into her from behind when she stopped short by ricocheting off each other.

After taking in the number of people in the office, Lady Vivian came to some sort of decision. "Ms. Niven," she said. "do you mind terribly if I borrow your staff for a moment?"

"Not at all," Sam agreed but stood to follow despite the lack of invitation, as did my Dad, Edward, and James.

With a sophistication I could only dream of, she held her hand to my father and, coquettishly tilting her head, said, "I do hope I'll see you for tea tomorrow?"

"I wouldn't miss it for the world," he said with a grin.

The exchange had the effect of stopping everyone in the office without insulting anyone. I wondered if she gave lessons on this stuff.

Removing the word "stuff" from my vocabulary would be top of the list.

Newspaper in hand, she held it above her head like a torch and led us in a direction I hadn't been before. When I pieced the route together, I concluded we were heading to the education area above the Heritage Center, which housed the lab.

Finally!

The makeshift cleaning and cataloging lab, tantalizingly displayed beyond a picture window, held a world of delights, including tesserae being assembled into a mosaic. I couldn't wait to get in there and soak up ancient Roman England.

We marched past and entered a learning room. With coloring books. "Sigh," I mumbled, earning a sniff from Simon.

Once assembled, Lady Vivian slapped the paper onto the table with dramatic flair. "Another one," she sighed, disappointment in me coming through every syllable.

"What?" Dolly asked.

Ignoring her question, Lady Vivian addressed Dolly and Simon. "I depend on the two of you to advise this," she paused, her gaze flickering to me, "this American on proper etiquette regarding private matters."

"Of course, Aunt Viv," Simon agreed while Dolly said, "What's happened?"

Point to Dolly for at least asking.

Pulling the paper toward me, I opened it to the Business section's front page. Splashed below the fold was another Jeffery Dailey article on medispas ruining the countryside.

"Ms. McGuire," Lady Vivian continued. "I know you are new to this country, but certain levels of decorum are expected, especially relating to the press."

Much as I wanted to protest, I knew it would be considered rude. And we were here to make me a better person, after all. I suppressed a growl and read the news item.

A rehash of the previous article, I clamped my jaw shut to keep indignant protests at bay.

Ignoring the continuing lecture, my eyes traveled over the page where a picture caught my eye.

"The De Valence Medispa..." Lady Vivian droned on, and at some point, Dolly interrupted her.

Time stopped. The picture in the paper filled my sight, blocking the raised voices. A man with bushy eyebrows and a hooked nose smiled at the camera in front of a world-renowned bank.

Simon poked me.

"Huh?"

"Maddie, I am really so very sorry," Dolly apologized.

"Okay," I responded dully.

"I knew Simon didn't want to sell Comer Manor, and I just thought, well, yes." Eyes downcast, she continued, "Absolutely no idea it would cause you so much fuss."

Lady Vivian's utterly appalled expression caused Dolly to shrink back.

"Gwendolyn. How could you?"

Dolly took the blow. Then, her spine lengthened, and she stood her ground. "There are other options. You need to consider Simon's feelings in your decisions."

Simon's hand floated to Dolly's shoulder, creating a united front.

With a shake, I brought myself back to the present. "You tried to get me deported?" I demanded, finally catching on.

"No," Dolly insisted, grabbing my hand and bringing me into their fold. "Of course not. Absolutely the wrong consequence. I do apologize. To both of you."

As Lady Vivian switched the focus of her displeasure to Dolly, I realized I was right about part of it. When I spied Dolly talking to Jeffery, she was giving him information about the medispa, but not to get me in trouble. Her goals were stopping the sale and supporting Simon.

Nice of her.

I really needed to work on my snap decisions about people. My hit rate in England so far was appallingly low.

"It's okay," I interrupted another of Dolly's apologies, more urgent things on my mind. "No problem." Turning the paper in her direction, I pointed at the photo. "Look at this."

Disregarding Lady Vivian's huffing, I took charge. "Who is that?"

"I," she began, then stopped and pulled the picture closer. "Why, that's Major Pickering." Keen intellect sparked behind her eyes. "You don't think—
"

Nodding, I said, "I do."

"Not to put any pressure on the two of you, but care to explain?" Simon asked, sounding bored.

Not answering, I read part of the article aloud. "Despite rumors of a debilitating illness, Randolph Ruthaven is back at his post, much to the relief of the financial world. Looking better than he has in months, Ruthaven's confidence is contagious."

Both Simon and Lady Vivian looked unimpressed.

"He was at our medispa," Dolly explained. "Under a different name."

"When I was there. After I found Sherrie, who had a recent surgery scar over her kidney."

"Surely you would have known if major surgery was going on," Simon protested, but Dolly shook her head.

"Winters, or White rather, handled all the scheduling, payments, and bookkeeping. We left everything to him." Dolly looked dejected.

"He said he had been there ten days. A long time for a spa treatment." I remembered wondering why at the time. "Do you think he knew?"

Simon offered, "I doubt it. If true, he is guilty of hopping the line and getting a kidney based on money, not need, but that's not a crime."

Still, he seemed like such a nice man. My first impressions radar was out of whack, but a plan formed at the back of my mind. And my dad could help.

* * *

Despite her protests of wanting to contribute, I kept Dolly out of my scheme. If it backfired, the last thing I wanted was for it to reflect poorly on her and her family.

Okay. Probably the second to last thing. The very last thing I wanted was to be deported. Having my dad at my side gave me the confidence to not worry about that.

Day of the Dead pictures of Sherrie in hand, we approached the bank.

"Do you have an appointment?" a severe-looking secretary asked, knowing full well we didn't.

Before Dad could turn on his charm, I tried, "Tell him it's about Major

Pickering."

She sighed and spoke quietly into the phone while I plastered an enthusiastic American smile on my face.

Moments later, Randolph Ruthhaven, also known as Major Pickering, emerged from his office.

"Ms. McGuire, wasn't it?" he asked, jovial but wary.

"You have such a good memory," I gushed in an attempt to match his tone. "And this is my father, all the way from Chicago, Illinois."

The men launched into handshakes and pleasantries while I edged around them to Ruthaven's inner office. When he noticed, I said, "I need to talk to you about the spa. Not more than five minutes," I promised.

My dad whispered something I couldn't hear, and the banker laughed, leading us in.

Once the door closed, Ruthaven took the power seat behind his heavy mahogany desk while we sank into squeaky leather armchairs.

Impatient, I took my pictures of Tori's sculpture and laid them across the desk. "These are for Sherrie. She had been dumped in the woods near the medispa, and I found her. I wanted her to be remembered, so my friend made this figurine."

Off track, my dad, of course, corrected. "Sherrie, about my own Maddie's age, had her kidneys removed."

The simple sentence triggered a spasm in Ruthaven. Face ashen, he fumbled with a decanter. Dad hopped out of his chair to assist, talking about trivial matters. He picked out bits of information, weaving together a bond between the two men that hadn't existed moments before.

Meanwhile, I wanted to scream at the injustice, threaten, and demand retribution, which is why I brought Dad along. Knowing my expression, he signaled me for silence.

Clutching the glass, Ruthaven continued to stare at the photos, but the color returned to his face. To me, it looked like the banker was beginning to trust Dad.

So far, my instincts about the man were playing out. Bankers were portrayed as evil money grabbers, but his reaction showed genuine shock.

Crossing my fingers that I got it right this time, I pulled out the last picture.

Setting it where his gaze couldn't miss it, I explained, "This is what Sherrie was like when she was alive." James dredged up the picture for me once Edward forced him to. Her face beamed, her arms around a friend's shoulder. I edited out the beer can and cigarette she held in one hand. Less gang, more happy teen. "Her kidneys were," I paused, unable to think of the correct term and not harvested. "Recovered," I practically barked, causing the banker to jump. "Uh, recovered for sale and transplant on the black market."

"I, I had…" Ruthaven stammered.

Before he could say anything else, Dad covered for him.

"My Maddie has a big heart and wanted to do something. She needed closure to heal after the horror of finding the girl. She told me you were a nice man, and I jumped at the chance to meet you."

At this point, I would have said, 'And no one else needs to know what happened.' A veiled threat of exposure and bad publicity. But Dad knew better.

"There is a society in Edinburgh that helps disadvantaged youths to stay out of trouble. Maddie's raising awareness for the cause in Sherrie's name."

It sounded cheesy to me, but Ruthaven visibly relaxed, allowing his hands to release. "The bank is always looking to sponsor a good cause. I like the sound of this one. Give the information to my secretary, and we will ensure a donation is made."

"Really?" I said, not believing it.

Dad jumped to shake his hand, sealing the deal. As we walked to the door, he added one more thing. "The police press conference will be tomorrow, and our friends, the De Valences, may lose everything in the fallout."

Ruthaven froze, but Dad kept talking and walking. Non-threatening, we were leaving when it was clear we should.

In just a few steps, he explained about Winters the butler and that the viscount was handing management of the spa over to his niece, Lady Gwendolyn.

"It would mean a lot to the family if you could book an afternoon there. Show the folks what an upstanding place it is. Help them move past this unpleasantness."

Palpable relief radiated off Ruthaven, who agreed that monthly massages made him a better CEO. As such, he would start including gift certificates to the spa for his Employee of the Month.

In less than ten minutes, Ed McGuire got everything we came for without ever hinting that we knew Randolph Ruthaven received a black market kidney. They parted on such friendly terms that the two would probably exchange Christmas cards.

Now that I had done everything I could think of for Sherrie, one last task was on my list.

Chapter Forty-Two: Saving Comer Manor

The workday at the Baths finished, I suggested we head to The Huntsman around the corner for a get-together. I popped into the Pump Room to invite Lily, but she declined with a wrinkle of her freckled nose.

"I don't really fit in with that lot," she told me.

"Well, you're my lot, and don't you forget it," I assured her.

As I walked away, I realized another one of my lot that I had forgotten.

Digging out my cell, I called Naomi to tell her that I wouldn't be coming back to Chi-Town after all.

"Woohoo!" she crowed.

"Thanks a lot," I responded.

"You were so excited about that internship that I couldn't see you coming home early. When your dad called me about getting you back in the dorms, I let him know there was no way you should come home."

"Oh, Naomi," I sniffled. "You're—"

"Amazin'. I know. Like I said, I got you, girl."

"Everything okay?" Simon asked when I joined him. Something about the chat with Lily reminded me about jail cells. On the short walk to the pub, I asked Simon why I was sent to Bridgewater and not Keynsham when he had me dragged away by the police.

"My idea, actually. Didn't want to embarrass you."

"Embarrass me? You thought that would help?"

He shrugged.

Before my righteous fury ruined our evening, Dolly interrupted. "You absolutely will not believe who booked an appointment for next week."

"The head of a world-famous bank?" I guessed.

Gaping, she asked, "How ever did you know?"

I explained about our trip to the bank, based on our assumption about the man we met as Major Pickering.

"I let my dad do all the talking. I would have been arrested for attempted blackmail after sixty seconds. Now, he and my dad are best buds."

After various congratulations, Dolly explained her new vision. "No more medical in my medispa."

I held a hand up for a high five, which she tentatively returned with a giggle.

"The new De Valence spa will be eco-based. Nothing artificial, nothing chemical. I have a friend from uni who studied chemistry, and we're looking at Druid remedies. Then we will expand to other ancient cultures."

The seed of an idea formed. While she talked about her plans, it germinated. I continued to look interested while I mapped out possibilities.

"Maddie, you are ignoring me."

About to argue, I gave up and admitted it. "For a good reason. You need a shop to sell the spa goods. And you should get everything locally sourced."

I turned to Simon. "Comer Manor has bees, yes?"

"A few hives."

"You'll need more. Sustainable, local hives and herbs that you sell to the spa. Consignment at first," I said, building steam. "Then, as the spa grows, they can buy outright. It'll be small, but all the profit can go directly to building repair for Comer Manor. And," I said, thinking of something else he said. "You can use your trust for investment in the hives and herb garden because it doesn't involve the house."

Simon and Dolly stared.

Doubting my logic, I asked, "Right? I mean, it's not an archeology center, but that's not off the table."

A few beats passed, and they continued to look at me blankly.

After an interminable pause, Simon agreed. "Right, but only if Dolly—"

"It's brilliant," she decided. "Totally," she added in a pitch-perfect Valley Girl accent.

The word, so different from her catchphrase, caused me to burst out laughing.

"Okay, now that we're all friends, I have to confess something." I looked down, unable to make eye contact. "Dolly, I overheard you talking in the Oversight Office one day. You said you wanted me back in America, and…"

Before I could ask the question, she answered. "Well, when Simon so absolutely prefers some American's opinion to his own fiancé's, of course, I can't help but be a little jealous. You are brilliant and a bit intimidating, if I'm honest."

"Wait, fiancé? When did that happen?" I glared at Simon, who had kept the engagement a secret.

"It will be official shortly. I didn't want the news to influence either my aunt or Dolly's uncle." Patting her hand, he stood and headed to the loo.

"Um, Dolly?" I said, allowing the compliment she paid me to sink in. "Wow, that's the nicest thing anyone has said to me."

She squeezed my arm. "All true. And no longer a problem as you are now my friend as well."

Aye, there's the rub, I quoted Hamlet in my head. As her friend, I needed to tell her about Simon. As Simon's friend, I shouldn't.

"So why do you look so miserable?" Dolly asked.

Cursing my overly expressive face, I started with, "Well, it's just about Simon. He's a great guy. Love him completely."

"As do I."

"Well, hear me out." I paused, hating to say it, so I implied. "I'm not one hundred percent convinced he is really into girls all that much."

"Oh, my giddy aunt!" she exclaimed. "Is that your problem with our relationship?"

Confounded, I nodded.

"I know, and we've discussed it. An heir, and a spare, and we can live happily as friends. It's ideal, really."

"But, what about love?" I blurted out.

"We do love each other," she explained as though I was a slow child.

"Chemistry, then," I pressed, thinking of my magnetic attraction for Edward.

With a smile, Dolly said, "I would rather be married to a wonderful, caring man like Simon than to any of the other playboy lads or sniveling twits my uncle has tried to pair me with." She took both my hands. "Really, we're happy."

"What are you two talking about?" Simon asked, suddenly reappearing.

Jumping out of my skin, I replied, "Nothing."

"You're an appallingly bad liar," he said.

"That's a good thing," I countered.

"Probably."

As the evening continued, another seed formed, this one concerning Jeffery the reporter.

* * *

The police press conference in Gloucester released information about White, kidnapping, and the black market organs. The uproar was loud but short-lived, as everyone in on the charade, including several spa staff members, were in custody. Mercifully, the De Valence name and medispa were not mentioned.

Jeffery Dailey saw me in the crowd with Edward and made a beeline. "Was it the De Valen—"

"Come with me," I interrupted, leading him out of earshot of other reporters. "Edward worked on the case. I'm supporting him."

Jeffery made to ask a question, but I didn't give him a chance. "I was hoping to run into you, though."

That shocked him into silence.

"About the article you wrote," I reminded him with a smile. "Lady Gwendolyn took it to heart. She is revamping the spa and wants to give you an exclusive."

"Wha'?" he stuttered, the epitome of eloquence.

"You could sell it to local papers and country living magazines," I said, handing him Jordan's card. "Contact this photographer. He can help."

Shrewd as ever, Jeffery reasoned, "That just gives her good press. What about my cuttin' edge reputation?"

"An exclusive is good for everyone." With a supreme effort, I didn't scoff at his so-called reputation. "Besides, the De Valence family wants to credit your article about spas ruining the countryside with the change in direction. The new spa will use locally sourced product ingredients, employ local workers, and extend a fifty-percent village resident discount." I smiled. "All thanks to you."

Chapter Forty-Three: The Next Level

After securing the reporter's cooperation and setting up a meeting time for the next day, Edward and I headed home to Bath on the train.

The setting sun turned clouds pale pink as we found ourselves walking along the Avon River.

"You hungry, lass?" he asked after kissing my hand. "I have something I need to talk to you about."

Usually, that phrase struck fear in my heart, but not when Edward said it.

Nodding in agreement, he smiled nervously. No one could out-stoic Edward, and worry crept into my mood.

"Is everything okay?" I asked.

"Be patient," he advised.

"This better not be a surprise."

Hand to his chest in mock horror, he exclaimed, "Would I do that? Knowing your hatred for all things spontaneous and joyful?"

Still distrustful, I slugged him in the arm as he led me toward a narrow boat moored on the Avon by Sydney Gardens. A table and two chairs perched on its flat roof, LED tea candles sparkled on every available surface, making it look like a fairy wonderland.

"How lovely," I gasped as Edward helped me aboard.

"It's not really a surprise," he rationalized. "It's just showing you where I live." His sidelong look tried to gauge my response to this news.

Grinning, I squeezed him. "I want the grand tour."

The boat was smaller than many on the water. Solid blue, clean, and well cared for, I realized I'd seen it before. "When you were in hiding, I saw James on this boat over by the train station."

"You have to move every three days. It keeps people from camping and making a mess," Edward said. "I find places with parking for my bike nearby. But it's cheaper than a flat, and the people are nice."

We entered at the front into a living room area complete with flat screen TV, a built-in couch, chairs, and a wood-burning stove.

"How can that possibly be safe?" I asked. I knew sailors hated open flames because when I was a kid, my candles were confiscated when my dad took me on a cruise ship. Many long lectures followed.

Edward's response didn't address the question. "Have to stay warm somehow."

Heading back, or aft as he called it, we passed through a kitchen that smelled delicious, by a shower room, followed by a double bed built into the wall. "James sleeps on the sofa by the TV."

The mention of his name summoned Edward's brother, who entered the boat from an aft door.

"Your dinner awaits," James said, waving toward the outside. "Out you go."

Obeying, we headed out and crawled onto the boat's roof. "This is temporary," Edward told me. "Just for you," he said, eyes down and looking shy.

We started with bruschetta made with tomatoes, feta, and balsamic. James served as a waiter, discrete and efficient.

"At the spa," Edward whispered, not wanting his brother to hear. "We were, uh, going to, um. I mean, before the tattoo fiasco, we seemed to be, you know, on our way to—"

Unable to bring himself to say it, I let him off the hook. "Yeah."

Relieved, he took both my hands and looked at me with a ferocity that set my soul on fire.

Holding my breath, I waited for his next words.

"I don't think we should." He rushed the words so fast that it took me a minute to register.

Once they sunk in, conflicting emotions fought for attention. Outrage at being rejected came first, followed quickly by disappointment. I put a lot of thought into the decision to be with Edward, and tons of conversations with Tori.

"When I took off to Edinburgh, I didn't feel like I could tell you because there was so much about me you don't know." He sighed, looking miserable. "You deserve the best, Madeline McGuire. You should know what you're getting into."

The final emotion warring in my brain won. Relief. Much as I was sure Edward was the guy, I didn't know him well enough.

Returning his gaze, I nodded.

James appeared with an amused smile in place. He took our plates and replaced them with spaghetti in red sauce, one giant meatball in the center. I felt like we were in "Lady and the Tramp," which wasn't a bad thing.

When we were alone, Edward asked, "Y'alright?"

Taking a moment, I considered before answering. "A bit of a blow to my general appeal," before he could protest, I finished. "But yeah. All good. Honestly, I agree."

However, he didn't look relieved.

"What?"

"One more," he said, poking at his meatball.

"What?" I repeated, my fork clattering to the plate.

"DCI Bray suggested that I apply to be a detective."

Rescuing my fork, I dug into the pasta, my appetite restored. "That's amazing! Aren't you young for that?"

Pleased, he answered, "Yes. DI Parikh said he spent six years at the constabulary before he applied to the detective branch. But he agreed, since I was so involved in the last two homicides, I was ready. It'll be more work. I have to take six weeks of extra classes. Which will take time away from you," he confessed, unsure of my response.

"Do it!" I insisted. "This is your career and your life. I've had enough people trying to mess with mine that I get it. This is amazing."

My grin faltered as I took in his expression. "But..." I prompted.

"But, there's more. DCI also suggested that Parikh move to the Tri-Force Major Crimes Investigation Team. MCIT."

"And?"

"And I want to follow him there."

"Would you have to move?"

"I have to move every three days," he said, crooked smile in place.

"You know what I mean."

"No, but there are times it would be easier to take my boat closer to the crime scene. Tri-Force is Avon/Somerset and Gloucester and Wiltshire."

"But you'd still be based here?" I asked, feeling him slip away from me.

He took my hand and placed his deck-shoe-clad feet over mine, grounding me.

"I'd be here every minute I could."

"So, you'd get to work directly with Parikh?" I asked, resuming my rapidly cooling dinner.

"I would be a Detective Constable. It'll be a few years before I can study to be a sergeant and then years after that before an inspector."

Confused, I asked, "Aren't you a constable now?"

"It's a lateral transfer. Same pay, worse hours, civilian clothes. But I feel like it's what I should do."

Agreeing, I searched his face for any sign of trepidation. Excitement sparkled in his eyes. "Of course it is. Go for it." The subject reminded me of something. "Why don't all police subdue suspects with the nerve pinch thing?"

"It's a risky move," he admitted. "The vagus nerve isn't easy to find, and if you get it wrong, you're not in a position to protect yourself from a blow."

"So you decided to experiment when I was in a headlock?"

His crooked smile appeared. "Nah. I knew right where White's was."

"How?"

"He taught me how to do it."

Okay, so, yeah. Edward was right in that I needed to know a lot more about him.

While I stared, open-mouthed, he explained that before his brother

William took over the gang, White was in charge.

We finished our plates with no more bombshells falling. When James brought up chocolate eclairs for dessert, I invited him to stay. With no way to sit on the side of the table without fear of falling into the water, he stood behind his brother.

"I realize your family is a mess."

The chorus of snorts and inappropriate language affirmed my assumption. I held up a hand to hush them. "Why not send the Day of the Dead doll of Sherrie to William? A memorial for the gang's lost members and a peace offering for you three."

After much huffing, denials, and other manly emotions, they agreed, and James left us to our dessert.

"Thank you for this evening." Our relationship moved to the next level. It wasn't the one I'd planned for, but the deeper connection meant more.

"I am pretty awesome, as you Americans would say."

Raising an eyebrow, I asked, "Too many deep emotions for one evening?"

"Maybe," he admitted, grinning at me. "But when you have a lassie like mine, you have to be prepared for everything."

A lassie like his - was that what I was? Did I consider him mine?

My stupid brain tried to be logical, but the warmth and giddy joy that bubbled through me answered my questions.

A Note from the Author

I have walked the Cotswold Way from Painswick to Bath, and it is lovely, safe, and unencumbered by horrifying discoveries.

Acknowledgements

My thanks to those in England start with deepest gratitude to Tim Stuckes, retired Police Inspector, and Andy Gwyther, retired Detective Inspector, both formerly of the Avon and Somerset Constabulary, for their insights into the British police force. In addition, Julie Reynolds, Cultural Heritage Curator at the National Trust, provided me with invaluable information about Roman archeology. Her contributions will be fully realized in Book 3 of the series. I also extend my thanks to Maddy of Mad Max Tours for providing delightful observations on Cotswold living. In America, my thanks go to Verena Rose and everyone at Level Best Books. Thank you to Sisters in Crime for its resources and support. Additional thanks go to Malice Domestic for introducing me to a fantastic group of authors and fans who love all things mystery and cozy. And finally, my profound appreciation to the Blackbird Writers for their treasured support and wealth of experience.

About the Author

Sharon Lynn was raised in Arizona, but it was living in England as a teenager, and every return trip since that inspired the setting of her Cotswold Crimes Mystery series. As a theater, film, and writing professor, she coaches and mentors aspiring artists. Her short stories are in anthologies from Malice Domestic and Desert Sleuths. She is a member of the Mystery Writers of America, Sisters in Crime, and International Thriller Writers. Please sign up for her newsletter at www.sharonlwrites.com and www.blackbirdwriters.com.

SOCIAL MEDIA HANDLES:
   Twitter.com/sharonlwrites
   Instragram.com/sharonlwrites
   Facebook.com/sharonlwrites
   goodreads.com/sharonlynnwrites
   bookbub.com/authors/sharon-lynn
   amazon.com/author/sharonlwrites

AUTHOR WEBSITE:

www.sharonlwrites.com and www.blackbirdwriters.com

Also by Sharon Lynn

Novel:

Death Takes a Bath: A Cotswold Crime Mystery Book 1 by Level Best Books (2022)

Short Stories:

The Professor's Lesson in *Malice Domestic 16: Mystery Most Diabolical* (2022)

Final Curtain in *Malice Domestic 15: Mystery Most Theatrical* (2020)

Carne Diem in Malice Domestic 14: Mystery Most Edible (2019)

Death on Tap in Sisters in Crime Desert Sleuths' anthology *SoWest: Killer Nights* (2017)

Death on Tap and *Carne Diem* are available as standalone short stories on Kindle